"A compelling page-turner of a novel that highlights the secrets that even good families keep from one another—with devastating, unexpected results. Johnson, a keen observer of peoples' foibles, has brilliantly captured Midwestern values, small-town gossips, and rebellious spirits in her remarkable first novel. Told from inside the mind of one accused of a crime of passion, you experience the torture of being charged with a crime you think you didn't commit. Finding this author is like discovering a young John Grisham. This is spell-binding courtroom storytelling at its very best."

—MADELYN CAIN, award-winning author of *Laffit: Anatomy of a Winner*, *The Childless Revolution*, and *First Time Mothers, Last Chance Babies*

"AGS Johnson's novel is a fresh new voice on family dynamics and, ensconced in a male dominated society, what it meant to be a counter-culture activist and budding feminist during the Vietnam War. But once Kip Czermanski is accused of murder in her conservative hometown, it stops mattering which side is right—just try to figure out who committed the murder."

—NANCY ELLEN DODD, author of
The Writer's Compass: From Story Map to Finished Draft in 7 Stages

"AGS Johnson's talent as a storyteller draws us in and shines throughout *The Sausage Maker's Daughters*. Page by page, chapter by chapter, Johnson transports us through time and ever deeper into the lives of her characters as we experience the pain of what is and the pain of what could have been, the mystery as it unfolds and the universal truths that touch us all. In the end, we experience *The Sausage Maker's Daughters* viscerally and personally."

—JAMES J. OWENS, Founder and CEO, The World is Just a Book Away;
Author of forthcoming anthology, *The World is Just a Book Away*;
Assistant Professor, Marshall School of Business,
University of Southern California

The
SAUSAGE MAKER'S
Daughters

The SAUSAGE MAKER'S *Daughters*

AGS JOHNSON

BiblioFile Press

Los Angeles, CA

BiblioFile Press

11693 San Vicente Blvd. #116
Los Angeles, CA 90049
www.agsjohnsonauthor.com

Aside from the historical events and figures from the era, this is a work of fiction. Any resemblance to persons living or dead is purely coincidental.

First Edition

Hardcover Edition: 978-0-9847341-0-8
Trade Paperback: 978-0-9847341-1-5
Ebook: 978-0-9847341-2-2

Publishers Cataloging-in-Publication Data

Johnson, A. G. S.

The sausage maker's daughters / AGS Johnson. -- 1st ed. -- Los Angeles, CA : BiblioFile Press, c2012.

p. ; cm.

ISBN: 978-0-9847341-0-8 (cloth) ; 978-0-9847341-1-5 (pbk.) ; 978-0-9847341-2-2 (ebk.)

1. Families--United States--Fiction. 2. Trials (Murder)--Wisconsin--Fiction. 3. Counterculture--United States--Fiction. 4. Feminism--United States--Fiction. 5. Fathers and daughters--United States--Fiction. 6. Mystery fiction. 7. Bildungsromans. I. Title.

PS3610.O318 S38 2012	2011960290
813.6--dc23	1202

Printed in the United States of America

BOOK DESIGN BY DOTTI ALBERTINE

For Mom, Margaret Edmundson Surmacz,
who made the field fertile with love.

For Dad, Joseph George Surmacz,
who exhorted me to grow!

And for Johnson
who loves me for all the wrong reasons.

You bless my life.

Part One

*When I can no longer bear to think
of the victims of broken homes,
I begin to think of the victims of intact ones.*

– PETER DEVRIES –

CHAPTER ONE

February 14, 1972 — St. Valentine's Day

> *How many deaths does it take 'til he sees that too many*
> *people—*

"'Fraid it's time."

> *—have died?*

"Miss Czermanski, it's time."

Time? Speaking to me through metal bars, a sad-eyed man in uniform interrupted me, singing softly to distract myself. I focused on the jangling keys in his hand.

Oh. Time. I plummeted back to reality—me locked in a jail cell. Mustering my indignation, I responded, "Finally, you've come to your senses. You're letting me out."

Not that this jail cell scared me—hell no. I've been clubbed, bruised, tear-gassed, arrested, and jailed too many times to count. And I have the scars to prove it. It's just, well … so much happened so fast. That must be why I'm a bit rattled.

"Van's awaitin'," the jail guard said, sliding open the cell door. Its crashing against the bars behind it, metal on metal, provoked my reaction. I jumped to my feet, tugging an old mothproofed coat over the other sartorial rejects I had dressed in. I looked as ridiculous as my being locked in this cell had been. How will they justify holding me? It was an outrage, and probably not even legal. Dad's lawyers would get to the bottom of it.

Charging from the cell, I strode the cement corridor in the only direction possible, dead ahead. "I'm more than ready to leave this creepy place," I told the guard, "for good."

Our footsteps echoed through the empty jailhouse, the old guard's plodding gait punctuating the rapid-fire determination of mine until we reached a metal door. Once the guard unlocked it, we were blasted by arctic air and blinding sunlight. "Go on ahead now," he prodded me. With my eyes adjusting, I stumbled toward a police van materializing at the base of a stairway.

Three uniformed men, shifting from foot to foot, waited beside a police van, their breath rising like smoke signals on frigid air. I gulped in the bracing cold to quell a sudden uptick in my pulse. One of my armed escorts offered me a hand into the rear of the van, but I climbed in on my own. He trailed me in and sat opposite, absently fingering his billy club. Doors slammed all around us, four consecutive concussions, both heard and felt. The van rumbled forward, and my teeth chattered as I fixated on his club.

I attempted conversation as we crunched and slid over rutted snow toward the county courthouse. "So, how long do these things take, Officer, normally?"

"Transfer to the courthouse? No mor'n a few minutes."

"No, I meant my appearance, the … arraignment." He shrugged with disinterest. Straining to see through the chicken-wired windows, I attempted another tack meant to divert me from the impending court appearance. Though clearly not my first, it would be my first all alone. "Looks like we got more snow last night."

"Couple inches's all."

"Right …" This was getting me nowhere. Besides, I should rehearse. I had only to state my plea, that's what Dad's lawyers told me—that, "and no more." *Not guilty, Your Honor. No way am I guilty. Man, I am so not guilty.* "Positively, unequivocally, not guilty! Get real, Your Honor."

"What?" The guard eyed me through the slits of his eyes as his grip tightened on his club.

"Sorry. I was just practicing my lines—you know, for court."

The man shifted away to further discourage small talk, his movement revealing a holstered gun beneath his jacket. Like a billy club to the head, it struck me that all these security measures—from the jail cell to his club and gun to his armed cronies in the front cab—were meant to safeguard greater Wausaukeesha, Wisconsin *from me*. As the significance sank in, I held back debilitating fear the way we did in the old days, with a protest song, this one sung in my head.

> *How many times can a man turn his head,*
> *pretending he just doesn't see?*

My stomach clenched like a fist when the van fishtailed to a halt in another razor-wired courtyard. At least it would all be over soon. My secret mantra cycled through my head as I exited the van. *Bravado, my old friend, don't fail me now.*

With my security detail, all three of them, I was escorted to a rear entrance of the Wausaukeesha County Courthouse, a building seen throughout my childhood from a distance, but never up close until today. Once inside, my entourage marched me through the ill-lit bowels of the building to a secure waiting area they called "the green room." Seated amid walls the color of pond scum, I pondered the room's theatrical name. Was it intentional, this allusion to a backstage area where actors waited to perform? Droll gallows humor?

"Kipe … Keep … K-I-P Czermanski," boomed a voice that filled the green room. Another uniformed official had entered and bumbled over not my last name, which was a handful, but my first. With him, the body count in the holding pen reached five—four official-looking and armed men and me, one childish-looking female.

I rose, ditched the coat, and tartly corrected him. "It's Kip, like 'hip.'" The officers gazed in obvious surprise at the now revealed outfit I was literally stuffed into—a nautical-themed white blouse with a navy blue tie and pleated skirt. Dad's lawyers assured me this mothball-reeking ensemble was the best my sisters could pull together after the lawyers had judged everything in my suitcase at home "unsuitable for the courtroom." I cheered myself, thinking that looking infantile was probably a good defensive ploy. All eyes in the green room traveled downward to my feet and stopped. Oh crap, except for the combat boots. Where did my sisters find them?

In a solemn tone I hadn't heard since I stopped attending Mass, the newly arrived official recounted courtroom protocol for me. I tried to listen but fidgeted with my hair, my clothes, and the damned boots, the protest song still wafting through my head.

"Okay, this way," he said when he'd finished. I prayed I hadn't missed anything important and forced myself in the direction indicated, chastising myself for allowing my habitual free-associating to seize my attention when, more than ever, I needed to be focused and present.

More echoing footsteps, another dead end before a locked door, this one marked Courtroom One, which the guard opened, and herded me inside.

CHAPTER TWO

My first courtroom visual, my family, inspired more tugging at the dark curly locks covering my scalp. My family was aligned behind the lawyers' tables in the first row of the spectators' gallery, but surprisingly, they weren't seated in order of age as was the Czermanskis' custom.

My mind flew to the ritual performed weekly at the back of our church, where Sybel lined us up from youngest to oldest for the Czermanski family entrance into Mass.

1952

Since I was about four, old enough to perform my role without Samantha holding my hand, I, as the youngest and least important Czermanski, would be first to enter the sanctuary's middle aisle.

My appearance was barely noticed until Samantha, eight years older than me, followed me down the center aisle for the farthest front pew available. Those were our marching orders: the farthest front pew. When Sybel, ten years older than me, trooped in behind us, worshippers began to notice. I don't think Sister Sarah was ever a part of these family entrances, but at Christmas and Easter Masses, Dad stole the show by bringing up the rear. We lined up in the pew before the good Catholics of Wausaukeesha and, at Dad's signal, sat in unison. Dad on the aisle with me at the opposite end made two dark-haired bookends for my eye-catchingly blonde sisters between us.

Even worse were the Czermanski family exits. Trapped in the sanctuary by those worshipers seated well back of our pew, Dad used the time to greet fellow parishioners as if they were his own personal flock. The old ladies who always outnumbered the rest of the people at Mass commented to Dad about his "lovely family, worshipping together." Their whispers, in fact, first drove home how unlike my sisters I was.

"Look at all the blue-eyed, Breck-blondes in one family."

"Tall and elegant just like their mother, with her glorious head of hair."

"Except that youngest one, KP. All Czermanski, that one, her father's spitting image."

"I agree, her black eyes and curls are JJ's, but the youngest reminds me even more of JJ's mother."

So much for the head covering required on worshipping females. I still stuck out like a sore thumb.

And so much for controlling my mind's free associations, I realized as the guard propelled me toward my family with me pulling at my frizzing coils—after all these years still striving for Breck shampoo-smooth. My sleek haircut, an *au courant* wedge, never stood a chance.

In Dad's traditional place on the aisle sat Sybel, the Widow Szyzyck, conspicuously draped in a black mourning veil, which still did not conceal her glare. "Damn it," I swore under my breath, "that getup won't help." Sybel slid her hand through Dad's arm and clutched him protectively while directing her formidable coldness at me.

I glanced at Dad who appeared to have aged a decade in the space of a day. Slumped between my sisters, the ruddy-hued man-in-charge was no longer evident. More gray hair seemed to sprout from his dark whorls. Our eyes, the same black-brown in color, met briefly before Dad's, reddened with grief and exhaustion, dropped away. I bit my lip, overcome by a foreign desire to put my arms around him and lie, tell Dad everything would be okay.

Samantha, wriggling in her seat next to him, absently coiled and uncoiled strands of hair around her forefinger. When especially nervous, Samantha often yanked whole coils from her scalp in one tug. She struggled to hold my gaze, which, in the effort, felt like some support. Then her blonde tresses, the ones I heard about on Sundays for years, flared out as her head snapped toward her husband.

Raymond, seated beside her, had undoubtedly made one of his biting comments. He upbraided his wife with yellow strands plucked from his clothing before discarding them with vehement finger-flicking. Samantha folded her hands in her lap as Raymond fell to primping the French cuffs that projected from his coat sleeves. From where I stood near the jury box, the *RCT III* monogram on one cuff was legible. What, I wondered for the millionth time, did sweet, natural Samantha ever see in the somewhat effeminate Raymond Chauncey Turner the Third?

Like a dog, I was ordered by the hovering guard to *sit* in the vacant jury box and *stay* until my name was called. Yet within moments, the same official shouted, "All rise. The Honorable Judge Dryburgh presiding." I rose hesitantly. "Be seated," he cried out, and I sat fast.

An encouragingly young judge in black robes billowed toward the bench. Sandy-colored bangs flopped over his eyes, and long sideburns, redder in hue, outlined his cheeks. Right on! A hip judge must be a good omen. He seated himself, perusing papers and files before announcing, "Bailiff, I'm ready for the custodies."

That apparently meant me as my name, "Kip Czermanski," rang throughout the courtroom. At least I'd straightened out its pronunciation ahead of time. Anxious to get beyond this travesty of justice, I sprang to my feet when out of nowhere, a seriously-suited stranger appeared at my side.

"I'm here to represent you," the man whispered.

"What? Where are—"

"I'll explain later," he said, shushing me. But like those church ladies, his whispers drew everyone's attention.

"Counselor," the judge demanded, drumming his fingers, "are you and your client quite ready?"

"Yes, Your Honor. Quite."

"S'cuse me, but this man is not my—" The stranger beside me squeezed my elbow hard. "Ouch!"

"Is there a problem, Miss Czermanski?" Hazel eyes beneath unruly bangs bore into me.

The pinching man spoke over me. "Your Honor, you see my client and I haven't actually met before this very moment. You'll find this amusing but it was the firm's partners—whom you of course know, Bob Stelzl and Art Polanski—who debriefed our client as I rushed home to represent her this morning. I'm afraid Miss Czermanski has been surprised—"

The judge thumped his gavel, shocking the pincher to silence. "Are you or are you not Miss Czermanski's legal representative?"

"I am, Your Honor. We—the firm, that is—represent Mr. Czermanski, my client's father, in all his legal concerns."

"Very interesting," droned the judge, "but you're wasting the court's time. Miss Czermanski, is he or is he not your attorney?"

I jerked my arm free, staring at the stranger whose pine-scented after-shave mixing with my mothball fumes did little to clear my head. "But where are the partners?"

The young lawyer tugged at his collar, nodding toward the row behind my family. And there they sat, Dad's lawyers for as long as I could remember, smiling reassurances in my direction. "They'll be behind us the whole way," he added.

I glanced from the partners to my dad slumping between my sisters to the fledgling advocate beside me. Was it a good sign that Dad and his legal team had entrusted my arraignment to an underling? Of course. It must imply their complete confidence in my immediate release.

"Miss Czermanski?" The judge's finger-drumming grew more insistent.

"Fine," I answered him. "I mean okay, he's my lawyer."

The judge shoved back his bangs and got right down to business. "Kip Czermanski, you are charged with murder in the first degree in the death of Dr. Stanislaw Szyzyck."

Murder?

"You have the right to an attorney, which we'll presume you have. But if not or you cannot afford one, the court will appoint …"

Did he say *murder?*

"… right not to incriminate yourself. And you have the right to a speedy trial."

In the first degree?

"Do you understand these rights and charges?" the judge asked.

"No no no, you mean manslaughter, don't you? It was an accident. Dad's lawyers told me the worst possible outcome today would be man—"

"Answer the question, Miss Czermanski. Do you understand the rights and charges as read?"

The lawyer beside me, wide-eyed at my outburst, whispered, "Answer yes or no."

"Yes, I understand what you just said, but—"

"If found guilty, you could be sentenced to life in prison with no parole," the judge spoke over me. "Do you understand the consequences of your plea?"

Life? No parole?

"Miss Czermanski?"

I clutched the lawyer's arm as the bottom dropped out of my world. He tugged at his collar as if he were the one on a choke chain, gesturing vehemently toward the judge with his eyes. "I-I guess I understand."

The lawyer spoke up. "Judge, may I take a moment to consult with my client before we enter our plea?"

"This too wasn't handled before court? Three minutes." Banging his gavel, the judge turned his impatience elsewhere. The lawyer plunked into a seat in the jury box and pulled me onto the adjoining one.

"He's …" I struggled to formulate a question. "The judge isn't saying—"

"Frankly, Miss Czermanski, I'm stunned. We hadn't anticipated the prosecutor going for anywhere close to the maximum here—an extremely bold move. Or perhaps it's a bargaining chip; we'll know soon enough. Regardless, I'm afraid you must plead the charges as read."

"I didn't kill Stan. Who could believe such a thing? The judge wasn't implying Stan's death was a murder, a murder committed by me? Why that's preposterous!" I exclaimed, my voice ratcheting up to a Tiny Tim falsetto.

"Keep it down," commanded the whispering lawyer beside me. "The last thing we need is a contempt citation after this faulty start." The lawyer plied his collar with his finger and checked his watch. "There's no time. You'll plead 'not guilty' then?"

"Of course I'll plead not guilty. What else—"

His gavel startled us. The judge demanded, "Your plea, Counselor."

"Yes, Your Honor," the lawyer said, rising. He dragged me to my feet. "My client is prepared to plead."

Chapter Three

"Not guilty, Your Honor," I stated my line as rehearsed on the drive over. "It was an accident," I couldn't help adding. The lawyer elbowed me to clam up.

The judge stared me down, daring me to speak out of turn once more. "Kip Czermanski," he began, his tone so stern, I forgot to breathe, "you will be held until trial in the first degree murder of Dr. Stanislaw Szyzyck. Preliminary hearing will be a week from tomorrow, pretrial motions in four weeks after that. The pretrial conference will be in six, and the trial itself will begin eight weeks from tomorrow." His gavel punctuated his pronouncements as I reeled at the words.

"Your Honor!" the lawyer shouted, "Your Honor, I humbly request the charges against my client be dropped as … as she was," he stole a glance at the senior partners, "yes, she was improperly detained with no bail hearing."

"You're asking me to drop a charge of murder one?" Judge Dryburgh scoffed. "Where was the bail officer when your client was brought in—" He rifled irritably through papers. "—at four o'clock Sunday morning?" He checked the wall clock mounted on the back wall. "It's now nine a.m. Monday, so twenty-nine hours ago."

"He went ice fishing over the weekend, Your Honor. He's so rarely called upon, as you can imag—that is, he left town and failed to leave a phone number or a backup officer. Which means my client was detained without a proper opportunity to post bail."

"Denied. Given the severity of the charge, arraignment within twenty-nine hours of arrest is hardly onerous. And bail is denied. The prosecution's complaint contends Miss Czermanski is a flight risk," said the judge, tapping the papers piled in front of him, "due to her known contact with a suspected felon, one Peter Replogel, who is evading arrest by the FBI just over the Canadian border." The lawyer's jaw dropped when he turned to me as if to say, *is this true as well?* The judge hurried him along. "Will there be anything else, Counselor?"

Both of us were overwhelmed by shock. I watched the lawyer struggle, his lips moving until sound finally came out. "No? No bail? Your Honor, my client, as you can see, is a twenty-four-year-old *female*. This is *her* first offense, and may I mention she's an upstanding member of *the* preeminent family of Wausaukeesha—perhaps the whole of Wisconsin." He glanced toward the Czermanskis, seated prominently in the farthest front pew. "The Czermanski family will vouch for her whereabouts and post any bond the court might require."

"Hardly a first offense." The judge lofted a thick file. "Your client has a police record a mile long, including assault and battery of a Madison police officer and—"

"If I may, Your Honor," the lawyer interrupted as if he had to speak now or forever lose his nerve. "My client was a student anti-war activist from 1966 to 1970 at the University of Wisconsin in Madison. You of all people, Your Honor, must surely recognize that characterizing her activities there, which were based upon practicing … her constitutional right to protest … government policies …" The lawyer ran out of nerve or conviction, I didn't know which.

The judge scowled at him. "I see where you're going with this, William, and frankly, it's beneath you. I'm aware of Miss Czermanski's anti-war activities, which is how she became romantically involved with the decedent in the first place."

The lawyer couldn't suppress a low groan, his eyes trained on the judge leafing through the file before him. "It's all here. Prosecution has been most thorough." He slammed the file shut and narrowed his eyes at us. "With the lifeless body of her brother-in-law found in the accused's bed the night following a family funeral, probable cause would appear to exist, regardless. You'll get your chance, Counselor—next week at the prelim." His gavel silenced all further discussion.

With my knees weakening, I gave the lawyer credit for one last try. "All hard evidence at the scene, Your Honor, suggests a grotesque accident. If you will allow me ..."

A buzzing in my ears drowned out their arguing. I staunched growing panic by zeroing in on the judge's drumming fingers. Weather-roughened and freckled, the judge's hands looked like he worked outdoors in Wisconsin's harsh climes instead of a courtroom. Perhaps he milked cows before court at one of the ubiquitous dairy farms surrounding Wausaukeesha.

My dad always said that farming in general, and cow milking specifically, figured large in the success he had become.

1958

"This is it, girls," Dad shouted, "where I grew up. Smell the country air, will you." We couldn't help smelling it. Country air smelled a lot like cow poop. As we drove under the humungous sign, Czermanski Farms, blazing across the gate in huge red letters, the stinky country air filled with the shrill noise of insects that made me cover my ears.

In a suit and hat, Dad took the time to tug galoshes over his shiny wingtips while my sisters and I stepped from the car. I wondered about that until, hurrying ahead, Dad's feet sank into and sucked up some glurpy farm muck. Sybel, Samantha, and I picked our way after him while Dad called out the sights.

"There's the old barn where we kept livestock, and there's the old homestead." The three of us stopped to stare in surprise at a crumbling bungalow alongside a peeling red barn. Dad flung his arms in both directions. "None of the rest a' this was here back then. I added the feedlots, industrial barns, grain storage, and all the rest after buying out the neighbors one by one. C'mon, I'll show you."

Dad's excitement dried up during our tour of the cramped quarters he'd shared with his parents until Granddad's illness forced their move into town. They not only lost the farm, Dad had to drop out of high school to go to work. Not to brag or anything, but Dad's old house would fit into the living room of our home on Moraine Drive.

"Let me show you the new operation," Dad suggested, already out the door. He paused before the tiny barn to let us catch up. "Wait a sec. My care-takers keep livestock just like we used to. Let's take a peek."

With the four of us—and the caretaker's three livestock, meaning cows—the barn was full to bursting. The cows looked gigantic this close up, especially to me, a short-for-her-age ten-year-old. They chewed and blinked in slow motion as we watched each other from a safe distance.

"Can't be good citizens of the dairy state, girls," Dad teased us for hang-ing back, "if you're afraid of cows. They don't bite, even when you milk 'em. I should know, I been milking cows since I was younger than you, Kip. Always had a special knack if I do say so. I'll show you." Dad grabbed a pail off a hook and shoved a stool alongside the closest cow, who mooed and scrambled sideways.

During their game of Dad placing the stool beside the cow and the cow dodging him time and again, Dad murmured to the beast, "Come on now, Bessie, settle down." The cow, who I bet wasn't named Bessie at all, just mooed louder and the other cows mooed back. "You just grab these," Dad said, at last making contact with the cow's milk-thingies and squeezing. But Bessie pulled away so suddenly, Dad toppled off his stool onto the hay and whatever gunk was mixed in with it. *Ick.*

Dad lay still a minute. Even the cows fell silent. When he stood to brush himself off, he stormed from the barn, yelling, "Let's go, girls." We figured our tour was over, but that was okay. As we made for the Buick, the mooing of upset cows rose along with the screechy-saw insect chorus that filled the country air.

⋘⋙

The judge bellowing at my lawyer corralled my attention to the courtroom and the business at hand. "Save the exculpatory for the hearing, Counselor, where—don't make me remind you again—it belongs. You and your client are dismissed." *Bangbangbang.*

Dismissed? I can go? But a courtroom official appeared to steer me from the room the same way I came in. I collected both my coat and my three prison guards at the green room. After one of them cuffed my hands behind me, I was trudged out to the waiting police van.

As we approached the vehicle, nearby church bells pealed out a childhood tune I remembered. I shook off the guards to listen.

Jesus loves me, this I know, for the Bible tells me so...

Then church bells sounded the hours.

...nine, ten...

From lifelong habit, I counted along.

1955

Since seven years old when I was first allowed to roam Wausaukeesha alone as long as I was home when dad arrived for dinner, I kept track of the time by the church bells that chimed the hours. When I heard five bells, Sybel had warned, I was to come straight home. If the chimes rang six times, I'd for sure be in trouble.

But one especially snowy afternoon, I lost all sense of time, pretending to be shot and wounded, falling backwards into huge snowdrifts formed by the wind. Sunk down in the snow, I swished out perfect snow angels while watching my breath float upward like tiny prayers. I crisscrossed Wausaukeesha, leaving a trail of snow angels behind while heading home like Sybel said.

Lights like moon glow lit the windows throughout my neighborhood, making even my house look welcoming in the early twilight. Oh-oh, all the windows in my house were glowing, including Dad's bedroom, meaning Dad was home already. Sybel would be mad I kept everyone from sitting down to dinner as soon as he arrived.

I couldn't help it, I practiced saying a few time while running for the back door, *the fresh snow made it slow going.* My icy mittens slipped on the knob before the kitchen door clicked open.

"You're late." Sybel's angry voice shattered the wintry silence. "That's it. I'm done with warnings."

I discovered myself once more with armed guards urging me up the jail-house steps. I staggered toward the grandfatherly jailer who'd deposited me at this same spot earlier in the day—before being accused of murder in the first degree, before being held without bail until trial. He waited in the doorway, the dark interior of the jailhouse looming behind him like an abyss. At the top stair, I collapsed, screaming, "No no no no!"

The jailer caught and held me. "Shhh. There, there, Miss Czermanski, no need for tears. I'll get you lunch right quick and some extra pillows and blankets. You take a good nap and you'll feel better, that's a promise. Need to keep up your strength now. Come along. Come along."

How surreal that at the lowest moment of my life, a stranger who happened to be my jailer comforted me. But with reality unraveling all around me, I'd grasp at any reassurance, clutch at any straw.

Chapter Four

My tears had finally stopped and my shock was beginning to give way to the reality of what had just happened, which was all a big mistake, a misunderstanding. I just needed to stay occupied until someone straightened this all out.

In the spirit of panic avoidance, I tried to eat whatever it was my jailer brought for lunch. I tried to nap with the extra blankets and pillows he delivered, which did little to improve the hard cot. But the judge's last words in the courtroom ricocheted inside my skull. *Murder in the first degree. Held until trial. Trial in eight weeks.* It had been but two hours since his words, and already the gray concrete walls beyond the cell bars closed in. How will I survive two months in this cage? And what did he say about prison for life? No, I cannot go there. That cannot happen. Dad won't let that happen. They have to let me out. Period.

"… since the new visitation room isn't finished?"

"What?" The guard I just noticed outside my cell was apparently talking to me. Who else would he be talking to, I thought, glancing around at the empty cells.

"Your family, they're here to see you. I can let them back here if you want. You are our only inmate, after all."

"My dad is here? Yes, yes, bring him back."

Dad, his vigor miraculously restored, made his normal storming-the-beaches entrance. His second in command, Sybel, charged in behind him. Raymond, outshining them all in his black overcoat and gloves, a tomato-red scarf draped about his neck, followed, his black hair gleaming under the harsh overhead lights as he moved. Lagging well behind, Samantha progressed unsteadily toward my cell, wincing at the clattering sound their footsteps made, struggling to take in the cells, the bars, the guard, the ominous grayness of it all. The first wave promptly filled up the cot opposite the one I sat on, beside a pile of extra bedding. Samantha trailed in, twirling hesitantly before claiming the only vacant seat left not counting the toilet, and collapsed onto the cot next to me. In the first awkward moments of no one knowing where to begin, she leaned in to pat my hand.

"A fine state of affairs—a Czermanski in lockup, right here in Wausaukeesha." Sybel eyed me up and down. "No prison stripes required here?"

I ignored her. "Dad, you have got to do something. Get me out of here! I can't possibly stay cooped up in this, this morgue—I'm the only inmate in the entire jail—for two whole months."

"Now see here, Kip, I met with my lawyers right after court today. They tell me there are simply no strings to be pulled in a case as serious as this one just turned." His sigh seemed to deflate him, as if upholding his image had quickly become too much for him. "We're all in shock. So much … now this …" Dad bit his lip, swallowing the rest of his thought.

"Dad, you've always bragged about knowing who to call to get things done. You own this town. Isn't that what you've always said?"

I followed Dad's eyes as they traveled the cell, from the cots to the toilet and basin against the back wall to the empty cells on both sides of the hallway he'd just traversed from freedom to captivity, his merely temporary.

Anger mottled Sybel's smooth skin. When she leaned forward, I braced for the venom that had surely been building since my arrest and arraignment. Sybel humiliated was most dangerous. But before she could spew, Dad held her back with a hand on her arm. Sybel slammed backward against the bars, her hair-trigger rage dissolving into tears. Real tears? I was astonished. But not many escaped before Sybel regained control.

"I'll make the calls, Kip," Dad promised unconvincingly, "to the mayor and police chief, our congressman and senators, though they all know I'm a dyed-in-the-wool Republican. And I've got my lawyers on it, believe me, Kip. But in the meantime, I'll see what I can do to make you more comfortable here—" He gazed around again. "—to make this less …" It was unlike my dad not to have plenty of well-worn phrases at the ready. "I'm sorry, Kip, I really am, but for the time being I'm stymied by this mess you've got yourself into."

"That's reassuring, Dad, put in those words. Can't your lawyers file some motion, demand another arraignment, call this morning a mistrial? You've got to save me, Dad." Desperation quavered in my voice.

"Like it's not happening to us?" Sybel cried. "At least here you're insulated from the disgraceful gossip this will inspire. We'll be the laughingstock of Wausaukeesha. *I* will be." Sybel's watery eyes iced over as she successfully contained her emotions.

"We have enough clout to weather this, too, Sybel. Look, Kip, we're all doing all we can," Dad insisted. So why didn't I believe him? "No one was expecting what happened in court this morning. Maybe the influence the Sausage Company wields in this town lulled us all …" Dad trailed off again.

"Oh please, I can't stand it another minute," Raymond broke in, unable to restrain his curiosity any longer. "Kip, is it true? You were 'romantically involved' with Stan? You were having an affair with Sybel's husband?" Raymond's dark eyes, bright with interest, faded to suspicion. "Or did you all know about this," he accused, studying Sybel and Dad to his right, "and chose to keep me in the dark? Again." His doubts shifted to Samantha beside me while Sybel's cold fury found a secondary target.

I stood for a breath of fresher air. "Stan and I were 'involved' as you call it, Raymond, in college. I hadn't seen him in years—nearly three—since the end of my junior year. No, I was not having an affair with Sybel's husband."

"You say that," Sybel blurted, "yet you can't explain why Stan was in your bed, how he got there, and how he happened to—" Sybel struggled to finish. "—to, to, to … die there," she whispered. This version of Sybel shocked me, regardless of the circumstances.

"Sybel, I've told you everything I can remember about that night. What happened to Stan is terrible… but right now, I've got to get out of this place.

Dad, you can't leave me here. Please. I will not survive it. Please, please do something." I could not keep the urgency from my voice.

Stampeding footsteps caused us all to turn toward the jailer, who was leading Dad's lawyers to my cell. Great, now on top of my family—suffering their public humiliations, unable to utilize their carefully cultivated influence when I'm the one in need—add Dad's incompetent legal team to the mix.

But wait. I bet they've come with news of my release.

CHAPTER FIVE

The lawyers' approach was telltale. The partners lagged behind the rookie on whom they'd pawned me off in court until they saw my dad. Then junior was overtaken by his bosses and the fawning began.

"JJ? Guess I shouldn't be surprised to find you here," rumply Bob Stelzl exclaimed, rushing to shake Dad's hand as soon as my cage was unlocked.

Silver-haired and -tongued Art Polanski followed suit. "Glad to find you here, JJ. We want to get right on your daughter's defense, not a moment to spare. We can get your thoughts before we begin."

"My defense?" I repeated. "You're not here about my release?"

Raymond stood, unfurled the red scarf he'd neatly folded in his lap, and slung it around his neck. His piercing dark eyes flashed at us when he spoke. "It's overcrowded in here. I'm going home and let you lawyers do what you do. Samantha, if you wish to stay, have Sybel drop you off." The guard let him out, closely followed by Samantha, as the junior lawyer stepped inside.

Sybel looked torn. She hated to leave before deluging me with her outrage, but none of us could stand Dad's sycophantic legal team—the partners who wished to be called Uncle Art and Uncle Bob when Dad was nearby. Sybel trailed out as well. Dad struggled to his feet, his emotional strain apparent. For an unguarded second, Dad seemed ready to implode in defeat.

Both partners gushed their disappointment.

"You'll stay of course, won't you, JJ?" said Uncle Art with an unctuous smile.

"The earlier we brainstorm ideas," Uncle Bob added, "the stronger your daughter's defense."

"No, the girls are right. We'll let you get down to business. I couldn't add that much," Dad conceded with questionable humility. What did they think my dad could contribute to his most troublesome daughter's defense when his power and influence had mysteriously dried up? Dad, nodding grimly at the partners, said, "But drop by the house when you two are done here. We need to talk. And you cooperate now, young lady," Dad said to me with a frown. "This is a serious fix you've gotten yourself into. Make this as easy as possible on all of us. None of your shenanigans, Kip, you hear?"

I stared in disbelief. "Dad, you're not going to leave me locked up in this place." I gazed at the cramped space, my home for the next few months, gulping back tears. "Please, please do something, Dad. I've never asked you for anything before, but please, I beg you, get me out." I held onto his sleeve as long as possible as he walked away, shaking his head.

Through the bars, I watched my family disappear, using the time to fight down the intense urge to collapse into a wailing wretch again. *Don't let them see your weakness,* I cautioned myself. *They'll only use it against you. Stay focused, Kip, on how to get back to California. You can cry when you get home.*

Fists clenched in determination, I swung back to face Dad's lawyers.

Part Two

Patriarchy's chief institution is the family.

– KATE MILLET –

Chapter Six

"Nice work today, gentlemen." Best to stay angry and on the offensive I decided. "'Manslaughter,' isn't that what you told me would be the worst the prosecutor would go for, 'if that?' And look where that gross error in judgment landed me: in this cage. And for two whole months the judge said."

The three lawyers, seated in a row in dark suits and overcoats, seemed unable to find a place to rest their gaze.

"I'd ask you to explain what happened in court today—good lord, you even failed to inform me who would represent me beforehand—but it's more important that you tell me what you've done about it since. When will they let me out?"

Finally meeting my eyes, the disheveled one with the oiled down hair, Bob Stelzl, said, "Rough going in court today, Kip, no getting around it. What happened was unprecedented in this company town. May I?" He stood to remove this coat, prompting the others to do the same. I hoped they were feeling the heat. Hesitating only a second, the partners piled bulky winter coats into the arms of the junior lawyer who, clutching them clumsily, eased onto the cot with a blush.

Once seated, Bob went on, "Our bad luck the rookie cop, who clearly doesn't know how things operate around here, was on duty that night. Then JJ, so distressed at losing Stan so close to Sarah, forgot to call us. By the time Sybel called for him, it was too late to get to the chief to nip this thing in the bud. The final nail in the coffin—" That phrase seemed to remind him discomfitingly of my predicament. "—um, so to speak, was the judge we drew for your arraignment—a young firebrand, full of ideals and out to make a name for himself." Bob sighed. "Bad luck all around."

"You mean my dad never called you about my arrest?"

"Sybel handled it for him, just a little too late."

Impeccably dressed Art Polanski, a vision in silvery grays from his hair to his tailoring, stepped in. "Besides all that, something pushed the prosecutor's office into overdrive. Amazing what they dug up in just over a day and over a weekend." Art's awe fizzled to a scowl when he turned to me. "You told us nothing about your police record, nor your association with a felonious draft-dodger—that cost us bail. Nor did you mention a romantic involvement with your brother-in-law. Frankly Kip, in terms of blundered forewarnings, that oversight is in a class of its own."

"This is not California," Bob drove Art's point home. "You'd best remember how such details scandalize this community."

These rationalizations of their pathetic performance in the courtroom prompted me to interrupt. "Wait a minute. You three are the legal pros here, not me. When we met after my arrest, I was in shock, not to mention mourning, struggling to piece together the events of the night—like Stan being found dead in my bed—events I still struggle with. Plus, I had just been jailed. I would have told you anything if you had just asked. Why didn't you ask? Or better yet, why didn't you do what the prosecutor did in 'just over a day and over a weekend'—find out for yourselves?"

"The milk's been spilled, Kip," Art said as if the cliché explained everything. "It won't easily go back in the bottle now."

"What we're saying is," the young lawyer spoke his first words over the coats he hugged, "bail was denied for several compelling reasons. It's all on the record now."

I slammed back against the bars behind me. "You mean to say you can't get me released? I have to stay here like the judge said, until trial? There's nothing you or Dad can do about it?" To think Dad's long cultivated clout had been squelched by an inexperienced cop and lawyer and an idealistic judge, none much older than me.

Bob ended the deafening silence that followed my questions. "The best and only strategy at this point is to vigorously pursue your defense—no more surprises. To start, let me fill in some background on our colleague who stepped in to represent you this morning. William, give Kip your card." The young lawyer juggled coats, futilely checking pockets until Bob added, "Just do it before we leave.

"Anyway, as I was saying, William earned his law degree at Marquette, specializing in criminal law. He clerked summers for *the* criminal law firm in Chicago. You can imagine the kinds of experience he gained there. He moved back home after graduation and joined our firm. So you see, William, the only criminally trained lawyer employed by Polanski & Stelzl, was our best choice to represent you this morning, a fact we weren't able to share with you as, after his rushed return from a business trip, we barely had time to brief William before court opened. I mean, murder, even manslaughter—well, they're not exactly kielbasa, if you know what I mean."

The partners stifled their guffaws at that witticism as my mind latched on the obvious point: What could the sausage company's legal team possibly have in the way of relevant experience? Hadn't they just proved that in the courtroom?

Art grew serious, apparently reading my thoughts. "Don't think for one minute that implies we are not able and qualified to handle your defense, Kip. In fact, William's very first case with us relied successfully on his unique skill set. Remember the Milwaukee woman who sued Czermanski Sausages for the wrongful death of her husband? She'd claimed he died from eating tainted sausages, but on the stand, William drew out her confession. She admitted injecting rat poison into Czermanski Polish sausages herself before serving them to him, rat poison being what she termed 'poetic justice' for the cheat her husband had been. Her suit came about when she discovered he'd left no money. Lucky for her, she won't be needing money where she'll spend the rest of her life."

Life. No parole.

I forced my thoughts into order. "You're saying that nothing can be done to change the outcome of the arraignment. It cannot be called a mistrial or contested in some way? No amount of money my dad could put up would hurry my release, not even a million dollars?" They sadly shook their heads as the reality of living in this cell for two months of my life leached all the fight out of me. With a long slow sigh, I acquiesced. "Okay… how do we begin?"

The partners glanced at each other before Art spoke. "You heard your father, Kip. He wants us to meet with him at the house. He, uh, hadn't said anything else about us, perhaps before we arrived? Good. We'll leave you two to begin working out your defense. Discuss the events of the night and start to pull all pertinent background information together. You take good notes now, William," he chided their protégé, who blushed once more. "We'll reconvene tomorrow, Kip, after William debriefs us this evening."

The partners stood, Bob stuffing loose shirttails beneath his belt, struggling to button his jacket. Art in marked contrast remained elegant and unwrinkled as they reached for their coats. In what must have been a prearranged signal, Bob used a thick ring of keys to scrape the iron bars. The second jarring trill summoned the jailer down the hallway toward my cell.

"You two probably have lots in common, both growing up here," Bob added in his folksy, avuncular manner. "Get acquainted, see where your paths may have crossed, while we begin the serious business of building a defense."

"No rock left unturned," Art cautioned the young lawyer they were leaving behind, effectively shifting blame for their poor preparations to him. The intensified color that directive induced on William's face spelled more than just humiliation. He was angry. The cell was locked with just the two of us within, my young legal eagle staring after his bosses long after they'd vanished.

CHAPTER SEVEN

I studied William Whoever He Was, futzing with his coat on the cot. His chubbiness might be downright fat without the constraining effect of his lawyerly charcoal-gray suit. A stark white shirt, buttoned at the collar, aided by a red-white-and-blue tie, cinched his neck too tightly. A discreet diamond stud tacked his tie. Standing next to me in court, he appeared to be about six feet tall. Despite thinning, dishwater-blond hair and his old-think garb, I now saw he was quite young—still in his twenties I'd bet, close to my age. Being this side of thirty made him—theoretically anyway—trustworthy, but his hyper-conservatism, completed by wingtips shining beneath his well-creased trousers, raised serious doubts.

He drew his briefcase onto his knees, raising its lid like a wall between us, and pulled out pencils and pads. Slamming the lid shut sent a wave of noxious pine cologne circulating through the cell. The thick lenses of his glasses had obscured the mud-brown color of his irises until he looked directly at me. The glasses eerily magnified and distorted his eyes, something I'd failed to notice in the throes of my arraignment.

He set about organizing perfectly sharpened pencils and legal pads beside him, glancing at me from time to time, but quickly breaking off eye contact. That caused me to examine what I was wearing. Upon my return to jail after court, I was given the option of remaining in the infantile sailor suit I wore to the arraignment, which made it even harder to breathe, or to change back into the clothes I had been arrested in—but only until they found a prison uniform "small enough for a small woman."

I'd opted for the latter, the college leave-behinds Sybel tossed at me as the police arrived at the house—a tattered red sweater covered with peace signs, jeans threadbare at the knees, and my old combat boots, all veterans of campus protests. Only Sybel, who had been scandalized by my counterculture garb, would nonetheless preserve them in mothballs for posterity. I created quite a sight for this conservative lawyer, as unnerved by my getup as I by his. There was nothing I could do about my hair gone wild, but I tucked the combat boots beneath my cot as an act of conciliation.

"Miss Czermanski," the young lawyer began at last, "perhaps we should begin all over again. Let's take nothing further for granted. I'd like to start with a quick review of the basics."

"You can lose the tie and jacket, loosen your collar if you wish. It's just you and me in this cell—in the whole jail—and I certainly won't mind." It would in fact be a relief.

"No, no, I'm fine," he insisted. "It's more professional. Now then, your full name is Kip Czermanski. Odd for a girl. No middle name?"

A girl? "No, I legally changed it several years ago to just Kip. I couldn't deal with the names my parents had bestowed upon me any longer."

His magnified eyes became owlish circles of surprise. "You're joking?"

"You try living with Knavere Priestley Czermanski, both my grandmothers' maiden names, thankfully shortened to KP early on. Knavere was my Polish grandmother's family name supposedly, but I suspect she'd shortened Knaveleski or something like it herself. She always wanted to be French, liberally dropping Frenchisms into her speech." This was more explanation than required, the lawyer's glazing eyes told me.

"Right," he replied, jotting a note. "And it's Miss. You are single?"

"It's Ms." The lawyer did a double take. "M-s-period. My marital status bears on my defense?" I demanded with good feminist conviction. But the bare facts of my case paraded before me—naked man, married to my sister, found dead in my bed. "Yeah, I'm single," I finally answered.

"And you're twenty-four years old?"

I nodded. "Almost twenty-five. How old are you?" Like the judge, the lawyer seemed shocked by two-way conversation.

"I? I am twenty-eight next week. To continue: Since your college graduation in May of 1970, you've lived in Santa Monica, California?"

I read the all too familiar Midwestern, anti-coastal attitude in the lawyer's sneer of disdain, which, come to think of it, was pretty much his normal expression. I replied with a nod, saying, "Let me guess, you've never been to California, yet you look down your nose at it. California is fantastic—no snow, cold, mosquitoes, or humidity, gorgeous ocean, beaches, and mountains. You should check it out some time. You'd be pleasantly surprised." As he appeared unconvinced, I enumerated California's other attractions to myself: *two thousand miles from here, no family, no small-town reputation or associations preceding me, warmth and sunshine all year round.*

William paused, staring at this notes. "It says here that you're employed by the Santa Monica Center for Women's Liberation." He glanced at me and laughed. "Not really."

"Yes, really. What's so amusing about that?"

He sobered, shifting on the cot. "Right. And your job at this Center for Women's Liberation?"

"Assertiveness Trainer. I coach pre-feminist women to get in touch with their deep inner needs and feelings, helping them discover and live more fulfilling lives, despite our society's ingrained sexism."

My cell mate removed his glasses and fastidiously polished the lenses. "I'm sorry, Miss, I mean Ms. Czermanski, I knew you were an anti-war activist during college. Am I to take it you're saying now that you label yourself a-a feminist?"

"Yes."

The lawyer studied his notes, pencil poised, before repeating as he wrote, "Assertiveness Trainer, the Santa Monica Center for Women's Liberation." He literally glared at the words he'd written before speaking again. "Excuse me, Miss Czermanski, maybe I've misunderstood it. Perhaps you could enlighten me about feminism, and while you're at it, explain what it is you women need liberating from?"

"You don't contend that men and women have equal opportunities and rewards in the home, in the work place, or anywhere else you might name, do you?" I bristled. "The basic precept of feminism is no more radical than equal pay for equal work. That and the freedom to choose how one lives her life. Perhaps we all need liberation from the customs and limitations built into our society, from the beliefs and expectations that inform all roles and relationships—women's subservience, men's breadwinning, for example. Sexism is woven into every strand of our existence."

His face betrayed total skepticism. "That sounds so reasonable. Yet the feminist diatribe—excuse the term—even we here in Wausaukeesha are exposed to employs other words, words like chauvinist, pig, castration—even death, once the sperm banks are filled. Are those the subjects unsuspecting women are coached in at your Liberation Center?"

I stamped my combat boot so hard on the floor between us, it hurt. "It's ludicrous for you to tell me what feminism means. Though hardly the radical-fringe feminist you describe, I am a practitioner. Try to remember you are the lawyer my dad is paying to defend me."

We glared at each other suspiciously. *What's with this guy?* But the bars I leaned against had begun to score stripes into my back. As I fumbled for a pillow to tuck between, I suggested, "Shall we get on with it?"

The uptight lawyer deliberated for a moment, his eyes moving from his notes to me, and back. "I'm sorry, Miss Czermanski, truly. But doesn't it bother you even a little to be responsible for the spread of ideas that threaten the security and structure of our country? First you undermine our government and military during time of war. Now you're undermining our homes and families?" Before I could react, he backpedaled, muttering, "We've gotten off track." He roused himself by shuffling papers and pencils. "Let's see, a more familiar term, perhaps family counselor, might sufficiently describe your professional duties? A judge, more to the point a jury, might relate more sympathetically."

"It's clearly less politically charged." *And the point was to get on with it.* "Fine," I allowed. "Family counselor will do for these purposes."

"You graduated from UW Madison in May 1970 with a degree in psychology."

"And a political science minor."

He glossed over my last comment. "And you're the youngest of Mr. Czermanski's four daughters."

"Three." It came out curt.

"Oh yes, three. I'm sorry about your sister," he paged through his notes to find her name. "Sarah. I never knew there was another sister." I made no response, I didn't dare. "Sarah was the eldest. How much older than you is—I mean, was—she?"

Like a well-trained Czermanski, my answer put us in age-order. "Samantha is eight years older than me, Sybel is ten, and Sarah was fifteen years older than me."

"How long had Sybel—she was the one with the mourning veils in court today? I get your sisters confused—how long were she and Stan married?"

"Of course it was Sybel under the veils. Sybel has always been known for dressing the part." That came across as cruel so I rushed to answer, "They were married six months, since last August."

The lawyer reviewed his notes. "That completes the preliminaries. Let's move on to your relationship with your—with Dr. Stanislaw Szyzyck. He was a doctor of …"

"Of political science, a professor, when I knew him. But that was close to three years ago, and for two of those, I had no idea where he'd gone or what he was doing."

"You two became romantically involved through the anti-war movement on campus during college, according to the prosecution complaint. You became, uh, romantically entangled again last week when you returned home?"

"No, we weren't 'entangled.'"

"But his body—it was found, unclothed, in your bed at the family home early Sunday morning?"

It did sound bad. The air grew heavy in my cell, thick like I'd sunk to the bottom of the sea. Exhaustion of every kind pressed down. It took effort to pace the small space to get some blood flowing. "I'm in big trouble, aren't I?"

Chapter Eight

On my next circle of the cell, I asked my pudgy counselor, "What did the judge mean by 'save the exculpatory for the prelim?'"

A more straightforward question of law immediately warmed Lawyer William. "The judge reprimanded me for attempting to introduce evidence at the arraignment which showed you did not commit the crime. Technically, that's done at the preliminary hearing. But I was floundering with all the surprises this morning."

He had floundered, I had to agree. "What happened this morning?"

"The arraignment was a fiasco, Miss Czermanski. That statement stays between us."

"Humph!" I snorted. "The partners hadn't prepared, nor did they prepare you. In fact, it would appear the entire firm of Polanski & Stelzl was out-matched by the prosecution."

William's eyes flashed momentarily behind his Coke bottle specs. "Frankly, even if I'd been here to prepare, I don't know whether your arraignment would have had a better outcome. The lack of preparation showed some arrogance, perhaps understandable given your father's position in this town. But the prosecutor went out on a limb with circumstantial evidence, though I haven't yet read the full complaint, it was so long. Harvey Debick in his least provoked state is a ferret, and for whatever reason, he appears to be highly provoked."

"Debick? The prosecutor's name is Harvey Debick? Not Mike Debick's father?"

"Yes, you knew Mike?"

"Did I ever tell you I hate small towns?" I paced again, risking further provocation of my temporary cellmate with each clomp of my combat boots.

"Wausaukeesha is hardly the small town you make it out to be," he responded. "Its population is almost twenty-five thousand."

Geez, everything I am, do, or say pisses this guy off, which was hardly productive. "No offense, William, it's just that everyone knows everyone in this town. I not only knew Mike Debick, I also knew his father, sort of. Mike's dad and I met years ago, and not under the best of circumstances."

I gazed down the hallway, which led not only out of this cell, but all the way back to my apartment with its glimpse of the Pacific and Santa Monica Beach from the balcony. "You better get comfortable if you want to hear this," I warned, standing before him. William pondered a second before nodding for me to go ahead.

When I closed my eyes, I felt hot sand beneath my bare feet. A screeching seagull swooped overhead. The fish-and-salt smell of the ocean filled my lungs. When I opened my eyes, there was only dead space beyond my cell and the touchy lawyer locked in with me.

"It had to be third grade in Sister Margaret's classroom at Immaculate Conception, 1956 ..." I sunk onto my cot, settling in before relaying the long-winded memory a name had dredged up from my past.

I was minding my own business, scratching initials inside my desk where they'd be hidden under papers if the sister made one of her surprise searches, when something slimy splatted on my cheek. "Yuck," slipped out as I peeled the stuck parts off. I glanced around to see who'd tossed the spitball and caught Mike Debick ducking behind the classmates seated between us.

Immediately, my name rang out in the classroom, Sister Margaret calling me to the front of the class to read my homework. I rubbed my cheek as I stood to explain. "Um, excuse me Sister Margaret, but I, um, didn't finish my homework last night. You see, I waited for Divine Inspiration for so long," I explained by using one of her favorite terms, "that I kinda fell asleep."

"Be seated, KP," she said and called out Mike Debick's name. Paper in hand, he trudged toward the nun from the boys' side of the classroom, noses wrinkling as he passed by. Mike was known to have what my nanny called a touchy tummy. I think he just lived on Twinkies and Coke, which was why he was so big for an eight year old—big and stinky. All the girls found Mike Debick dis-*gusting*. Was that what made him so mean?

Mike faced the classroom in his scruffy uniform, his scent lingering. I let him see me holding my nose. A deep blush seeped up his neck and over his face, covering his scalp under the blond bristles that never seemed to grow. Even his chubby hands clutching his homework turned red. But his watered-down blue eyes dared us to make fun of him or his paper. He read, "We're lucky to be Catholic, the One True Religion"—he too buttered up Sister with her well-worn phrases—"because we get a lot more school holidays than public school kids 'cuz of all the Catholic holy days. We're lucky to be Catholic because Catholics breeze through Purgatory and get to Heaven fast when they die. We're lucky to be Catholic because we don't have to pay attention during Mass 'cuz we can't understand the language anyways." Sister stopped him there.

Wow, Mike had written the paper of his life. Or maybe he swiped it. Or maybe he made someone smaller than him, which could be anyone in class, write it for him.

"See me after class," Sister said. "Be seated. And KP—" I looked up when Sister said my name. "—see me after class as well." Darn, I thought she'd forgotten all about my missing homework.

When school bells sounded the end of the day and the hallways filled with kids making their escape, Mike and I remained in our seats on opposite sides of Sister's classroom. Paying no attention to us, Sister kept us waiting for fifteen minutes. I forced myself not to squirm, as past experience taught me it would only slow her down more. When at last she called us both up to the front of the room, she directed me to sit in the closest desk to hers, which belonged to the teacher's pet, Katey Rudeshiem.

I hated being this close to a nun—it served teacher's pet right. Their witchy habits smelled like mothballs and their skin like lye or bleach or something they probably bathed in for their Daily Penance, another of Sister's favorite phrases. I wondered what nuns had to repent every day, besides being mean. She quizzed Mike, who was not paying close attention. He fiddled with papers on her desk, trying to act tough. He failed to notice that Sister's black eyebrow, which ran from one side of her forehead to the other with no break in the middle, had stopped moving and settled low—a sure sign to wise up before it's too late. One blow with her metal ruler to Mike's shoulder made his chin quiver and lip pout.

"Look at me when I'm speaking to you," she threatened. Before he obeyed, he received two more blows almost too fast to see.

I knew what to do. I raised the lid of Katey Rudeshiem's desk and slunk down behind it, checking out its contents while I was there. A white Bible, neatly stacked papers, clips and pencils, a picture of Jesus with a halo taped to the lid, and not an initial to be found. *Bor*-ing.

"KP Czermanski, you pay attention." Did the sister know what she was asking of me? Mike Debick would bully me without end if I caught him crying. But I lowered the lid as directed to the tears brimming in Mike's eyes.

The Sister's brow lifted a bit. "It is a sin to disregard the privilege of being raised in the Catholic Church and the great privilege of attending Catholic school. You make a mockery of Immaculate Conception's third grade class of 1956-57. Mike, you blasphemed," she hissed, whispering the last word, "when you counted Latin Mass a blessing you don't have to pay attention to. Have you both forgotten that upon your seventh birthdays last year, you reached the official Age of Reason? God has kept Permanent Records on you both ever since. I shudder to think how those records read in their very first year." The sister actually shuddered before continuing.

"Before first bell tomorrow, I expect on my desk your papers enumerating the blessings of being Catholic. Do you understand? And you know I have the Sixth Sense. Did you really think you could create a disturbance in my classroom I wouldn't detect?" She glared at us, and with her eyebrow settling low, it took all my willpower to not react. "Before first bell. You may go."

We raced from Sister's classroom onto the playground, me crossing to the girls' side with Mike following, slinging his usual stupid taunts: "KP, KP, isn't that some kind of punishment you get in the army, KP duty?"

"Really funny, Debick." I did not slow down.

Neither did Mike. "Kitchen Patrol, Kitchen Patrol, Kitchen Patrol Czermanski is … the Sausage Queen." Even as Debick's little gang ran toward us, I stopped to face him. He chanted, "Kitchen Patrol Czermanski is the Sausage Queen." Then he sang my dad's theme song from the radio, which he'd just started using on TV. *"And we know that science is the secret of Czermanski's great meats."*

I stomped up to Mike in the circle of his buddies and said, "At least I didn't cry when some old nun slapped me with a ruler. And I am not the Sausage Queen."

I was never the Sausage Queen, a fact Mike and I had been over many times. Samantha was the one who for years rode in the homecoming parades in the convertible car shaped like a Polish sausage on a bun, complete with oozing sauerkraut. To help him remember this time, I punched Mike on the snout. "Boogerhead."

Debick's nose gushed blood so badly, he fainted. We stared down in shock at his bleeding body. Holy moly, had I killed him? That really would look bad in the first year of my Permanent Record. My next confession sprang to mind: *Forgive me Father, for I have sinned. I didn't do my homework 'cause it was, well, so dumb. And I sassed my sister, Sybel, but she already grounded me for another month. And oh yes, I killed Mike Debick but it was an accident, Father, really. And he started it.*

"What's going on here?" Sister Margaret surprised us from behind. "KP, you are not allowed on the boys' side of the school playground. You—oh my heavens, what's happened?" She muscled through our circle, drawing a Kleenex from inside her wide sleeve. *What else did she keep up there?* She tried to stuff it up Mike's nose but lucky for me, he came to and pushed her away, holding her Kleenex himself. We watched it turn red in his hand. The sister ordered me to run to the office for help. By the time I returned with the young novice and her emergency kit, Mike was standing, still fending Sister off.

Once he for sure wasn't going to die, Sister marched the two of us to Sister Mary Principal's office, where we were told to sit in the waiting room until our parents arrived. I settled into the chair nearest the window so I could at least look outside, knowing it'd be a long wait for my mom and dad. Debick slouched in the row of chairs opposite me, ignoring my whispered, "I'm sorry I made you bleed."

The hallway door burst open and in stormed a Mike Debick look-alike, only old. "What's this I hear," the man demanded of Mike. "Some girl gave you a bloody nose? You fainted?"

When Mike glanced to where I'd been hidden behind the open door, I scrunched down in my seat, making myself as small as possible. But Mike's father slammed the door and stood before me.

"You?" he cried. "Are you the culprit behind this hooligan act?"

I thought I'd wet my pants, watching Mr. Debick burn a furious red from his prickly scalp to his fingertips, just like his son. Except for their age difference, they could've been twins.

I glanced around for some protection, but there wasn't even a desk for "duck and cover." I was out in the open and all alone until Sister Mary Principal appeared from the inner office.

"Oh, Mr. Debick," she said, stepping between us, her size and habit hiding me completely, "I thought I heard you arrive. Thank you for coming so quickly. As I told you, there was some trouble on the playground after these two scamps were detained after class by Sister Margaret. Please come wait in my office until KP Czermanski's parents arrive."

Sister ushered Mike's mom, whom I hadn't even noticed, toward her office door, but his dad didn't budge.

"Czermanski? Sister, did you say Czermanski?"

I kept Mr. Debick's huge balled-up fists in sight until Sister pulled him away. "Yes, JJ Czermanski's youngest, KP. We'll just wait in here, Mr. Debick."

"This is not over," he shouted over his shoulder at me. "I promise you, this is far from over."

CHAPTER NINE

I realized I'd been staring at Lawyer William but seeing instead Mr. Debick from years earlier. "When you referred to the prosecutor as a ferret," I asked William, "you were simply implying that he's thorough, not that he's vindictive, right?"

"You're worried about that childhood incident at Immaculate Conception? I doubt it would prompt his overzealousness. That would be overkill, even for Harvey Debick."

"Of course you're right. He would never remember me after all these years." *Though I would never forget him,* I thought, shifting uncomfortably in my seat. "But, well, there was just a wee bit more to the story I'm afraid."

As William's bespectacled eyes met mine, his brows arched above his thick frames, I determined to complete for him the childhood tale that had thoroughly changed my life—even changed my name.

My Polish nanny during the third grade had tried to protect me. "Sybel ist steamink mad," she warned me that evening. "Stay in your room."

But I was well aware of Sybel's state. After meeting with Sister Mary Principal and the Debicks, Sybel, as my stand-in parent, could barely control herself in the car on the drive home, despite her firm policy against public punishment. I'd been staying out of striking range since, waiting in my bedroom, knowing what was coming. I'd even made my bed and hid my dirty clothes beneath it. For extra protection, I'd seated myself behind the small white desk I inherited from Samantha, who inherited it from Sybel, and which Sarah had probably passed down originally. I had just begun my homework by writing, "We are lucky to be Catholic," when my bedroom door burst open and in stalked Sybel with Dad in tow.

Dad had removed his jacket and tie and loosened his collar, but his curly hair was still dented from the hat he always wore in public. "What's this I'm hearing, KP? You picked on Harvey Debick's boy at school today? Bloodied his nose?" Dad did not look all that mad, though his tone was serious.

"I didn't pick on him, Dad. He picked on me, like always."

"Not what the nuns told me," Sybel said, "not even close. You really got yourself in deep trouble this time, KP. Mr. Debick is demanding that Immaculate Conception expel you for assaulting his son, doing him 'bodily harm,' he called it. He's threatened to sue the school if they don't take immediate action against you."

Sybel turned to Dad. "Imagine the humiliation of having a Czermanski, the first Catholic family of Wausaukeesha, expelled from Catholic grade school. How will we uphold our position in the church and town? Our importance will only ignite more vicious rumors and gossip—" She paused to eye me with open contempt. "—thanks to you, KP, always at the center of trouble. How could you do this to us, KP? Do you ever think about the rest of us?"

I wasn't following everything Sybel was saying. My mind had stuck on the word "expel."

Checking his watch, Dad sat before me on my pink-flowered bedspread and pulled Sybel down next to him. She tossed her head to spread her blonde waves over her shoulders and glared at me as Dad asked, "What have you got to say for yourself, KP? Let's have it, the whole story, and be quick about it."

I told him what happened, from spitball to principal's office, as fast as I could, knowing no matter what I said, it wouldn't make any difference. It never did.

"Wrong family to pick on," Dad commented when I finished. "Harvey Debick and I go back a long, long way, back to Immaculate Conception ourselves in fact, and on through St. Hedwig's." Dad chuckled. "And even beyond."

I didn't get the joke, but I liked the sound of Dad laughing. I chuckled too, raising Sybel's alarm, which Dad didn't notice. "We competed for everything, and it killed Old Harv, the silver-spoon rich kid from town, to lose to me, the dumb Polack farm boy. But I bested him in every instance except one, when I had to drop out of high school after my dad got sick. Harvey made captain of the football team that year, something we both wanted badly. As it turned out, St. Hedwig's had its worst season in history."

Dad laughed out loud and I joined in. This wasn't going too badly after all.

"The final straw between us was my new plant," Dad continued. "Sure, I got some zoning variances pushed through to build my new processing plant, nothing unusual about that. But to this day, Harvey thinks I knew that he owned all the land around it and the nearby lake. Seems he'd bet the family fortune on a real estate development he was going to call Wausaukeesha Shores." Dad guffawed, shaking his head. "You can't even say it. How the hell would he have sold it?"

"Daddy," Sybel interrupted, reminding him why they were sitting across from me, hunkered behind my desk.

"Huh-hem, right. The point being, KP, that Harvey lost everything on that scheme when my new sausage assembly plant went into operation. Seems the plant created a little odor pollution problem for Harv's development, and it failed. He went bust, which is why I said, 'wrong family to pick on.' There's nothing I can do—no free sausages for the school or the rectory, no donations like I made when you refused to cover your head for Mass because the boys didn't have to, nothing. As assistant county prosecutor, Harvey's in a position to make good on his threat against the school, and they know it. My hands are tied. You're out, young lady, out of Catholic school. Now what do you think of that?" Dad glanced at his wristwatch, always ready to bolt when it came to such messy family issues.

I tried to look dejected for Sybel's sake, but my mind was spinning. No more Catholic school? No more nuns and priests, novenas, and Hail Marys? No Our Fathers, except on Sundays of course? No more Sister Margaret? No more school uniforms? I bet public schools allowed bobby socks like my sisters wore, and penny loafers and maybe even patent leather shoes. No one besides a nun would worry about patent leather and pennies reflecting upward, right?

As a storm gathered in Sybel's sky-blue eyes, I forced myself to reply, "I'm sorry, Dad, but it wasn't my fault."

"Nothing is your fault," Sybel hissed, coming to her feet, "yet you're always involved." I shrunk backwards in my seat.

Dad rose with her. "I don't totally hold with this other cheek stuff myself," he said, I guess referring to the spitball? "Regardless of who started what, life isn't fair, KP, and sometimes you've got to pay the piper. Sybel will take you to the public grade school tomorrow morning on her way to school and get you enrolled. No telling how hard you'll have to work to catch up with your new class." He looked from me to her. "In this instance I think that will be punishment enough."

Dad talked over Sybel's protests. "You've brought great shame on yourself and this proud family. You'll be the first Czermanski ever who isn't Catholic school educated. I'm just glad your mother isn't here to see this." He ushered Sybel through the door. I remained seated, listening until their footsteps reached the bottom of the stairs and faded completely. I used my best cursive to finish writing the sentence I'd begun when Dad and Sybel stormed in. "We're lucky to be Catholic … because we can confess our sins and be forgiven."

I sprang from behind my desk and rushed to my closet, tossing my homework in the trash on the way. I rummaged through my shoes for the patent leathers that had started me off on the wrong foot with Sister Margaret the first day of third grade. Pulling them out, I used the plaid skirt of my former school uniform to make them shine.

Chapter Ten

Evidently comfortable with my counterculture attire, or at least putting its offensiveness behind him, the lawyer stared at me, his lens-distorted eyes wide with apprehension. But he wasn't seeing me at all, and a blind silence stretched out. His alarm began to alarm me, and I moved to the sink for a plastic glassful of water until I finally had to plug the noiseless gap.

"The history between my dad and the prosecutor, it can't affect my case, can it? I mean, I was only eight years old, a lot of years ago, and my involvement was just kid stuff, like you said."

His staring into space unnerved me, so I again leaped into the void.

"I'll tell you one thing about my expulsion from Immaculate Conception that is important to this day. When I enrolled in the third grade at public school, I gave my name as Kip Czermanski." To his continued lack of response, I emphasized the point. "I added the 'i' and I've been Kip ever since."

William the Lawyer, somewhat green around the edges, at last reacted. "I'd heard that Harvey Debick became a county prosecutor after a financial setback of some kind. I always assumed it was malicious gossip since Harvey is known for being difficult, but a vendetta?" William flopped backwards with a thud. "Could that explain the excessive preparedness, the high-risk charge?"

I drank the glass dry and set it down. "As I think back on that meeting in Sister Mary's office, he seemed like a hard man, hard on everyone, including himself. He was kind of tough on his son that day. Whatever happened to him—Mike, that is? You obviously knew him." The lawyer's plump physique reminded me of Mike. "What's become of him? I haven't seen him since that fateful incident in the third grade."

"You don't know?" My question had stopped the lawyer cold. "Mike Debick enlisted at eighteen. He was killed in action in Vietnam his first week of active duty."

"Oh! Oh no, he's dead? Mike's dead six years now?" I plunked down on the cot and covered my face with my hands, remembering what was surely a premonition of this years ago—perhaps while it was happening. "And he enlisted. Doesn't that totally figure …"

William nodded noncommittally. "Mike was their only child. Though it was hard on Harvey I'm sure, he never showed it, but Mike's mom fell apart. I've heard she rarely leaves their home anymore. Harvey apparently channeled all his grief into his work. To call him a formidable adversary is to put it lightly.

"I thought I'd seen Harvey at his most exhaustive," William continued, "but today's complaint at your arraignment surprised even me, who knows the man too well." Respect if not awe infused the lawyer's tone. "You can imagine the fervor with which Commander Debick executes his drill sergeant duties at our monthly Guard exercises."

I gasped and backed away, my whole body surging with adrenalin. I could not look at the man locked in the cell not two feet from me without hot anger and cold fear coursing through me, one after the other. He suddenly seemed huge and threatening.

"You're not telling me … you don't mean to say …" I hugged myself in a corner for protection. "You're National Guard?" Saying the last two words made my old wounds throb all over my body.

William straightened up, an indignant flush displacing the green. "Indeed I am. Despite the responsibility of three little ones at home, I'm proud to do my part for my country."

It had been several years since I'd been on the front lines of the anti-war movement, but the bruising clashes my comrades and I experienced at the hands of the National Guard called onto campus to disperse or arrest us remained visceral. I had braced, I realized, unconsciously.

The lawyer watched me as if weighing how cornered and vulnerable I was before closing in for the kill. It wasn't the first time I'd seen that assessing look in the eyes of the cops and guards, steeled with clubs, tear gas, and shields against us unarmed demonstrators as they surrounded us. Assessing weaknesses must be the first step in combat training.

The lawyer struck with words. "I don't aid and abet our enemies during time of war." He became so steamed, his glasses seemed to fog over. "Honestly, Miss Czermanski, how can you be proud of being one of those spoiled, lawless students fomenting violence and anarchy right here in our own country, right here in Wisconsin?" The junior lawyer from Dad's firm on Dad's payroll couldn't stop bullying and bating me, in his eyes a home-wrecking feminist and enemy-abetting anti-war activist.

"You were ROTC as well," I stated without question. The worst those spit-and-polish student reserve officers did was shove us around when we were fewer than them on campus and taunt us as "fucking freaks." Still, they weren't my best memory of college either.

"Of course I joined the R-O-T-C," he answered. "I have always taken my patriotic duty seriously."

"And you're pro-war naturally—a brave stance when you serve your country by playing at war games with your buddies once a month in the dangerous jungles of Wisconsin."

"I resent that, Miss Czermanski."

"As do I your implication that it is unpatriotic to hold any opinion other than yours, that all activists are spoiled children rioting for the fun of it, that all feminists are would-be murderers of men."

I stood and circled, playing for time to weigh consequences before a decision that suddenly seemed inevitable.

"Okay, explain it to me, Mr. Pro War. You successfully avoid real combat by first prolonging your education, then getting married, having kids, and joining the Guard. That's a lot of exemptions you've used—your draft lottery number must have been really low. Yet you self-righteously claim to be fighting the domino theory of communism from right here in Wisconsin. You're pro-war—in concept? Someone else can do the real fighting and dying?"

"That is not fair," William shot back, tugging at his collar.

"'Like life,'" I quoted my dad from many years earlier. "'And sometimes you just have to pay the piper.'" A dangerous realization had overtaken my brain and there was no more delaying it.

My head ached, my body ached, I felt nauseous. I hated this cell, I hated the lawyer's aftershave and his narrow-minded condescension. I hated the stink of my old clothes, I hated this town and every second I would be held in it. And none of that changed a thing, nor would the full backing of Dad's law firm—that had become undeniable.

I sat down before him with a sigh. "William." *What are you doing, Kip?* "William, I don't think this will work." He studied me. "Though I have no doubt you'd do your duty as commanded, your heart won't be in the defense of a spoiled, lawless activist turned home-wrecking feminist whose future and freedom will depend upon it."

He blinked rapidly. "Miss Czermanski, my firm has an outstanding track record with your father in all his legal matters," he reminded me. "I did not seek this assignment," he huffed, "nor you me," he conceded, "but I can assure you this case will be no different—"

"It is different, William. *I* am different. Your partners admitted earlier that this was well outside the norm for Polanski & Stelzl—something about kielbasa?"

William shifted in his seat, dropping his eyes but I detected a softening in the lines of determination around his mouth.

I began speaking, despite the questions running through my mind. *What was I doing? What would I do?*

"Please tell my father and your bosses," I began tentatively. "Yes, tell them that the services of Polanski & Stelzl will not be needed." *Kip, are you crazy?* flashed in neon before my eyes.

"Miss Czermanski, I must advise you to carefully consider such a decision." William's expression vacillated between concern over consequences and a joyous relief he could not mask.

"Thanks for the advice, but I'll find my own lawyer." *And just how will I do that from this cell?*

"Have it your way. The court will appoint—"

"Thank you, but that is no longer your concern."

William the Lawyer stood, yanked on his coat, and swiped the bars with the metal reinforced corner of his briefcase, champing to get out. Once released and bounding away, he added as if convincing himself, "It's completely the client's decision."

Silence rained down on me after he'd gone. I'd probably played right into my ex-lawyer's hands. Where, how, would I find a lawyer other than another reluctant local the court would appoint, hardly the best option, given my reputation in town and Dad's sudden powerlessness.

I paced, collapsed on the cot, stood, collapsed on the cot, paced some more to stimulate my brain. *Think,* I commanded myself, when on my next brief loop of the cell I noticed a business card, creased where William had been sitting on it. He must have found it while juggling overcoats but forgot about it as we clashed. I picked up the small white card and smoothed it out, flipping it into the air as soon as I read it.

"*No.*" It fluttered to the floor. "It cannot be. No way. Not *Billy Beneke.*"

The heat of humiliation prickled my skin. I threw myself on the cot facedown and buried my head in the pillows. "I hate small towns." At least I'd fired him.

Part Three

How does it feel
To be without a home
Like a complete unknown
Like a rolling stone?

– BOB DYLAN –

CHAPTER ELEVEN

"Awful quiet back here. You all right, Miss Czermanski?"

I awoke with a start to the kind-faced jailer whose arms I'd collapsed in earlier in the day. I'd drifted off, not quite sucking my thumb, pondering my latest legal dilemma: the no-lawyer part.

"I'm still here," came my feeble response, "and for eight whole weeks before trial even starts. How long will the trial take, do you think?"

"No tellin'. Depends upon your lawyers, the judge, a whole bunch of stuff. But these things take a while, even once they get started."

"Like a month?" My arraignment seemed like a month ago, not mere hours. "More?" The rasping in my voice said way more than I intended.

The jailer shrugged. "Likely you'll be with us somewhere around three months, maybe more—that's if your lawyers take the quickest trial date."

"'*Take* the quickest trial date?'" I stared at him, dreading his implication. "The judge set the trial for eight weeks, other dates in between, too. What do you mean 'take?'"

"Sure, but court dates and such change, drag out for one reason or another," the jailer explained. "Why I can remember one case … well, I'll just leave you be."

"No, don't. Don't leave, Mr. … Jailer. What should I call you?" Might as well get acquainted with one of few people I'm likely to see for who knows how long. Oh man, he can't be right about three months. Or more?

He removed his guard cap to expose a shiny bald head encircled by a crescent of white fringe. "Timothy Rudeshiem, Miss. Pleased to meet you."

The melancholy of his smile was repeated in his eyes as he extended a large, dry hand through the bars.

I stood to shake it, certain most jailers weren't this congenial. "Kip Czermanski." He nodded until I realized I was clutching his hand and released it. "Right, you knew that—your only inmate. Timothy Rudeshiem, you say? Meaning you're related to Katey?" Damn small towns.

"Barely. Katey's some kind of cousin so many times removed, can't say as we're real relatives. Heard, though, that she's married, has kids, lives in a real nice house not far from the square. Not that I'm complaining, mind you. Got a real secure job here, good benefits, and retirement not far off. Then you just watch me head up north lickety-split and fish my life away, summers and winters."

"You're a fisherman? I never understood—I mean, how interesting. Maybe I'll try it, uh, when I get out."

"You should. So still and peaceful, the water rocking your boat in warm weather, the sun dancing all around—it's like heaven itself, I hope. Why, you hardly care if you catch anything."

"It sounds beautiful, Mr. Rudeshiem." That idyllic description inspired an unexpected surge of emotion. *Get a hold of yourself, Kip.*

"Timothy, okay?"

"Timothy," I heartily agreed. Reminders of Katey Rudeshiem every time I addressed my jailer were hardly welcome. Immaculate Conception's prime example of feminine piety flashed before me. Katey Rudeshiem kneeling to show Sister Margaret that her plaid pleats brushed the ground, that her white blouse was buttoned to the collar, that barrettes and bows held her hair off her face—another nun-thing.

"Call me Kip."

"Deal. You hungry, Kip? You hardly touched your lunch."

"Not in the least." In the subsequent awkward interlude, I grasped that my jailer was about to leave me. "Timothy," I improvised, "I was supposed to be on my way home by now, back to California. My boss will be worried, or worse, when I don't show up for work. Could I call her to tell her what's happened, that I won't be in for … a while?" He couldn't possibly be right. "I'd hate to lose my job over this, uh, delay."

Timothy scratched his shiny skull before replacing the hat. "S'pose I can let you do that. You're a Czermanski, after all. I'm sure you're more'n good for the long-distance charge. I'll hav'ta dial, though."

I couldn't believe it. My jailer was unlocking my cell—for me. I crossed the threshold to freedom, however fleeting. Should I make a run for it, cross the state, get to Canada, find Peter, and hide out … for the rest of my life? No way. Besides, I'd be pretty conspicuous slogging through the snow in this Ms. Nineteen Sixties getup. I'd be spotted, shot in the back, my blood staining virgin snow. What movie was that from—*Dr. Zhivago?* I imagined stoic Sybel at my funeral, secretly thrilled by my demise and the sympathy it garnered her.

One is the loneliest number that you ever do.

Timothy guided me along the hallway toward the front of the jailhouse, but I could have followed my nose and ears. The strains of pop music and the stench of burnt coffee intensified with each step.

No is the saddest experience you'll ever know.

We reached a room with a large window onto the jail's lobby entry in which a uniformed receptionist sat beyond the glass, filing her nails, wide eyes on me. Beyond her, another window allowed me a glimpse of the outside world. Timothy tossed his hat on the closest of the two facing desks furnishing the inner office. It landed next to the playing radio that he directed me to sit in front of, opposite him.

Two can be as sad as one,
It's the loneliest number since the number one.

With a twist of a dial, I snuffed out the song. Timothy asked for the center's number, glancing from me to the squelched radio. "Need to be sure I can hear," I explained after relaying the number. "Long distance, you know." He handed me the ringing phone. Okay, now what was I going to do?

"The Santa Monica Center for Women's Liberation," sang Cece's secretary after the second ring. "The time is now to take charge of your life," she added our new slogan, making it sound like a toothpaste commercial. I was put straight through after asking for the boss lady.

"Hey there, Kippy Girl." Cece's greeting carried with it California sunshine glittering over the ocean. "You home? I called your apartment a while ago and no answer. Figured you might've gotten waylaid by weather somewhere between here and the winter hinterlands. How is she, your sick sister, okay? When will you be in?"

"Cece, hi … My sister … um, I'm still in Wisconsin."

"Storm? Man, I can still remember those blizzards socking in O'Hare—"

"That's not exactly the reason I'm still here." With Timothy watching and my employer on the line, I was determined to maintain self-control. "Cece, I've been—How's Malcolm?" I asked about my cat.

"Unbelievable. X and Casper are best buddies, like pepper and salt. Misses you though. So when will you be back?"

"Cece, I … I've been detained."

"Detained? What the hell does that mean? Till when?"

"I can't say, Cece."

"Kip, what's going on? You sound weird. You upset about something?"

"I'm fine," I insisted, hardly pulling "fine" off. "I just don't know when I'll be back. The trainee can take over for a while, can't she?"

"Kip, what's wrong?" Cece demanded.

Tears gushed as I choked out an answer. "I'm in some trouble here, Cece." She kept encouraging me—*just tell me, I can help*—until I confessed, "I'm in jail. Yeah, you heard right, jail." Timothy handed me a Kleenex as Cece fired questions. "Yes, arrested. Charged with," *sniff*, "ah, murder. Yes, murder, Cece. They think I killed my brother-in-law."

"Not that schmuck you told me about, the one who up and married your sister—"

"The very one. Cece, I need help. I need a lawyer, a good lawyer."

An uncharacteristic silence stretched out on the line. I sopped up my eyes and nose and tried to breathe. "Okay Kip, here's what we're going to do.

The lawyer who does pro bono for the center, our most sensitive cases, Phil Benedetti—don't think you two have ever met, but anyway—"

"But I need a lawyer now, Cece, and here in the 'winter hinterlands,' remember?"

"I'll call Phil right away, soon as we hang up. I'll get a referral for you at least. Be back at you ASAP. Wait, how will I do that? Call your home number when I know something?"

"I guess you'll have to, but don't talk to Sybel. Ask for Samantha. She'll be there."

"Check. Now don't worry about a thing. Phil's the best, *the best*. Be cool, Kip. Try some visualizations, some chanting, TM, a mantra. You gotta stay cool now."

"Sure," I sniffed. "Thanks, and kiss Malcolm for me." But Cece was gone. The line buzzed dead.

CHAPTER TWELVE

I handed the telephone to my jailer, severing my brief connection to my real life. Blotting up humbling tears, I thanked Timothy for the call and the Kleenexes.

Nodding wearily, he reached for his cap. "Well then, guess I better get you back."

But I didn't stir. "You know, Timothy," *sniff,* "I could use some coffee. Could we make a fresh pot?"

My jailer emptied the burning pot and, too quickly, fresh coffee was brewed and poured for us both. I sensed a fellow coffee addict in Timothy and liked him for it. *Ugh.* The first sip which I had to force down tasted more like hot water with brown food coloring than the coffee I learned to drink in Madison, but at least the burnt coffee stench had abated. I sipped slowly, gazing through two large plate-glass windows at the now pallid winter day.

Funny what smells bring to mind.

Wisconsin's bitter cold often chased my schoolmates and I into the ubiquitous State Street coffee joints near campus. There the odors of coffee, cigarettes, and wet wool blended in the thawing heat of packed bodies, and intellectual banter abounded. Bequeathed to us from the prior-generation's "drop-outs," the beatniks, coffeehouses galvanized the Sixties' social movements, which were spawned in the disillusionment that followed the Kennedy and King assassinations.

Civil rights, already well underway by then, proved to be the mother movement of them all. It established the nonviolent resistance patterns that would be copied in turn by the anti-war and, finally, by the feminist movements. Each borrowed Dr. King's protest practices of marches, demonstrations, sit-ins, vigils, and consciousness-raising. Perhaps inevitably, impatient factions within each movement resorted to violence over time.

Still, everyone had a rallying cause in the Sixties, it seemed. Would the Seventies sustain such passions? Or would causes and commitments dissipate like the steam rising from my coffee cup?

I stared at the darkening day, the wind scaring up tiny shards of ice that would feel like pinpricks were I not so insulated from the great outdoors by my captivity. Timothy stood and donned his cap, and I realized my phony freedom was at an end. I drained my cup and docilely followed him. But before being locked in my cell, I tried another tactic to avoid being left alone in the deafening silence.

"Timothy, I'm your only prisoner, right? I mean, obviously." Our eyes swept the empty enclosures. "We could both pass some time, oh, I don't know, playing cards. Yes, cards. Bridge perhaps, two-handed bridge?" Did such a game exist? I had no idea, but now that my fate was once again out of my hands and in Cece's in California, time would drag.

"Don't know bridge," Timothy replied. "How 'bout canasta?"

"Sure, great, canasta. You can teach me."

Given my inability to concentrate, Timothy beat me unmercifully at canasta until a buzzer pierced the quiet of the jailhouse. "Good heavens," I said, fumbling cards on the cot between us, "what's that?"

"Someone callin' me. Sorry, Kip, but it's about time for shift change anyways. Anything you need before I go? Or something I could bring you tomorrow?" Timothy rose, wielding his keys on the cell door

"Hmm. Oh, law books, Wisconsin's penal codes and criminal procedures. Is that possible?"

When the buzzer blasted again, he pulled on his cap and nodded. "Think that can be arranged. Oh, and we're supposed to have a prison uniform for you within a day or two. Night now, Kip. Don't forget to eat your dinner when it's brought to you. Need to keep up your strength."

I thought about napping, but instead went to the sink and splashed my face with water, the warped image in the mirror absorbing my attention. Moving side to side caused my face to spread and separate like blobs in a lava lamp; up and down stretched my square features thin. Dark circles exaggerated the chocolate-brown of my eyes. My sleek wedge haircut was a riot of black whorls. In short, I looked like shit and even more like my discombobulated father in the courtroom.

"Kip."

I nearly jumped out of my combat boots. "Timothy, you snuck up on me."

"Sorry. The buzzer was for your sister on the phone."

"Which sister?"

"'Mrs. Samantha Czermanski Turner,' she said. I told her I'd deliver a message if she wished. Technically, I'm not supposed to let you out of your cell without extra precautions except under extreme circumstances. This close to shift change—well, anyhow, I took a message."

I was relieved, I discovered, to not have to talk to Samantha or anyone in my family just then. I was in no mood for more drama and innuendo through the family's customary point person. No matter the words, their accusations always bled through. "It's just as well, Timothy."

"I know family would be a big comfort at a time—What? You're not disappointed about not talking to her?"

"Not in the least." Timothy's shock turned to suspicion as he tried to deduce the meaning behind my words. "What did she want?"

With head-shaking disapproval, Timothy replied, "I told your sister no calls for the inmates." I'd become an inmate, the sole inmate of Wausaukeesha County Jail. "She wanted you to know your boss called from California to say the lawyer you two spoke about would catch a flight and be here tomorrow evening or first thing the next day. Think I got it all."

Although the lawyer flying to my rescue was a total stranger, tension drained from my body with Timothy's words. Help was on the way.

Chapter Thirteen

As if I were losing my last friend, I gazed after the jailer's diminishing form until the darkened corridor snuffed all traces of him. I flopped backward on my cot and shook out some blankets. The morgue-like stillness amplified my breathing, reminding me of the TV scuba diver on *Sea Hunt*.

I stared through the bars above my head. If I lay here awake, random memories will plague me while details of what happened with Stan just two nights ago still eluded me. Yet if I dozed, I risked disquieting dreams.

It seemed I had reached a time and place in my life where there were no good choices.

Twelve steps led to three vaulted double doors of the Cathedral of the Immaculate Conception. The warm breeze swirled brittle leaves in autumn hues as I approached. Someone was burning fallen leaves nearby. I smelled the pleasant scent, but the air remained crisp and clear. I kicked up the dying foliage, destined to be transformed by fire—first into smoke, then into nothing at all.

Sybel stood in the doorway to the right, motioning me to hurry. The exasperation apparent in her jerky movements said, *why are we always waiting for you?*

"Coming," I shouted, crunching leaves in my path. "Coming." But the smoke-tinged breeze, carrying hints of distant fields of hay and the wet, green tang of a freshly sprinkled lawn, smelled like heaven. Protestant church bells added peals of sheer joy to the air. I was in no hurry to enter the cathedral.

Starting up the stairs, I discovered Sybel had disappeared but my father stood in the left doorway. A hint of indulgence crinkled the skin around his eyes and mouth, though my dawdling exasperated him. "Everyone's inside," he shouted. "It's time for our entrance, KP. Hurry." But when I reached the entry, Dad had disappeared as well.

I stepped inside. After the blinding autumn sunlight, the darkness was impenetrable. Slowly the sanctuary, illuminated only by daylight filtering through rows of stained-glass windows, took shape. When it did, I found it empty. Across vacant pews and upturned kneelers, dust motes danced in slanting, multi-colored light, morphing like a kaleidoscope as I moved cautiously down the center aisle.

Admiring the shifting colors and patterns on my skin, I noticed the goose bumps on my arms. Oh-oh, my arms weren't covered. My breathing added clouds to the tinted air, making me wonder why the sanctuary was so cold. I felt for my headscarf required for Mass and—more trouble!—found only curly hair. I never understood why uncovered arms and heads offended God. Didn't He make us, bare body parts and all? But I wouldn't be seen in an empty sanctuary, so I might as well find out why I rushed to be here.

The stench of incense intensified as I neared the front of the nave. On the dais where altar boys performed each Sunday, a bright light illuminated three caskets. A funeral? I was hurrying to a funeral? Who died? Knowing Sybel would ground me for a year for my bare-head and –arm infractions if she found out, I eased onto the dais.

I crept toward the closest casket and peeked into the open upper half only to find it empty. The casket beside it was empty as well. A sudden premonition warned me to leave—I wasn't supposed to see this—when a noise made me freeze. Giggling? I heard it again and peered around, afraid of who might find me alone in the vacant church, improperly dressed and peeking into caskets.

Two women, twins or sisters, stood arm-in-arm on the dais, their blonde hair lit from above like shining auras. Forgiving smiles illuminated their faces. Sarah? Mother? My sister and mother opened their arms to me, and I burrowed deep into their embrace, laughing until I cried.

When the chill of the sanctuary penetrated the warmth of our desperate hug, I opened my eyes to find myself alone under the bright light. They had vanished. Where was everyone? Why had I been summoned to Immaculate Conception Cathedral where three empty coffins stood before the empty church? Unlike the others, I noticed that the third casket was fully closed. Suddenly, I had to make certain it was empty as well.

Knowing it was a sin to uncover the casket's secrets, knowing the knowledge could somehow kill me, I crept forward and clutched its lid, jerked it open, and gazed down. "No," I cried, stumbling backward.

I made myself look again. Inside the third coffin, *I* was laid out.

The waxy version of myself felt cold and hard as an ice cube when I touched my hands, steepled on my chest for my eternal rest. My hands, something was wrong with them. Dried blood and deep gashes disfigured both of my hands.

I backed away, stumbling off the dais before turning to run. *Run, before it's too late.* I raced down the center aisle of the church, now miraculously filled with worshipers, past the Czermanskis in the farthest front pew; past Sister Margaret who, like Sybel, wore a smug expression as she watched me.

Dusty swirls in the slanting light danced feverishly in my wake when I glanced back over my shoulder, then checked my hands, both sides, as I made for the exit. There were no wounds.

Run, before it's too late.

CHAPTER FOURTEEN

February 15, 1972 — The Ides of February

"Someone t'see you, Kip."

I sat up so fast, my head spun. "What?"

"Some lady," said the nice guard I played cards with, "a stranger to town. Wanted to make sure you were up first, though."

Timothy ... Rudeshiem, that was his name. His sly smile inspired me to ask him for the time. "Five?" I reiterated. "You mean, it's five o'clock? In the evening?"

"Just after five p.m. You been out like a log since before I came on. We just let you sleep goin' on twenty-four hours now. Looked like you needed it. Think you were dreamin' though, from your thrashing and grunts when I checked on you."

Dreaming. I turned my hands over and over again. There was nothing wrong with my hands. Nothing.

"You hungry? I can bring—"

"Timothy, I slept that long?" No wonder I felt groggy. "Who'd you say is here?"

"Someone you were expecting, she said."

In the radical getup I'd worn for how many days now, I rose to move about the cell and force blood to my brain. Who was I expecting?

"Timothy, I was sleeping really hard. Give me a minute, okay?"

Tossing aside the afghan I'd used like a cape since my arrest, I assured myself before the mirror that I was somewhat intact, despite the ridiculous clothing. I smoothed down my kinky locks and the peace signs on my sweater as I slipped into my combat boots. I was expecting … a lawyer from California, but Timothy said it was a woman. Oh, it must be Babs, the local gossip columnist, sniffing out a scoop for *The Dairyland Diary,* Wausaukeesha's weekly "news" rag.

I pictured Babs, solid build, thick-soled shoes, pencils stuck in her hair as footsteps announced Timothy with … a stranger indeed, and definitely not Babs Howenhauser. In contrast to Timothy's paunchy six-plus feet, the woman looked child-sized. Dark hair, stylish and short, pretty in a businesslike way, a look too "city" for these parts. Maybe New York? She paused outside the cell as Timothy twisted keys in the lock. The overcoat slung around her shoulders was rich cashmere. Her black boots gleamed. Impenetrable shades concealed her eyes.

Studying me all the while, the woman stepped around Timothy into my cell, juggling a briefcase and gloves to extend a small, manicured hand for a surprisingly firm handshake. Two nights running, I'd slept in these old clothes, and my hair was in all-out protest against the wedge. This better not be important.

"Hello, Kip," flowed the small woman's resonant alto. "I'm Philomena Benedetti. Cece warned you I was coming?"

"You're … *You* are *Phil*?"

"Philomena, aka Phil." Her piercing gaze took in my blatant shock. "I see Cece didn't paint the entire picture."

"You're a lawyer? I mean, *the* lawyer? From the center? From Santa Monica?"

"The very one. You're … disappointed?"

Caught in the act of sexist thinking, I flooded with embarrassment. A woman lawyer, why hadn't I thought of that? Obviously even I hadn't gotten passed my own unexamined assumptions.

"*Au contraire,*" I replied, "I … oh man, I'm thrilled." I giggled stupidly, strangely close to tears. "Cece referred to Phil, the center's best lawyer, and I just assumed—"

"Of course. People do. But if it's going to be a problem, I need to know now."

"No, absolutely not, it's … You are a most unexpected pleasure." Anticipating my dad's and his lawyers' reaction to this news—they'd be speechless, at least initially—lightened the overwhelming and emotional relief I felt. My knight in shining armor was a "girl." I had to laugh.

When Philomena Benedetti smiled, her big city varnish gave way to a guileless, almost girlish, warmth. "Mind if I lose the coat then and have a seat? I've been here a while, getting searched and cleared by the guards, who were more than a little suspicious of who I said I was."

"Oh, sorry. Please." I sat and faced her, propping my jaw on my fists.

From the doorway to my cage, Timothy interrupted us. "You missed your breakfast and your lunch, Kip, and I'm told your dinner the night before. Shouldn't I bring something back?"

"Go ahead," Phil encouraged me. "I ate, if you can call it that, on the plane."

"I really can't just now, Timothy. But if you've got some coffee, fresh coffee?"

He sighed at my dietary bad habits and turned to Phil—my lawyer, Philomena. "Could bring you some, too, while I'm at it."

"Black coffee would be great," she said, taken aback.

"I'll bring the pot and some cups," he said and sauntered away.

While Philomena Benedetti rummaged through a doctor's bag-like briefcase that dwarfed her, I studied my female lawyer. Petite like many European women, she wore a perfectly tailored dark jacket and skirt, at once flattering and serious. A closer inspection revealed sprinkles of gray threading her black hair, which pixied around a face enhanced by character lines. She could be mid-forties, I guessed. Putting her sunglasses away, Phil caught me staring. Curious brown eyes dominated a face stamped with an Italian heritage: a

Roman nose and full mouth. She wasn't pretty the way my sisters were pretty, but more worldly and chic. Her warmth or empathy softened the whole picture, making her appear approachable.

"Fifty-one, first generation Italian-American, uncharacteristically for Catholics, especially of the Italian variety, an only child. From Boston originally, on the West Coast since high school. First in my class at Stanford Law after honors from Berkeley undergrad. Following a ten-year stint practicing criminal law in New York, I opened my own practice in Los Angeles, developing a specialty in family and women's issues. Call me Phil, Philomena, Miss Benedetti, as you wish. Anything else you need to know right now?"

"I was staring, I'm sorry. But I gather from that thumbnail CV, I'm not the first."

Timothy returned to pass two mugs through the bars along with a coffee thermos decorated with fish jumping out of a pond. He left us without a word. I poured two steaming but watery coffees for my new lawyer and myself.

"You're hardly the first," Phil responded, accepting a cup. "'Phil' really threw you, huh?"

I nodded. "It's crazy, I know, me a devout feminist. But I've never seen a female lawyer before."

"There aren't many of us, almost none in visible positions, a factor that greatly influenced my decision to work for myself some years ago. You're certain it's not going to be a problem, Kip? Now is the time to discuss it."

"No, I'm only sorry I'll miss the reactions your presence will inspire throughout town, especially from my family and Dad's lawyers. They'll leak back to us soon enough though. You … well, I haven't had a nice surprise in a while."

Phil weighed her next words. "I'll let you in on a little secret of success. Being underestimated almost always works in your favor. But let's keep that between us." When she laughed, Philomena became impishly pretty.

I laughed harder and longer than warranted. Exhaustion? Unlikely after sleeping for a day. Did I dare hope that this stranger could make the difference, that I could actually trust her, rely on her? "Well, thank you for coming all this way, but understand this might take three months. And the preliminary hearing is Tuesday."

"Don't worry about it. We'll probably waive it anyway—most likely waive the judge's calendar altogether. Your right to a speedy trial is rarely the best strategy for a defendant. But we'll get to that.

"As far as my being here," she continued, "your case came perfectly timed. I just settled an enormous suit unexpectedly, and quite favorably I might add. With nothing critical or even interesting on the docket that my staff can't handle, your case had added appeal. Plus, I hold the utmost allegiance to the center and to Cece personally. Without her, I might still be …" As her thoughts trailed off, Phil blinked, remembering me. "Cece speaks highly of you, though she warned me of your youthful inexperience and rough edges."

"My what?"

But Phil, warming her hands on the cup, focused on my clothing. "They don't require prison uniforms here?" she asked, avoiding further comment on my Fuck No, We Won't Go getup.

"They're looking for one to fit a small woman, I'm told. Till then …" I camouflaged the open gaps in the knees of my jeans with my hands.

"Really? Where am I?" Her amazed laughter lured me in.

"Oh, you have no idea where you've just landed," I responded with a chuckle.

"No, I meant how do you pronounce the name of this town? Wausau-*kee*-sha?"

"Wau-*saw*-kee-shaw, emphasis on the second syllable."

Philomena repeated the Indian name several times until it rolled off her tongue. "As I was saying, having handled the center's legal needs over the years, I admire and support the work you do there. All of which means I have the time, I've made arrangements, and I'm all yours. Shall we get started?"

"Your fees, shouldn't we discuss them?"

"My hourly is standard, the going rate, and my expenses here should be reasonable compared to say Los Angeles or New York. But if you wish, of course, let's discuss it."

"'If I wish?'" I repeated. "What you earn is more important than that, isn't it?"

"Very important, and I appreciate your being upfront about it, Kip. I had understood that money wasn't an issue for you."

"I do have the money my mother left me, somewhere close to $100,000 by now, and if that's not enough, I swear I'll work the rest of my life—Wait a minute. What do you mean, 'not an issue?' Cece told you that?"

Phil reacted as if I were joking. "Yes. She mentioned that you were an heiress to the Czermanski Sausage fortune."

Not once had I mentioned my family to my boss or anyone else in California except in the most oblique ways. Now that Czermanski sausages were sold in California groceries, I evidently didn't have to. "I'm afraid the sausage fortune just shriveled up where I am concerned. It is no longer a fall back here ..."

I tried to explain. "I've been on my own since college. I can't, I won't, take Dad's money, not with the strings he'll attach—in this case, the use of his lawyers and, through them, total control over me and my trial with an eye toward minimizing embarrassment to his name and company.

"I tried to revert, to go along with Dad and his lawyers—call it shock and fear following the incident—but even in that state, my reverting lasted all of a day." I sucked in my breath. "I'm terribly sorry, Phil, but I'm afraid you've been misled."

"Fine," she said. "Shall we get started?"

"Do you think that $100—"

"It's more than enough to start. Look, should we near that figure, and that will depend upon how quickly we get through this process, we can negotiate the rest. Kip, I'm not being cavalier. In some respects, I owe Cece my life, both professional and personal. I might still be struggling ..." Phil shook her head and went on, "Cece is deeply concerned about you and asked if I would help personally. I've got the time and feel certain my fees and expenses will be covered. I've read your personnel file and am confident we can work together. And of course the publicity this case might bring won't hurt me either." She held my gaze.

"Okay." My sigh of relief sounded melodramatic even to me. "Can the bank arrange—"

"You're obsessing, Kip. I'll bring in a form and take it to the bank for you once I settle in. What I'd really like to do is get a quick synopsis of your case before I figure out how to live here for the next little while." She waited for my nod of assent. "I can get a copy of your arraignment proceedings and the police report tomorrow. Summarize for me why, when, and where you were arrested."

I settled back against the bars after offering Phil a pillow for her back. Though I dared say the word only to myself, having this no-nonsense female lawyer to defend me gave me hope. She impressed me as a seasoned woman of great competence. And Cece's endorsement carried great weight as well.

At the same time, I worried how she'd feel about defending me after hearing the summary she'd requested—the why, when, and where of my being charged with the premeditated murder of my brother-in-law, recently discovered in my bed in my bedroom at the family home where the whole family, including his wife, slept nearby.

Chapter Fifteen

"They say, that is, they claim that I murdered my brother-in-law who is, was, married to my sister, Sybel." Once started, the story tumbled out haphazardly for the lawyer. "Because, well, because they found him dead in my bed at the house the night of Sarah's funeral—that was my oldest sister—which is why we were all staying at the house and why I came back to Wisconsin in the first place, to see Sarah one last time. But I didn't kill him, I couldn't, I wouldn't. I don't know how Stan wound up in my bed, nude, but I think the vase—there were funeral flowers in a huge vase next to my bed—fell on him and killed him. I think he was trying to rape me, that our struggle upended the vase."

I took a deep breath. "More coffee, Phil? It may be watery, but it is the best the Wausaukeesha County Jailhouse has to offer."

Philomena shook her head, clearing it or refusing the coffee, I wasn't sure which. "Kip, why don't we start with the incident," she said, extending her cup for more. "Take your time telling me what happened."

I refilled our cups and took a fortifying gulp. "In the early hours of Sunday morning … No, let me start again."

Discombobulated by the unexpected presence of a female lawyer, not to mention her intense concentration and the possible consequences of what she was about to hear, I took a moment to regroup.

"Okay. Last Saturday after my sister's funeral, most of Wausaukeesha stopped by our house to commiserate or whatever those 'receptions' are for."

It had been only four days, I realized, since we buried Sarah, and that miserable day would prove to be Stan's last.

"By late evening of a very long day, a long week, only my family and a few close friends remained."

"More brandy?" Dad had repeated, wandering among the black-clad guests strewn about the living room like fading flowers, wilting in the overheated quarters like the ubiquitous funeral arrangements.

"Just think," Mrs. Kleinschmidt had commented, "Sarah lived but thirty-nine years, while her mother, Norma, died even younger at just thirty-seven-years old."

Mr. Kleinschmidt changed the subject after a thoughtful interlude. "What ever happened to that beau of Sarah's? Weren't they engaged way back when?"

Sarah—my sister the nun—had a beau? At four years old, I was too young to understand Sarah leaving for the convent. I remembered very little about her at all. I struggled to imagine my nun sister having a life complete with a "beau," let alone a fiancé.

I waited for someone to add to these revelations, but in the ensuing silence, angry whispers diverted our attention. We craned our necks toward Dad and Sybel at the far end of the living room. Their gesticulating ceased, their disagreement squelched when they felt all eyes on them. Sybel worked up a smile and, retrieving used glasses along the way, headed for the kitchen. "I sent the help home," she explained as she disappeared into the dining room.

Remembering the brandy bottle clutched to his chest, Dad said, "Stan, you're empty. Surely you'll have more."

The somber atmosphere, heavy with memories and regrets, grew oppressive. I shook it off, standing and offering to lend Sybel a hand in the kitchen, which surprised even me. Rare were the times I voluntarily sought out Sybel. We'd always been an explosive combination. But the things Sarah said to me before she died were haunting. *Sybel's running, still. You'll see it if you just look.* I suppose I should at least attempt talking with her, perhaps find out what Sarah had meant.

Sybel froze when I picked up a towel and told her I'd dry. She clutched a soapy glass suspended in midair, disbelief cocking one eyebrow before she resumed thrashing dirty glasses in dishwater and setting them to drain in the empty side of the divided sink. Her mourning costume—black hose, heels now kicked aside, a black jacket and skirt—looked ridiculous with the sleeves rolled up over bright yellow rubber gloves. Soapsuds clung to her forehead where she'd pushed back strands of her new "shag" haircut.

A cynical "Interesting" from my sister was the extent of our conversation until I committed the egregious error of putting dried glasses away in the wrong place. "Those go in the dining room hutch. You still don't know that?"

"Geez, sorry, Sybel, but except for a few summers, I haven't lived here in over six years."

"They haven't moved during your absence, Kip."

This was not going to be easy, Sarah. "We're both just exhausted," I decided out loud. "I know I am." I reached for another glass. "So, Sybel, did Stan ever mention that we knew each other in Madison when I was in college?"

"Hmm …" Glass thrashing slowed. "… I think so. Yes, you took his classes."

That's what he'd told her? "Yes, but—"

"Sisters." Stan's voice from close behind made us both jump. "The Kleinschmidts and that nosy Babs Howenhauser are leaving, finally. Come say good-bye."

I pivoted to find myself within kissing distance of Stan and flinched.

"Make excuses for us, won't you, dear?" Sybel spoke the last word with an emphatic chill. She grasped a glass in her yellow glove like she might crush it. I checked Stan's reaction, but he was staring at me.

"Yeah, make our good-byes," I added, backing away.

"I poured these for you." Stan spilled some of Dad's brandy, pressing glasses into our hands. "*Na zdrowie!* Or as they say in these parts, 'bottoms up.'" Stan waited. "Drink up now, ladies. It's your father's best. God knows we can all use an extra swallow of brandy today."

I held the amber liquid to my nose. To me, the best thing about brandy, the Wisconsin state drink after milk and beer, was its clear-your-sinuses smell. Sybel noisily drowned glasses in suds until we both sensed Stan lingering. A meaningful look from his wife encouraged his retreat through the swinging door. Turning back to my task, I found Sybel doubled over the empty side of the sink, choking.

"Are you all right? Sybel, did you just puke?"

Sybel ran water and shook her head. "Of course not."

Samantha bustled into the kitchen, loaded down with funeral flowers of every color and type in sharp contrast to her black dress.

"So many beautiful arrangements," she commented. "Everyone's been so kind, haven't they? Of course, everyone loved Sarah. I'll put flowers in each bedroom, if that's okay with you both. There's no place left to put them down here. And I think … I think they'll be a nice reminder of her."

Banging cupboard doors, on hands and knees unearthing vases, Samantha's activity glossed over the awkwardness in the air. Sybel concentrated on dirty glasses as if making them clean again had become her life's mission.

Samantha arranged flowers in various vases to a running monologue on their colors and scents. "Let's see. Dad loves gladioli," she said, considering the gangly stalks, "though I can't think why. These will go in his room. You'll love these roses, Sybel." The red hothouse roses had been stripped of both thorns and scent. "I'll put them in your room."

When Samantha carried off her first floral creations, Sybel spoke rapidly, as if she'd been holding it in too long. "Of course Stan told me he knew you outside the classroom." I was surprised and pleased Sybel was taking that fact in stride until she completed her thought. "You joined the anti-war movement he led back then."

Samantha hustled in with more funeral flowers and began her next concoctions. "Look at this vase, would you." She maneuvered an unusually tall cut-crystal vase onto the counter. "So regal, ooh, and so heavy. It looks old. It must've been Mother's. But weren't there two of them, a pair you used at your wedding, Sybel?"

Sybel shook her head. "They were a wedding gift to Mother and Daddy but one was broken after our ceremony."

Samantha gathered red-orange trumpet-shaped flowers unfamiliar to me, blowing their own horns, so to speak, atop long stalks.

"What are they?"

"I had to ask, too, Kip. Amaryllis," Samantha replied. "Aren't they … unusual? And no strong odor, see?" Samantha extended a flower for me to smell. Strong scents had always bothered me. "For both those reasons, I'll put them in your room, Kip, in Mother's and Dad's surviving vase. I'd never negotiate the stairs with it anyhow." Samantha picked up the vase and plunked it back down again. "Better put it on your nightstand first and fill it there."

Hobbling under the weight of the yard-high vase, Samantha tottered down the back hallway toward my room behind the kitchen, returning for the amaryllis and her watering can before disappearing again.

The gurgle of draining water signaled the conclusion of our clean-up effort, and Sybel and I had barely spoken. She took her time drying her hands on the dishtowel I held, the blue of her narrowed eyes an inscrutable gray.

"Stan told me all about your puppy love infatuation with him, if that's what you were driving at." She smirked. "I can just see it. Your professor, thirteen years your senior, slight European accent, harrowing survival tale stoking his passionate beliefs in 'The Cause.' Which, by the way, just like you, he's since left. So much for causes."

Sybel slipped into her black heels. "He must have struck you dumb, a small-town freshman, first time away from home, fawning after your professor, an 'older man,' transparently scheming to be near him."

Samantha returned to the kitchen and began another flower arrangement. "I sent Raymond home," she told us, mixing white carnations with sprigs of baby's breath in a small vase. "Told him I needed to stay close to Dad for at least the night. You and Stan are staying, right, Sybel?" She paused to smile at us. "It'll be like old times—the three of us under one roof again, except …"

Samantha paled at a second thought, undoubtedly involving Sister Sarah and other old times. "I'm off to bed," Samantha said, hoisting her final composition. "Night, you two."

Footsteps retreated up the back stairs as I reacted to Sybel's belittling. "'Fawning? Schem—'"

"Okay, what was your point?"

"Just that—"

She cut me off. "I'm exhausted. Tell me tomorrow—if you must." Sybel unrolled her sleeves at the foot of the stairs, preparing to follow Samantha. "I think your little crush on Stan, while utterly ludicrous, was kind of cute. Get the lights, Kip, and don't forget to lock up before you go to bed." Flipping the switch as she started up, Sybel left me seething in semi-darkness.

"'Puppy love? Cute?' Oh Sybel, you have no idea."

CHAPTER SIXTEEN

My hands had clenched into fists, I realized, while my lawyer watched intently, noticing everything. Pretending the need to stretch my legs, I rose and paced.

"Sybel was married to Stan, whom you knew in college," Phil recounted her understanding. "From your description of your interchange with her, I take it the two of you were less than close sisters and that Samantha was the sister caught between you two in more ways than just age."

"Right on both counts. Sybel and I could barely be in the same room without getting into it. It got worse with every passing year. Samantha ran interference, even defending me when she felt she could do so without reprisals from Sybel."

"We'll get into the family dynamics, but first let's get through the whys and wherefores of your arrest. Pick up where you left off, after everyone went to bed."

"The rest is sketchy. I remember things here and there, but there are holes and other parts are vague. Do you think it's shock?"

"Could be. Let's start with what you do recall. Then we'll know where we have to fill in."

"At first, I thought I was dreaming. That I do remember." I plunked onto the cot and poured us both more coffee, hoping a big gulp of the now semi-hot liquid would jog my memory and get me through this once and for all.

Heat had spread throughout my body from my core to my extremities. My heart raced, my breathing shallow. *Oh… Oh that's… Hold me, don't let me go. Never let me go again.*

I seemed to be moving in slow motion through a thick darkness, as though an ocean pressed down on me. Yet it was a place I wished to stay. Limbs entangled. Lips and tongues pressing. Two bodies generating heat and moisture. Every particle of me opening. *Hold me.*

But I seemed to be floating upward against my will toward a distant light above, as if rising from the ocean floor. *No, no, hold me. Hold onto me. Stay with me.* But I continued upward through murky waters, the light growing closer, harsher. *No, let's stay here forever.*

My lungs began to burn with my ascent. I needed air. I was rising too fast. My lungs felt like they might burst as I gathered speed. I needed air. Air! I broke the surface with a gasp and opened my eyes, not to the harsh light I wished to avoid, but to darkness, total darkness. What was happening?

It was a dark but somehow familiar place. My old bedroom? I was at home in bed. But not alone. Who? Stan? Stan in my bed? No, stop, stop it. "Stop it, Stan!"

A hand clamped down on my mouth, muzzling my outburst. Squirming against him only increased the pressure until I thought I'd suffocate. I was desperate for air. "Make no noise and I'll let up," he whispered. His words, rushed and low, smelled of old liquor. "You promise?"

It took everything I had to nod. Stan's grip loosened, then lifted. I gulped in air and blinked back the water spilling from my eyes.

Stan's face hovered over mine in the darkness, two hard glints for eyes. "Oh baby," he whispered, "that felt so good, you welcoming me to your bed after all these years."

All these years. Oh my God, Sarah's funeral. Stan in my bed. Everyone upstairs. "Stan, are you crazy?"

He stifled my words with his palm, crushing both my mouth and nose. "Shut it, Kip, or I will silence you." I began to make out his face in the gloom, his feral eyes gleaming with determination. I nodded weakly until he let up.

"Stan, Sybel, your wife, up-upstairs," I stammered, trying to breathe and reason. "And Dad. Leave … you must leave."

Stan began to move under the covers, wrangling his way over my body. "You were always ready for me, weren't you, baby. You're ready for me now, aren't you?"

"Stan, don't. Not here, not like this. We'll meet. Tomorrow. Anywhere you say. Don't. Don't." I screamed until a crushing palm silenced me.

Couldn't move, couldn't breathe. *Help someone. Help me. He's going to rape me. Suffocate—Kill me.* Desperate for air, I worked one arm free. Clawed. Punched. Flailed at anything. Hit. No air. Help me … Dying …

A distant noise penetrated a dense fog. Drip. Drop.

Dazed, I lay on a cold floor, heart pounding against my ribs, aching all over, fighting for air.

Drip, drop.

I groped in the darkness, found a bed. Pulled myself to my feet. Steadied myself with the bedpost. I stared into the darkness. Someone was in the bed.

A blinding flash stabbed at my eyes. Overhead lights flooded the room. Dad stood in the doorway, Sybel and Samantha huddling behind him. I followed three shocked expressions to the body in my bed. A man lay face down amidst jumbled bedclothes.

Stan? Sybel's husband was in my bed?

In a flannel nightgown, her hair in rollers that lumped over her head, Sybel disentangled herself from Samantha and approached the face-down figure, half covered by a sheet. She shook his bare shoulders, hissing, "Stan, get up this minute. Stan, I'm warning you."

But Stan didn't stir. Sybel glared at me. "Now what have you done?" She bent over Stan and, with a groan, rolled him onto his back.

We all gasped. There beneath the sheet, like a tent pole propping up canvas, poked the slowly deflating evidence of Stan's arousal. Sybel's face darkened. "God damn it, Stan, wake up."

But there was no movement except for my father staggering toward the bed, white as the sheet and clutching the bedpost opposite mine. Sybel leaned over to listen to Stan's heartbeat, but the hollowed-out orange juice cans she rolled her hair in prevented contact. She tugged several out to lay her ear on Stan's chest. Sybel bolted up, lurching for the bedpost I clung to and shook her head.

"No? No-no heartbeat?" I stuttered. "Is that what you mean, Sybel? Stan, wake up. Get up. Dad, Samantha—someone make him get up."

But nobody moved except Sybel, more closely examining her husband. Again she bolted upright. She extended her fingers to us to see, crimson with blood.

"Oh no, oh no," Dad moaned over and over, staggering backwards and tripping into the chair.

Only the bedpost kept me standing as Sybel turned Stan's head to the other side. There on my pillowcase beneath it spread a bright red Rorschach blot of blood. Georgia O'Keefe's poppy bloomed on a pure white canvas.

"Oh my God," Sybel shouted, glaring at me. "You killed him. You killed him."

"No, Sybel, no, I didn't, I couldn't, I wouldn't."

"Stan's dead." Sybel slumped against the bed, sobbing. I had never seen Sybel shed a single tear and could not pull my eyes away from the spectacle. She sniffed and turned on me directly.

"You did this, Kip. You were insanely jealous that Stan married me, weren't you? You'd do anything to get back at me—admit it. Seduce my husband and then what? This?" She gently placed Stan's arm against his body as tears welled in her eyes.

"An ambulance." Samantha came to life, circling the bed for the telephone. "I'll call." Something scraped against the floor as she moved around the bed.

Sybel grabbed Samantha's arm. "No, don't. Stan …" she faltered, "… no longer needs help. We'll let his …" Stan's erection wavered beneath the covers. "…go down first. Before we call anyone, we agree on what we're going to say."

She shot a meaningful glance at me. "Some of us have to live in this town for the rest of our lives."

Samantha appealed to Dad. "Shouldn't we get some help, Dad?"

Bewildered, Dad gazed at Sybel. "Shouldn't we?"

"Need I remind even you, Daddy, what this could do to us—our company, our standing in the community? A suspicious death in the Czermanski home? Do I have to do everyone's thinking?"

"Sybel," I struggled to explain, "I think I was dreaming, about college—"

She spoke over me. "It's clear what went on here. Your plot for revenge backfired. Once you got Stan in bed, your anger over him choosing me over you boiled out of control." She turned her back on me.

As I tried to make sense of the situation, I heard that noise again. Drip, drop. Drip, drop. I realized water was dripping from the bed to the floor and onto my feet. My nightgown was soaked through. The bed was wet and strewn with flowers. Only then did I notice the vase filled with funeral flowers Samantha had placed on my nightstand was gone.

"Where's that old vase, Samantha?"

Dad made an anguished groan, shifting in the chair in which he'd collapsed to avoid seeing Stan's body. His movement started that scraping noise again. The three of us peered over and around the bed at the shattered glass surrounding Dad's feet. The floor on the far side of the bed was covered with jagged shards, which crunched under his slippers.

I answered my own question. "That vase must have crashed onto Stan, then rolled off to the floor, breaking into pieces."

Sybel whisked away a tear as it formed and gazed sidelong at me. "Pathetic, Kip. We're to believe a broken vase is responsible for what happened here? You can do better than that."

"Sybel, you're not seriously accusing me of intentionally—"

"Shhh," Samantha overrode us. Clutching the blue princess phone Dad had granted me in high school to her ear, she said, "Police? Something terrible has happened. Yes. Yes, an accident. Samantha Czermanski Turner. The Czermanski household. Yes, Moraine Drive, yes that's the one. Stan. Stan Szyzyck. My brother-in-law. He's hurt and bleeding. He may be dead."

CHAPTER SEVENTEEN

I took a deep breath before plunging on, now anxious to get that pre-dawn scene from just days ago out and behind me. Then I'd allow myself time to worry about Phil's reactions.

Footsteps had clomped down the back hallway. "Back here, Officer." Samantha's voice.

Sybel urged me out of my revealing, water-soaked nightgown that was also freezing cold. But the dry clothes she grabbed from my closet did nothing to stop my shivering. I zipped my jeans as Samantha and a police officer entered my bedroom. Dad, uncomprehending and unmoving in the chair, acknowledged no one. Everyone but me and the uniformed officer wore bathrobes, but Sybel had removed all the OJ cans from her hair.

Samantha made the introductions. "This is Officer, ah Officer, I'm sorry, Officer, I've forgotten."

"Dougy—Douglas Rankin." The officer, his cheeks rosy, his skin baby-perfect against the blue uniform, gaped at the scene before him. "Officer Rankin, sir, uh, ladies. And ah, and this would be the vic—the man you called about."

A violent blush filled the space between his roomy collar and the cop hat that slid low over his forehead. He approached Stan's still somewhat excited form. He checked for a pulse, then a heartbeat. He examined Stan's nose and mouth for signs of breathing. The officer opened Stan's eyes, which were rolled-back and unresponsive. He peered beneath Stan's head for the source of blood. His blush paled dramatically.

"Can I use a telephone?" he asked my father.

My dad didn't respond. Wiping his eyes on his bathrobe sleeve, running his fingers through his hair, Dad's gaze was now trained on Stan, truly the son he'd always longed for. Sybel nodded to indicate the phone to the policeman.

Between princess phone exchanges of information and holding for instructions, Officer Rankin told us he'd need to get our statements. "Okay, an ambulance is on the way," he said and hung up. "So … oh yes. Now I'd like to start with Kip. Which one is Kip?"

"Me?" I made a weak signal. "Why me?"

"Your sister here said 'the accident happened back in Kip's room.' Didn't you?" Samantha bit her lip. "Okay then, um, the rest of you, can you excuse us? I'll need each one of you when I'm done here, one at a time."

My dad couldn't pull it together so Sybel seized control. "We'll wait in the kitchen, Officer," she said, muscling Dad out of the chair and through the door before her. "I'll put on some coffee."

Samantha trailed them out, communicating something with her eyes until Officer Rankin closed the door and motioned me to the chair Dad had vacated.

He winced at the orange walls. "Okay then, you're Kip Czermanski. That much I already got." He pushed up the brim of his cap with a pencil while pacing around the double bed, which took up most of the floor space, steering clear of the broken glass as best he could. "Would you care to make a statement?" He produced a small notebook.

"I don't feel right. Some water maybe? There's a glass in the bathroom next door."

"I'll get it. You stay." He returned in seconds with the glass he handed me. "Where were you tonight, and what you were you doing for the last, oh, hour or two?"

"I was in bed, here, sleeping." Our fleeting glances at the body occupying my bed made us both wince.

"And this is, er, was?"

"Stan Szyzyck."

"And Stan Szyzyck is?"

"Him." I pointed but kept my eyes on the officer.

"Yes. I have the name of the, the deceased. I meant, he was in your bed because, well because he's your husband? Fiancé? Boy—"

"Brother—"

"Oh."

"In-law."

"Oh."

"Sybel's husband."

The officer stared where his notes should've gone. "Sybel, who let me in?"

"No, the other sister."

"Have trouble telling them apart. And, and Sybel was where during this timeframe?"

"Upstairs in bed, I guess."

Officer Rankin blinked rapidly while I gulped down water. I felt so strange, not all here. A sharp rap on the door heralded the arrival of the ambulance team that trailed in, focused on the body, circling, questioning, discussing with the officer, then examining and probing. I was still thirsty and out of water. Officer Rankin reluctantly dismissed me. "I'll need to talk to you again when we're finished here. Wait with your family in the kitchen."

I opted for the living room, burrowing under the afghan on the couch. A constant murmur of voices from the kitchen played in the background. I couldn't get comfortable or warm. My head, my whole body, ached. My mind felt dull and slow, unable to piece things together. I'd been sleeping, dreaming about Stan and me in college. Then he was there, for real. I wanted him to stop. Didn't I? I woke up next to the bed. Everyone was there in my bedroom, and Stan was dead. Does that make sense? Mother in a golden frame gazed down on me from over the fireplace. I burrowed farther beneath the afghan.

A shrill note—Sybel's voice from the kitchen—startled me from my lethargy. I must have dozed. The ambulance was leaving with Stan. The police officer with them?

From my cocoon I spotted two shiny black shoes trampling the carpet's roses. Peeking up, I found Officer Rankin speaking to me. "… the station … further questions … take you in." He helped me to my feet. Bundled in the afghan throw from the sofa, I followed him in a daze.

A Wausaukeesha Police Department squad car was parked in our driveway. The officer held open its back door. I slid onto the frozen seat, brittle and crackling under my weight. He backed out onto Moraine Drive, our house—the only one lit on the block—receding from view.

Samantha stood in the doorway in slippers and robe. In the frigid predawn air, her breath made visible streams until Sybel's hand jerked her back inside and the front door slammed shut. I swear I heard it lock.

CHAPTER EIGHTEEN

Recounting the events of that night, such as my memories allowed, made me shaky, but it was my lawyer who looked ashen. Philomena Benedetti blinked a few times before finding a place to begin.

"Well," she exhaled, standing to pace the cell, three steps away, three steps back. She drew a deep breath every time she pivoted, lost in thought. "All right. Your family entered your bedroom all together?" I nodded. "Who else was in the house that night?"

"No one. Raymond went home."

"Raymond—Samantha's husband, right?" I nodded. "You're sure?"

"Yeah, pretty sure. I locked the house and doused the lights myself before collapsing into bed."

Phil paced for a very long time, the beat of her small feet brisk. I braced for the excuse as to why she couldn't take my case after all, to be followed by a hasty retreat to sunny California. Who could blame her? Instead she posed a question. "You think a vase of funeral flowers fell onto the bed and gashed your brother-in-law in the head? That's what killed him?"

Boy, it sounded dumb when she said it. "It was huge and heavy and sharp, cut-crystal. What else could have happened? I remember struggling, I think for real. We must have knocked the nightstand and toppled the vase. Flowers and water were spilled everywhere, I was soaked, and the shattered glass to one side of the bed clearly indicated where the vase crash-landed."

Phil's pallor wasn't improving. She glanced at her watch and announced, "I'm all turned around with the time change, and it's getting late. I better settle in somewhere. We could both use a good night's sleep. Let's call it a day and dig in tomorrow."

"I'm not going anywhere." I didn't bother telling her I'd just awakened from a twenty-four-hour nap before she arrived. Secretly I felt relieved she had mentioned returning.

"Where shall I stay?" she asked.

"Only one decent choice, I'm afraid, the Howard Johnson's off the square, but there are several good places to eat."

I hated the way she looked at me like she was secretly reevaluating her new client. Or was it just my paranoia?

"Besides the usual assortment of fast food joints," I continued, "there's a Big Boy's, which has everything from omelets to spaghetti to burgers. Then there's the frozen custard stand called Jimmy's Sundaes, a drive-through and walk-in with way more than good frozen custard."

To her perplexed expression, I explained, "Frozen custard is like extra-rich ice cream. Welcome to the dairy state. Jimmy's burgers and brats, served on kaiser rolls, were great when I ate such things. And they make the best skinny onion rings. Kleinschmidt Haus is the one sit-down restaurant worth mentioning. All three serve Czermanski sausages, so you can't avoid them."

Phil's raised brows caused me to cease my prattling. "That's about it. Welcome to Wausaukeesha."

"I'll try some Czermanski sausages tonight. Research." Phil gave me a reassuring smile as she shrugged into her coat. She dragged the metal case she kept her business cards in over the bars to signal the jailers. Neither of us spoke until she was safely locked outside my cell by the night guard. "See you in the morning."

"You really shouldn't," I advised as she turned to go, "try Czermanski sausages—or sausages, period. If you knew how they made them, you'd be a vegetarian like me."

Philomena circled back at that last statement. When she saw I wasn't kidding, she laughed out loud and left.

Too soon my world reverted to the crypt-like silence that my over-caffeinated brain wasted no time trying to avoid.

1958

When I started at Kosciusko Elementary School on Milwaukee Avenue in the middle of third grade, Miss Hanson was my first-ever non-nun teacher and a huge improvement over Sister Margaret. She welcomed the expellee from Immaculate Conception without question. In return, I often treated the class to Czermanski sausages. After all, there were no more schools in Wausaukeesha if the public grade school didn't work out. Plus, Dad loved every chance to demonstrate his generosity and importance, though he wouldn't admit to that last.

No matter, it eased my way some when no one else was about to. My requests to Dad to send the sausage wagon to treat the class, even the whole school once, was, according to Sybel, "pathetic. Do you have to try that hard, Kip, at the *public* school? That should tell you something." Sybel really hated it that Dad enjoyed "gaining converts," as he called it.

I had Miss Hanson again for fourth grade, through the '57-'58 school year. One spring day in fourth grade, she sent a note home with me for my father, suggesting my class tour the Czermanski Sausage factory. We were studying economics, which I guess had something to do with making sausages. I hid the note from Sybel to give it directly to Dad that night. He happily agreed.

The day was set, May first. I remember because of the May Pole with colored streamers set up on the playground. A yellow school bus that picked up the farm kids and brought them into town drove my whole class to the flat building with Czermanski Sausage Company in big red letters perched on top. Those letters created a funny red glare that could be seen in the sky for miles.

Dad's secretary, Miss Jennifer, greeted the bus as we unloaded before the front doors. "Good morning, children. Welcome to Czermanski Sausage

Company. We're delighted you're touring our facility today. When your tour is complete, there'll be lunch: Czermanski sausages, sauerkraut, German potato salad, and Kool-Aid, plus Jimmy's frozen custard for dessert." We all cheered. "So you can enjoy the warm day, we'll serve lunch outdoors. But first, please line up here while I talk to your teacher a moment."

The boys in class started nudging each other and making faces like: wow-wee, she's pretty. Dad's secretary looked like all the Polish nannies I'd had so far. Blonde, square-faced, blue-eyed, and pretty in a clean, simple way. Standing next to Miss Hanson, whose silver hair puffed out all over her head, Miss Jennifer looked like Sandra Dee dressed for the office: flipped-up hair, buttoned shirt, fitted skirt to the knees with high heels. She kind of looked like Sybel, just not as tall or thin. I hoped all the nine-year-old boys would act their age today.

We trooped inside to wait in the hallway by the Executive Offices sign for my dad to come out. Miss Jennifer introduced him as "our President, Chief Executive Officer, Chief Operating Officer, and Owner, Mr. JJ Czermanski."

He seemed to wait for applause or something before Dad offered to "say a few words about the company." I tuned out. I knew it all by heart. The boys were ogling the secretary again, and watching them whisper and poke each other was more interesting anyways.

Next thing I knew, Dad was charging down the hallway with us following single file as directed. Miss Hanson stayed behind to speak to several of the worst boys, mostly those dumb Thallensen twins. They straightened up after that, but only because Dad's secretary left us at the Executive Offices.

At a big door to the "plant," we were handed paper hats and booties to wear as Dad explained the need for cleanliness wherever sausages were "in process." We filed into a space where everything changed. It was freezing, for one thing, with two competing smells: dead and sterilized. The antisepticy smell reminded me of our bathroom after it had been cleaned to Sybel's sat-isfaction. Men in white coats with head coverings and gloves were working at high tables.

Dad explained that, unlike most sausage makers, Czermanski had its own "rendering facilities" behind the plant, which none of us understood. "Livestock is both raised and shipped in, finished according to my secret methods for feeding and fattening, then 'rendered' into parts that are passed along to the kitchen. Cuts are then selected, ground and seasoned, and brought here for final assembly."

Dad continued, "Now as you may know, sausage casings are often made from sheep innards, which are cleaned and processed and stuffed with seasoned meats that vary by the type of sausage we're making that day." Dad led us to a table close by. "Here for example, we're making bratwurst." An older man all in white smiled at us, then went back to a machine that, at the push of a button, oozed ground meat into casings—sheep innards.

"Now follow me," Dad commanded after we'd watched bratwurst being spit out by the machine one by one. He headed for the next room, equally cold with the same two odors. "Here is the future of Czermanski Sausages, where we test the latest casings, preparatory equipment and methods, as well as fillings." Big machines filled the room with just a few white-coated men watching them. The hum of motors kept drowning out my dad, who talked the whole way through the room. "...someday all our sausages may ... cost efficiencies ... same superior quality ..." *Maaan,* this was just like dinner conversation at home.

When we arrived at a back door, Dad led us to an outdoor courtyard set up with picnic tables. A man grilled sausages in one corner, which smelled really good after the factory stink. Dad told us to line up, take a plate, and help ourselves to the food piled on a long table beside the grill. The boys ran to the front of the line even though Miss Hanson reminded them of their manners. I hung back. I'd never been to the new sausage factory before—I mean, Dad's processing plant. On the far side of the courtyard was a caged area filled with young animals under a sign: Nursery.

"What's that, Dad?"

He said with a grin, "You know, the birds and the bees." We waited for him to explain. Instead he encouraged me and my friends to go over to pet the baby animals through the wire mesh and followed us.

"Ah-hum, as will happen in nature, sometimes animals in our feedlots have young 'uns. They're brought here and cared for by special handlers. Cute, aren't they?"

Dad put his square hands through the wire and the lambs scattered. Dad soon lost interest and wandered back to Miss Hanson and the food, as did the last of the kids. I stayed behind to watch one lamb trot around in the warm air. I offered it my own hand through the fence. Slowly the lamb came closer and closer. It sniffed my fingers, gave me a little lick, then bounded back to his own buddies, peeking back at me now and then. I wondered if Dad would let me take him home. Sybel wouldn't allow "filthy" dogs and cats in the house, but the lamb looked clean, and we could keep him as our pet in the shed. I'd take care of him. Sybel wouldn't have to. I'll ask Dad tonight.

Miss Hanson was calling me to line up for lunch. I was last to fall in, taking one bratwurst with grilled onions, sauerkraut, brown mustard, and ketchup, just like at home, plus loads of potato salad and cherry Kool-Aid. At my first bite, my new pet lamb made a bah-bahing cry, and I straightened up in my seat to watch it. When it hit me: Casings are sheep innards. Lambs are baby sheep!

There was no place to go, it came on so fast. I leaned over the table to ask Miss Hanson if I could be excused, but instead, threw up all over my plate and a few others' close by. A stunned silence caused my dad to notice what happened before he disappeared into the building. Soon Miss Jennifer, not looking upset or mad at all, came out to organize the cleanup and more food for anyone still hungry.

We didn't see Dad again that day. A grinning Miss Jennifer bade us good-bye before the Executive Offices "on behalf of Mr. Czermanski and the whole Sausage Company staff." But Miss Hanson insisted on thanking Dad person-ally while we loaded onto the bus. Guess she didn't want to lose her access to the sausage wagon due to one of her student's puking, the student with the same name as those free sausages. The warm ginger ale I'd been given had settled my tummy, but I felt ready to get away.

Dad didn't show for dinner that night, not even before I went to my room. I never did get to ask him about keeping the lamb as a pet. Sybel ranted for weeks about my accident at Dad's factory. "You totally humiliated this family by your barfing performance—right at Daddy's plant." Sybel could keep trouble boiling on the front burner long after the pot should've gone dry.

I knew Dad would never agree to my keeping a pet lamb after that anyways.

CHAPTER NINETEEN

February 16, 1972

"I forgot to tell you," I addressed my lady lawyer, still crossing the dead space toward my cell, "that I want—I insist upon—the earliest trial date, 'the calendar,' I believe you called it yesterday. I wish to exercise my 'right to a speedy trial.'" More thrilled to see Phil than I dared admit, I still needed to set some things straight right from the beginning. I planned to lay them out fast and then see how committed she remained to me and my case.

Philomena Benedetti stepped into the cell, glancing up from the file she perused as we were locked in. "Let's not be too hasty here, Kip. I have to petition the court to appear on your behalf since I hold no Wisconsin license. No telling how long that might take. I might be required to join with a state-licensed firm. Besides that complication, I'm going to need time to learn my way around, understand the characters, and—"

"No. It's important that you agree to the earliest possible trial date."

Phil removed her overcoat and shook snow from it. It amazed me that my lawyer was shorter than me. She wore a fitted pantsuit in soft gray cashmere with a shimmery white blouse tied in a looping bow at the neck, casual but elegant.

"Why?" she asked, seating herself and avoiding comment on my stiff powder-blue jail-issue pants and shirt, three sizes too big.

"'Why?' Because confinement in this place one minute longer than necessary is asking too much. I'm claustrophobic," I confessed with a shiver.

"Plus, it'll be easier on you—"

"Most likely tougher, at least in court."

"And well …"

"And?"

"It would be smart to get this over with quickly."

"Only if 'quickly' results in your acquittal, wouldn't you agree? What am I missing, Kip?" Without taking her eyes from mine, Phil opened the oversized briefcase on the floor before her and withdrew a thermos.

"You brought coffee?" I plunked down on my cot, nearly drooling at the rich scent the thermos released.

"In neither of the flavors you mentioned you get here—weak or burnt. I bought a coffee pot for my hotel room at the Howard Johnson's—the store next door carried everything I needed and stayed open late. I made real coffee for us since we share the habit. I couldn't survive on the stuff I sampled yesterday, although it's nice your jailers are so … accommodating."

She produced two paper cups and poured. The aroma itself was enlivening. Handing me a cup, she looked me in the eye. "Now what's this all about, beyond claustrophobia?"

I inhaled aromatic steam. "Sybel's pregnant."

Phil controlled her expression. "With … her dead husband's—"

"You don't know her. She'll use this, she'll find every way of turning it against me, I guarantee it. It's going to be hard enough with her in the courtroom, draped in widow's black, without a burgeoning stomach drawing more sympathy for her—"

"And harsher judgment for you."

"If that's possible in this town." I gulped coffee, feeling the heat travel to my stomach and spread its warmth from there.

"Why do you say that?" she asked.

"My reputation in Wausaukeesha has always been troublemaker and fuck-up of the first order. And that was before my association with the counterculture movements in college. I never fit in around here. Plus, I don't need to be around for the joyous event, okay?"

"I see what you mean about a pregnant Sybel in the courtroom. Yet her presence will be critical for your defense. A show of familial solidarity, especially from the wife, could prove vital. This information does change things … How far along is she? When did she tell you?"

"She's not showing at all, and I don't think she's told anyone yet."

"*Except* you? I got the idea you two weren't close."

"Very perceptive." I took a slow sip. "She didn't exactly tell me, but I'm sure it's true, now that I've thought back on it. She's been queasy since I got home, complaining of an upset stomach. She hasn't been eating much, and I realized I've not seen her with her current drink of choice, her *tres chic* white wine. Nor has she been sneaking beer in the kitchen. Sounds like pregnancy, doesn't it?"

"She didn't tell you? You're surmising her pregnancy?"

"I think she threw up that night in the kitchen sink." Perfect Sybel Czermanski Szyzyck's own barfing performance. "And I was told—just not by her."

"If she hasn't told anyone yet, then by whom?" I blew on my coffee, watching steam curl and disappear until Phil pressed me. "We're wasting precious time here. Kip, I'm on your side, remember? Let's establish a ground rule for working together." She leaned across the space separating the cots. "You trust me with complete and honest answers, regardless of the question. Your confidences are protected by lawyer-client privilege after all. And I do better work defending you because of it. Agreed?"

"By Stan."

"Stan told you?" Phil thought for a moment. "When did he tell you something your sister hasn't told anyone?"

I knew that alone looked bad before I answered, "That night."

"The night Stan died? In your bedroom?" Her careful control didn't quite mask disbelief. "While attempting to rape you?"

"I know how this sounds. I can't remember parts of that night, but for some reason, I do remember him saying, 'Big sis was cold before the pregnancy. Now she's an ice cube.' I thought I'd dreamed it. But last night, thinking about how Sybel's been acting, I suddenly remembered with clarity Stan saying it. In my gut, I know he told the truth."

After another thoughtful pause, Phil asked, "How did you react?"

"I can't remember."

Phil watched me. "What else came back to you from that night?"

"Just that."

She grasped her cup with both hands and leaned back. "You do understand how this appears?"

"Yeah." I collapsed against the bars, tearing up. "Like it drove me over the edge." I met her gaze, penetrating as it was, anxious for her reactions, too. Would she stay after realizing my case's publicity could cut two ways?

Phil sipped coffee and studied me while I braced for the proverbial other shoe. "We better start at the very beginning of your relationship with Stan. Tell me everything about it." Phil slipped off her jacket. Using it as a buffer against the bars, she settled back with a legal pad in her lap.

"You'll stay with the trial date then? We won't waive it?"

"Kip you must understand the defense commonly prolongs the trial date. The longer it takes, the more memories blur, evidence deteriorates—in short, the better a defendant's chances grow. Given Sybel's situation and likely reactions from the jurors, a speedy trial does make some sense now. Let's think about it along with our other options such as a change of venue—"

"No!"

Phil sighed. "The most I can agree to at this moment, Kip, without fully knowing what I'm up against, is that I will not petition to waive the calendar now or until we've agreed to do so."

"Good. Thanks."

Phil put her pad and cup aside and her elbows on her knees. Balancing her chin on her fists, she trained her formidable attention on me. "All right, Kip, from the beginning: Stan Szyzyck—am I saying that right? *Siz*-zick?"

I nodded, toying with my cup. The information I was about to impart would further incriminate me with all of Wausaukeesha who'd tried and convicted me years ago of being a misfit. But I had to trust this woman. I'd fired the other options.

I filled my lungs to capacity before diving head first into my nonconformist life.

Chapter Twenty

Stan ...

"December 1966, that's when it all started, and innocently enough, near the end of my first semester of college."

I hadn't allowed myself to think about this in years. It was proving difficult to put into words. I had no desire to relive my relationship with Stan, now or ever. But my lawyer, demonstrating the patience of Job, waited expectantly, all ears.

The freezing wind had been paralyzing. Blowing down from the Rockies, it swept a thousand miles of plains, reaching ultimate ferocity over the lakes that surrounded Madison's campus. The churned-up waves actually froze in mid-break.

Huddling with my comrades around the campus Selective Service Office, we did our duty, despite Wisconsin's crushing winter, by shouting down the cold. "Ban the Draft, Stop the War." Only a deep commitment to the cause could drag us out in this weather. Only our shouting and chanting could divert our minds from the penetrating wind chill factor. Through the stinging ice gusting in our faces, I peered down our line at the wild combinations of fake furs and bell-bottom jeans, feathers and psychedelic colors, the counterculture uniforms of our unbreakable human chain.

By locking out the "SS," as we dubbed the Selective Service officials, we prevented drafted Army inductees from reporting for duty, our contribution to slowing the war machine which was devouring our generation along with thousands of Vietnamese citizens and warriors. We determined to stay until our demands were heard or we were disbursed by clubs and tear gas or we were carted off to jail. When the unforgiving elements challenged that resolve, and chanting, "Hey, hey, LBJ, how many kids have you killed today?" no longer counteracted the bone-freezing wind, we sang to keep our minds from numbing like our fingers and toes.

> *Yes 'n' how many times must the cannon balls fly*
> *Before they are forever banned?*
> *The answer, my friend, is blowin' in the wind ...*

Joining the anti-war movement early in the first semester of college made me one of few eighteen-year-olds among the demonstrators this early December day. I had been easily convinced that sending many of my friends against their will to make war in a place none of us had heard of was hardly worth the risk forced upon them. Not only that, the war and the draft that supplied it was based on a questionable theory about containing communism, not about any direct threat to our country or our interests. And frankly, it seemed doubly unfair that I, an eighteen-year-old female, was exempt from the dangers of both the draft and the war.

Perhaps the only person over thirty we could still trust, Professor Stanislaw Szyzyck, organized and led, more like exhorted, us ragtag anti-war activists. His standard uniform consisted of faded denims and a khaki shirt with rolled-up sleeves and an open collar that hinted at the professor's taut physique. A rolled up bandana worn Indian-style around his head held his long hair off his face while drawing attention to his feral eyes, two green glints of fanatical determination. With snow and ice scudding over the ground like a low cloud, the professor had added a fraying leather bomber jacket, though unzipped, and socks beneath his sandals.

He moved frantically along our line surrounding the SS building, commanding us to make America hear that "drafting eighteen-year-old boys to die halfway around the globe for questionable reasons was unconscionable." As the hours mounted and the cold inevitably wore us down, someone in a nearby building encouraged us by blasting out our theme song on a Peter, Paul, & Mary LP:

Yes and how many ears must one man have
Before he can hear people cry?
The answer, my friend, is blowin' in the wind.
The answer is blowin' in the wind.

My comrades and I waved placards as Stan approached our sector. "Stop the Killing." "End America's War of Imperialism." "Bring Our Boys Home." The power we created as a united front was way more intoxicating than the pot that passed down our lines.

Stocking feet in sandal straps stopped before me and my hunkered comrades. I looked up as Stan pulled me up and out of earshot. He whispered that he wanted me to help him keep order. Me? "Things," he added, "might get ugly." Stan indicated Madison Police vans on both Orchard and Charter streets with a nod. Cops in riot gear and gas masks streamed into the streets, hemming us, their prey, in the middle.

With bug-eyed monsters rushing us, there was no time to figure why Stan had chosen me from the others. Fear charged the air and our determination faltered. Chants faded, then stopped. Doubts grew audible: "Look at those clubs." "Should we run?" "We're going to be gassed!" "Run!"

As I stared at the onslaught, a memory, or a premonition, blotted out charging cops and terrified demonstrators: an inexplicable vision of Mike Debick, a guy I hadn't seen since he got me kicked out of Catholic grade school, fighting back tears as he lay in blood gushing from his nose, a playground scene that morphed into Mike, full grown and fallen, never to rise again.

I shouted at my comrades to tighten the line and their resolve. "Remember why you're here. They can't take our brothers against their will. We're their conscience. We won't let them forget."

Demonstrators near me picked up the chant. "We're your conscience. We won't let you forget." It reignited our ranks. Clinging together, we wouldn't give in without a fight. "You can't take our brothers against their will."

The first tear gas canisters hissed their venom into the air. Eyes burned and streamed in torrents. Noses ran blood and snot. Throats gagged on the suffocating poison seeping in. We grew lightheaded. Still I struggled to keep everyone united, arms interlocked. Resist. Until the chaos dimmed to silent black.

Light stabbed the back of my skull when I blinked, and I groaned. Finding myself wedged against Stan on the crowded floor of a Madison paddy wagon, only the crush of bodies kept me upright. Thawing heat from crammed demonstrators and the just-in-from-the-snow smell of wet wool were the next sensations to penetrate my consciousness. When the police van lurched, Stan steadied me, preventing more bruises like those throbbing all over my body. Whatever preceded our arrest had also left a wicked red welt on the hand steadying me, and I noticed Stan had lost his headband. His slow smile softened the fervor but heightened the curiosity in his khaki-green eyes.

"Oh no, Profess—Stan, what happened? Was everyone rounded up?"

"Most, yes, but nothing to worry about," he said, his Polish accent bleeding through in the aftermath of the melee. I found it sexy. "They can't hold us long. I'll demand we be charged or freed. They never want to house and feed all of us. We'll be released long before these bruises clear." With a finger, Stan gently traced the sensitive outline of a ragged bruise I envisioned down the side of my face. "It hurts?"

I shook my head to loosen the memory. Had I blacked out, bouncing my skull on ice and concrete, or had a bug-eyed monster's swinging billy club slammed into my face? Stan leaned in, his loose brown hair tickling my skin, and kissed me gently on my bruised cheek, the other cheek, then briefly but squarely on my lips. "I was so proud of you today," he said. "You inspired us, Kip. We stood our ground."

When he drew back, Stan's arm remained around my shoulders. I was conscious of his hand dangling close to my breast. I made no unnecessary movement to prolong contact with the controversial professor I fantasized about. With sidelong glances at him, I ensured my injuries hadn't induced incoherence as well.

As the truck jostled us toward the jailhouse, my comrades erupted into claps and cheers—imagine!—for me.

CHAPTER TWENTY-ONE

When Timothy carried in my food tray, Philomena excused herself to grab lunch and make phone calls. I studied Wausaukeesha County Jail's nutritive offering. Like a school lunchroom all over again, hot ground mystery meat was drowned in gloppy gravy beside overcooked vegetable-mush and a carton of Wisconsin milk. I used the latter to wash down a dry apple dessert that was the most edible thing provided. When Timothy returned for my noticeably untouched tray, he quizzed me about a vegetarian diet, demonstrating his determination to "keep up my strength." As he lumbered off with most of my lunch, I realized dying of starvation was one way to shorten my jail time until that heartening thought was overshadowed by more footsteps.

"You're the last person I would expect." I bolted to my feet, looking past Raymond for Samantha or something to explain his voluntary proximity. Yet Raymond was alone. "What are you doing here?" I didn't mean to sound unwelcoming, but Raymond's open hostility toward me and my "humiliating antics" was historical. Everything about me embarrassed Raymond Chauncey Turner, III since long before this latest antic.

"I can imagine your surprise," he said in a contemptuous tone that matched his expression. We understood each other too well. Raymond said no more until the guard locked him in and he was certain we were alone. In the meantime, he folded his overcoat on the cot, sat, and primped his tie and cuffs. His thin black hair was severely parted and his high cheekbones were colorless. I observed his foppish tailoring, from pocket square to handmade shoes, wondering again what about this mannequin had ever attracted Samantha.

Sitting bone-straight, he finally spoke. "Look, Kip, you've never liked me and vice versa. But I'm not here for me. I've come," he said, standing up to pace in his glistening shoes, "for your sister. Look, just confess and get this over with, will you? A public trial and its attendant gossip are too much for all of us, particularly Samantha. She's falling apart, and she's driving me nuts!" He sank onto the cot.

"You expect me to confess to a murder I didn't commit because your wife is driving *you* nuts?"

"Look, personally I could care less about Stan Szyzyck, JJ's Polish *wunderkind*. But it's pretty obvious, whether you remember or not, that you did away with him." A brief chuckle escaped. "Not that in all likelihood he didn't deserve it. But Samantha is barely functioning. She's pulling her hair out, literally. And she's not the only one suffering—"

"No, I imagine you and Sybel are equally disturbed by this blow to the family's superiority complex."

He ignored me. "JJ is graying before our eyes. He's losing weight, even losing some of his bluster—" Raymond chuckled again. "—which isn't all bad. But anyways," he rushed on, "it seems obvious that to delay the inevitable only hurts everyone more—you included, I might add—dragging out your time in this God-forsaken place." He glanced around until his eyes riveted on my uniform. One brow flew up with his assessment.

"Gee, Raymond, thanks for remembering me. I'm sorry you're having a hard time but I'm pretty sure Waupan State Prison won't be a noticeable improvement over my current digs—for the remainder of my life!" We glared at each other.

"Fine. I knew you'd never be reasonable. Let the trial drag on. Drag all the Czermanskis, your family, through the mud along with you. You'll end up being convicted, that's inevitable. On top of the murder of your brother-in-law, you'll have the health and sanity of your sisters and father on your conscience those long years you'll be locked away. You know how childlike and sensitive Samantha is—nothing like you or Sybel. How she survived the family as well as she has is a wonder." He glanced down the empty hallway. "How do I get out of here?"

"You just got here, Raymond." But I scraped the bars with the rings of the notebook in which Phil asked me to record any and all recollections. The sound caused Raymond to leap to his feet. He turned an accusing eye on me. "Just calling the jailer for you, Raymond." He turned away to calm himself.

"Confess, Kip," he swung back to say, "and get this behind us. Allow the rest of us some chance at normalcy again. Samantha's on the edge, Sybel's never been wound up tighter, and JJ's aging by the moment. You could end all of it and not change by one iota your own fate."

He stared me down. "You've been chasing your own self-destructive finale for as long as I've known you. You're there, Kip. Arrived! Congratulations." Steeliness crept into Raymond's expression. "Now end it—before you destroy the rest of your family."

There was real threat in his words. For the first time, prissy Raymond scared me. I slumped on my cot as he stomped away, the jailer locking up and hurrying after him. Squeezing my eyes shut and burying my head under the pillow didn't hold off the image of Samantha, pulling her lovely blonde hair out—one coil after another wound around her finger.

CHAPTER TWENTY-TWO

I was doing laps around my cell when Phil returned, snow dusting her hair and coat. "That dime store is impressive," she began. "I saw this on my coffee maker excursion and went back for it. The guards said we could hang it, but only with glue on cardboard, which I'll go back to pick up tomorrow."

After dropping her coat on the cot, Phil revealed what she'd protected beneath it, unfurling a print of a Chagall painting I recognized. A solitary figure floated over rooftops and a fence that marked a snow-covered road, the skewed perspective making it even more evocative.

"Well?" she asked.

I took the print and studied it. "Chagall. A museum in Los Angeles held a retrospective of his work, which I attended several times. I love the fantasy of intimate family life he often portrays. Thanks," I said, glancing at my drab cell. "This will brighten up the joint. Ha. The Joint." Though the painting was mostly black, brown, and white, there were hints of blue sky and tepid winter sunlight.

"You know his story," Phil asked, "at least why I think his figures float over barriers?" I shook my head. "Chagall was a Russian Jew, confined to the ghettos where Jews were walled away from the others. The Russians occasionally whipped themselves into a frenzy and invaded the ghettos to kill, maim, and terrorize its occupants. That insanity was called a 'pogrom.'"

"I know. Poland had pogroms, too. It might even be a Polish word."

"You mentioned being claustrophobic, but this place would strain anyone. I hoped Chagall's reminder that nothing can lock in your mind—"

"I see." 'Study for *Over Vitebsk*, 1914,' read the inscription. Nineteen-fourteen, the start of the Great War. "Thanks, Phil," I struggled to say, fearing this poster might demonstrate the only freedom I'd experience from now on, the kind in my head.

"All right then," she said, settling down to business. "We left off where you and Stan became, as you called it, comrades-in-arms."

"Right …" I placed the poster on the cot beside me and tucked its corners under covers and pillows to keep it from rolling up. After a good long stare at it, I returned to the history my lawyer required, as if all this background would somehow prove my innocence.

Early in my second semester in Madison, early 1967, Poli. Sci. 102 had ended, and the crowded lecture hall emptied to the music of muffled conversations and shuffling feet. From my seat high in the back of the room, I descended toward its pit, dodging exiting students, adjusting my nearly straight bob and my sweater covered with peace signs, my eyes all the while riveted on Professor Szyzyck. He crammed papers never once referred to throughout his impassioned lecture into his battered briefcase at the lectern.

Today his subject had been "Apathy in the Political Process," or as the professor distilled it, "Americans taking their freedoms for granted." If I hadn't already embraced the anti-war movement in my first semester, I would have signed on immediately after our professor challenged us apathetic Americans to "live your beliefs, no matter the cost."

A spirited debate had ensued on justifying the means to one's philosophical ends. The SDS, the Students for a Democratic Society, provided the highly charged example. They pursued their well-known stance against the war's violence through any means available, including violence.

Professor Szyzyck stoked the discussion by paraphrasing his personal hero, John Locke, whom he often referred to as "the precursor to the science of politics." He reminded us, "The sole justification for any government is its ability to protect individual rights better than the individual himself can. If a government does not accomplish that, the people have the right to replace it.

"If we agree with Mr. Locke," the professor argued, "then one might ask whether our government is properly protecting individual rights when it drafts men into the armed services against their will. In light of the dubious threat Vietnam presents to our national safety, the question becomes more profound. Let me ask what the eighteen-year-old males in the hall think?"

The room exploded with guffaws and commentary. The professor added over the buzz, "The SDS, the Weathermen, other anti-war factions—are they not simply exercising their right to undermine and replace a government that has failed in its fundamental purpose?"

Despite my reticence, I had rashly popped out an answer in that huge hall. "It's the violent way they exercise their rights that is in question, not whether they can or should."

Stan had flashed an indulgent smile at me. "Our government liberally utilizes violence to put down peaceful protest, which is guaranteed under the Constitution, do they not? You of all people, Miss Czermanski, might recall government-condoned violence right here on campus not many weeks ago."

When snickers died and I'd sunk down in my seat with all eyes on me, the professor continued, "Just another instance of our government doling out violence that it justifies, the primary example, of course, being Vietnam itself. Which brings us right back to the question of justifying the means to an end."

These arguments confounded me, but as I drew near the professor, more pressing thoughts pushed them aside. Specifically, Stan's lips on mine in a jostling paddy wagon, a scene replayed more or less continuously in my head since before the Christmas break. My breath quickened, thinking of it for the millionth time over the winter recess. Did it mean anything, that kiss, beyond gratitude for my impromptu stand at the lockout?

"Um, Professor, I mean Stan—"

His eyes, the exact color of his faded green headband, brightened when he glanced up. "Kip!"

"I, uh, just wanted to ..." *Get your shit together, Kip.* "... oh yes, thank you for watching out for me after the roundup at the SS—"

"Thank me? No, no, Kip, I must thank you. What courage you displayed."

He extended his hand, so I stepped forward and clasped it. He pulled me uncomfortably close, searching my face as it began to burn. When I dropped my eyes, Stan released me. "It's healing well."

My hand went to my barely bruised cheek. "I just wanted you to know I appreciated it."

He studied me until, again, I glanced away. "You have class now?"

"Not until late this afternoon," I answered.

"Good. You'll help distribute flyers for our next demonstration on your way past the dorms?" Not waiting for a response, Stan helped me into the plaid overcoat I'd balled in my arms, slid into his bomber jacket, and guided me up the stairs by the elbow. "Come with me to my office to get them."

Exiting Social Sciences and all the way to Bascom Hill, Stan hummed an old tune I recognized from something my dad used to sing on occasion around the house. Something about making the world go away.

Greeting grungy students dressed much like him, as well as bow-tied professors on our climb to his office in ancient North Hall, Professor Szyzyck didn't release my elbow until he fumbled for his keys and pushed open the door.

His office appeared unoccupied, the desk facing the door bare. Only a battered couch against one wall, jumbled with books and papers, showed signs of use. I was drawn to the single window that looked out over the statue of President Lincoln presiding over the hill in front of Bascom Hall. Before snow-dusted hills in the other direction lay frozen Lake Mendota. The idyllic view seemed incompatible with the unrest plaguing the campus.

Stan's proximity when he spoke made me jump. "It's an illusion," he said, his breath tickling my ear.

I bumbled into him when I turned. "What?"

"The peacefulness perceived from here." Having slung his jacket over his desk chair, Stan rolled up his shirtsleeves and stepped to the window, drawing me alongside. A hardy ice sailor skated his little boat over the frozen surface of the lake before the winter winds. "One might forget people are being blown to bits at this very moment, dying, with no one to comfort them as they breathe their last."

Just then, the ice sailor failed to execute a tack, and his sails flattened and the bladed skiff blew over on its side.

"The children," Stan added, "the ones who survive, will never ever be free of it."

"We're doing our part to stop the war, aren't we, Stan?"

We brushed against each other when he faced me directly. I could not control my blushing with each inadvertent touch. That, plus the stifling radiator heat in his office after the bitter cold, had me sweating. Wrangling me from my coat and tossing it over the chair that faced his desk, Stan slumped against the sill.

"Truthfully, Kip? I grow disheartened with every protest. We've *progressed* from being ignored to being beaten and arrested, yet our efforts haven't formed a blip on the radar screens of the men running things, from this campus to the war in Vietnam. We're dismissed as the radical fringe, an insignificant splinter group of the Left. Do we make a difference? You tell me."

Open doubts from my leader rattled me. I considered for some moments before responding, "It doesn't matter." Stan's head snapped in a double take. "'Live your beliefs, no matter the cost.' Your words from today's lecture."

"Someone listens," he exclaimed, lunging as if to hug me, but I stepped back. His smile vanished. "I appreciated your comment in class today, Kip. You're an obvious proponent of nonviolence. But you'll pardon my saying it's naïve."

"Oh no, not John Locke again," I said, teasing him. The way the professor sobered, I feared I'd crossed a line until his stern expression softened into mischief.

"I suppose I over-reference Locke, but one shouldn't ignore a man who believed a good life is one of pleasure."

"He thought that? How does that relate to political science?"

"It underlies it all. It's what attracted me to the subject—the science of how best to control man's natural impulses."

"Violence being a natural impulse?"

"One of them, of course. You Americans in general have no idea what violence or war really means. How could you? Wars have been so far away. I must admit I envy that naiveté. I barely survived the war, only doing so shamed and hounded by my past."

"Shamed?"

Stan came to his feet. "All so long ago. Forgive me, I shouldn't go on like this. I'm just discouraged."

"Tell me what you meant." I said, interested as well in delaying my departure.

Stan returned to the view from his window, silent for so long his next words came from another world. "The place I lived then was similar, gentle hills, small farms, little lakes …"

He appeared to track the ice boat once again as it skimmed frozen waters, but apparently he saw something else altogether.

"I was a small child in September of 1939 when the Germans invaded Poland. My father, armed with a sword, rode off on horseback to halt the foreign invader. It's my last memory of him, my proud father in dress uniform from *The Great War*, an ancient plumed hat strapped beneath his chin, straddling his stallion. With every stride of the horse bearing him away, his dangling sword flared with sunlight until he disappeared."

Stan abruptly faced me, his voice flat. "In mere weeks, German tanks rode over the pathetically outmatched, foolishly heroic Polish homeland defenders. The entire world watched Poland stand alone against the resurrected German war machine. When Russia joined the pillaging from the east, strongly worded 'objections' from Poland's allies rushed to her defense." Stan shook off his bitterness. "So, Kip, you're here for flyers." He began a dispirited search of desk drawers, slamming each one as he went.

I sat down on my coat in the chair before him. "Your father, Stan, what happened to him?"

"Never knew. If he didn't die in battle, he died in a work camp in Germany as a forced laborer, or he was executed as an example to those who would resist their captors."

"You never saw him again?"

Stan collapsed into his chair, his only response, his darkening features. My own half-memories tumbled out. "Vanished, as if they never existed … Your mother, Stan?"

"My mother … Mother," he repeated at length, "kept our farm going as best she could with no grown men to work it, until the *Wehrmacht,* German army officers, commandeered the place." He snorted indignantly. "The officers magnanimously allowed us to live in our own barn like the farm animals we'd become. My mother cooked and cleaned for them day and night. I carried water, pail by pail, from the well for them to drink and bathe in, carrying out pail after pail of their garbage and their shit.

"That winter was brutal. I can still feel the cold. Sleeping in the loft above the animals, only the warmth of my mother's body kept me alive." In counterpoint to the deathly cast of his face, the chords in Stan's neck throbbed.

"How old were you, Stan?"

"Four—"

The office doorknob jiggled. Neither of us moved until an abrasive knock roused Stan from his chair. He flipped the lock and wedged the door open a crack. At the end of a muffled exchange, Stan thundered at the intruder who was blocked from my view, "A LOCKED DOOR IS NOT RESPONSE ENOUGH FOR YOU? ARE YOU A COMPLETE IDIOT?" He closed and locked the door as footsteps hurried away.

To my shock, Stan sheepishly explained, "I keep my office locked when in conference," as though that clarified what just happened. He moved to the sofa and motioned me to join him there. "Forgive me, Kip," he said once seated, "but interruptions are distracting. See, I've forgotten where we were."

I squeezed into the small space beside him not claimed by textbooks. "You were four years old," I reminded him, catching his clean scent, something citrusy.

In a heartbeat, Professor Szyzyck reverted to war-haunted Stan. "The Germans treated us worse than the cows and pigs *Matka* and I lived among. Farm animals had value—provided milk, cheese, meat. We Poles were vermin—all Slavs in fact made up the Reich's so-called second inferior race—to be exterminated, quickly or slowly, it didn't matter.

"Official Nazi policy for 'reclaiming' land for the Reich called for ridding Poland of Poles through work or starvation or both. They didn't need us, least of all me, a crying brat who stole my mother's attention. Her determination alone kept me alive."

Stan's harrowing story played like a movie in my head. "How did you survive?"

"Oh, our situation improved," he said with sarcasm, "from imminent starvation and overwork to constant hunger and overwork. One of the German officers, the one who spoke intelligible Polish, a Catholic himself *Matka* told me, saved me, I suppose. Saw we got scraps of food, a treasonous act on his part, showing humanity to a subhuman Slav. Of course about that time, my mother stopped sleeping with me in the barn." A tear tracked Stan's cheek, leaving a shiny trail. "I never forgave her. I blamed her, I hated her, for leaving me alone in the dark and the cold."

I watched his lone tear. "You were a scared kid, Stan. Once you realized the sacrifice she made for you—"

"She died, two days before the liberation of the camp we'd been shuttled to as the Germans retreated. I never …"

Slow tears trickled down my cheeks as well. I turned away to the clouds gathering beyond the window, but what appeared before me was Stan's uniformed father on horseback, his sword glinting in the sunlight. The image then bled into the flickering candlelight surrounding my mother, dressed for church and sound asleep in our living room.

Stan took my hand. "Imagine these fine Polish fingers worked to the bone by captors bent on your death." He pried open my fingers and kissed my palm.

"Half-Polish," I muttered as heat prickled up my arm and throughout my body.

"Forgive me." Stan released me. "I don't know what dredged up those memories. Maybe your hair, so unusual for a Pole, curly and dark like *Mat-ka's*." His eyes gleamed a little, thinking of his Polish mother.

My hand flew to my head, finding my bob was still mostly smooth.

"The truth is," he said, "we must fight the illusion perceived from this window and remember that at this very moment, people are frightened, starving, and dying. It must be stopped, Kip."

Wartime death and suffering vanquished my foolish fantasies. "You're right, Stan." I said, standing. "You wanted me to distribute flyers?"

Stan held out his hand for me to pull him up. We came face to face, Stan crowding my space.

"Something very special about you, Kip Czermanski." He pronounced my last name as it was in Poland, the first syllable coming out "shshur." "It draws me to you, draws me out—a kindred fighting spirit I sense, determined despite what the head-in-the-ground majority wishes to believe."

Stan stood so close, I was afraid to breathe. "I kissed you that day," he whispered, his breath caressing my face. "You remember?"

I reddened furiously. *Oh yeah, I seem to recall.*

"I meant it, Kip. I'd like to kiss you again." He raised my chin to his.

Eyes closed, I anticipated his unforgettably soft lips. *I'd like to kiss you, too, Stan.*

But he stepped away, retrieved a stack of flyers from a desk drawer, and piled them in my arms. "You know what to do," he said. Draping my coat around my shoulders, Stan stepped to the door and opened it to people passing by in the hallway.

I blundered out the door, my arms full, my head spinning, my heart pounding. What was I supposed to do? Kiss him? I'd blown it? Glancing backward in confusion, I collided into a friend on his way to see the professor, scattering flyers in every direction.

"Man, Kip, watch where you're going," Peter Replogel shouted as he knelt to help me gather papers. When Stan joined us, Peter glanced back and forth from me to Stan until I colored. Stan told Peter to wait for him in his office as he stood. Peter rolled his eyes and shook his head at me—*what?*—before acting on the suggestion.

Tweaking my chin, Stan advised me to be "more wary." He called out as I stumbled away, "Kip, about that matter we were discussing—call me when you're ready to pursue it."

CHAPTER TWENTY-THREE

As a second semester freshman, I had understood that Stan was taunting me to call him when ready to pursue his offer of a kiss, but I played it cool for a whole week. Virginal terror of an experienced man inspired the delay until, one evening, I showed up at his office, knocked, and stepped inside before I chickened out again.

Stan, in shades of khaki from his headband to his pants, dropped his pen on the desk. "Yes Kip?" he said, not unfriendly, but far from what I'd imagined.

I stood my ground. "You told me to call if, that is, when, I, ah, wanted to pursue, ah, what we talked about."

Stan rose and circled the desk like a cat closing on its prey, his feral eyes hypnotizing. "And we were talking about?"

That was it. My sexually liberated co-ed resolve to call my flirtatious professor on his blatant proposition evaporated. I lunged for the door, muttering, "Never mind," but Stan's hand closed over mine on the knob, preventing my tail-between-the-legs flight.

He greeted me with a kiss on the cheek, grinning as he said, "I'm glad you came, Kip."

He pried my grasp from the doorknob, tugged off my coat, locked the door, and switched off the light. We both knew why I'd come. I struggled to swallow without choking while we studied each other in the twilight filtering through the window.

"We don't want any interruptions, do we?" Stan asked, holding my hand. He had to feel its clamminess.

"No," I gulped. "No, we don't."

"How adventuresome are you, Kip?" Without waiting for my response, Stan pulled me toward him and held me against his body. Heat surged everywhere we made contact, which was everywhere.

"I don't have much exper—" His lips stopped me. I had never been kissed like that—hadn't been kissed much at all—purposefully, as though he sought my every nuance. He entwined his fingers in my flipped-up bouffant and pressed me to him. I concentrated on his lips and tongue seeking mine, the earthy hint of beer he must have drunk at lunch pleasing.

Stan and I stood smashed against each other until my knees threatened to buckle. He maneuvered us to the sofa and we sank down in each other's arms, knocking books and papers to the ground. Stan released me to move heavier texts aside before turning back to unbutton my blouse. Guided by example, I freed the buttons of his shirt. When he stood to tug off my blouse, I rose before him, braless. I'd burned my last bra at the Betty Friedan convocation.

Stan traced the curves of my breasts with gentle fingers, murmuring all the right things to ease my self-consciousness. "You're so beautiful, Kip." For the first time, I believed it.

He slipped off his shirt and laid it alongside my coat and blouse on the floor, then pulled me down with him. His hand skimmed my bare belly to my breasts. His lips brushed along my ear and down my neck. He tortured me with his lips and tongue. Heat swelled throughout my body. Wetness beaded on my skin everywhere at once. I felt lightheaded and fought to control the groan seeping up from deep inside.

Stan struggled to undo my jeans while I fumbled to release his belt and zipper. When he stood to step from his pants and shorts, I gasped at the sight of him from my angle below, all hard and fierce looking. Stan, intent on liberating me from my tight-fitting bellbottoms, tugged and yanked until he drew them off by turning them inside out. He slid my panties down, kneeling beside me, his fingers tracing the changing terrain of my body. I found myself unashamed as if animal instinct opened my entire self to him. All sense of time and place, all control, was lost. I stuffed my fist in my mouth to stifle the sound when Stan lowered himself over me.

Heat, hunger, yearning, love, lust, and connection combined with our bodies. A million sensations bombarded me. They crescendoed, leaving brief pain and lingering ecstasy. Stan covered my mouth with his hand to silence me until, with a throaty gasp, he went still.

I longed to remain forever in this delirium of union, acceptance, and belonging. But little by little, it slipped away. Awareness of the world we'd left behind crept back in. Ragged breathing, intermingled sweat, blooming musk, pounding hearts—all slowing. I blocked out Sister Margaret reminding me of my Permanent Record, inhaling deeply Stan's masculine scent.

My raw emotion turned to overflowing tears which Stan, nestled against me, traced as each one crossed my cheek. He murmured praises of my beauty and my passion as we lay intertwined. Only when the floor turned hard and cold did Stan ease us up to sitting. I brushed back his hair caught in the damp of his face and neck and smiled dreamily, never wanting to leave this place. But my drying skin chilled as the room came into focus, and I laughed out loud.

Stan studied my face. "Kip? You're laughing?" I pointed to the poster hanging on the wall above us. "Make Love Not War" read the slogan printed over entwined flower power and peace symbols. Stan wrapped his arms around me. "Advice we will heed at every opportunity."

Chapter Twenty-Four

That was more than enough on my lover, Stan—my *ex*-lover. Now only loss, regret, and confusion accompanied that subject. I came to my feet to out-maneuver a sudden wave of sadness and pressed into Phil's hand a letter I'd received that day. "Convict mail, opened, read, and delivered," I told her.

Phil flipped it over and back, perusing the return address. "*The Dairy-land Diary*? Babs Howenhauser?"

"The local gossip columnist for Wausaukeesha's weekly newspaper, if you can call it that. She's been the self-described 'society editor' for as long as I can remember."

Phil read snippets of the typed letter aloud. "'... perhaps best to leave the dead to their peace, but I never trusted that Stan ... your voice to the community ... wish to make a public statement ...' What's this?"

"Trying to win my trust, plain and simple, to extract gossip, the slimier the better, anything to fill her column. And I suspect ol' Babs wouldn't mind embarrassing the Czermanskis either, especially Sybel."

Philomena reread the note and tucked it into her doctor's bag briefcase. "I'll pay Babs a visit sometime soon. But no 'statements to the community,' all right?"

"Check."

"Let's finish up your history with Stan today." Phil's brusque business manner redirected the conversation. "So you and Stan became lovers, which lasted through your college career. Then what happened between you?"

"Not quite through my college career," I corrected her. "The last time I saw Stan, that is before returning to Wausaukeesha last week, was the end of my junior year—that would be May of '69, almost three years ago. At the time, I thought we were saying good-bye for the summer." I plunked onto the cot and covered my ears to stop the tune that instantly blared in my head.

> *Though we've got to say good-bye for the summer*
> *Darling, I promise you this*
> *Let us make a pledge to meet in September*
> *And seal it with a kiss.*

"Stop!" I cried, startling Phil. "Sorry. What I mean is I never really understood what happened and now it's clear I never will.

"We said our good-byes before my father packed me off to Europe for the summer preceding my senior year," I explained. "I still can't believe I went along with it. Though fascinating, it was a lonely summer for me, I missed Stan so much. By fall as my senior year was beginning, I couldn't wait to get back to Madison and to Stan."

Phil, apparently anticipating the disastrous tale of my return to campus I was about to cobble together for her, settled in and looked on with interest and a bit of sympathy as I bumbled forward toward heartbreak.

Taking the stairs to the top floor of North Hall two at a time, I bounded toward reunion with Stan after my three month tour of Europe which my dad had hoped would finish me off like a proper young lady. Boy, was he dreaming, or my activism really had him worried, or perhaps Dad simply couldn't face another summer of Sybel and me at each other's throats.

Once I'd left home for college and became in my mind an adult and Sybel's equal, I resisted her domination even more stubbornly. She redoubled her efforts to rule me and the roost. Nothing was too insignificant for her to bitch about: "You left the TV set on." "I just went to the bathroom." "Don't leave your half-read books lying around." "This is the study, isn't it?" "Can't you tone down that outrageous hippie garb of yours, at least while you're home?"

"It's a free country, they say." "When did you get in last night? Who were you with? Where are you going?"

Et cetera, et cetera ad nauseam. Europe had turned out to be way better than another three months of that.

I'd faithfully sent Stan a postcard from every country I traveled to. From his first home, Poland, where I visited my nannies, I wrote him often. Paris, Europe's most romantic city where I mooned for him constantly, inspired any number of postcards, correspondence that reflected a sterilized version of my hunger for him.

In anticipation of our reunion, I smoothed my blown-straight tresses over my shoulders, checked that my denim skirt fell most flatteringly above my knees, and adjusted my top to accentuate my breasts. I noticed the name plaque at his office door was missing, leaving a white square on the yellowing wall to mark the spot. Must've needed a new one, I thought, the tightening in my loins overwhelming such trivia.

I burst through the door, shouting, "Stan!" to find a middle-aged woman sitting behind his desk. I stopped, stared, apologized for barging in, then stepped back into the hall. I doubled back but this time, I knocked and peeked in.

"'Scuse me, but I'm looking for Dr. Szyzyck. I've been away a while, but I'd swear this was his office last May."

The seated woman's black hair had the most dramatic silver-white streak running skunk-like down the middle to a loose gathering at her neck. I found myself studying it while she fumbled through a file cabinet drawer, which happened to stand on the hallowed ground of my sacrificed maidenhood. I flushed at the memory. When the silver-streaked lady held out a paper pulled from a file, I noticed the intelligence in her warm brown eyes.

"No, I don't see the name on the new roster. Szyzyck, you say, spelled S-Z-Y, right? You're the second person this morning. No. No one in the department by that name."

I have been away a long time. "Am I in the wrong building? I didn't accidentally enter South Hall, did I? This is the Poli. Sci. Department?"

"Yes, you're in the right place."

"Well then, your roster's wrong. Dr. Szyzyck's taught Political Science here for years."

"There certainly could be an omission," the bright-eyed woman reassured me. "I'm Dr. Snashl. I'm new here and was assigned this office, which, I was told, had been empty. But perhaps I misunderstood. Would you like me to call the dean's office? Or you could go there. Do you know where it is? Maybe someone there could help you."

"I'll walk down to the dean's office, thanks."

I stumbled out the door, inexplicable panic closing my throat. I made myself walk-not-run to the office, where the dean's secretary kept me waiting before I asked her for the location of Dr. Szyzyck's new office.

"He must have moved while I was away for the summer," I added hopefully.

Arching one brow, the dean's secretary eyed me without speaking. Her appraisal made me feel self-conscious, even ashamed. Could everyone read my randy thoughts? A look akin to condescension settled over her pointed, fox-like face. Her beady eyes narrowed, her lips compressed.

"What?" I demanded. "Could you just tell me where he is? Please."

"And you are?" She spoke each word as though it pained her to part with it. "A student? A *friend*?" I really hated the way she said "friend."

"I'm a student and a friend. What difference does it make? Are Professor Szyzyck's whereabouts a university secret, *Madame*?"

She donned the glasses held around her neck on a faux silver chain. Her lips separated into a snarl that substituted for a smile, all the while continuing to scrutinize me. "I'm afraid Dr. Szyzyck is no longer employed by the university. So sorry." She let her glasses drop on their tether and spun back around on her chair to her typewriter.

"What? Wait a minute. You're telling me that Dr. Stanislaw Szyzyck, Professor of Political Science, left this university? Why? When? Where did he go? Another UW campus?"

"I'm afraid," the secretary replied cheerily, "that all I can tell you is he's no longer with us."

Something cold coagulated in my gut. I took a deep breath. "I wouldn't ask you to divulge university secrets, but I need to reach him. Can you please tell me how to do so?"

"Oh, no, I couldn't," she smiled-snarled. "However, you may leave your name and personal information, and I'll see if it can be passed along to Professor Szyzyck. I'm sure he'll contact you." The dean's secretary was enjoying this, but why?

I signed the clipboard at the bottom below at least twenty-five names, from comrades in the movement to some geeky sorority girls. I had no idea Stan's following was so broad—wide, that is. But it wasn't funny, especially to me. My stomach flip-flopped until I banished momentary suspicions. *Don't be ridiculous, Kip. Good relationships are based on trust.* And ours was the best relationship I'd ever known.

I checked with everyone I could for information about Stan. His disappearance left me in such a fog that I gave almost no thought to a weird new attitude from some of my male comrades in the anti-war movement. Only vaguely I sensed a sort of diminishment, a disdain I wrote off to my bourgeois heartbreak.

I besieged Stan's former landlord. "He broke his lease in May," the landlord told me flatly, despite my repeated attempts to glean more information. "No forwarding address. That's all I know, as I have told you again and again." Stan had vanished.

Weeks later, I went back to the dean's office for one last, desperate attempt to locate Stan. I hung in the hallway until his tight-assed secretary left for lunch, wearing the most surprising bright red pleated skirt. The scent of cheap hairspray hung in the air in her wake. I entered the vacated office and called out, "Hello? Hello?"

The dean stepped from the inner office and asked if he could help me. Something about him, a gentleness, made me relax.

"Yes, I'm sure you can. I'm a former student of Dr. Szyzyck. We were working on a research project together until summer break last May. We planned to finish the project this fall. However, now that he's gone, I need to return his texts and research materials. I'm sure he'll need them. Some are very valuable." I flashed my most innocent smile at the dean as I lied.

He nibbled the stem of his glasses, rocking back and forth on unusually large feet, considering me. The thinning gray hair—no, more the empathetic eyes—reminded me of photos of sickly Grandpa Czermanski.

"It's an awful lot of stuff," I added, "very heavy and unwieldy, quite an expense to mail. But I'm happy to do so if you could just provide an address? A phone number?"

"I am sorry, Miss," the dean said, "but we don't have that information. Dr. Szyzyck told us he'd contact us when he established himself somewhere, but so far, we've heard nothing. He's probably taking an extended vacation. I'd be happy to take your name and number and pass it along when we hear from him. That's the best we can do for you, I'm sorry to say." He meant it.

"Look, Dean. I was a very close friend of St—the professor's." I rushed to speak before desperation broke down my voice completely. "I need to know what's going on. Can't you tell me what happened? Why Stan left? Anything? Please." The dean looked miserable, shaking his head, avoiding eye contact. Inching my denim skirt down my thighs, I blushed, I wasn't sure why. "You already have my name."

I turned to leave, more confused than ever, and scared. Something in the dean's expression, something beyond sympathy, warned me I'd never see Stan again. As if he'd died.

Chapter Twenty-Five

Footsteps pounding toward my cell ended my recounting Stan's disappearance to Phil. I was almost happy for the distraction until I saw the entourage that approached. I leapt up to grasp the bars preventing the guard from opening my cage for them. "What are *you* doing—"

"Morning, Miss Czermanski."

"Morning, Kip."

"Um, hi."

A flash of color heated my skin when the young lawyer, William, and I made eye contact. Lagging behind Polanski and Stelzl, William colored as well.

"May we come in? We need to talk to you. It can't wait," Bob Stelzl said.

Dad's legal team, looking rather desperate, caused me to relent, stepping back as the guard eased open the barred door. My little world got very crowded with the three of them, plus Phil and me, in the cell.

The lawyers stared down at Phil, who sat on her cot and took her time extending her hand. "Philomena Benedetti. And you are?"

"These are the—"

"I'm Bob Stelzl," he spoke over me, taking her hand and kissing it. Puh-*leez*. "Meet my partner, Art Polanski, and our associate, William Beneke." After hand-shaking all around, he extended his business card, and the others followed suit. "Our firm exclusively handles all legal matters for the Czermanski Sausage Company as well as its founder, JJ Czermanski, and his family." He shot an accusatory glance my way. "Except this

Czermanski, it would seem." His joking manner failed to conceal the barb in his words.

"These are the lawyers I told you about, Phil," I said, "the ones I fired after the fiasco at my arraignment."

"What can we do for you gentlemen?" she asked.

Bob Stelzl ignored my criticism. "We've come to offer our services to Miss Czermanski and yourself. We heard there was a female lawyer in town, and frankly we were more—that is, we wanted to make your acquaintance. And offer our assistance, as I said."

"We've already been through this." I inserted myself between the lawyers and Phil, gagging on a whiff of William's overpowering aftershave. "As you see, I've gotten my own lawyer."

"Oh, we see that, Kip." They barely looked at me, Phil intrigued them so. "Where do you practice, Miss, Miss …"

"Benedetti," Phil and I replied in unison. I sat down beside her.

"Benedetti? Italian, isn't it? And you go by Phil? Now that's downright deceiving." Art Polanski forced a chuckle.

"You mean based on your assumptions about lawyers?" she said with a broad smile. "It's short for Philomena."

"Very pretty, that name, Philomena," Bob Stelzl chimed in. "You're not from around here, are you? Chicago?" His voice dropped. "New York?"

"Los Angeles," she replied. Stelzl and Polanski exchanged glances that effectively said: that explained everything. "If I may be direct," Phil continued, "my client and I are quite busy preparing for trial—"

"We're here at JJ's request, Kip's father," Bob broke in, patting down his heavily Brylcreemed hair. "We took on Kip's case at the arraignment, fully planning to continue her defense. However, she told our protégé, William here, that she would hire her own lawyer. Well," he peered at Phil, who held his gaze, "I must say we were caught off guard by that, and frankly, again by you."

"I sensed that," Phil replied.

William looked ready to bolt at the first opportunity, Polanski had difficulty speaking in front of a female lawyer, and Stelzl was playing for something, but what?

The two partners seated themselves across from us and Bob Stelzl continued, "Now Miss Benedetti, Wausaukeesha is nothing like LA, as I'm sure you've noticed. You might need some assistance, some local knowledge, you being an outsi—being new to the area."

"No way," I cut in. "*I* know Wausaukeesha, only too well."

Phil shot me a meaningful expression that surprised me. "My client is reticent, as you see, and it is her decision. This assistance you're offering, exactly what form would it take?"

"This form." Stelzl pushed William forward until he stood halfway between the opposing camps. "William is young, yes, and somewhat inexperienced, but he was top of his class at Marquette Law, as you'll see."

He produced William's résumé and handed it to Phil. "It's all there for you to read. I'm sure you'll find it impressive." He then quipped, "Now here's one of those differences between Los Angeles and Wausaukeesha: not much need for criminal law in these parts. So we're lucky to have someone like William on staff at a time like this."

Polanski waved a manila folder at Phil. "I brought a copy of William's complete file for your review." Phil let it drop in her lap, so he pressed on. "William was born and raised here, knows all the players, the prosecutor, the judges, and their, shall we say, quirks. He could prove invaluable to you in that regard while also providing extra hands and feet as you wade into the case."

"No fucking w—" Phil sat back against the bars and stymied my outburst by pulling me along.

Restraining me by the arm, she asked, "Who would pay for these services?"

As if we were considering it?

"Mr. Czermanski has offered to pay."

"But William would be under my direction—both in and out of court? My sole direction?"

The partners rushed to agree: "Yes, yes." "Of course, of course."

"And I could expect your total discretion?" she asked William. "You'd be working solely for Miss Czermanski and me, remembering not only your fiduciary responsibilities to the client, but complete confidentiality outside of this cell?"

William licked his lips and swallowed, glancing at his superiors. "If that's what's agreed upon," he finally responded, "yes." He was sweating and kept toying with his collar.

"Phil, I—"

She cut me off. "Kip and I will discuss your offer and get back to you. Thank you, gentlemen." When they didn't move, she added, "We really must get back to work."

The partners stood, all three lawyers looking unsure of what to do next as they waited for the jailer to free them. Only as they filed out did Phil add, "Oh, one more thing. *If* we take you up on your offer, I'd require a document releasing William from all duties at," she glanced at the business cards she held, "'Polanski & Stelzl' for the duration of the trial, as well as all of your signatures on a strict confidentiality agreement covering these proceedings."

Panicking, William's jaw dropped as he appealed to the partners, who themselves suffered obvious shock at Phil's words, to do something.

"That wouldn't be a problem for you, would it?" Phil asked.

They blinked until Bob jerked out a nod. I suppressed a giggle. They'd be steaming by the time they returned to the cold February weather. "Good," she responded. "We'll be in touch."

Chapter Twenty-Six

Following the eager stampede for the exit of Dad's legal lineup, I let out the laughter I'd been suppressing.

"Impressive as that was, Phil, I hope it was just a demonstration of feminine capability for those chauvinists," I ventured. "You're not seriously considering allowing my dad's henchmen a toehold here—no, more like a front row seat? Wait a minute. I'm the client and I won't have it."

"Yet you are the one insisting on the earliest trial date, little more than seven weeks from now," Phil shot back. "Your insistence adds a dimension that must be dealt with realistically. I can track all leads, interview witnesses, learn the players and their predilections on my own, even secure additional help, had I the time. But I don't. Nor do you. I'm merely exploring all options in light of the reality we face."

"But Billy Beneke—that's not reasonable. He's a chest-thumping, domino-theorizing, feminist-bating Neanderthal who quite eloquently expressed his disregard for me and my anarchistic kind. You saw how thrilled the prospect of working with us made him—boss-lady lawyer and feminist girl murder suspect."

"Billy?" She reread his card. "You know William ..." she tried my pronunciation, "Ben-*neck*-kee?"

"*Ben*-ne-kee, emphasize the first syllable. One of the joys of small town America, Phil—of course I know him. We both grew up here." I moved from my close proximity to Phil as my mind filled with visions of Billy Beneke in his Head Hall Monitor insignia—an official-looking white shoulder sash that ended at his waist—guarding Immaculate Conception's entrance.

With a severe look, Billy Beneke could stop even the feistiest boys from running in the hallways or shoving in line at the bubbler. He was the handsomest hall monitor at school, at least to me. I was beneath him by both three grades and untold coolness levels. Billy Beneke, my first heartthrob, whose name filled the margins of my notebooks. I used the school's main entrance each day to catch a glimpse of Billy, who never once acknowledged me.

I leaned back, wedged against a corner of my cell and smiled at Phil. "You wouldn't believe how cute, how cool Billy Beneke once was."

The march of time had added the thick-lensed glasses, the thirty pounds, and his thinning, darkening hair, all of which had made him unrecognizable to me. But ten years ago, Billy was downright hunky and I … well, I was about to perfectly portray a complete ass.

Even as a lowly fourteen-year-old ninth-grader, I had zero interest in dating Lanny Krousy. He was the guy next door who hung around our house a lot, even though he was a high school senior and somewhat of a basketball star at St. Hedwig's Catholic High School for Boys. Lanny was tall and spindly, with ever-present pimples splotched across his face and neck. We were friends, kind of, so when he needed someone to go to his senior dance, he didn't ask me. He asked my father. What was he thinking, that we lived in the previous century? Dad assumed I'd be thrilled to go out with an athlete and older guy and accepted for me. Neither my ranting nor sulking got me out of it.

At the appointed hour, instead of his usual unannounced appearance through the back door, Lanny walked across our side-by-side driveways to ring the front doorbell. I forced myself from my bedroom behind the kitchen, wearing the bubblegum-pink gown passed down to me by Samantha, who'd gotten it from Sybel, who previously had it passed down to her by Sarah, I suppose. My arms itched where the gauzy material encircling my chest rubbed against them. And with my olive skin, I looked terrible in pink.

Since I was neither tall nor slender like my sisters, the mid-calf-length gown dragged on the ground. Only the fact I still had no boobs allowed me to zip the strapless thing.

Lanny's jaw dropped when I stumbled from the kitchen on dyed-to-match pink heels, itching at my armpits. Resembling upside-down cotton candy, I figured I'd have no more worries about Lanny asking Dad for another date with me.

Lanny's white tuxedo jacket with ruffled shirt that gapped around his neck made him look gawkier. I noticed his shiny black cummerbund over black pants when he forced a red wrist corsage in a clear box on me and planted a peck on my cheek. Honestly.

Holding the door, he guided me by the elbow out and across our driveways to his waiting VW. My gown overflowed the front seat as I sank into the center of a poofy pink cloud. *Shit.* Why hadn't I taken the opportunity to buy something new in exchange for going to this dumb dance? Dad wouldn't have cared about the cost at all, but Sybel would have insisted upon accompanying me, which explained it completely.

When we arrived at St. Hedwig's Catholic High School for Boys and finished the beers Lanny had snuck under the front seat, I knew I was done up all wrong. The girls crossing the parking lot looked like grown-ups in their tea-length gowns, their breasts burgeoning beneath spaghetti straps. They wore thick eyeliner and pink lipstick, smooth hair parted and flipped up at the bottom. In comparison, the pink barrettes exerting control over my mane were childish and hideous.

"Lanny, maybe this is not a good idea," I hesitated. "Why don't we blow off the dance and go to the drive-in?"

But it was too late. Lanny's basketball buddies and their dates circled our car. *Hey Lanny,* the guys were calling, *who's the girl?* Lanny came around and held my door so long, I had to get out. I tugged at my personal version of the flip, lacquered into place on my head, while trying to keep my top in place, my arms from itching, and my skirt from tripping me. Gadzooks, what had I ever done to Dad to deserve this? If I hadn't already felt ridiculous, the stifled smiles and shared glances among the girls, the embarrassed hush among the boys, would've done the trick.

"This is Kip Czermanski," Lanny announced.

One of the girls with glowing blonde hair, a golden gown to set it off, whispered loudly, "Jimmy, we really must get inside. I'm catching a chill in this bare thing." Jimmy leered at her modestly revealed cleavage while leading her away. Lanny and I trailed them into the gym, where I bet he wished he were playing basketball instead of dragging me around. Ditto that, by the way.

Crepe paper in St. Hedwig's blue-and-gold school colors hung in uneven swaths from a mirrored ball rotating on the ceiling. It cast ghastly specks on those dancing to the music produced by Buddy Holly-esque band members, all flat-tops and crew cuts, lining a temporary stage. Groups encircling the dance floor added their shouts and laughter to the music.

With a sweaty hand, Lanny pulled me out to dance. The top of my head didn't even reach his shoulder, which made it impossible to dance and talk. When he tried, I heard nothing but smelled beer-breath, so we lumbered around the floor without conversation until at last the music stopped.

I wiped the clammy hand Lanny had been holding on my dress while the couple next to us greeted him. I should have recognized them, but the six years since our Immaculate Conception days had changed us all.

Lanny said, "This is my date, Kip Czermanski."

The girl zeroed in. Only then did I recognize Katey Rudeshiem, Sister Margaret's favorite and her overused example of feminine goodness, now standing before me in slightly revealing, tight blue silk.

"KP?"

"It's Kip now."

"Well, my my ... Whatever happened to you? You stopped showing up at Immaculate Conception in the second, no, wasn't it the third grade?"

"I changed to the public school," I replied, as if she didn't know the details. "So how are you?"

I could feel Katey's eyes taking me in, from my outfit to my disobedient mop topping it all off. Katey's my age, I thought. Why does she have breasts and hips, well displayed in that gown, and a self-confident, sexy smile? Why did she get smooth shiny hair, flawless skin—

"Kip," Lanny said, "this is one of the basketball greats of St. Hedwig's." He punched the shoulder of Katey's date worshipfully. "Meet the captain of the team, William Beneke."

—and get the guy I used to dream about? Ignoring Katey's scrutiny, I smiled hello at William—Billy back at Immaculate Conception. Billy hadn't lost any of his devilish good looks—sandy blond hair, eyes a similar light brown, a square jaw, and a star athlete's body. He still looked down his nose at the world, which on him just seemed cool. My pulse quickened, remembering Billy at his hall monitor post, speaking only to the In Girls while keeping order in the school.

I sighed inwardly at his dismissive "Hi," marking as it did the first time we'd conversed. Katey grinned at me and whispered to Lanny before being squired off to dance. Lanny's blush only underscored the pimples spotting his skin.

"What did she say?" I demanded, expecting something mean. People never changed.

"Katey told me to cut in for a dance sometime, that's all." He was obviously shaken by the attention. Geez.

Lanny and I danced again, that is, we shifted from one lead foot to the other. I watched Billy and Katey, gliding 'round and 'round, outpacing everyone as the band switched from "In My Room," to "Don't Let the Sun Catch You Crying," one of my current favorites.

When Lanny pulled away, I realized too late that he was cutting in on Billy and Katey. Soon she was rocking woodenly back and forth with Lanny, focusing her flirtatious smile on him, and I found myself in the arms of the coolest boy from Catholic grade school. I didn't care how much my dress itched my armpits—they could just wait.

Remembering Lanny's beer-breath, I avoided all conversation as Billy tried to lead me around the floor in sweeping movements I couldn't follow.

When a strangely sour-sounding rendition of "I Want to Hold Your Hand" blared out, Billy suggested we jitterbug. I watched, then imitated, his quick moves until he glided in and grabbed one hand. I tensed as he swept me under his arm and caught my free hand as I passed by, snapping me back the other way. When I got those moves down, he tried a few more turns and reversals. People around us began to notice, stopping to clap as Billy executed a mean jitterbug, and I kept up, kind of.

I relaxed into the groove of the music, the fun of being twirled one way and then the other, forgetting the irritating fabric, my unflattering dress, the clumsy shoes, the pink monstrosity of it all. We danced face to face, Billy holding both my hands, until he dropped one and backed off. I sensed a turn-under-his-arm move coming. Push back, twist under, snap back around. I loved this! Imagine me dancing with Billy Beneke, and enjoying it.

Totally exhilarated, I twisted under our upheld hands and back again. When he caught my free hand, I heard a rip as I felt my gown shift. On the swing-through move, my dress slipped, tangling in my feet and dragging me down, still holding tightly onto Billy. To a chorus of gasps all around us, Billy and I piled up over crumpled pink gauze on the dance floor.

Although he couldn't catch himself, Billy the Athlete recovered quickly. He sprang to his feet and pulled me up with no effort at all. I rose to standing in the center of a pink mound of gauze in only my underwear—slightly padded AA strapless bra, once-white panties, garter belt holding up pink nylons rooted in color-coordinated heels.

A hush fell; even the band whimpered to a halt.

Lanny rushed over. "Kip, good God, cover up." I looked down as snickers mushroomed into giggles, laughter, and catcalls, with a few congratulatory slaps to Billy's back. I felt myself burn the color of the dress puddled at my feet while Lanny helped yank the gown up around me.

I kicked off the heels and ran. I didn't stop until I got to his car. I waited for Lanny, who arrived with my shoes, blush-pink himself as he held them out to me. We avoided eye contact.

"Open the door!" I screamed.

Gentleman to the end, Lanny helped with the gown I held up by my arms smashed against my sides before closing my door and slipping into the driver's seat. I would not allow myself to cry in front of him.

"Just take me home, will you," I snapped. But as soon as the ignition caught and he turned to back out, I burst into tears.

I didn't stop sobbing into my pillow until well into the night.

CHAPTER TWENTY-SEVEN

The snap of Phil fastening her briefcase jarred me back to reality, my eight-by-ten-foot cell. She stood to slip on her coat and check her watch.

"I have an appointment with the arresting officer at the station before he goes on duty tonight. It was difficult to get." To my quizzical look she explained, "The authorities couldn't believe I'm your legal counsel. They required I produce my credentials before approving the meeting."

Phil brushed the bars with her briefcase until the jailer's footsteps sounded. "It's a big problem, exacerbated by my lack of Wisconsin credentials. That in itself is an excellent reason to consider taking on William. Working through Polanski & Stelzl's state license would save precious time."

She faced me directly as Timothy came plodding down the hall. "The trial date is closing in while this technicality goes unresolved. I implore you to give serious consideration to William assisting us. We can't afford *any* delays, Kip, unless you're willing to waive the judge's calendar."

I shook my head. "No way."

Phil asked Timothy to give us a moment. A huge grin broke through her irritation when she pivoted back to me. "Don't think I don't sympathize with you over that tragic high school dance. But," she turned serious, "view that embarrassment from the perspective of your upcoming murder trial. I'm thinking if Polanski & Stelzl provide the license, we'll agree to accept their offer with our stipulations in signed agreement form. As an added precaution, I'll interview William *Ben*-ne-kee before we sign. Otherwise, I'll have to import assistance from Milwaukee or Chicago—I've made a few calls—who, if I read this place correctly, would still be suspicious outsiders, though perhaps not female."

Phil left me with, "William might prove valuable to us. Let's think it over."

"But—"

"Just think it over."

Being the sole inmate of the Wausaukeesha County Jail had advantages. It didn't pay to staff a cook for a single prisoner, especially one with my odd eating habits. So I was given the menu from the Big Boy's restaurant near the jailhouse and told I could outline what a vegetarian eats. Then nutritious meals, planned with the assistance of the School of Home Economics at Wausaukeesha College, would be arranged.

Tonight's dinner was spaghetti reminiscent of canned Chef Boy-Ar-Dee, cold banana cake that looked suspiciously like thawing Sara Lee, and in a nod to the dairy state, milk. I couldn't be happier—about the food, that is. Tomorrow, I planned to wheedle from my jailers a Jimmie sundae with bananas from the frozen custard stand. It was dairy, after all.

The sound of voices and footsteps in the hallway reached me before my dessert warmed to room temperature. I pushed aside the tray to see my father approaching, schmoozing the guard, of course—my dad, never too big to forget the little people. Dad nodded at me while thanking the guard, shaking his hand, and clapping his back. Before locking my father in, the jailer asked if I'd finished my dinner.

"Not quite." Banana cake was the best part. "Any fresh coffee up there?"

"Ol' Rudeshiem left a thermos before shift change," the guard said. "I'll bring it back."

"Geez, Dad, what's with all the buddy-buddy stuff?" I asked, embarrassed as usual by my father's excessive insincerity.

"Just greasing the skids. Offered to send some sausages over for the staff before asking the night guard to bend visiting hours for me. And I'll point out the obvious: worked like a charm. Usually does, Kip."

In an expensive overcoat, its fur collar, like his silvering hair, glistening with snow, Dad's imposing figure seemed to fill the cell. But once the guard disappeared, Dad collapsed onto the cot. "This is terrible, just terrible." The deflated old man from my arraignment languished before me. "You doing okay, Kip?"

"Holding up." I glanced over his head at my Chagall poster, the figure floating free of earthly bonds. "Yes, holding up."

Dad struggled to assume control. "Now what's this talk I hear from my lawyers, Kip. You've hired your own lawyer and kicked them off the case?"

"Something like that." I rose before him. "Dad, this is not disclosing the animal parts you stuff in your sausages. This is murder one. You know I could—"

"But a *girl* lawyer? From *California*?"

It was impossible to know which of those two sins was worse in Dad's purview. "A woman, Dad, hardly a 'girl.' She's smart, well credentialed, and I … trust her." I realized I did trust her, as much as I trusted anyone. "She came highly recommended."

"It's bad enough, a girl—*woman*—standing trial for, well, you know the circumstances. But who's going to take a woman lawyer seriously? Kip, this is crucial."

His glancing around the small cell to emphasize the point infuriated me. I'd been living the situation's seriousness since my arrest. "You're telling me? We may be 'girls,' Dad, but we get it. We know what we're up against."

I wondered if Phil really did understand just how far from California she'd wandered. Of course she did. She'd made it in a man's world in a man's field against all odds. Of course she understood.

"Well, who is she? What's her background? What's this woman lawyer charging you?"

Phil might need to begin carrying her degrees and CV with her. "She graduated from a top law school and has years of experience—relevant experience," I emphasized. "She worked in New York for ten years before setting up her own practice in Los Angeles. She represents the center where I work. And I'm paying her. You needn't worry about her charges."

"New York, Los Angeles? What does that have to do with us?" Dad, rising to pace, inspired my taking a seat. "You getting enough to eat around here?"

"Yes, Dad."

"Frankly, I'm worried …"

Touched, I gazed up in surprise at Dad expressing concern for me and my health. Demonstrations of affection or concern were frowned upon in the family, especially by Sybel.

"… you're not making one of your statements, are you, with a woman defending you? People are riled up enough with all the goings-on you read about: flag burnings, bra burnings, draft card burnings. We don't need any of that now, Kip. For once, don't make it harder. We have our position in this town to uphold."

He sighed. "I should say rebuild after … after everything. My reputation is the same as the Sausage Company's. I've got a lot of people depending on me beyond the family, you know. You need to protect them, as well as our own future."

Wrong. Dad was worried about the scandal's effect on his beloved company, that ego-extension of himself. "Rest assured I have a vested interest in taking the situation seriously, Dad." Testing the banana cake with a finger, I found it the right temperature to eat. "So don't worry about it."

"I want to meet her. At least, let that smart young lawyer who Bob and Art are so high on help out. These people have worked for us since the beginning. I'd feel a whole lot better if someone on your defense team knew the difference between Wausaukeesha, Wisconsin and Los Angeles, California. Someone I trust to watch out for our interests as a family should be on board at the minimum."

"William's ROTC, Dad, and he … we … Never mind."

"I'd pay for him, Kip, and the other one, too, the gal, if she checks out once we meet."

"No!" I rose to face my father. "I've made arrangements with Phil. As far as William Beneke, Esquire goes, I will only say … we're considering him. Trust him or not, Dad, how much applicable experience could he have at his age, working for the Sausage Company?"

"Law is law. Now how much is she charging you, Kip? You've seen this lady lawyer's credentials? You *know* she's got her law degree from some … reputable place?"

"She doesn't travel with her diplomas, Dad, but you can check up on her at Stanford Law and UC Berkeley undergrad if you wish. She's staying, Dad. *We'll* decide about William's assistance. And you'll meet Phil in due time."

Dad glared at me, and hard as it was, I held his gaze. He eventually added, "I beg you, Kip, none of your shenanigans now, none of your grandstanding or causes. For once, don't make this any harder on us than it already is." He sighed and shook his head. "Well then, how do I get outta here?"

I dragged the metal cup from my tray across the bars. The jailer appeared with Timothy's coffee thermos in hand. Once locked outside my cell, Dad swung back with a new angle, which I cut short with, "I'm not trying to make things harder, Dad." Dad clucked in disgust and walked off. "I'm finding things quite hard enough," I half-shouted after him. I dropped the cup onto the tray, suddenly no longer in the mood for banana cake or fresh coffee.

I never tried to make things harder. I never had to try. I clunked backwards against the bars and stabbed the cake with my finger. Dad's words gave form to something that had been niggling me since my arraignment. That childish nautical outfit—I'd worn it to Sybel's college graduation. That was twelve years ago, when I was twelve. No wonder I could hardly breathe. It was so tight it could have been sausage skin.

My first assertion of adulthood—that was where that ridiculous outfit came from.

1960

Beep-beepbeepbeep.

The honking horn caused me to fumble the belt and start again. "I'm coming, I'm coming," I shouted from my bedroom window, a story above the anxious occupants of Dad's car in the driveway.

The honking kept up: *beep-beepbeepbeep, beep-beepbeepbeep.*

At last I got the belt to hold the navy pleated skirt in place above my knees, instead of inches below like some Catholic schoolgirl. Though the skirt wasn't plaid, pleats always reminded me of Catholic school. Man, I'd hardly thought about Immaculate Conception since I left it four whole years ago. To think I'd still be stuck a whole 'nother year through the eighth grade with the nuns, instead of finishing seventh at Pulaski Junior High.

Beep-beepbeepbeep.

The shoes I'd hidden under my bed, the exact navy blue of the skirt, were too big, like the rest of the outfit. I slipped into them and admired myself in my mirror, until my first wobbling steps shattered the adult image. If I kept my toes scrunched up, I could still keep them on when I moved. And no matter what Sybel thought, by twelve years of age, it was high time for high heels. I tried a few steps back and forth until I walked almost normally.

Beep-beepbeepbeep, beep-beepbeepbeep. Beep-beepbeepbeep.

"Coming." I stepped out of the shoes and dashed down the stairs, slipping back into them at the front door.

The moment I appeared, listing toward the driveway, Dad shouted from behind the wheel of his new 1960 chrome-and-yellow Cadillac. "We're going to be late, Kip. Hurry on up now."

Dad gunned the engine as I slid into the backseat behind him and Samantha. To block out Dad's scowling as we careened across town, I focused on tying a perfect square knot with the navy blue tie that completed my nautical-themed white blouse.

May was proving unseasonably hot and humid. Just a month before, we had a blizzard that blanketed the state in drifting snow. An icy mound sealed our back door shut until spring warmth returned and melted the hill-sized drifts to grimy clumps, which Sybel sent me out to shovel away. I'd minded none of it. We'd gotten one last snow-day from school.

Dad steered his humungous Cadillac onto the ivy-covered campus of Wausaukeesha College to his VIP parking space behind the Czermanski Hall of Animal Husbandry. It's not like we had to search for a place to park or walk any distance. What's the big hurry?

As soon as I stepped from the car, Samantha gasped, "Where did you get those shoes, Kip?"

I wobbled on heels as high as hers. "Gimbel's?"

"Kip, at twelve years old, you are way too young to be wearing high heels. Goodness, they're Sybel's new shoes, aren't they?" Samantha glanced at her watch, at Dad impatiently jerking his dark jacket over his short-sleeved shirt and tie.

"No time," Samantha sighed, lugging me along behind Dad. "Why do you always make it harder on yourself, Kip? Prepare to catch hell," she whispered.

"You look nice," I told her. The sleeveless dress hugging her frame was the perfect color of rose on pale Samantha, a nice change from her usual white.

Samantha shook her head. "We'll all hear about it from Sybel."

Hurrying to keep Dad in sight, we rounded the concrete-and-glass-cube building bearing Dad's name, the only building on campus that wasn't red brick with ivy. The Sausage Company jingle, "Science is the secret of Czermanski's great meats," was meant to remind the locals of the college that bore his name—not that the College of Animal Husbandry influenced his sausage recipes, so far as I knew.

We entered the stuffed and sweltering auditorium, but of course, had VIP passes to descend to the front row. We'd be right under the podium when the chancellor handed Sybel her diploma. She couldn't miss us and vice versa. My father made his usual halting entrance, stopping to shake hands and make phony conversation. Yeah yeah Dad, everyone knows you're *the* Czermanski of the Sausage Company and the College of Animal Husbandry. *Geeez.*

I slunk ahead to an open seat while Samantha dutifully stood by Dad throughout his slow descent. Samantha held the roses we'd brought for Sybel, which happened to match the dusty pink color of her dress. When they reached the first row, Dad and Samantha made me move back down to sit beside them. Man, this was starting to feel just like going to Mass.

The chancellor appeared on the stage, the lights dimmed, and he asked us all to stand for the national anthem. Then the college band struck up a discordant version of the Wausaukeesha College school song, which made people around me tear up. Gads, I'd never understand grown-ups. Next came the school fight song. *Rah rah rah. Go Blue Devils.* The Mayor of Wausaukeesha gave a speech about civic duty and "steering" the future, though he never exactly explained how. Finally, with the band playing the school anthem as a backdrop, the chancellor began to read the names of the graduates as they marched across the stage to collect their diplomas.

The moment my dad had been waiting for arrived, recognition of the family's first college graduate.

"Sybel Norma Czermanski, Dean's List, College of Home Economics. Congratulations, Miss Czermanski."

I snuck a peek at Dad as Sybel grasped her diploma. He grinned and clapped, even blew that ear-piercing whistle he makes with two fingers in his mouth. Sybel did not approve and shot Dad a meaningful glare. He shut up.

I watched him watch her, one of the few girls who looked pretty in cap and gown. The shiny black fabric billowed as she walked, proud and erect, her long blonde waves swishing back and forth across her shoulders. When she returned to her seat on stage, diploma in hand, she flashed a smile our way that staggered me, completely erasing the Sybel I knew. She became what the guys at school called a knockout. Sybel looked happier than I could remember.

I looked at Dad with a sudden realization about that smile. It was my mom's smile all over again. I noticed his eyes clouding while he sniffed back unmanly tears. I clapped and sat down—they were only finishing the Cs after all. Samantha followed my lead, tugging Dad onto his seat.

The minute the ceremony ended, I slipped up the stairs and out to the courtyard ahead of Dad and Samantha—not that I was over-anxious to congratulate Sybel, but to avoid Dad's chatty exit. I hung around the fountain in the middle of the courtyard, dipping my hands into its splashing water and touching them to my forehead and neck. Man, this May day was August sticky-hot.

Samantha coaxed me over to where Dad and Sybel, now holding the roses, stood BS-ing several men in flowing black robes—the chancellor, the dean of the College of Home Economics, and the dean of the Czermanski College of Animal Husbandry, I learned upon introductions.

The home economics dean studied me and gushed, "My my, I see we can look forward to another Czermanski. I hope Home Economics will be your choice as well, dear girl. We could use more serious students like your older sister." He hugged Sybel, who flashed that smile again.

I played with my square knot till Sybel, who ran our household like a drill sergeant long before her diploma in home economics, elbowed me to respond. "Uh-huh."

The dean pretended shock. "Does that lukewarm response imply you're not interested in following in the footsteps of your elder sister here?"

"You could say that." I bit back the nastier comments that sprang to mind, noticing the dean was more interested in my Dad's reactions anyways.

"Oh come now, young lady," the dean pressed on, faking surprise. "What does your lack of interest in the latest in scientific home care suggest about your future?"

A Sunday school story about a wrathful god in sheep's clothing flashed through my mind, a good description of Sybel's approach to running things. I was beginning to suspect where she'd refined her methods. A string of comebacks, any one of which I'd pay dearly for, tickled the tip of my tongue as the lengthening silence and waiting eyes implied the next move was mine.

"I could never be like Sybel, even if I wanted to," I said. "When I get older, I think I'll study animal husbandry." I had no idea what it meant. "And help Dad out at the Sausage Company."

Sybel's smile froze, her dean's eyes widened, and I went back to playing with my navy tie, peering up when I heard snickers. Both Dad and the dean of the Czermanski College of Animal Husbandry erupted into backslapping laughter. Samantha and I joined in, leaving Sybel and her bow-tied dean, sour-faced and trying to ignore us.

The Animal Husbandry dean, whose gown looked too small for his large body, nodded approval at me. "She's the precocious one, JJ, that's evident. Young lady, we'd welcome that. You come see me when it's time, you hear?"

I nodded and concentrated on my tie, knowing without looking that things had gone too far for Sybel. Sybel must have focused in on me, though, because she noticed my high heels. Actually, they were her high heels, which

I borrowed for this very special occasion, but I was pretty sure she got them at Gimbel's in Milwaukee.

Pretending to smell her roses, Sybel leaned in to whisper, "You little shit, how dare you wear my shoes *and* do your best to ruin the biggest day of my life. Little bitch, you'll pay for this. Everything ends up being about you, doesn't it? Not even today is mine."

She straightened to full height, tossing her hair over her shoulders and pasting a smile on her face, her skin blotched with anger.

I'd catch hell as soon as we got home, no question, but it was too late now. Might as well enjoy a moment of payback while it lasted. I undid the square knot I'd been practicing and retied a loose bow that drooped down the front of my sailor blouse, all the while maintaining perfect balance on Sybel's new navy-blue high heels.

CHAPTER TWENTY-EIGHT

February 17, 1972

I shouted the obvious point at Phil, "William 'Billy' Beneke will be a leaky sieve to Dad and Sybel through Dad's 'trusted' lawyers, Billy's bosses. I can't believe you'd give this—him working with us—serious thought. Lawyer-client privilege does not exist in a one-sausage-company town."

I leaned across the space that separated my cot from Phil's to demonstrate my decision had been reached. "I'm the client, and I say NO. In fact, I say: fuck no. Besides, Billy's heavy-duty aftershave gives me a pine-infused headache, and I can't exactly open a window."

"Let's not rile ourselves," Phil said, unimpressed by my vehemence. "How about we talk it through before spouting slogans?" My lawyer met me half way across the no man's land between cots. "Why they've made their offer will be immaterial once the partners sign a document delineating the conditions of William's employment with us—release from all responsibilities to them for the duration of the trial, continuance of his full salary and benefits, plus wording to construe any fiduciary breach as direct intervention by the firm of Polanski & Stelzl, as well as its partners and William personally."

Phil was keeping a tight rein on her frustration, I could see. "Listen, Kip, I know you and William are opposite ends of the spectrum, but he is a trained criminal defense attorney. He's been taught to put aside his personal opinions—a necessary part of the job, although I see you both struggle with that."

"Excuse me?"

"Inexperience, I suppose. But he may rise to the occasion. When I spoke with him alone, William struck me as someone who deeply respects the law and would honor any legal agreement he signed."

"You spoke to Billy? When?"

"Early this morning. I stopped by their law office to see about drawing documents, should we agree to proceed. He's very stiff, Kip, I agree with you on that. When I asked him why he chose criminal law only to practice corporate, his answer was surprisingly naïve. Criminal law is the most 'black-and-white,' he said." Phil chuckled. "Yes, definitely inexperience.

"As for his practicing corporate law, his wife wanted to raise their children near her parents and his mother, which meant moving home and foregoing the form of law he loves best. It's hard on him, I could tell, as is providing for his wife and kids. He has a six-year-old and twin three-year-olds already and he's not much older than you. Despite your evident differences, I'd bet William would get into this case."

When Phil stood and began to pace, I studied her black pantsuit, black boots peeking out beneath, with a silken blouse the most amazing color of blue-green, which perfectly set off her features. She looked beautiful. "You really need him, Phil?"

"*We* need him, Kip. He'll know the judge who will preside at your trial, he'll know the police and coroner and other officials who have been slow and uncooperative with me, a foreigner to town and a woman. It's causing unacceptable delays. He can spend time in Madison or wherever needed. Plus, I can represent you in court under his firm's license with no more precious time wasted on that technicality. I don't know how we'll do this without him, Kip. Our trail date is seven-and-a-half weeks away. Unless of course, we waive—"

"William would be personally bound to confidentiality, no matter who pays him?"

"Positively, with real teeth that make him, his firm, and its senior partners vulnerable to suit for any breach."

Going against all my instincts, I relented. "If you really think he can help, then … then I suppose I must agree. But I don't think you're right about him. He despises every uppity feminist, every anarchistic activist, and just about everything else about me. I'll never trust him. I've run into plenty of his type, too, usually on the receiving end of a nightstick."

Phil drew in her breath as if she'd been running a marathon. "A wise decision, Kip. William will join us after we execute documents at the offices of Polanski & Stelzl over lunchtime."

"Lunchtime? You knew all along I'd agree?"

"I knew something had to give, and I was pretty certain you cared more about the calendar than anything else. We'll give him a try, Kip. We have nothing to lose."

Late that afternoon in his first appearance at my cell as an official member of the defense team, Billy Beneke looked like he'd been sentenced to the gallows. He avoided direct eye contact or acknowledgement until locked in with us. After deliberating, he perched on the far end of the cot from Philomena and without pleasantries began, "Miss Benedetti—"

"Phil, please."

"—briefed me over lunch as to the ground covered thus far. I'll review details tonight to catch up. You can pick up from where you left off with her." When neither of us responded, his nervousness provoked some rambling. "You're causing quite a stir around Wausaukeesha, Miss Benedetti—"

"Phil!"

"—Phil. And you, too, I don't need to tell you, Miss Czermanski. To think one of the Czermanskis—"

"Ms," I insisted, which stifled him less effectively than Phil's wide-eyed surprise at his digression.

"—ah, yes Phil and, and … anyway, my wife's quite interested in this case."

"I bet," I said. "So who isn't?" William had thankfully dispensed with the heavy aftershave. Had Phil written that into their signed agreement?

"Well, yes, but since you went to school together, she's taken a more personal interest."

I had to ask, though I really didn't want to. "I know your wife?"

"You did, way back when. Katey. Katey Rudeshiem. Katey Beneke now, of course."

Dear Lord, please spare me this—on top of Billy! I shot an accusatory glance at Phil. Katey Perfect-Catholic-School-Girl Rudeshiem was my new boy-lawyer's wife? "Perfect."

Billy looked a little confused by that comment. "We've been married for …"

As he rattled on about his wife, the vision of Sister Margaret cutting off Mike Debick after he'd read but three lines to the class on why we were lucky to be Catholic blotted out William's words. Hoping to end her class on a positive note following two off ones—my forgotten homework and Debick's unacceptable paper—Sister called on Katey Rudeshiem to show us how it should be done. From her desk fronting Sister's, Katey stood, waggled her braids into place, smoothed her pleats, straightened her fully buttoned white blouse, smiled at Sister, and began: "We are blessed to be Catholic because—"

Puke! I tried tuning her out, knowing she'd say just what Sister Margaret wanted to hear. "… the blessing of the sacraments …" Gadzooks, did Katey really believe it or just say this stuff to please the sister? "… educated in the one, true religion …" Perfect Katey Rudeshiem, who used bows to hide the gum bands that secured the ends of her braids, was always at the ready with the right answer. Making it known she wanted to be a nun one day only cemented her title of exemplary Catholic schoolgirl for all the rest of us to hate.

Becoming a nun had apparently been a passing fancy for Katey. She *married* cool Billy Beneke. Was there no justice in this world? Perhaps there was. William had become a stiff-assed, holier-than-thou creep. As I said: perfect.

While Billy chatted nervously, Phil occasionally responding, third-grade Katey morphed in my mind to grown-up Katey at St. Hedwig's senior dance, sexy and confident in strapless blue silk, cleavage evident. Quite a change from her braided-and-bowed, heading-for-the-convent look.

"You *married* Katey Rudeshiem?" I tried not to wrinkle my nose. Apparently I'd interrupted my lawyers, both of whom I now doubted. Phil couldn't appreciate what she'd done with this addition to my defense. And to think I allowed it.

"Yes, as I said, just as I was entering law school. You do remember her?"

"How could I forget Sister Margaret's … ah … Katey?" I edited myself. I'd only agreed to give it, i.e., Billy, a try, I soothed myself. Phil would realize the obvious soon enough.

Flipping pages of her notepad, Phil directed the conversation to a safer subject, my murder defense. "Now then, I'd like to review with co-counsel any prior discussion of change of venue. You surely considered it?"

"Not seriously because—"

I spoke over William. "We might've discussed it, I really can't remember, but my father owns this town, Phil. I'm sure none of us thought such a move would help." William nodded agreement. "Of course at the time, I didn't really think I'd be held, let alone charged."

"Then we should revisit it," Phil said. "'Owning' can cut two ways, Kip. And didn't you mention your reputation here?"

I gazed around at my hated cell to discover Timothy outside the bars, holding his jumping-fish coffee thermos. "Sorry to disturb you, but I made some fresh coffee. I doubled the amount of Maxwell House since you like it so strong, Kip. Brought three paper cups, too." Timothy passed them to me.

"You read my mind, Timothy. Thanks." As he loped away, I distributed cups, opened and poured for Phil the best-looking jailhouse coffee yet, excluding the coffee she imported each morning, long since gone.

I held the thermos out to William, who grimaced. "I never developed a taste for coffee."

"Humph," I snorted at Phil. Figured. No coffeehouse debates for this young lawyer. Might such undeveloped tastes suggest an under-active brain?

Phil pressed ahead. "So as far as petitioning for change of venue—"

"As bad as this place is, I think we're better off here," I said. I took a long sip of decent coffee. "We've got my speedy trial date, which a change of venue would surely delay. Beyond the other reasons we discussed, Phil, here I'm like my jailers' only child. Let's leave it." Lord help me, I was adjusting to this cell.

Phil and William exchanged rapid-fire sentence fragments: "If we didn't get a fair trial due to some provable bias—" "Yes, I see what you mean, but without a petition on record, recourse might not be—" "An acceptable chance we'll have to take per the client's request." "Yes, I suppose you're right."

I required translation. "So, it's settled? I stay here? Trial will begin early April?"

Phil nodded with some bitterness and went back to her notes. "Okay Kip, after your fruitless search for Stan as your senior year at UW began, tell us how and when you first learned he was here in Wausaukeesha—" Phil smiled in triumph at her flawless pronunciation. "—had in fact been right here since he left Madison some time the previous May."

I found myself circling like a caged animal, each loop ending with Billy Beneke in the flesh, awaiting my every word, with his wife's image conjured up at the opposite turn. I sure as hell can't outrun them. Oh, why did I ever come back here?

"Phone calls from Samantha," I blurted out, starting smack-dab in the middle, "that's how this all began."

Chapter Twenty-Nine

"I've learned to dread phone calls from Samantha, the family go-between who constantly bugged me to come home for every holiday or long weekend. That never changed, even after I moved from Madison to California and put two thousand miles between me and them," I told the lawyers, who looked a little confused.

I plunked down on my cot before them. "In answer to your question, Phil, about how I discovered Stan was here in Wausaukeesha, I'd been living in LA just over a year when Samantha began to campaign for my return home. 'You must come for Dad's sixtieth. We're having a surprise party. The whole town will be here. You must, Kip, you must come home.' I pointed out it was too far to come for a weekend and that Sarah wouldn't be there either, close as she was. Samantha told me to stop being ridiculous. Still I begged off, knowing Dad would hardly notice and that no one cared, not even Samantha really.

"When Sybel herself called to convince me to come, I got suspicious but still refused. Sybel wouldn't give a damn if I ever came home again. Her calling made no sense—unless something else was in the offing."

I drained the remnants of my cup, refilled it, then offered Phil more. That done, I had to continue. "Umm, Bill—William is now constrained to keep my every confidence, right?"

Phil looked exasperated, but William nodded, "'Constrained' is appropriate. Besides the agreement we signed, it's a case of lawyer-client priv—"

"Fine. Remember that newspaper lady who wanted to be my voice to the community?"

Phil bobbed her head as Billy guessed, "Babs Howenhauser?"

"The one and only. I didn't come back for Dad's sixtieth, but received excruciating detail through Babs' coverage in the *Dairyland Diary*. Samantha, or maybe Sybel, sent it to me, probably Sybel now that I think back on the envelope with no note inside. My suspicions had been valid. Sybel had planned way more than a surprise birthday party for Dad last August."

"August '71," Phil noted, "two years, three months since Stan's disappearance."

Billy unclasped the briefcase he clutched on his lap, propping the lid between us like a demarcation line—sides established, them against me, good versus evil, white versus black—the tidy concepts that drew him to criminal law.

"I should have that article," he said to our astonishment. Rummaging through a thick folder, he explained, "When the partners directed me to prepare for this case, due diligence required I find out everything about the vic—er, the deceased. A natural first step: the local newspaper." He pulled a folded article from a file overflowing with clippings and copies and flattened it over the closed lid.

Phil gasped, "William, that stack of articles is about Stan Szyzyck since his arrival in Wausaukeesha not even three years ago?"

"No," Billy corrected her, "the file contains articles about anything Czermanski." He offered her the article dated August 3, 1971. His 'diligence' impressed me. He'd been conscientious enough to retain the front-page photos under the headline: *Local Magnate's Celebration Ends in Surprise Wedding*. Phil slid closer and read photo captions as I stood to peer over William's shoulder.

> *In the gown passed down from mother to daughter, never more apparent was Sybel Czermanski's striking likeness to her late mother, as if beholding our much beloved and long-missed Norma on JJ's arm again, like so many years ago at their nuptials.*

Even in grainy black-and-white, Sybel with her hair twisted up on her head, looked stunning in the old-fashioned dress, which fell to mid-calf. Another photo captured for posterity the couple's first married kiss. A way-straight Stan—gone his Jesus-length locks—mugged for the camera. In the pictures, his hair scarcely brushed his collar, though a moustache and long sideburns hinted at his counterculture past. Dad's emotion was captured in the next picture as he watched an ebullient Sybel greet the mayor of Wausau-keesha among the celebrants. To think how narrowly I'd missed bearing witness to all that.

"Read the article," I encouraged the lawyers. "It's as good as being there. Given Babs' flowery prose, perhaps even worse." I slithered onto my cot in sudden need of a nap. As if the images weren't burned into my brain, my lawyers took turns reading the overwritten piece aloud.

JJ Czermanski's surprise sixtieth birthday celebration culminated in its cake-cutting finale. Candles blazed in the darkened dining room before being gustily extinguished. Toasts to the sixty-year-old bandied forth from all corners. Eloquently delivered was a brief thank you speech from the honoree, which referenced his eldest daughter, Sarah, whose devotion to the church prevented her attendance.

"No 'reference' to his youngest, also not in attendance," I commented. I knew I wouldn't be missed.

Phil looked up. "You stayed in California, but where was Sarah?"

"She's a … was a nun, cloistered up north."

No sooner had cake been passed when Sybel, who had changed into a white tea-length gown embroidered with pink roses, called for silence. The gown should have tipped us off. As she waited for the crowd to still, she repeatedly checked her watch. Again, dear readers, none of us knew what to make of it until she cried, "Daddy, I have another surprise for your birthday." Sybel reached into the crowd and drew Dr. Stanislaw Szyzyck, her father's up-and-coming protégé, to her side. "Daddy, everyone, Stan and I are to be married!"

A chorus of congratulations were sung at the couple as the name-sake of Wausaukeesha's own Czermanski Sausage Company, JJ, succumbed to the emotional surprise. But Sybel's surprise was not yet complete. "Wait, wait everyone," Sybel shouted over the buzz of excitement, rechecking her wristwatch. Frankly, this reporter began to wonder at that distracting mystery when she added, "Stan and I plan to marry—right here, right now!"

Phil gazed over the paper at me, shaking her head in disbelief, so William took over the reading.

On cue, the doorbell chimed throughout the sprawling Czerman-ski household on Moraine Drive. Motioning Stan to answer it, Sybel explained, "That will be the new priest, Father Biaggio, Father Dub-chek's assistant. Sadly, old Father Dubchek's in no condition to perform our ceremony today as we'd planned. Everyone," Sybel continued, her arm sweeping the crowd, "you're invited to our wedding. Please join us in the backyard."

Following a moment of stunned silence, what had been a birth-day gathering veered off in a din toward the rear of the Czermanski household.

Phil's look suggested the beginning of comprehension as William con-tinued to read.

Wrangling a few moments with the father of the bride before the ceremony, your Society Editor uncovered the following, which I share here with my loyal readers.

SE: You brought Dr. Szyzyck to town to work at the Sausage Com-pany. Did you ever imagine this wondrous result?

JJC (with a knowing smile): "Originally recruiting him for Wausaukeesha College, I realized as soon as I met Stan, he was just what the Sausage Company needed. It was almost like he and I both realized it at once. Stan grew up on homemade sausages like me. He's more than street-smart with his Ph.D. from Harvard—and worldly—Stan's originally from Poland! A blue-blooded education and Polish to boot! I'd never beat that combination. So I offered him a position with the Company. Only later, when I brought the lonely bachelor home for a home-cooked meal, did I introduce him to Sybel. And now they're marrying—that about makes everything perfect. A son at last to follow me in the business."

"This Babs is quite a reporter," Phil interjected.

The myriad guests, "tous Wausaukeesha" one might say, (Billy pronounced Babs' Frenchism with the ending 's') *took their places on the folding white chairs that defined Sybel's open-air wedding chapel, which for my readers who might be wondering, had been specially consecrated by Father Dubchek for this occasion, I later uncovered. Handkerchiefs and tissues fluttered like butterflies amongst the flowers and congregants when Sybel, on her father's arm, paused at the top of the aisle. Looking like her mother's twin, Sybel's appearance caused generalized "déjà vu" amongst those of us who'd attended her mother's wedding to JJ, too many years ago to count.*

A white tuxedoed guitarist, longhaired even for a musician, strummed "Here Comes the Bride," as father and daughter promenaded down the white-carpeted garden path toward the young priest waiting at the flower-bedecked altar. Two enormous crystal vases, which a number of Norma's friends, this scribe among them, had given her and JJ as a wedding gift, brimmed with peonies on either side of the altar. The bride's sister, Mrs. Raymond (Samantha) Turner, as matron of honor, along with her husband, Raymond Chauncy Turner III, as best man, took their places beside the bride and groom, as a joyous but reluctant father gave up his most beloved daughter.

"You can say that again," I sniped before William continued.

Standing side by side, the Czermanski sisters' similarities were indeed striking—tall and thin, blonde, and blue-eyed. Like them, Sarah, too, was the spitting image of their dear, departed mother.

Phil studied me. "Is that true? Your sisters look that much alike? You don't follow that description at all."

She'd noticed, before ever seeing my sisters. A noncommittal "Right," was all I said.

Billy read on.

Sybel's bouquet of white and pink peonies was reiterated on the altar and down the center aisle. Before describing the glorious ceremony itself, I, your Society Editor, must again digress. I happen to know personally that the peony was Norma Czermanski's long-standing favorite flower. Looking around Norma's garden at the numerous pink and white peony bushes, which spread their spicy scent when in bloom, provided both testament and legacy that Norma had been with us. Nobody's peonies grew as big and as densely petaled as Norma's, big as an outstretched hand. Most unfortunate was the seasonal fact that peonies were well past flowering this August day. Thus, to faithfully mimic her parent's nuptials, Sybel imported hothouse peonies for her ceremony, mere runts compared to those from her mother's garden, scentless blooms no bigger than a closed fist.

One final aside, loyal readers. The wedding presented many of us Wausaukeeshans our first good look at the young priest brought in to assist Father Dubchek at the Immaculate Conception Parish. I have it on good authority that Father Dubchek has been warned by his doctor to rein in his indefatigable rounds. Cherubic Father Biaggio's Adam's apple bobbed charmingly above the priest's collar of his short-sleeved black shirt, practical in the August humidity. Exposed were his hairless arms completed by rather delicate hands. The initial impression, suggesting Little Brother Biaggio, vanished when the young priest spoke.

"They are no longer two, but one flesh," he boomed in a resounding bass. "Let no man separate what God has joined." Sotto voce, the priest averred, "Christ abundantly blesses the love of a man and a woman, an abundance we experience here in the midst of this earthly garden."

I confess I feared the priest referencing the story of Adam and Eve in the Garden of Eden, with Eve tricking Adam into trying the forbidden fruit, eternal banishment resulting. But no, Father Biaggio moved on to vows, pronouncing the young couple, MAN AND WIFE in the thundering voice of an archangel. As the guitarist commenced an overwhelming rendition of "Ode to Joy," the bride and groom lingered in their first kiss.

"So there you have it," I said, stretching and yawning, "the inside scoop inquiring minds need to know."

Billy glanced around, wondering if he should go on. "There's a bit more."

"Enough."

"Why not?" Phil spoke over my protest, glancing at me. "We've gone this far." She settled against the bars.

Within moments, musicians led by an accordion player ground out somewhat raucous Polish polkas to draw the multitudes inside. There, well-rehearsed hired hands had moved the furnishings as well as the living room carpeting to create a dance floor where—

"Does she elaborate on the cleaning crews' procedures, too?" Phil interrupted.

"Almost done," answered Billy.

"—where JJ polka-ed with daughter Samantha and Stan with his new wife, all executing the Old Country dance with surreal elegance. Meanwhile Sybel's staff passed mini-quiche lorraines and rumakis …

"That's enough," William stopped himself.

"Amen," I added.

Phil studied me until the article and photos dubbed by Reporter Howenhauser as "Wausaukeesha's social event of 1971" that William held out for her slipped and fluttered to the floor.

"This is how you found out that Stan was still alive?" she finally asked. "Not only that, but that he was living in your hometown, working for your father for two years, and married to your sister? An anonymously sent newspaper article you received six months ago?"

"Actually," I said, wiping back an escaping tear Phil's words had prompted, "right before that bombshell arrived in Santa Monica, I received a postcard from Sybel, a strange occurrence in itself. The front showed an unspoiled beach against darkening stripes of aquamarine. The back read: 'Too bad you missed Daddy's birthday party, which if I do say so, was a fabulous surprise. You also missed an even bigger surprise, my marriage, which followed. I did all I could to prevent your missing both.'"

"What did she say about Stan specifically?"

"This is all verbatim. I read that card so many times, it's forever etched in my brain. Even burning it didn't erase it. 'Perhaps you remember my husband who taught Political Science at Madison during several years you were there, Dr. Stan Szyzyck? We're here on our honeymoon.' She signed the card from a resort in the Caribbean, 'Sybel Szyzyck.'"

Phil exhaled long and slow. "I'm glad you were so stubborn, Kip, staying away." I nodded. "Do you think Sybel knew everything?"

"I don't know what she knew about Stan and me, or what she knows now. As her postcard burned like an offering to the demons of fate, I solemnly swore I'd never, ever return to Wisconsin."

Phil retrieved the article and pictures from the floor, glancing through the clippings in disbelief. I was introducing her to a concept of family she didn't care to meet. "I'd like to take your file with me tonight, William." He passed over his folder, which she secured in her doctor bag. "So you vowed never to come home again. I'm beginning to understand why, Kip. Yet you're here. After all that, why? What brought you back?"

"Damn it!" I cried, launching to my feet and scowling down at them both. "More questions? Do your questions ever end? Is everything in my life fair game for the two of you to dissect? Is no subject sacrosanct or private?"

Stunned at the outburst, the lawyers looked from me to each other and back to me. "We've inadvertently stepped on a landmine," said Phil, "But the answer is yes, the prosecutor will delve into your whole life and we—"

"Of course," I cut her off, twisting away from them as a deluge of conflicting emotions engulfed me. Damn their questions.

Chapter Thirty

Sarah. The one-word answer to why, despite my vow never to return, I had come back to Wisconsin.

Sarah, my eldest sister and the one I barely knew.

Why had I so readily flown home when my one clear memory of Sarah centered around our embittered good-byes?

1964

The Czermanskis driving anywhere all together was rare enough, but singing together as the car sped north—unheard of. Dad had turned up the car radio to Brenda Lee singing:

> *All alone am I ever since your good-bye,*
> *All alone with just the beat of my heart.*

Everyone except Samantha joined Brenda's warbling:

> *People all around, but I don't hear a sound,*
> *Just the lonely beating of my heart …*

It showed how excited we were about visiting my oldest sister, Sarah, my first visit ever.

What would she be like, this sister who in eleven years had never come home once? "Rules of her order," I'd been told. Did such rules make her a better Catholic, I wondered, a better nun? Though my memories were faded, I remembered Sarah's creamy skin and shiny blonde hair. Okay, that described all my sisters, but in the back of my mind I seemed to remember Sarah making everything feel better somehow.

I'd taken extra care dressing for this sister I barely remembered, starting with the medium-high heels Sybel had allowed as of my fifteenth birthday last fall. Turning fifteen had been a big deal and not just because of the heels. At fifteen, the rule of Sarah's order which banned children from visiting no longer applied to me. When the invitation came these many months later, I was more than ready.

My new paisley dress stuck to my body in the prickly heat held down by dull cloud cover. Despite the serious risk to my smooth pageboy hairdo, I rolled down the car window to a gush of humid air. Sybel from the front seat yelled immediately for me to roll up the window, saying the draft messed her hair. That helmet-shaped bubble, ratted and sprayed stiff on her head? Fat chance. But Dad's glance back said clearly: Don't make me say it. I rolled up the window. *Maaan.*

Sybel imitated Jackie Kennedy, wearing a square hat stuck into her bouffant flip, flesh-colored lipstick, thick eyeliner hidden beneath her oversized sunglasses with stacked-heeled shoes that matched her purse. A strand of pearls, about as real as my old pop beads, hung down her body-skimming yellow sheath. In contrast, Samantha, seated beside me, had dressed in a white shirtwaist and heels, her hair loose to her shoulders with only a touch of lipstick, making her appear much younger than the two years in age separating her from Sybel.

Samantha had pulled her yellow locks forward to cover her face. An ever-present Kleenex pressed to her nose hid the rest of her features. Samantha was acting just plain weird since we left home. Something was on her mind, I could tell. Miles back, I idly commented on all the white farmhouses and all the red barns we passed. "It's all so perfect," she had cooed, giggling unstoppably in a brief appearance from behind her hair curtain. Noticing my confused reaction, Samantha immediately retreated again.

"Are we almost there?" I whined, raising my arms to dry out my armpits. I took the opportunity to inspect the job I'd done shaving them since I'd only recently begun. No one answered anyways.

Beyond the car windows, the landscape grew more rugged the further we drove north. White birch forests stretched away on both sides of the highway, parting here and there for small lakes fringed by bogs sprouting reeds and cattails. The unmistakable whiff of cows still scented the air now and then, though there weren't many dairy farms in this part of Wisconsin. Wasn't much of anything, making it a perfect place for Sarah's nunnery. We'd come across that term in Shakespeare's play *Hamlet*, which we were studying in ninth grade English. When someone asked the teacher what it meant, Miss Boedeker turned all weird and blushy.

The car slowed and Sybel lowered the radio right in the middle of a Dionne Warwick song I loved:

Don't make me over now that I'd do anything for you.

Skeletal birches crept close enough to claw our car as we crunched down a gravel turn off. Just at the very best line of the whole forty-five:

Take me for what I am—

Sybel switched the radio off altogether. I didn't even bother to complain. Except for the ping of stones spewing up beneath the car, all fell silent.

Dad steered our new Buick into a clearing beside a high stone wall that blocked whatever it guarded from view and parked beside a large gate. "We're here. Yay!" I shouted, happy the long drive had ended. No one else said a word. Dad donned his jacket and straightened his narrow tie before he clanged a kind of cowbell hung from the stone wall. Its ringing bounced off more stones in the inner courtyard now visible through the gate's iron slats.

A nun in black-and-white habit appeared to float over the cobblestones toward us, her footsteps making no sound. Just like the nuns at home, this sister must be wearing those rubber-soled boots they used for sneaking around. She even looked like Sister Margaret from Immaculate Conception, suspicious and mean, but it wasn't her. *Phew.*

From behind the gate, the nun studied each of us and after thorough inspection, said only, "Yes?"

"Hello, Sister," Dad said in the phony voice he used with officials in our Parish, doffing his hat like a Shakespearean actor. "I'm JJ Czermanski." His pause was the nun's cue to exclaim: *Czermanski, of the sausage company?* But apparently not a lot of sausage-eating went on in these parts. Dad continued, "These here are my girls. We've come to see my daughter, Sarah. Sister Sarah Joseph, that is. Got an invitation for the whole family to visit today. Drove all the way up from Wausaukeesha."

"Oh yes, yes of course," the Sister burbled, now glad to see us. She produced a huge, medieval-looking key from the folds of her habit and worked the lock. "Yes, Sister Sarah Joseph told me." Over the loud squeal of the gate being pushed open, she shouted, "Please do come in." Once the gate creaked shut again and the nun had locked us in, she crooked her finger for us to follow her.

The nunnery's hush exaggerated our footsteps over cold stones. We sounded like an invading horde hurrying after the sister, who skimmed along toward a small stone structure, where she encouraged us inside. She told us to be seated on the wooden benches facing each other along the two longer walls of the rectangular room.

"Sister Sarah Joseph will be along presently." Lowering her voice, the sister added, "The door at the far end of the room is a lavatory, should any of you need to-to-to wash up after your long journey."

Twirling his hat in his hands, Dad squirmed on the pew-like bench. Despite the day's heat and mugginess, the stone quarters felt dank and stale like our basement. Its silence and emptiness made me squirm, too. I didn't like it here.

With no footsteps to warn us, another sister materialized in the doorway, her features unreadable, her hands hidden in her habit. She studied us until a small smile lit her face. She glided toward Dad, who stood and reddened while she hugged him. My real sister, Sarah.

Sarah looked each one of us up-and-down before hugging first Sybel, then Samantha, who dabbed at her eyes with her crumpled Kleenex. Even Sybel and Dad looked a little teary, but Sarah's clear blue eyes never wavered.

She shook her head in disbelief when she focused on me. Her smile broadened as she enclosed me in a hard hug.

"KP," Sarah murmured, "oh my, you've become a young lady."

"Yeah," I responded, enjoying her hug a lot, "but my name is Kip."

"Kip?" Sarah glanced from me to the others. "Really? Kip? Well then, Kip it is. I like the sound of it, and it fits you somehow, doesn't it? Look at you, all grown up. You're how old now, fifteen?" Sarah held onto my hand, and as fruity as it was, I let her.

Sarah no sooner mentioned that the sisters were bringing a light lunch for us after our journey than several nuns carried in a folding table and trays of food, setting up a yucky looking buffet of apples, cheese, and bread alongside a pitcher of water. Gross. Sarah insisted we eat, so we all put something on a plate and bowed our heads while Sarah thanked God for this "manifestation of His abundance." She'd lived in this place a long, long time.

My first nibbles tasted like chalk. I scattered bread and cheese around my plate, hoping we'd find an A&W Root Beer stand or a Dairy Queen on the drive home. Sarah looked content to watch us play with our food until Dad set aside his untouched plate.

"Sarah, you look good," he began. At twice my age, Sarah didn't have a line on her face, not even a crease between her brows like the one I'd had forever. "They're treating you all right up here?"

"Yes, Father, of course," Sarah answered with a laugh. She clapped her hands together like a little kid. "I love it here. It will be so hard to leave."

"You're leaving?" Dad repeated as we all stared. "Oh good heavens, you're coming home. It's about time."

"Oh, no, I wouldn't … I couldn't do that …" Sarah sat down between Dad and Sybel, patting their hands to soften the determination in her voice. "No, no, not that. Well, I didn't intend to jump right into this but, well, I gained special dispensation for your visit today so I could tell you my plans in person."

Sybel and Samantha placed their plates on the folding table. I'd finished playing with the cheese long before.

"I've prayed for guidance for many years now," Sarah began, "and at last I've received my calling. I'm joining a smaller order which requires, as part of its acceptance of me, full renunciation of my worldly life."

No more bread and water?

"Full renunciation?" Dad said, looking alarmed. "What's left to renounce?"

My point exactly.

We waited for Sarah to answer. "I will be withdrawing from active life in the cloister."

It's a cloister, not a nunnery?

"I will go into complete seclusion and have no further human contact—"

"What?" Dad exploded. "What the hell kind of—"

"—with only strictly enforced exceptions."

Coming to his feet, Dad roared, "Now Sarah, I've had just about enough of this foolishness of yours. This is going way too far."

"Father—" Sarah stayed him with a firm hand on his arm. "—I called you here today to say good-bye. I hope you'll come to understand and accept my decision. Please give me your blessing and remember me in your prayers, all of you, as I do each of you every day."

"What will you do with no people around?" I blurted into the stunned silence that followed Sarah's announcement. "Come to think of it, what do you do now?"

Sybel shot me a zip-it glare, but Sarah just laughed. "I'll pray and I'll meditate. I'll imagine what you'll be like when you're my age, thirty." Sarah laughed again. No one else even smiled.

"Why don't you stick around and see for yourself," I responded, unable to stop myself, "instead of imagining."

Samantha sobbed, "I came to ask you to my wedding. You won't come now, will you?"

Sarah rushed to Samantha's side, stroking her hair as she cried on Sarah's shoulder. The rest of us gaped at Samantha's bombshell, the second in as many minutes.

Sybel was first to voice our surprise. "You're getting married, Samantha? Good Lord, when?"

"I'm sorry, Sybel," Samantha sniffed. "I thought it would make a nice surprise to tell you when we were all together again as a family. I don't have a ring yet, but Raymond and I are engaged. We plan to marry as soon as he finishes school. Couldn't you wait, Sarah?" Samantha pleaded, searching for a dry corner of her soggy tissue, "and join this new order after my wedding? Please Sarah, let us be together one last time as a family."

Far from comforting Samantha or any of us, Sarah's faraway smile made clear her intention to go where she'd been called—a place that didn't include her family, or anyone else for that matter.

Sarah asked us to step outside so she could speak with Father alone. Samantha numbly led the way into the stone corridor, wiping her nose and coiling strands of hair around her finger. Her sniffles became the only sound in the "cloister." So what is a nunnery then?

Unaware of me behind her, Sybel muttered to herself, "Married? Samantha's only twenty-three. Raymond isn't out of college either, though what's taking him so long is a wonder. Daddy should do something, like before ... She should be made to wait. Samantha's too young."

A sudden vision of life in the Czermanski household with no Samantha running interference rose before me. Oh boy.

Moments later, Dad staggered back into the corridor a broken man. Eyes downcast, he mumbled for Sybel and Samantha to "go on in to your older sister." He slumped against hard stone and raked his fingers through the tight curls on his head as if it might loosen a solution in his brain.

No one had imagined this—our last farewells, forever. I couldn't even ask Dad what he thought about Samantha's engagement. I was too stunned to talk. I paced for an eternity in the creepy stone hallway. When can we go home?

The door opened and Sarah ushered my sisters out, one under each arm, Samantha still crying, Sybel holding in all feeling, assuming there was feeling to hold in. Sarah kissed them both, then fixed her sweet smile on me and asked me to join her for a moment alone. Like a zombie I followed her inside the airless little room, thinking: *shouldn't be much to say. Hadn't seen her eleven of my fifteen years. Wouldn't see her again ever. "Hi. Bye. Oh, yeah, remember me in your prayers that will take up the rest of your life."*

"You're so young, KP—I'm sorry, Kip." She edged onto the bench, drawing me close into the folds of her habit where hints of mothballs and that antiseptic smell I associated with nuns were hiding. "I don't expect you to understand my decision, not completely, but believe me, it wasn't an easy one to make. Still, I hope you'll come to understand and to think of me with love. I'll send my blessings every day. I won't forget you, not ever."

The pleasantness of Sarah's expression took on an emptiness that began to bug me. "You don't even know me. Of course you'll forget me." I struggled to my feet. "It would've been better if I'd never seen you again."

I lurched for the door, but with surprising speed, Sarah blocked the way. I shouted in her face, "You should've gone on remembering me as a dumb little four-year-old, hanging on your neck. And I could have gone through my life almost but not quite remembering you." Hot tears sprang from my eyes. I didn't even try to hide them.

"Kip, why are you so angry?" Sarah moved closer.

I dodged another upsetting hug. "Don't," I warned her. I didn't need another phantom memory of love.

Sarah stumbled backwards, sinking into the dark puddle her habit made as it spilled over the bench.

"Kip, I have a calling. Try to understand, this is bigger even than family. I heard and obeyed. After Mother, I knew. I ..." Sarah seemed to sink further and further, looking to me like she was drowning. "It must have been hard on you, to be motherless so young," she at last said. "But Sybel and Samantha, and Father, of course, took good care of you. You've become a bright, and I daresay, precocious young lady." An attempted smile twisted her lips. "My presence would have added nothing."

"That's what you think?" My tears stopped in that instant. "People see what they want to make their own lives easier. You may be a nun, but you're no different, Sarah. Believe whatever you like, but if you couldn't have improved on Sybel as my substitute mother, then I'll have to quit imagining you as nice." I rushed on before I lost it, "Now let's just say hi and bye. Quit making a big deal out of it. We don't even know each other."

Sarah dropped her head, black fabric veiling her face, her hands wringing each other white in her lap.

"I'm so sorry, Kip," she choked out. "I...." She sighed and stood to accompany me to the door. "Good-bye, Kip. And God's speed."

I grasped the door handle but spun back to the sister for one last look. Her empty smile had vanished, and Sarah's eyes expressed something deep and raw. Sadness? Fear? Perhaps no more than the shocking discovery that this nun's baby sister committed the original sin—she'd outgrown unquestioning obedience.

"At least you learned my name, Sister Sarah, so those blessings you'll be sending for the rest of your life won't be wasted on someone who doesn't even exist anymore."

CHAPTER THIRTY-ONE

I needed a brisk walk in freezing air. I needed to crunch, slip, and slide over treacherous frozen ground, concentrating to stay upright, all other thoughts driven from mind. Instead, I faced the expectant gazes of my lawyers requiring more on the last subject on earth I felt able to cope with: my recently deceased sister.

Seeing my troubled gaze, William tried tactfully to encourage me. "You were about to tell us why you came back to Wausaukeesha, why you are here."

"Right. Just the facts, ma'am," I said in my best Sgt. Joe Friday imitation, which at least lightened my own bitter mood. "Samantha's phone calls ..." I tried again. "Samantha called—was it only ten days ago?—and I caught a flight back to Wisconsin. When I heard why she called, Samantha didn't have to nag."

Who had I been expecting, nearly breaking down my apartment door to get to the ringing phone inside? In response to my three-flights-up, breathless hello, I was greeted by, "Sarah's dying."

Adrenaline surged through my veins, prickling to my fingertips. I stared through my balcony doors at the faintest glow on the horizon where the ocean had extinguished the sun, trying to absorb Samantha's words. They felt familiar, Samantha's words, like an echo returning from a distant past. *Mommy's dying. Do you know what that means?* I squeezed my eyes shut.

"What do you mean, Samantha? Sarah's up north, praying or something. She's too young to die." I calculated fifteen years over my age. "She's only thirty-nine, and she's a nun for God's sake."

Samantha's voice garbled out, "She's here in Wausaukeesha. She wanted to come to the hospital here, to us. Sarah has cancer, cancer of the ovaries, and, and they say—"

I slumped to the floor, holding the phone at arm's length, back to scanning the darkness for a clear line separating heaven and earth. But with the sun's complete disappearance, they'd merged seamlessly. I'd missed my nightly ritual of watching the sunset from my balcony, my contemplating the waves which mirrored the clouds through each day's final, flamboyant act.

I raised the receiver to my ear to hear Samantha saying, "She wanted to come home to die." Samantha's quiet sobbing induced the first twinge of emotion pressing the back of my eyes—two sisters, separated by two thousand miles, grappling with unspeakable loss, another unspeakable loss.

The first stage of grief is denial. "How's Dad taking it?"

"Badly," Samantha answered. "Sybel says you should come home. I told her you would, of course. You'll come, won't you, Kip, as fast as you can?" As if she'd intuited my vow never to set foot in Wisconsin again, she added, "Sarah asks for you."

"*Me?* Samantha, that's imposs—"

"She wants to finish a conversation you two had on our last visit."

I exploded, "Damn it, Samantha, for once, get real about this family. Sarah made her glib good-byes years ago."

Samantha sniffed. "I know you barely knew each other, Kip, but you're sisters. Her asking for you proves it: The bond between sisters is stronger than distance or years that may separate them. Sisters—"

"Spare me your rose-colored views on family," I snapped. Rubbing my throbbing temples, I willed down my venom. "I'm sorry, Samantha. Tell me what her doctors said, exactly."

While she talked, my gaze returned to the inky waters of the Pacific, where its movements created glints and winks, flashes that vanished just as quickly as they appeared.

"Kip," Samantha pressed, "you must come home for Sarah's sake. This is your last chance to see each other."

I cracked the sliding glass doors open and filled my lungs from a wintry gust off the ocean that bore the odors of fish, salt, and decay. *I can't go back there. I won't.* My throat clogged when I tried to swallow while the rest of me seemed to liquefy—my eyes watered, my nose ran, sweat beaded and dripped, a noise like breaking waves pounded in my ears. Malcolm brushed against me, and automatically, I stroked his black fur. He began to purr as I forced my words, "I'll get a plane ... call when I know my arrival." I let the receiver slip to the floor. If I never hung up, no one would ever reach me again. But it was too late for that now.

Malcolm curled up in my lap, oblivious to the tears pocking his smooth coat. I was returning to Wisconsin, despite my solemn vow.

Samantha's skin blotched and her lower lip quivered when she caught sight of me amid bleary travelers stumbling off the overnight flight. Until removed, dark glasses concealed her red-rimmed eyes underscored by bruises of fatigue. Her stringy hair straggled back to a bare rubber band. In an unusual moment of solidarity, we hugged each other as if our lives depended on it, me burying my nose in the wet-wool smell of her overcoat. She handed me my old winter coat, an ugly plaid from college, which I threw on as we grabbed my bags and hurried out to Samantha's old Oldsmobile.

With the wind gusting in our faces, the windchill factor made it feel like miles and hours before we sheltered inside her car's interior, celery-green like its exterior. The drive from Milwaukee began uncomfortably with emotion too raw to voice. To cover the awkwardness, I flipped on the radio, listened to John Denver croon:

> *Take me home*
> *Country roads*
> *To the place I belong—*

And at that lame sentiment, I switched it off fast.

After a while, the well-tended farms and rolling hills of Wisconsin's countryside reassured me. Some things—Samantha's odd choice in a car, the neatly delineated fields—hadn't changed. I at last ventured, "Is Sarah—"

Samantha kept her eyes on the road. "Waiting for you."

"Why do you say that, Samantha?"

She glanced at me, then back at the road. "She asks where you are, Kip, if you're coming, when you'll be here." I watched Samantha's eyes mist. "It is the only thing of this world Sarah shows the slightest interest in."

I counted the lakes blurring by the window—seven, eight, nine—as our final visit to Sarah, a long drive like this one years before to her cloisters, recalled Brenda Lee from the recesses of my mind. Over and over again in my head, she sang:

> I'm sorry, so sorry.
> Please accept my apology,
> But love is blind and I was too blind to see.

Though the car heater blasted away, I cinched my overcoat tight when at last Samantha veered up the curving driveway of Wausaukeesha Hospital. Except for the sign, Emergency Room Entry, and zigzagging wheelchair access, the brown brick building looked no more ominous than my high school. Neat rows of windows ran along three floors, save for the entry portico under which we drove.

Samantha patted my shoulder supportively. "You go in, Kip, while I park the car. No use both of us freezing to d-d-d … See you up there, the cancer ward."

With a resolve I didn't feel, I sprang from the car and jerked open the double doors of the hospital's main entrance. A wave of antiseptic odor mixed with the singed-dust smell of overheated buildings stung my nostrils. My hesitating in the doorway, neither in nor out, created an imbalance where warm, pungent air rushed to escape while dry, frigid air howled to get in—the whole world restless to be elsewhere. Battling currents screamed as I tugged the doors closed behind me, wondering on which side of this entryway lay the vacuum that nature abhors.

My immediate recognition of the lobby made me lurch, grasping for the corner of the reception desk to steady myself. The nurse behind it looked up in shock at my clumsy entrance.

I remembered, hearing again Sarah whispering, "Don't be afraid of the dark, KP. We're playing a game to surprise Mommy." She had covered me with her cape and held me tight against her shoulder, telling me to stay very still, to not make a sound until we got off the elevator and inside Mommy's room. Then Sarah had said that she'd pull the cape off, and Mommy would be so surprised. "Quiet now, KP, and keep your head down. Here we go."

"What is it, Miss? Miss?" The nurse-receptionist's name badge pinned at her heart read, Joy Daily, RN. After my careening arrival, she eyed me suspiciously.

"The cancer w—"

"East elevator, third floor."

But my stomach grumbled ominously and I turned back to Joy Daily to seek the bathroom. Nurse Daily tore her attention away from her paperback, hitching a thumb over her shoulder to indicate the passage clearly marked "Restrooms" and "Cafeteria."

I hurried down the dim hallway and crashed into the first stall of the ladies' room, banging the door behind me as I vomited in the bowl. I felt better after flushing away airplane food until I caught my image in the mirror above the bank of sinks—ratty plaid coat, haggard black eyes, smooth-wedge haircut madly askew. And I thought Samantha looked old. I had aged ten years on an overnight flight.

I found the east elevators and pressed three. Even before the doors parted at the third floor, I heard my dad's shouts ricocheting down the corridor. "Can't you at least make her more comfortable? Good God, man, this is inhuman." The doctor Dad was venting on acknowledged my approach with a nod over Dad's shoulder. Dad pivoted. "Kip. Finally."

The fury that appeared to hold my father together did not mask the fear in his eyes. Words felt risky and inadequate, so I simply kissed Dad on the cheek. "Kip's here," he announced.

At my name, Stan who paced nearby headed toward us. I froze.

"Stan," Dad said, "this here's my youngest, Kip, all the way from California."

"You're Kip?" the doctor mercifully intervened. "You better go right in."

Stan extended a hand to me, concern etching his brow. "Kip, I'm so sorry you have to deal with this, all of you." He glanced at Dad. "It's so hard. Will you be all right?"

"I guess," I stammered, shocked at the establishment look of him, an oddly familiar stranger. I ignored Stan's proffered hand, moving off in the direction the doctor indicated.

In a chair with a magazine ignored on her lap, Sybel guarded the door to Sarah's room. She appeared as composed as always until I drew near. The harsh fluorescent glare exposed worry churning in Sybel's eyes. They shifted toward the door. "In here, Kip."

I swallowed to ease the tightness in my throat. One hand on the cold metal door, I mouthed my first Hail Mary since my last confession ages ago, before college. *Pray for us sinners, now and at the hour of our death …* I stepped inside and the heavy door swooshed shut behind me.

Wan winter light from a single window cast Sarah, propped up in bed, in silhouette. A monitor made a low, steady beep. Its screen, flickering ever-changing graphs and statistics on the patient it was attached to, added a strobe effect to the gloom. A smell like pine disinfectant didn't quite disguise a rotting stench I prayed to God was not my sister. Casting aside the coat that had suddenly become too warm, I conjured a smile and approached my sleeping sister.

Though I detected no indication of breathing, she was just sleeping, right? Or, was I too late after all? I touched Sarah's arm, flinching at the heat of her jaundiced skin. She turned back from the window she had been staring out of, not sleeping at all.

"You're here." Her voice sounded hoarse, unused.

"Hi Sarah." Freed of her nun's habit, I saw irrefutably Sarah was my sister. Blonde hair, chopped in short tufts, blue-water eyes, a labored smile exposing small, perfect teeth. A tear slid down my cheek as I recognized not only all my siblings, but a vision of someone else on her deathbed.

"The chair …" She swallowed with difficulty several times. "Sit." She closed her eyes.

While Sarah battled for breath, I sat and scrutinized her. Skeletal, her skin discolored, Sarah couldn't weigh ninety pounds. Her hands showed every bone and vein. When she opened her eyes again, the pain heightening the vivid Czermanski-blue stung my heart. "Oh, Sarah, I'm so sor—"

"No time, Kip. Let me speak …" Her determination silenced me. "You were right, those years ago, Kip. You needed us … when Mother was gone … all of us. My leaving after her passing must have felt like abandonment to you … another."

She sank into her pillow, shifting her gaze out the window at the monotonous grays of Wisconsin in February and whispered, "So many mistakes."

My eyes following hers, I remembered February in Wisconsin, the month the dirty snow and overcast skies became indistinguishable, the month winter seemed to dig in against spring.

Sarah glanced back to me. "'People see what they want to see to make their own choices easier.' You said that back then. How wise for a fifteen-year-old. How sad you grew up so fast. You called me on my selfishness, and … in part you were right. I did run away, Kip."

This I wasn't prepared for—me being right? Wise? Her astonishing words provoked me to interrupt, "No no, Sarah, I didn't mean—"

But Sarah forced her words over mine. "Father fell to pieces after Mother died. I resisted filling the void … so many reasons. Sybel seemed capable and willing to step into Mother's shoes. I wanted to believe that, so I did."

"Please, Sarah." This was what she wanted to say to me? Her words coaxed something up in me so long buried, I'd forgotten it was there. I took her hand, and she grasped mine tightly. "Hush now, Sarah. You'll tire yourself. You had a calling. You told me you did."

Something deeper than contentment crept over Sarah's features. I leaned in to catch her next words. "God will judge my motives. With that, I'm at peace. But I could not go until I apologized to you, the sister I hurt most … after Sybel."

Sarah's words intensified that strange stirring within. Beneath layers of protective camouflage, resentments, and even deeper doubts, did vindication glimmer? I needed time to navigate these emotional torrents, time to let her words in one by one and examine them safely, in private. Then all of Sarah's words sank in.

"'After Sybel?' Did you say, 'after Sybel?'"

Sarah nodded. "I let her down, more than you, if that's possible. Sybel … had to be medicated … even talked of institutionalizing her—"

"Sybel? Institutionalized? After Mother died?"

"No—" Sarah gasped, clenching her fists. The monitor broadcast a warning that cast my sister's grimace in an intermittent red glare.

I panicked, unable to decipher the screen's meaning. "Sarah, should I call the doctor?"

Contorted with pain, Sarah shook her head. "No," she gasped. "Don't."

I felt sick all over again, watching Sarah suffer. Eventually her fists relaxed, her eyes opened, and the machine began to drone as before. Though drained, Sarah attempted a reassuring smile. When she could speak, she continued, "Sybel's depression lifted when … when she took up the challenge of running things. We all thought it a miracle. I thought … auspicious." Sarah abruptly turned back to the window.

Was she hiding tears or searching for something out there? With feeble winter daylight all but gone, the view from her hospital room resembled a black-and-white snapshot of life in limbo: bare trees, frozen ground devoid of vegetation, darkening skies close and foreboding. It hit me, gazing out, all I was about to lose, and I fumed inwardly, *Don't just bully and threaten us, God. Bring it on, unleash your worst. Send us a blizzard. Bury the roads and bring down the power lines. Strand us all here while You coerce life—and death—to a halt. Surely You can do that.*

I looked down at my sister with deep regret, remembering that sooner or later all snowstorms spent their fury, and life, though numb and slow-moving, scratched its way back to normal. Life apparently knew no other way.

With a sad sigh, Sarah looked back at me. I squeezed her hand. I didn't want her to go, least of all now. How I hated her obvious acceptance of this fate. "Why did this have to happen, Sarah? You're too young, and you're a nun. Where's the justice—"

She waved me to silence. "Need to finish. Sybel assumed the helm of our lives … with a vengeance." It was almost funny: a vengeance indeed. "Do you see?" Sarah searched my face. "We were freed by Sybel's competence. She was buried by it."

I shook my head. "Sarah, I don't know about any of this. Sybel loved the power she wielded over everyone, especially me, the least able to withstand it."

Sarah waggled our joined hands to force my attention. "She's running, still. Just look. You, Kip, so strong …"

Strong? Sarah's bony fingers clung to mine with astounding strength. "I let you down," she gasped, "all my sisters. And Father too, even Mother. We need your forgiveness, Kip. Please forgive me. I am most to blame." Her grip suddenly relaxed and her eyes fluttered, then closed.

"Sarah? Sarah?" I cried, trying to hold her there. "No, it's so unfair."

"Unfair?" Sarah blinked as if considering the word. "Yes, perhaps it was … I love you, Kip."

"Sarah, I never blamed you. I never knew. I-I love you, too, Sarah."

I didn't know what to do. The relentless machinery hooked to her body seemed louder and slower, the last ticks of a clock winding down. *Let her stay, please God, just a little longer.*

I lost all sense of time sitting beside Sarah's bed. I stared at her shriveled body beneath the covers, her cropped hair, her thin fingers folded in mine. The droning machine, the dripping intravenous, the strobing screen, the turmoil buzzing in my head—it all lulled me into an altered state. Occasionally Sarah's breathing made a perceptible rise and fall beneath the sheet, or maybe

I imagined it. Her untroubled features reminded me of my impression of her ten years earlier—an angel floating high above earthly entanglements.

Sarah's crucifix hanging on the bedpost glinted with the changing light. It eventually refocused my attention. I pried her fingers open and closed them over her cross. "Good-bye, Sister Sarah." I kissed my sister on the forehead. Samantha had been right: there was nothing further for Sarah here. "Thank you for waiting for me."

A gust of wind rattled the window. I noticed that the bare branches clawing at the low clouds had at last released the storm. Snowflakes spiraled on currents as a new sound penetrated the gloom—a low, steady beep from the static monitor. I stumbled away from Sarah and the window and the storm to make my way back to the remains of my family. A nurse brushed by me at the door.

By the time I reached the waiting area, a full-blown winter storm was unleashing itself over Wausaukeesha.

Perhaps over the whole world.

CHAPTER THIRTY-TWO

Had that been only ten days ago? What was I saying? It had been ten of the longest and strangest days of my existence, starting with Samantha's call, with no promise of them ending soon. Having relived Sarah's death, heading into a detailed recounting for my lawyers of her funeral, burial, and the events surrounding, all of which involved Stan, I couldn't suppress crippling pain.

If one searched hard enough for some distracting good news, it can usually be found: Sarah's death made my arrest almost trivial in comparison. Surviving trial preparation with my lawyers might make the actual trial, should it really come to that, a relative snap. At least I had to hope so.

While they had discussed "arrangements" for Sarah—Sarah's remains—with hospital officials, Sybel held Samantha in a motherly embrace as my father stood stoically beside them. I sat in the hospital wait area, staring out at the storm, agitated and in shock. Sybel's surprising tenderness disturbed me further. In our fleeting moments together, Sarah had raised so many questions, loosened so many intractable emotions, and then she had disappeared forever for the second—no, for the third and final time.

I needed to regroup, so I stole off to the cafeteria for some bracing coffee and a moment alone. But hospital coffee soon churned up my queasy stomach and again I rushed for the bathroom I used earlier, and for the same reason. Convinced there could be nothing left to throw up, I reentered the shadowy hallway where someone grabbed my arm.

"Hold on there, Kip." Stan's arms closed around me in an embrace meant, perhaps, to comfort me. "Are you okay? Sarah wanted so badly to see you. I'm glad you got here in time. Was it terrible?"

I failed to stifle my tears, crying, "I no more realize how much I love her, and she's gone." A lifetime of tears gushed forth and Stan let me sob on his shoulder. Sarah's death and all that we'd missed as sisters streamed out. Stan's familiar scent of lime soap mixed with the new smell of starch on a scalding iron encouraged the deluge I'd kept dammed so long.

His consoling words aided my unraveling. "There, there, Kip. Let it go. I'm here. I'll do everything I can to help you through this."

Once the flash flood slowed, I extricated myself from Stan's embrace. While sopping my eyes and catching my breath, I caught Stan frankly appraising me, which only reminded me of my ghastly reflection in the bathroom mirror.

I tugged at my curls while studying him as well. Shorter still than in his wedding pictures from six months earlier, Stan's haircut gave him that "tool of the Establishment" look he once ridiculed. He wore a dress shirt with rolled-up sleeves and loosened collar over suit pants that I bet accompanied the unthinkable—a jacket and tie. Men no longer wore hats but if he'd held one in his hand, it wouldn't have surprised me. Stan was becoming a JJ-clone except for his moustache. Like the headbands he once wore, the moustache served to emphasize his green-olive eyes.

"Kip, please." Stan maneuvered me into the darkest corner. "I saw you speed from the cafeteria and realized we may not get another chance. We may never be alone again. I've longed to talk to you, to explain, to just be near you again."

"What?" I wriggled away.

Stan's wheedling tone hardened into all business. "So I'm sure you understand and have forgiven me." He extended his hand like a peace offering. "Kip, it's more important to me than you can know. You ..." he faltered, "... you're more important to me than I ever realized. I can't get you out of my mind."

It was his astonishment that really pissed me off. "You're telling me this

now? Realizing this *now*? It's all about you, isn't it, Stan, and always has been."
I shoved his hand away. "I was such a child not to see it. It's too late, Stan,
and now is not the time. I have far more important things on my mind. You'll
excuse me."

Stan barred my exit and inched in. "I got *fired* from the university, Kip,"
he rushed on, "while you traveled abroad that summer—they used our radical politics to trump up charges against me." He tilted my chin up until our
eyes met. "Understand how humiliated I felt, too embarrassed to contact you.
I didn't know what to say. The truth is I still can't fully explain what happened
to me."

Stan glanced down before saying, "I was blackballed—throughout the
UW system and beyond. No legitimate school would interview me. I had no
money, there was nowhere to go, no one to help. I, I was alone and suddenly
overwhelmed by things so basic, I'd forgotten their importance."

His breathing grew shallow. He remembered me. "I should've turned to
you—I wish I had—for the comfort you always gave. But I couldn't go back
there, to campus." Stan cupped my cheek with his hand. "You're so different
from your sister—"

"*Trumped-up charges?*" I mimicked him, slapping his hand away again.
"You commanded an organization that would have marched, demonstrated,
closed down the university if necessary, had you but given the word. No,
Stan, I don't buy it. You disappeared with no explanation and showed up
again two years later married to my sister—Sybel, of all the women in the
universe. What's to understand? The times, make love, not war, free sex—
that's all I was to you."

I broke free but stopped. "Do you have any idea how I felt? I truly loved
you, as well as what I thought you stood for. When you disappeared, I became
convinced you'd died. I've grieved for you, Stan. I've been unable to trust anyone since you, starting with myself. No, Stan, I'll never understand what you
did or why." I swallowed hard to keep my stomach under control. "Did you
ever love me, Stan? Do you love Sybel?"

"Yes of course, I loved, love … Oh Kip, don't be so—"

"Forget it. I'll never forgive you. What you did hurt and set me back too much. Leave me alone, Stan, I mean it. I want nothing to do with you. Now get out of my way."

In the dim light, Stan's eyes glittered like pools. Could this be for real? A single tear tracked a shiny path down his cheek as I watched it, trying to recall what it reminded me of. Apparently misreading my hesitation, Stan smothered me in a reckless hug.

"You haven't forgotten how good we were together, the good we accomplished together. That was the real Stan Szyzyck. It could be that way again—*we* could, Kip."

He grabbed my shoulders as if to shake some sense into me, but slid his arms around me and clasped me to him.

Though tired, sick, and undone by sorrow, I watched myself as if disembodied reacting to Stan's familiar touch—as if years hadn't intervened, as if sisters hadn't married or died. His clean scent bore the memory of feeling safe and loved. He kissed my forehead, my eyes. Moist lips brushed mine, then kissed me hard. With his mouth on mine, I was back in college, satisfying my hunger for my lover after a demonstration, or meeting in his office between classes for this purpose. Tingling prickled up beneath my exhaustion. My arms closed around him. I'd never let him go.

"Dr. Millen, emergency room, stat." Speakers blared over our heads. "Dr. Millen, stat."

Hospital corridor. Kissing Stan? Wait a minute.

"Stop it, Stan." I shoved him hard. "The college girl you once knew died. She's reincarnated as the Kip Czermanski who teaches assertiveness to yielding women." I pushed past him, pausing to hurl one final insult. "Go on pretending you don't know me when my family's around. Because you don't."

Stan's body tensed with fury, his fists went white with pressure, menace sealed his mouth in a tight slit. Like a wild animal preparing to pounce, Stan frightened me, but still I couldn't resist a last blow. "You're nothing to me now, Stan, nothing but Sybel's husband."

CHAPTER THIRTY-THREE

Sarah's funeral was held on February twelfth, just five days ago, four days after her death.

The funeral had been one long, Latin ordeal. The numerous nuns in attendance were subdued but not teary like most everyone else, including my dad and Sybel. Apparently these insiders of God's earthly hierarchy understood the necessity for my sister's premature death—which infuriated me. I for one questioned *their* God, who in His Omniscience "recalled his angels," as the priest labeled it, regardless of age or whom they left behind, "the survived-bys" in his patronizing terminology. That meant us survivors, unclear about how to carry on, let alone why. The priest's platitudes, liberally sprinkled throughout the service, provided zero comfort and even less guidance.

Coughs, wheezes, and sobs from the crowded sanctuary provided the backdrop. The incense-laden air was barely breathable before the cloying scent from the white lilies Sybel had surrounded the coffin with reached my nostrils. It was hard to sit still. Sarah's death released a bitterness within that surprised me, given I'd hardly known her. But I kept it to myself. Who would I share such disturbing feelings with, especially before I'd had time to figure them out for myself? At long last, the priest signaled the family to file out behind Sarah's coffin for her burial behind the church.

The rest of the congregation needed no direction to the burial site in the sprawling cemetery. The grandiose Czermanski mausoleum towered over the other crosses and headstones of Immaculate Conception's burial grounds. It could in fact be seen from blocks away. The priests, nuns, and my family formed the first ring encircling Sarah's casket, placed on a bier in the center of the mausoleum's shiny granite forecourt. Diverting myself from choking emotion and the bone-chilling cold, I realized the polished granite on which we stood resembled a smooth ice skating rink. Oddly, it reminded me of Catholic nuns' horror of things that reflect upward. Perhaps the pantsuit craze had ended Catholic worries over female exposure. Or was the worry male excitability?

The large burial monument by which my father intended to immortalize himself and the rest of the Czermanskis drew my curiosity as the crowd continued to assemble. Three facing granite benches defined the outer edges of the forecourt slowly filling up. The proud Czermanski name was etched in stone at the center, now beneath the coffin. Steps led to a granite mini-chapel, the actual mausoleum, which formed the fourth side of a square. Circling our name both in the courtyard and above the "chapel" entrance were carved amoeba-like shapes I hoped no one recognized for the sausages they were. Glass-and-wrought-iron doors, also surrounded by decorative carvings of fruits, leaves, and an occasional sausage poking through the foliage, opened into the mausoleum. The names of those interred to date appeared under our name: Grandpa and *Grandmere* Czermanski, Josef and Magda. Norma Jane Priestley Czermanski, my mom. And in testament to Sybel's organizational skills, Sarah's names appeared as well: Sister Sarah Joseph, *née* Sarah Magda Czermanski.

The back wall opposite the clear-glass doors of the mausoleum was one huge stained-glass window, fragmenting the day's dull light. My dad had commissioned the window to portray his favorite parable, the prodigal son. I thought that odd coming from an only child, unless it was how he imagined his final voyage, his death: After a lifetime of largely ignoring the church, God would nonetheless welcome Dad, and hopefully the rest of us sinners, when we needed it most.

Just when I couldn't bear another moment of this February day, Father

Dubchek, direct from his sickbed, spoke. The vapor of his words rose over his head to disappear like the Holy Ghost Itself. So mesmerizing were the smoky shapes of his incantations, I forgot to listen.

At Father Dubchek's signal, only the family and church officials followed the pallbearers inside the chapel-tomb behind Sarah's casket. It, she, was lifted into one of the vaults that ran from floor to ceiling along the walls to either side of the doors. A plaque above, repeating her names, read: Born December 26, 1933, died February 8, 1972. Beneath was the biblical quote Sarah had specified: "*And Jesus said, Suffer the little children to come unto Me.*"

More than enough spaces remained for the entombment of all the rest of us and then some. Dad must have anticipated more progeny from four daughters than had been forthcoming. Now that I thought about it, it was odd for four Catholic girls, nary a child between them. Had my married sisters, like me, sinned against the church by using The Pill? If so, why?

Under the stained-glass window, a large sarcophagus doubled as the altar with an identifying plaque: "Norma Jane Priestley Czermanski, Beloved Wife and Mother, 1915 to 1951," the latter date just three years after my birth. Dad would eventually share the large stone casket, resting forever with Mom under the ever-changing variegated light. Imagine resting here for eternity in the dead air and cold stone of these cramped quarters. How creepy. I suspected my mother would have been more comfortable in the ground beside her parents in the Protestant cemetery than in this monument-to-self. But that was pure projection on my part. I'd never known her.

Samantha's nudge caught my wandering mind off guard. Sybel, behind Dad with Samantha following, approached Sarah's casket for the symbolic burial preceding her interment. The young priest who'd married Sybel had black Wisconsin dirt in a small pail—both items most likely had dignifying Latin names. He held it out to Dad, who hefted soil in his palm, hesitating before sprinkling Sarah's coffin. Dust and ashes. Sybel repeated the rite, and I realized my turn was coming. So instead I fled the mausoleum through the crowded forecourt for the church bathroom.

Pressing cold water on my face and swollen eyes, I willed myself to calm. Sybel would be disgusted at my show of weakness, but I felt certain Sarah would understand that these rites and formalities were not my way to say good-bye.

I decided to walk home, despite the forlorn winter weather. Perhaps I'd find a sign of spring buried beneath the snow on my way to the reception Sybel had planned—another command performance in an already endless day. Ritual number three, coming right up.

Since Czermanski Sausage Company was by far the largest employer in the area, most of Wausaukeesha stopping by the house for the final death rite had been anticipated. Wisconsinites would never be deterred by the slushy residue remaining from the snowstorm that ended three days earlier after raging for two days. Sullied snow was merely a fact of life here. Perhaps Sarah would have felt honored by the presence of the bishop from the diocese along with the parish priests, but their sanctifying presence only riled me more. Too many died young, no matter how good they were or how much they were needed. What kind of loving God allowed that?

Steered through the mire by their husbands or children, the women carried in casserole dishes, cakes, or steaming platters piled with their personal specialties for this, the final ritual. From a safe distance, I observed the female migration to the kitchen while the males congregated around the television set in the living room. Dad, with Stan at his side, formed the nucleus of men exchanging reflections with teary eyes and loud sniffles. A flurry of handkerchiefs flitted in and out of jacket pockets. Dad's frayed composure appeared on the mend, aided by the Scotch he sipped from a coffee cup. Sybel would disapprove, but to me it was simple: whatever gets you through this.

Our living room was redolent with the odd combination of funeral flowers, mostly lilies, and the yeasty odor of beer. Sybel had arranged a keg of Schlitz and hired servers to help with the turnout. Beer steins in hand, men settled into sofas or chairs, the TV set droning in the background. Had the men worn baggy peasant pants and the serving girls pigtails dangling from *babushkas,* the old-country religion I'd witnessed on my travels through Germany and Poland would have been faithfully recreated. That kind of observance—high on celebration, low on sanctimony—I could get behind.

Meandering toward the kitchen, I puzzled over why Dad idolized, more like deified, Stan. Sure, Stan fawned over him, another sycophant to add to Dad's retinue, and they spoke Polish together, which Dad really dug. Still, Dad not only treated Stan like the son he'd obviously longed for, which had to bug Raymond immensely, but he also bragged *ad nauseum* about Stan's Ph.D. and where he earned his degrees. How much did Dad really know about Stan? How much did any of us know about Stan?

The rioting aromas of sauerkraut and sausages trapped in a soggy cloud swept over me when I pushed through the kitchen door. There the clustered women performed their own rites for the expiation of grief. Perhaps they chose the steamy kitchen for the proximity it forced, a comfort in itself. They fussed over each other and the food, ignoring the fact we'd hired people to prepare their dishes and set them out on the dining table and sideboards.

Food—creating it, serving it, sharing it—seemed to be a critical aspect of women's coping. As revealed through my work at the center, both physiologically and psychologically, most women never ranged far from their fundamental nurturing nature. Food to laugh by, food to cry by, food for any occasion that brings people together, including funerals. Food to fill the vacancy left by death, to remind us we're still alive, that we've survived yet another passing.

"Here, Mrs. Wiegel," I said to the neighbor who followed me in, "let me get someone to help you with that."

Cradling a steaming bowl swaddled in a dishcloth, stout Mrs. Wiegel insinuated surprise at my offer. "My, you've grown up, Kip. Poor Kip," she sniffed. "Sarah was an angel, just like your momma. An angel! God wants all His angels near Him," she repeated the priest's inane message. "It must be true. Ah, poor Kip." Shaking her head, which waggled her chins, she added, "but this will be hardest on JJ."

"Yes. Thank you for your concern, Mrs. Wiegel. Now let me take this for you." As short as I was, it was unusual to peer down at someone's frizzy gray hair. Mrs. Wiegel's body, testing the black dress she wore at every seam, gave the impression of girth equal to height.

Clutching her dish to the large breasts that squared her stocky figure, she insisted, "No, no, I must make sure it's served hot. Nothing worse than warm *golomki*. Your papa loves my *golomki*, you know."

"You're Polish, Mrs. Wiegel? I had no idea. *Golomki*—it's cabbage roll, isn't it?" I asked politely, as if the aroma rising from her guarded treasure didn't broadcast *eau de chou*. The entire household reeked of a dozen dishes spewing the fetor of pungent cabbage or briny sauerkraut into the air.

"Wait 'til you try my g*olomki*, KP—oopsy, Kip. Just you wait." Judging from the concern in her eyes, Mrs. Wiegel meant to say: Will you be okay? Do you know we care, that we love you—even if you were always different?

"I'm sure I'll love it, though I like *holubky* just as much." I said that to impress Mrs. Wiegel with my Polish, now all but used up. All I knew of *holubky* was that it contained cabbage as well. What I meant to say in response was: Thank you for caring.

The name of my dad's favorite Polish dish, *holubky,* brought to mind the sour cabbage odor of every Czermanski Christmas Eve. Placing the dish before Dad, who sniffed and nibbled thoughtfully, Sybel anticipated his annual pronouncement: Just as good as your mother's—why, even your grandmother's. Sybel would color a seasonal red when Dad kissed her on the forehead to reinforce his praise. My whining, "Can't we eat? I'm hungry," always drew a sneer from Sybel down the long dining room table.

"*Holubky*? Child, you must try my *golomki*." Mrs. Wiegel touched my cheek with great tenderness. "Kip, will you be all right?"

"Of course," I snapped, drawing back from her touch. "I hardly knew—" When Mrs. Wiegel placed her dish down in order to comfort me in the great, flabby arms I'd always thought looked, well, comforting, I escaped the heat, fumes, and ant-colony activity of the kitchen, not to mention prying eyes and good intentions.

In the dining room, ladies jockeyed their dishes into prime locations on the buffet table, deftly blocking competing dishes. Watching their strategies restored my slipping composure. The game was, apparently, to be first to find your dish empty. The winner could then parade her scraped-clean serving dish around the house, lamenting she hadn't the foresight to make enough to meet the high demand.

Sybel pushed through the kitchen door in her black mourning suit, minus hat and veil. *Au courant* in her shag haircut, she frowned in exasperation: of course, Kip wouldn't be helping. "Kip, would you mind telling the men the food is on, to come while it's hot? If it's not too much trouble."

"No problem, Sybel." She disappeared behind the swinging door.

As I walked through the dining room, I again reflected on women's tunnel-visioned focus on food, how it encouraged each one to carry on despite what life handed out, and despite what life took away. It stopped me in my tracks. Suddenly I envied them, this community of wives, neighbors, mothers, aunts, and cousins who'd grown up together and would die together. Liberated or not, these women were able, through simple physical activity, to pacify grief for a time.

Blaring whistles from the football game on TV reached my ears before I passed through the entry hall into the living room. There, no one watched the tube. Dad, sitting on the couch with Stan on its arm beside him, led a debate that heated the faces of its participants: Could anyone fill the shoes of the great Vince Lombardi, God rest his soul, and restore the Green Bay Packers to glory? Unaware of detection, Stan did not quite conceal his boredom.

"Dad," I interrupted, and the dispute died. Guilty eyes glanced at me as the sounds of the football game surged into prominence. Dad looked sheepish, caught in the act of not concentrating on his grief. "Food's hot. Sybel wants you all to come." So thoroughly had I infiltrated the male domain, no one reacted except for Stan. who jumped to his feet, too willing to follow. I repeated a vague, "Come on," and hurried off.

I moved through the house, speaking but not conversing with whomever I bumped into. I thanked them for coming, for the nice things they said about Sarah and the family, for the food and flowers. Most commented on how I'd matured, which said loads about meaningless conversation. These people would never understand me, my rebellion, my college radicalism, nor my devout feminism. Nor would they ever forget. But at least it diverted me from thoughts of Sarah.

The serving girls kept up their rounds, filling beer steins from my dad's prized collection for the heartier mourners, passing tea and coffee in my mother's bone-china cups for the more reticent. As the gathering settled down with food and drink, I noticed the oversized platter, which had been piled high with Czermanski sausages, held only one Polish sausage, wrinkling as it cooled.

Above the hum of conversation, I heard music and tracked the sound to the living room, now usurped by people crowding around old Mr. Koblecki, his accordion in his lap. This I hadn't expected—after a funeral? He played familiar polka tunes while the oldest contingent of mourners, mostly Poles and others Slavs, tapped toes, bobbed heads, and hummed with the music. A few sang along in English, Polish, and heaven knows what other languages, swaying to the rhythm of the old country songs. For the first time I heard how those simple tunes spoke of resignation and determination, of both life-long sorrows and momentary joys, all at once.

"Celebrate life, Kip," advised a voice from behind. "Live each moment. It's a good custom." I tensed at Stan's presence, so close his breath felt warm on my ear. "Don't make me beg, Kip. After all we've shared, can't we at least be friends?"

"'Friends?'" I repeated, wheeling around to face him. "We're relatives now, Stan." I marched off as he sputtered, deciding to take advantage of this rare opportunity to talk to Dad without Stan's chronic hovering. I found my dad at the fringe of the gathering, intent on the music. "Dad?"

It took seconds before he registered my presence. With a wistful smile, he nodded toward the accordion. "It's for Sarah," he said. "He taught Sarah to play."

I followed his eyes. Mr. Koblecki ended a song with a sustained, mournful note that sounded like a train whistle—the keening made as a train rushed headlong into the future. Or was it a wail for the past even a locomotive couldn't outrun?

"Sarah played the accordion?" I asked.

"Till your mother died."

When Mr. Koblecki switched to a more modern tune, a memory stung me: Sarah playing boogie-woogie on the accordion and encouraging her toddling baby sister to dance—more like twirl, in dizzying circles. "Look at KP dance, will you? Go, KP, go."

Dad didn't seem to notice the room whirl suddenly as I steadied myself on his arm. I fought the lump in my throat, forgetting altogether why I wanted Dad alone. No wonder I'd been mad at Sarah my whole life. When she left, the music stopped.

"She loved Fats Domino the most," Dad said, glancing at me. "Glad you're home, Kip. Did you and Sarah ... Well, did you two say what you needed to say to each other, before ..."

"I guess so."

"What was it she was so desperate to speak with you about, if I can ask?"

"She was sorry we'd known so little of each other, that kind of thing."

Samantha's face buried in her husband's shoulder made it harder for me to dam back my emotion and concentrate on accordion-style boogie-woogie. Raymond stiffly patted her back as he glanced around in embarrassment.

"That kind of thing?"

"Mm-hmm." I studied him. "Why, Dad?"

"She didn't talk about ... about her leaving ... going to the convent? About that time?"

"She apologized for letting us down, all of us, she said, including you."

Dad blanched at that, but continued to study me as if convinced I was holding back. I ached to talk freely about Sarah, the effect her strange words were having on me. But with the plug she'd pulled from my heart, I simply couldn't trust myself to speak. Messy emotions would only embarrass Dad in this public setting, and somehow, cost me in the end.

"Sarah blamed herself for abandoning me, her word. Still, it was obvious she was more than ready to go." Dad's façade crumpled in despair. The collapse, the depth of his wound, startled me. "Due to her pain," I reassured him. "I'm sure it was her pain."

Just then several mourners approached to make their farewells. Dad pivoted around to say his good-byes as his persona, suitably sad but emotions held firmly in check, reassembled itself right before my eyes.

CHAPTER THIRTY-FOUR

February 18, 1972

Nights especially dragged, as if the earth itself ceased rotating. Without the normal rhythm of light and dark, I learned to tell time by jailhouse routines. When two sets of footsteps closed on my cell, I was thrilled it was at last nine a.m. It turned out to be Timothy escorting Billy back, while a glance at the hall clock showed only eight o'clock. With a fatherly comment on how well I'd eaten, Timothy retrieved my breakfast tray and locked Billy in. This was awkward—Billy and me alone. And now whenever I saw him, Katey also miraculously materialized.

"Um, hi, Billy."

"Billy?" He spun around with his coat half-off. "It hasn't been Billy since the eighth grade when I graduated from Immaculate Conception."

Oops. "Of course, William. It's far more lawyerly." I blundered along, "People outgrow names. I did myself, from KP to Kip." I rubbed out the wrinkles in my blue uniform. "So … where's Phil?"

Billy checked his watch as he lit on the edge of the cot, clutching his briefcase in his lap. "I don't know. She said to be here at eight, which was two minutes ago." Was he perturbed by her directive, her lateness, or being stuck here with me? He toyed with his briefcase, releasing and locking its clasps. Click-snap. Click-snap. Click-snap.

"So … you married Katey Rudeshiem." Billy eyed me suspiciously, so I covered that inanity with, "I mean, she was always so pretty, and you know, 'in,' cool. Even the nuns loved her." His cynical snicker surprised me. "What?"

"Yes they did. The nuns loved her. I wonder what they'd think about her
…"

"Her … what?"

"Nothing. It doesn't concern you. Well actually, it does. My wife has been talking nonstop about you since your dramatic return to Wausaukeesha."

"I can imagine. Is she at least lighting candles for my immortal soul?"

William studied me, all seriousness. "You don't understand. Katey's fascinated with all you represent."

"'Represent?' And to her that means?"

"Oh, let's not be coy, Miss Czermanski. You clearly represent dissidence, rebellion, the general undermining of all authority—both the church and state—of piety. And let's not forget your feminism—" He spit the word out as if, given the list, it was my most heinous crime. "—which threatens every normal home in America today. You can't deny—"

"Sorry I'm late," Philomena gasped, approaching the cell with another powdering of snow sparkling on her hair and coat. "I had to find some rubber boots for this weather. The desk clerk got the owner of the shoe store to open early for me so I wouldn't ruin any more leather shoes or boots. This snow! Isn't it beautiful?"

"No." William disagreed.

At the same time I responded, "How would I know?" Philomena paused, palpable tension reaching her before she entered my cell. "William was just enumerating for me what it is I represent to his wife."

Phil shot him a quizzical look. Billy fidgeted with something inside his briefcase. "Okay," Phil said, settling in, "before we begin, I know I need strong coffee. Kip, too."

She made more than the necessary fuss, pouring cups from the thermos withdrawn from her briefcase. The scent the dark brew gave my cell made my stomach grumble, though I'd just eaten. I inhaled it before letting the hot liquid fill my mouth and warm my throat. *Ahh.* Who gives a damn what William and his Perfect-Catholic-School-Girl wife think I stand for?

With Phil and I engrossed in the pleasant stimulation of our first real coffee of the day, William waited, stiff and prim, subdued on the surface but obviously seething just below. Ha. Working for two women just might kill him.

"Why eight?" I asked.

"Eight? Oh eight o'clock. Why are we here early, you mean," Phil translated. "We don't have much time to start with, and both William and I scheduled appointments for later. We'll need to start at this time from now on. Not a problem for you, is it, Kip?"

"Not at all." Yay, the endless nights just got shorter. The earth just might spin again.

"Okay, Kip, before we get into your police record, I want to round out my understanding of your family. You've only mentioned your mother in passing. What actually happened to her?"

I shrugged.

"You don't know? Well, what do you remember about her?"

"Remember? Not much, not much at all. She died in 1951. I was only three …"

1951

The house smelled icky, like church. And lots of people were there. My sister, Sarah, held me up to see Mommy, but Mommy was asleep. Everyone was crying, or most of them, even people I never saw before, and Sarah was, too. I knew 'cause of her jerky breathing as she held me against her chest. They cried and looked at Mommy and some even touched her.

Mommy looked so pretty, white skin like vanilla ice cream, hair wound up on her head so light it glowed like the angel's halo that topped our Christmas tree. Dressed like on Sundays—gloves on her hands, little hat on her head with a little veil that didn't hide her closed eyes—she was lying on a bed-thing right in the middle of our living room.

When Sarah held me out toward her, I touched Mommy, too. But she was so cold that it scared me. And Mommy didn't even move. She wouldn't even open her eyes. The people around us made signs with their hands. Some talked to themselves on their knees around Mommy's bed, holding long necklaces. Some of them cried over me, too, kissing and patting me till I wanted to squirm out of Sarah's arms and run away. But Sarah held me tight and shushed me, even though I wasn't making a sound.

What was making the icky smell? The white flowers everywhere? The smoking pots around Mommy's bed? With the smell and Sarah squishing me, I felt like I might throw up. Then Daddy came downstairs with Sybel under one arm and Samantha under the other. Both of my sisters had silver wires on their teeth with little rubber bands on them. When they sobbed, candlelight made a funny gleaming in their mouths. Sybel was wearing those turquoise sweaters, one over the other, that she wore all the time. Ick, I hated that color.

Dad with my sisters and me stood together around Mommy. Daddy's face turned red when he covered Mommy's folded hands with his. Then he walked away through the crowd, stopping to shake hands, to kiss the ladies and get kissed back on his cheek, a sad smile on his face. He stayed away from Mommy after that, and all of us, too. I didn't see him again in the bunches of people coming and going for, it seemed like, forever.

But nothing bothered Mommy. She slept right through it all.

"Mother died in 1951 when I was three," I repeated. "She'd been bedridden basically since my birth."

"Why?" Phil asked.

"Complications related to giving birth is all I've ever known."

Phil considered this for some time before dashing off a note and handing it to William. "Would you find out more about that—cause of death, Mrs. Czermanski's doctor. See if he's still available to interview."

"Why?" William and I both asked.

"If nothing else, background," she answered. "Now then, where were we ..."

"As you directed," William spoke up, sounding peevish to my ears, "I reviewed Miss Czermanski's permanent record. It's heaviest her senior year of college."

"'Permanent record?'" I repeated with a chuckle. "Spoken like a good Catholic school kid."

"Permanent record?" William blushed. "*Police* record," he corrected himself.

"Good," Phil said. "Let's start there. Kip, how do you explain that fact?"

I didn't look forward to sharing my frenzied year of sex/drugs/rock-and-roll with Billy William Esquire. But there they were, my lawyers, waiting for me to explain the least explainable year of college.

"My p-police record for that year shows, I'm sure, nothing more serious than my three previous years of college. Perhaps higher volume?"

"Significantly more arrests and citations," William filled in.

"Frankly," I sighed, collapsing back against the bars, "I don't know how to explain. I suppose I was trying to lose myself. Stan's inexplicable absence was so ... close to home somehow." I rose and paced the tiny space. Even my Chagall wasn't going to free me of this task. "I'd risen to the top of the anti-war movement my senior year, though that relationship was destined for a dramatic change. Plus, I participated in everything from Zero Population Growth to Planned Parenthood and finally the budding feminist movement as it was taking root on campus and across the country.

"All of which resulted in some arrests," I minimized, "disturbing the peace, inciting to riot. Oh, one charge for breaking and entering when we occupied Administration in Bascom Hall. We went to jail for that, too, but they let us out later the same day. A few other campus incidents, disorderly conduct and the like. Kid stuff." I offered, gesturing airily.

My cell had grown suddenly warm, I realized, slipping the old sweater I wore over my blue uniform onto the cot, peace signs down.

When neither lawyer spoke, I felt compelled to try again. "You in particular, Bi—William, would be familiar with how radical Madison's campus has been since the mid-Sixties. Black Power, Vietnam, the draft, feminism. Tom Hayden didn't label Madison 'the third coast' for nothing." I immediately wished back my reference to the SDS leader as well as his references to the extremist campuses of Berkeley and Columbia, fearing those red flags would provoke half my legal team to charge. I hurried on, "You're just a few years older than me. You must've known lots of kids at Madison then."

"Yes, as a matter of fact, I did," William responded, stiffening even more, "quite a few. And not one of them has a criminal record to show for it, nor would they be proud they'd gotten one."

"You seem to think we latched onto any excuse to rebel against our parents and all authority," I countered. "You think we were just having fun?"

"Truthfully Ms. Czermanski," he shot back, "how many of your so-called *comrades* were motivated by serious ideals? Admit it, most of you were bucking the system, disrupting classes, taking drugs, and partying with utter disregard for accepted norms of behavior. It's called lawlessness."

I shook my head and closed my eyes. Instantly, police in gas masks rushed me. Tear gas seared my nostrils. Chants blared in my ears.

"It was the most important experience of my life," I asserted, standing up to his sanctimonious glare. "I feel blessed by participating in something so meaningful as activists practicing civil disobedience, fighting for what we believed in, flaunting authority when it had gone so wrong."

William shifted in his seat, a visual harrumph. "Pardon me for not applauding that irresponsibility, whatever you label it."

"Just hear me out," I shouted. "I belonged to a cause bigger than any one of us, yet a cause that inspired each of us to know and defend our beliefs. It was an empowering but awesome responsibility."

As I spoke, I saw Stan as he was then, a fiery idealist, handsome and passionate, inciting the crowd with his words. Had they been only words to him? I pushed Stan from my mind.

"In those years at least, I knew I could make a difference—together, my comrades and I could make the world a saner place—nonviolently, mind you, and we did. A ragtag group of misfits made a difference. President Nixon's current rhetoric about 'Peace with Honor' is nothing less than an admission we don't belong in Vietnam. We never did."

William regarded me as he would a naïve child who refuses to grow up. Plummeting from my soapbox, I blasted him, "Damn it, man, you're a lawyer. Regardless of politics, surely you can appreciate the right—the duty—of living what this country was founded on. Weren't those your very words at my arraignment?" I knew he'd lacked conviction. His initial defense of me had been no more than a lawyerly debate, words hardly believed in, simply an argument to win.

My indignant glare caused both lawyers to shift in their seats, Phil quite interested in the interchange, William disgusted by it. Phil seemed satisfied to observe us interact without intervening but as the pregnant pause lengthened, she reminded me, "Okay Kip, your senior year. Prosecution is likely to go over it with a fine-toothed comb, so spare us nothing relevant."

Chapter Thirty-Five

Right up to my graduation in May of 1970, senior year was a blur of causes. After tracking Stan to no avail the prior semester, I threw myself headlong into activism my last. The anti-war movement still came first, but increasingly its sexist leanings, apparent to me only since Stan's disappearance, rankled. I suppose the feminist movement had raised my consciousness. Though the causes helped, Stan was still gone, like sisters and mothers and people you dared to love.

Was it bourgeois to allow love's attachments? Old-think, monogamous relationships were dangerous, my friend Peter Replogel often reminded me. Look at the flower children offering flowers and kisses to everyone, making love in the streets, if what I'd heard about Haight-Ashbury and the Summer of Love was true. I'd missed that as well as Woodstock, being properly finished off via three months of European travel, but I'd heard of the sexual openness, the good vibrations, these people believed they created for the world. Maybe they knew something: the more you loved, the less love hurts? Quantity versus quality? They weren't doing any harm, were they, especially since The Pill? Maybe all love was good love?

At the opposite extreme, the radical feminists advocated death to men after stocking the sperm banks. The one thing we women needed men for and vice versa remained uninfluenced by ideology. Personally, I thought my dad acted pretty lame most of the time, but I'd never advocate his murder, nor Peter's. Nor Stan's.

A fellow activist and friend since freshman year, Peter hung out with me a lot our senior year, despite my melancholy, or maybe because of it. I treasured his friendship since my all-encompassing relationship with Stan had prevented my getting to know many of my class- and cause-mates. In the spirit of comradeship, Peter accompanied me to my first major feminist rally—a day so unseasonably warm, he probably just wanted to be outdoors.

Rally rhetoric rose steadily in vitriol to a crescendo of "Male Pigs, Male Chauvinist Pigs! Kill the Pigs!" All feminists' eyes locked on the presumed example in our midst, and it became clear Peter risked attack by the *longhairs*, Peter's label for feminists who let their armpit and leg hair breed unchecked—those zealots whose unadorned faces flashed more anger than I could muster. As I saw it, men hadn't done anything worse to me than my sister. I'd be far more fearful of a world with only Sybels in it.

Peter and I made our getaway by slipping into the endless parade of students skirting the rally as they passed up and down Bascom Hill. We skulked off to the safety of a secluded green spot near the shoreline path that circled Lake Mendota.

"Thanks, Kip," Peter said, sprawled on spring grass, catching his breath. "Like, that almost cost me my life, or my *cojones*, or both."

"No way, Peter. Don't be melodramatic. They wouldn't kill you—until they figured out how to get your sperm." We laughed so hard, I felt almost like I had before Stan's disappearance—good.

"Man, it's nice to hear that crazy laugh of yours, Kip." Peter, propping himself on one elbow, turned to me, lying beside him in a sheltered alcove.

"Hmm," was all I said, thinking of what had caused that laughter to dry up. Determined to practice the Zen approach to happiness, staying present, I concentrated on the lapping sound of the waves and the loamy aromas of Madison in early spring—fertile black earth, new green grass, lilacs in bloom—all spicing the breeze. I stayed present admiring crocuses pushing toward sunlight, the shade tree that hid us, the comfort of a good friend's presence. Don't allow the past or future to intrude on the now. The past and future can take care of themselves.

"Like wow, Kip. You don't believe that bullshit, do you?" Peter interrupted my Zen moment.

"Bullshit? Oh, the thing about killing men? Nah. I'm nonviolent to the core. But their ideas on equality of the sexes and equal opportunity are right on."

"Man, Kip, we've fought too many battles together for me to have to start calling you the enemy."

The anti-war protests and rallies Peter and I, along with thousands of others across the country, had organized and participated in appeared to be having some effect. President Nixon's Peace with Honor was pure political rhetoric for finding an end to the Vietnam War.

"Pot?" Peter asked.

I never admitted to my comrades that I couldn't stand the reek of the stuff—one of those gag-me scents that stuck to the inside of my mouth—so I faked a drag and rolled onto my elbow to face Peter. He got high, mellow, out there, faster than anyone I knew, an angelic smile forming on the baby face his stringy beard and dishwater-blond hair couldn't mask. Instead, his expression conjured a humorous vision of him as a toddling two year old—sweet grin, Nordic-blue eyes dancing under what was most certainly a towheaded thatch. The peace signs splashed over his wide jeans, vest, and T-shirt brought me back to the present. We shared the joint, me faking it while Peter sank into peaceful pot-reverie.

"Like wow, Kip, I've hated seeing you so bummed," he said, the toddler smile gone. "This is much better." His fingertips traced the curve of my lips and twined a wisp of my hair, which I'd let go wild and bushy in an imitation Afro, a damned good one for a white chick. "Man, I'd give it to you if you wanted it."

"Hmm? What?" I blinked.

"My sperm," he answered. His finger slid down my throat to tickle the skin above my low-cut T-shirt above its printed motto: Zero Population Growth! Stop At Two!

I got goose bumps. "For the cause?"

"Yeah, of course. You could brag to your feminist friends."

We stared at each other for an indecisive moment before Peter leaned in to kiss me. When his amazingly moist lips landed on mine, my mind flew to kissing Stan. But I recalled Zen—staying in the moment—and concentrated on soft lips, the feel of Peter's tongue pressing against mine, exploring fingers tugging at my T-shirt, the ache growing in my groin.

Peter had my skirt up, my panties off, his zipper down, and his pants loosened around him before I realized what we were doing. This staying-in-the-moment stuff appeared to be quite effective. Soft lips and tender touching just felt good.

Good, good, good, good vibrations…

When Peter rolled on top of me, my legs curled around him, holding him against me as if it were the most natural thing in the world, which actually, it was. For the cause or otherwise, Peter donated his sperm with abandon. To think, that tiny pill I took made all this spontaneity possible.

We lay catching our breath afterward until voices reminded us we were in a public park. We fumbled into our clothes and sat leaning against each other, watching boats bob out on the lake. Now, along with the other smells borne by the spring breeze that ruffled the waters, were ours.

"Far out, Kip," were Peter's first words. "And I still love you." When my chin dropped at those words, he reddened and dissolved in laughter. "Bourgeois emotions aside, Kip, you're … far out."

"Uh, thanks. And you—"

"And we're still best buddies, comrades in arms. Nothing's changed, right? That is the way you want it?"

"Sure," I nodded. "Of course."

Peter spaced on the hypnotizing rhythm of the waves lapping the shore for some moments before he exclaimed, "Man, we did it, proved we're free to follow our feelings and conscience, to make love, not war."

I winced at the slogan that transported me to Stan's office, but realized Peter was right. What could be wrong with this? And since I'm not madly in love, he probably won't disappear any time soon. I can handle this. Sexual liberation was enjoyable, no denying it. Attachment was bourgeois, and its lack, certainly less painful and frightening.

Chapter Thirty-Six

Phil broke the silence relating that escapade had induced in my cell, commenting, "So many causes, Kip."

"And all worthy," I exclaimed, my defensive retort surprising even me.

"Certainly, but ... what's that about, do you suppose?"

"I have no idea what you mean, Phil." I glared at her and William both. Right, so why did I sound so pissed off? "Oh all right, at the risk of sounding pathetically idealistic, I wanted to make a difference, leave the world better than I found it. I still do."

"I admire that in you, Kip," Phil added.

"But what?" I demanded.

"It just occurs to me, listening to you, that all your work for all those good causes may have filled some need in you, too."

I had a hard time maintaining eye contact with Phil, and William, who was smoldering over something, was no easier. I glanced about, stammering, "I-I don't ... I-I'm not—"

"It's not a criticism," Phil was quick to explain. "We're all human, motivated by our needs. Life is just easier if we're aware of them, that's all. Surely the psychology major in you would agree?"

Phil's humbling insinuations called to mind the oldest student in my assertiveness group back in Santa Monica at the Center for Women's Liberation—Betty. Betty had told us how she'd finally stood her ground and demanded some time for herself away from her duties to husband and children. But when her enraged husband stomped out of the house, Betty had caved immediately and chased after him, begging him to come back and let her get supper on, supper evidently being a foolproof method for keeping a man.

"What should I have done?" Betty had asked me in the same defensive tone that had just escaped my mouth. "Let him leave me, me with three kids? Raise them on my own? He'd find someone in no time, but me?" she'd choked, "with three kids?"

My staunch belief in my standard response: *What's wrong with being on your own?* stuck in my throat as it dawned on me that I knew nothing of husbands and children to support. How could *I* help Betty? I'd wondered. The first gray area in my tidy, independent, adult life had penetrated my assumptions.

An equally murky area now spread out before me. Why did I join so many causes? To belong, of course. To belong.

"'Leave the world better than I found it.'" William mimicked me as if reading my thoughts. "What a load of … of hooey." He rose, along with his indignation. "You really believe your own rationalizations? This feminist …" He thrashed about for a word. " … tirade of yours undermines the family unit upon which our entire social order depends. Good religious wives and mothers are being told by you, Kip Czermanski, to overthrow the taskmas-ters they married and—"

He had read my thoughts.

"Now, William," Philomena interceded, "that's an oversimplification of feminist—"

"You have no idea how insidious your message is," William thundered over Phil, "how it seeps into women's consciousness until they feel they must rebel, though they're rebelling against the life they chose." William glared at us. "Oh what's the use?" he snorted, storming my cage door and rattling it loudly even after the jailer's footsteps approached. Once safely outside the cell, he stammered, "This, this just isn't going to work. We can all see that. I'm, I …" William hurried down the hall before shouting over his shoulder, "I quit."

I settled back on my cot, trying not to gloat overmuch. "He has a point, Phil, about this not working, that is."

Phil replied after some thought. "Safe to say William's having some marital problems, but things may work out yet. What do you know about his wife?"

"Nothing," I said a bit too quickly. I didn't share Phil's optimism nor care if it worked out. "I knew her years ago in grade school."

"With all the small-town interconnections you've mentioned, I assumed—"

"Okay, Billy's wife, Katey, was the quintessential Catholic school girl, yet despite that moniker still one of the cool kids, blonde and pretty. She wanted to be a nun when I knew her. That about sums it up."

I began to giggle, reliving the moment Phil had chosen to intervene with Billy. "Phil, were you about to elucidate feminist doctrine for your assistant?" The title I'd given him added to my amusement. It would incense William no end to be Philomena's assistant. "You consider yourself a feminist?" I hadn't meant the question to sound so incredulous.

"I avoid such labels, Kip. Too limiting. But what woman wouldn't believe herself conceptually equal to a man, deserving of equal opportunities in whatever endeavor she chooses. What thinking *person*, I should say. But a feminist, like you? No. I don't put much faith in group causes, not that there were any such groups or support movements when I was your age. I've had to rely on the individual approach to surmounting obstacles."

"You don't believe banding together wields more influence? That more than just calling attention to ills, it brings more rapid change?"

"Hmm." My lawyer tapped a pencil against her skull as if stimulating the synapses as she considered. "I grew up in a very different time than yours, which I daresay, is unprecedented. I was never like the kids I knew. I was always too old, too serious, for my peers, a result of being an only child, I suppose, and very close to two parents who were such hagglers for the truth. Discussion around my home was lively, to say the least. I grew up thinking Socratically: question, debate, disagree, but seek your truth at all costs. It hardly made me popular."

Phil smiled at me as if we shared some secret. What?

"Females distrusted me even more than males," she continued, "as if my choice to apply myself throughout school and pursue a career somehow denigrated their choices—choices that were largely limited to marriage and kids, or to becoming a nurse or teacher before marrying and having kids. But some good does come from evil."

"Yeah? Like what?"

"World War II gave me my opportunity. After the Japanese bombed Pearl Harbor and the country united behind President Roosevelt to fight the Axis powers, all able-bodied men enlisted and were sent to all corners of the globe. The drastically reduced numbers of young men not only allowed me to go to law school, it was the only reason I got in."

Phil thought for a moment. "Some of my professors weren't even aware of their biases. I had to be battle-ready every day of law school, even more so afterward in the workplace. Maybe I was once more of a crusader like you, Kip. I took it very, very seriously being the first woman honors graduate of Stanford Law, the first female partner. I thought I was proving something for all women I suppose. How ironic that they resented me more.

"I'm not saying it wasn't tiring, proving myself over and over again to the men I worked with and my predominately male clients, but eventually we established workable relationships. Not so female clients, nor the few female lawyers I came across then.

"Suffice it to say, Kip, I've never been a joiner. In my experience, groups— of men or women—are dangerous and unpredictable. I've experienced firsthand the truism that a group plummets to the intellectual level of its slowest member."

"The power of groups," I insisted, "makes my generation totally different from yours. We band together to demand change in ways that cannot be ignored, at least for long. Groups against the war, against racism and segregation, against the inequality of the sexes, are changing the world. And I wanted to be a part of it. What's wrong with that?"

A silence lengthened. This, I was discovering, was Phil's method for forcing me to think.

"Okay," I confessed, "so I'm not free of all selfish motivation. Yes, I want, uh, wanted, to belong somewhere. I'm human, was that your point? Okay, guilty. Regardless of that mortal weakness, it doesn't erase the good that's been served."

With William's word, rationalization, taunting me, I was wearying of this discussion. "You obviously cannot understand, Phil," I huffed at my pseudo-feminist lawyer. "The generation gap thrives right here in my cell. Let's agree to disagree on methods and motivations and stay focused on my case. After all, it's just the two of us again."

CHAPTER THIRTY-SEVEN

After Billy quit and walked out, my strained exchange with Phil caused her to wind up for the day.

My pre-feminist female lawyer psychoanalyzing me—me, a psych major!—was way more than I bargained for. I didn't appreciate it one bit. Phil hadn't seemed upset to me, though, more like distracted by the loss of the help she counted on from William; perhaps more importantly, what she was going to do about it. The clock was ticking.

But our dispute bugged the hell out of me, reminding me of the last time I trusted someone over thirty. They really just don't get it, do they, no matter how "with it" they act?

While arguments formed in half of my brain against Phil's generationally limited views, her description of the underbelly of group dynamics awakened just such an incident in the other half.

As my final, final exams of college neared, all hell had broken loose.

1970

The two things intensified throughout my four-year stint in Madison—the war in Vietnam and the increasing violence at home employed by those determined to stop it. The Summer of Love's good vibes disintegrated into fear, outrage, disillusionment, and finally, to death.

A previously buried story of a massacre of the entire village of My Lai—the men, women, and children—by regular US soldiers marked the beginning.

Next, President Nixon announced that our troops had invaded Cambodia to "weed out Communist sanctuaries and strongholds," an incredible *expansion* of the war after years of peaceful protest and resistance. In the same breath, Nixon referred to us campus activists as "those bums blowing up campuses," paradoxical coming from the man responsible for blowing up people and countries. He contended that we bums were "utterly naïve" if we didn't recognize an obvious fact of life, which is that if we "got rid of the (Vietnam) war, there'll (just) be another one." The president understood the undeniable human trait of warmongering we pacifists had yet to comprehend.

The incendiary issue of the draft exploded at the same time with the revocation of the dependency deferment, wherein men with children were exempted from the military draft. The draft had expanded as well.

Reactions escalated. On Madison's campus, someone "trashed" the Monroe Street Draft Board and firebombed the Old Red Gym where ROTC—Reserve Officers' Training Corps—headquartered. One stupidly misguided protestor mistook the Primate Research Center for the Selective Service Office and firebombed it, too. After Jerry Rubin of the Chicago Eight spoke at the student union, rioting erupted on the Isthmus, the strip of land between Lakes Mendota and Monona that connected the campus to the state capitol.

The low point, however, was yet to arrive. May 4, 1970 felt to me like our entire country lost its last vestiges of innocence, if not its democratic ideals. The Cambodian escalation fomented the firebombing of the ROTC building at Kent State University in Ohio. The building burned to the ground when demonstrators prevented the dousing of the flames. The National Guard was called in with guns and live bullets to face down unyielding crowds shouting, waving flowers, or throwing rocks. When the Guardsmen opened fire on the protestors, among the injured lay four students, shot dead.

The war had just spread from Vietnam to Cambodia to home.

Reactions among my comrades were chilling. Several guys who'd jock-eyed all year to fill the leadership void left by Stan contended that working within the system—practicing our first amendment rights to march, protest, resist, raise consciousness, and demand change—had failed. The only change we'd seen, they asserted, was our own miserable evolution from being discredited, beaten, violently suppressed, to being killed. If the government lumped all dissident groups together and intended to silence us with bullets, then we must respond in kind. So ran their argument.

The debate raged. Peter and I among the old guard decried this violent turn, insisting it brought us down to our enemies' level. We were openly disparaged for that logic. The subtle snickers and raised eyebrows of earlier in the year had grown into guffaws and snipes now when I spoke. To these guys, my leadership position had come solely from my relationship with Stan. Their sexist language and innuendo became intolerable, but the school year as well as my college career neared an end. In deference to the bigger issues, we avoided head-on confrontation—that is, until Kent State.

I never surrendered my hope for peacefully reaching *détente* with the authorities, but I proved powerless in steering my comrades from this wrongheaded course. I prayed Stan would return to us now since I had totally lost my grip. The violence increased with each demonstration until Governor Warren Knowles, repeating the Ohio precedent, brought the National Guard onto campus, stationing sharpshooters with loaded weapons atop key buildings. Nightly, helicopter searchlights chased down trashers. UW Madison became our own Vietnam.

The last stand for protestors, rioters, and authorities alike occurred on Mifflin Street, known colloquially as Miffland. It held up within its barricades against the odds until the Establishment's long-range gas bombardment forced its end. The authorities dismantled Miffland as the last cornered resistors eluded arrest, me among them, slipping out as cops stormed in for the occupation. Weeks of rage and outrage ended, final exams were cancelled, and most kids simply went home for the summer.

Not me. I stuck around for graduation. My dad had paid for my education so I felt I owed it to him. But the semi-deserted campus with buildings bleeding smoke felt like I'd survived a war to wander the battlefield in search of what had been decided, and at what cost.

If he were alive, Stan had to know what was happening. Madison's stand-off had made national, even international, news for weeks. But Stan never returned and I realized that unless he reappeared before I left Madison in mere days, our chances of reconnecting were zilch, like two straws borne along by the unpredictable winds of a new decade.

On the day of my graduation, I, along with thousands of others, some who had stayed, others who'd returned for the ceremony, entered the stadium for the ritual officially marking our passage to adulthood. The glorious, sun-drenched day was surreal in comparison to the fitful weeks that preceded it. My Afro frizzed in the heat my black cap and gown greatly intensified.

My comrades and I rationalized our attendance at this establishment gig. Peter justified his presence "among the bourgeoisie" by his parents, who'd driven up from Janesville to watch their only child graduate. "Plus," he whispered as we plodded in line, "this'll be the last time we're together for a long, long time."

His eyes looked haunted when he squeezed my hand. Peter's low draft-lottery number meant immediate induction into the Army after graduation or an illegal alternative. I squeezed back hard.

Families, faculty, the university band, and we graduates filled the stadium as if for a big game. The crowd stood, swaying in unison to the school song, "Varsity," arms waving back and forth with the final notes: U Rah Rah Wi-i-issss-con-onn-sinnnnn. My dark glasses hid the fact that on this, my final day of school, the sight and sound made me mist up. Though I couldn't wait to leave Wisconsin and my dependency on my family behind, then again, what next?

As a former state senator spoke to us about individual responsibility for our collective future, a motley contingent of Vietnam veterans, a few in wheelchairs, aligned themselves beneath the stage we grads would cross to receive our diplomas. Dressed in faded combat fatigues plastered with peace symbols, the long-haired vets, some with missing limbs, brandished flags and placards while chanting their message: One More Trick, Dick, Bring Our Boys Home."

One of them wore a bandana the way Stan had, Indian-style, on a clean shaved head, a peace symbol painted on his skull. With the watered-down blue of his eyes, he looked like a grown up Mike Debick from my third grade class. I was sickened to see he'd survived the war with neither of his legs. When he shouted, his whole head blushed red. He could have been Debick's twin.

The time finally came for Peter and me, situated toward the rear behind our more aggressive anti-war comrades, to cross the stage. We found ourselves totally misplaced directly behind a uniformed ROTC contingent, which the Vietnam vets worried mercilessly, wildly waving placards in their faces and shouting taunts. One ROTC guy wrestled a poster free and splintered it over his knee before tossing it back at the protestors. The veterans reacted by redoubling their efforts to disrupt the proceedings, screaming and indiscriminately using their signs to harass anyone they could reach, including my group as we moved onto the stage.

More ROTC boys joined a counter-offensive, and even my battle-toughened comrades—those peace-determined activists—leapt into the fray, shouting, "Pigs of the Establishment, tools of aggression, Nixon's warriors." They jeered, "Ho, Ho, Ho Chi Min," and they, too, wrested signs to splinter.

"We're on the same side," I shouted at my comrades, pulling them back from the edge of the stage and the veterans below. I begged them to think. But the jittery mood of the past few weeks boiled up fears and frustrations, seeking anywhere to vent.

Dumbstruck and motionless in the midst of the melee, I witnessed someone spitting on the veterans below. I wanted to die when a few of my friends joined some of the ROTCs spitting on those war-crippled men. Oblivious grads, unflappable in their scramble to the future, jostled me left and right where I stood rooted to the stage.

I noticed campus cops closing in and the shaved-headed kid, tears standing in his eyes, wiping spit from his face. He was shouting himself purple: "Hippie freaks, fucking freaks, long-haired dope addicts. What have you ever done for this country? I fucking fought for it. I gave—"

I lunged into the thick of it, screaming, "Stop! These guys aren't the enemy. The war wasn't their idea. Can't you see how they've been used?"

But my friends, now indistinguishable from our ROTC foe, stomped, spit, taunted, and cursed. One of our own shoved me out of the way, shouting in my face, "Get the fuck out of the way, you cunt. You're the worst of all the do-gooder cunts in the movement. You think your brain gives you power over us?" He laughed as he stomped a stolen placard and went looking for more.

I reeled back, dizzy, hot, shocked. Pissed. I barely kept myself from being trampled as campus cops scattered combatants who blended into the black-gowned throngs. I, who exhorted people to live their beliefs and stand their ground, had failed to make those same people use their heads. Misplaced anger, crass and sexist cruelty, and base crowd mentality had won the day.

I turned my back on the mob my friends had become and left the stadium without my diploma. All the tricks I used for staunching tears—think of the worst thing Sybel had ever done to me, remember how she slapped my face, pinched me until I bruised, grounded me for no reason—had no effect against hot tears of shame. Even Peter had gotten caught up in the free-for-all. I felt more alone than ever.

In a manner of speaking, I turned in my anti-war credentials that graduation day. The time had arrived for moving on in every way.

Perhaps we had accomplished some good. Nixon's Peace with Honor sent Henry Kissinger to Paris to negotiate with the Viet Cong. Perhaps we'd contributed to the end of the killing.

CHAPTER THIRTY-EIGHT

February 22, 1972

Footsteps? I couldn't believe my ears, then my eyes. Philomena had an appointment with the county coroner that would occupy at least the morning. Like me, she probably needed a break after our little psychotherapeutic session. I'd spent the long weekend of Washington's Birthday fuming alone in my cell, while she for certain waived the preliminary hearing—otherwise, that's where we'd be right now.

Staring at the daunting-looking volumes of the Wisconsin Penal Code, expecting no one for hours, it horrified me to see William trudging toward me. I jumped up to bar my locked cage from him.

"Now what?"

"I'd like to come in and talk. Apologize." William glanced down as the jailer waited for my assent. I nodded tentatively, I'm not sure why, and took a seat.

William waited until we were alone before facing me. "It would appear my job, for the time being, is here."

"Polanski & Stelzl wouldn't take you back? Interesting." They were up to something.

"Your dad insists that someone he trusts, uh, knows, remains on your case. Phil needs the assistance. So," he glanced about, "where is she?" Hemmed in alone with me again caused William to back away until he tripped onto the cot.

"Not good enough, William. It's my decision who works on my case, not Dad's, not even Phil's."

"But you're insisting on the earliest trial date. You need me, you both do." It sounded rote.

"I question the help you bring when you're blaming me for … well, for what? Your marital problems?"

He reared back as if I'd slapped him. "Marital problems? Who said anything about marital problems?"

"Phil. Oh wow, it's true. You accused me of 'insidious preachings altering the minds of religious wives' or some crazy mumbo-jumbo right before quitting and stomping off." I slumped back on the cot. I'd been so sure Phil was wrong.

William leaned forward with jaws clenched. "Before this case, my wife never entertained these notions you feminists espouse in your assertiveness training camps: Men are worthless autocrats, subjugating women just because they can. Stand up for yourselves, women, and dump the bastards if they don't show appropriate sensitivity to your needs." He leaned in even closer to hiss, "There are times, *Ms.* Czermanski, I wish I'd never heard of you or your case. You're ruining my life."

"Ruining *your* life? Given the current state of mine, how dare you blame your marriage on me. That's a stretch."

"You think so? My career slipped out of my control the day I was assigned this case. The partners have been double-talking ever since—why, I don't understand. Then out of the blue, my wife finds 'inspiration' in all you represent to her."

"The partners' double-talk? About what exactly?"

"'What you represent?' Is that comical?" William went on talking about his wife, "Let's see, would we be talking sex, drugs, or rock-and-roll?"

"That's it. I've had it, William." I rose to tower over him where he sat. "That's more than enough of your holier-than-thou, sexist bullshit. I've ignored your narrow-minded, uninformed barbs and tried to focus on you strictly as my duty-bound defender because … because, well you know why. But you not only barge in here following your wimpy, childish 'resignation,' acting like I should be thrilled you've come back—which you've only done because my father made you, and still you can't resist goading me.

"Why would anyone goad someone in my position, William? I'll tell you why: because from the first, my activism threatened the very foundations of your hopelessly conformist life. How can *I* stand up against the war, you insinuate, when our elders and leaders tell us it's both necessary and good for America. Are you forgetting, William, that our current president got himself elected on his 'secret plan to end the war?' Am I to surmise he's come close enough for someone like you, who doesn't have to war outside the state of Wisconsin?"

I shouted over William's retort, "But it's far more than war that comes between us, William Beneke. It's a more basic belief that women should concentrate on 'domestic' concerns. Have you asked yourself why women gaining nothing more than equal opportunity in the workplace threatens you? Couldn't you compete in the meritocracy an even playing field suggests? Do you need the crutch of male superiority and preference? Is that what you're trying not to face, William, by antagonizing me?"

"'Level playing field,'" he repeated. "If only that were the case."

"The world is changing around you, William, and you can't understand it, let alone cope. Forces have been unleashed …"

"I don't have the same luxury you women have of 'reexamining roles and expectations.'"

"… cannot be recalled. I'm not so egotistical I believe I could influence …"

"I have a family to support. How do you *reexamine* that?"

"… your wife into questioning her marriage. Weak thinkers look outward, William. Might her questions have something to do with your condescending attitude and that hair-trigger temper of yours?"

As if to prove my last point, William smashed his fists on his briefcase and cried, "Oh, it has plenty to do with me. Katey says 'it's no longer enough.' What she means is *we're* no longer enough, the kids and me. *I'm* not enough for her anymore …"

For a moment I'd managed to forget that this on again, off again lawyer of mine was married to Katey Rudeshiem. I chuckled, "Rest assured, I have no sway over women like Katey."

"That's what I thought when I mentioned your case initially. Imagine someone like you—her antithesis—having such effect on my wife?"

"I'd have to agree with you on that one," I said, picturing Katey in pig-tails before Sister Margaret's desk. "But I refuse to take responsibility for your marriage or your career. I hardly begged you to take my case."

"Everything about you impresses her. Your degree, your work with women, the life you built away from your family's support."

"We are talking about the same Katey Rudeshiem, Sister Margaret's prime example of pious femininity?"

"Feminism, you mean. Katey's done with piety and obedience. Can't see what it's gotten her. Just a husband, kids, a home? Not enough. She's liberat-ing herself from—"

"Katey Rudeshiem? A feminist? Impressed by me? That's ludicrous."

"Katey Beneke," he shouted. Then his voice dropped. "Unless she's going to change that, too. She now claims she always secretly admired your 'spirit' in grade school with the other kids, but especially the nuns and priests. She now wants to 'make a difference,' too, your very words the day I quit." He dropped his eyes for a moment. "She wants to go back to school, finish her degree, and open the business she's always dreamed of, not that I ever heard of it before."

"Okay William, what's wrong with what she wants?"

He clambered to his feet, his briefcase crashing to the floor between us. Standing eyeball to eyeball with me, he ignored the clattering mess. "What do you women want? My wife is the only woman I've ever loved, and I don't know who she is anymore, let alone what she wants."

William broke away, only to swing back to exclaim, "I've done what was expected of me. No, I've done more. I married her and had the kids she wanted. Borrowed so much money to support them while putting myself through law school, I'll never get out of debt. Gave up the offer of a lifetime to practice criminal law in Chicago so she could come home to Wausaukeesha. And it no longer satisfies her? Now with my life going to hell all around me, *she* needs more?"

He collapsed on the cot with a thud. "I'm … I'm about to lose everything I've worked for. Everything." His eyes misted before he glanced away.

I studied him, thinking Phil had been right—again. This wasn't about me, per se.

When his eyes met mine, I spoke as calmly as possible. "It seems to me, William, you need to be clear-headed about your wife's actual statements versus what you're projecting between the lines. Is she unhappy in your marriage, or is she just under-stimulated staying at home? Is she talking divorce?" The Katey in my head would never entertain such *verboten* behavior. "Or are you letting your fear of her needs extending beyond you and your children run away with you?"

"Katey says she's capable of handling the household *and* finishing her education. She says she's dreamed of opening a bookstore where people can exchange views, think, and debate."

No way! But I resisted drolly observing, *No one could change that much.* "What you just said about her dreams and desires hardly sounds as threatening as the pictures you've been painting."

William bristled. "I don't want my kids humiliated at school because theirs is the only mother who works outside the home. You have no idea what that was like."

"No, of course, I wouldn't." His thoughtlessness acted like a self-imposed splash of cold water. William dropped his head in his hands as I sat across from him. "'*Times they are a changing,*' William. It's not the Fifties anymore. Your kids will understand and adapt—if you can."

"Right back in my lap," he flared up again. "I *must* change because my wife now wants to."

"No, you don't have to. You have choices—you both have choices. You can try to satisfy both parties in the relationship, or you can call it quits. Simple as that."

"'There's no divorce in the Catholic church," William rebuked me. "Another detail of your upbringing that slipped your mind?" He slumped against the bars as if taunting me no longer energized him. "I'm sorry, Kip. That was unnecessary."

"Apology accepted." I intended to leave it at that, but William, his anger spent, looked downright pitiful. "You both have to make it work, William, and what do you risk by trying, if, as you say, you 'lose everything' dug in where you are?" I couldn't look at him in his lost condition, so I paced to give him a moment. But the anguish in his voice stopped me cold.

"Would she still love me?" William searched my face. "If Katey didn't *need* me anymore, would she still *want* me around?"

There it was: the simple human fear at the bottom of it all. I sat down again and admitted, "I don't know Katey any more than I know your history together. But if she is the 'only woman you've ever loved,' start there when you talk to her. Admit your fears and listen to hers."

William dropped his eyes and appeared to drift in thought. I conjured up Katey Rudeshiem inviting my pimply date, Lanny, to cut in for a dance. "Imagine, at that damned high school dance at St. Hedwig's."

"St. Hedwig's?" William glanced up on the alert. I'd spoken aloud and held my breath. "You *do* remember our bumping into each other in high school, don't you?" William accused me, his eyes narrowing.

I shook my head and turned away from him. But William's wording got the better of me. "'Remember bumping … bumping into each other." The vision of me mired over poofed pink organza with Billy Beneke stretched on top, the ring of dancers surrounding us silent, made it hard to suppress my amusement at his choice of words. A giggle escaped as I replayed Billy righting himself and tugging me upward *sans* gown. I repeated, "'Bumping into each other?' Droll understatement, William?"

Stern William disintegrated into laughter. He gasped when he could speak, "I knew you remembered that pileup on the dance floor at St. Hedwig's." We both blushed the cotton candy color I'd worn that fateful day, but neither of us could control our laughter once it had begun. In retrospect, the incident was pretty damned funny.

He choked out, "I thought you'd forgotten it and/or me, I hoped, which suited me just fine. In all this time, you never said a word."

"I lived in fear you'd bring up the most embarrassing moment of my life, until recently that is."

William's self-control was returning. "You were the worst dancer," he said with a grin.

"Thanks. And you were the most conceited jerk I ever tripped on a dance floor."

William sobered. "Fair," he owned, "that might be fair. The fact I only wore my glasses, disguised as safety goggles, on the basketball court throughout high school didn't help. I didn't know you'd tripped until I stumbled over you." William removed his spectacles, thick lenses held aloft between us. "You can imagine how much I missed without these."

"So you weren't ignoring the multiple trips I made each day past your hall monitor post at Immaculate Conception."

He looked dumfounded. "You did that?"

That he was touched made me feel ridiculous. "In the third grade I had quite a crush on you, Mr. Sixth Grade Head Hall Monitor." As unexpectedly as shared laughter had come, it vanished. William blanched. I was quick to add, more self-conscious than ever, "It was a really long time ago, William."

He rose and banged for the jailer. "I … Sorry, I have to … sorry." His words trailed off as he hurried away, shrugging on his overcoat.

I backed up toward my cot, staring after William, wondering what had just happened, when I stumbled over his briefcase. He always clutched the thing as if it contained all his magical lawyering powers. Yet here his precious case remained behind where it had crashed to the floor and its contents scattered—as if he no longer needed it.

CHAPTER THIRTY-NINE

February 23, 1972

Phil and William arrived at my cell the next morning all buddy-buddy smiles and warm hellos as they approached. I knew my last meeting with William had been thoroughly rehashed. But I was pissed, being left in the lurch by William two times running.

"We need to quit meeting like this, William," I snarled, "especially since we never seem to find the time for proper good-byes."

The climate outside my cell changed precipitously. "Ah, Kip," Phil began as she was allowed into my cell, "over breakfast William told me what invaluable advice you gave him yesterday. He and his wife talked like they haven't in years. Didn't you tell me that, William?" Pure Phil the Pragmatist, smoothing over our differences until she could convince us there weren't any.

William stuttered with embarrassment, "I-I intended, first thing, to thank you. Your advice yesterday was simply brilliant."

"That explains your rushing out yesterday? To talk to your wife?"

"Before she picked up the little ones and there were distractions. Before I lost my nerve. Before anything else could come between us, yes." Emotion garbled his voice. "I don't know how to thank you." Wow. He meant it.

"Well, all right," I mumbled, standing back to let him enter. William's eyes fell on the briefcase he'd abandoned the day before, upright at the foot of my cot. "I put your stuff back as best I could. Nice pics of Katey and your kids, by the way. Three towheads—they're cute."

Pleasure at the compliment was offset by the obvious fact I'd looked through his stuff. "I wasn't prying, William. The contents spilled all over the floor. I did read your signed confidentiality agreement since it pertained to me." It had been the only legal thing in the case, the rest all sharp pencils, pads of various sizes, and empty file folders. I handed him his case. "Reading that gave me more confidence."

He cleared his throat. "Look, Miss, I mean Ms.—"

"Kip's fine."

"Kip. We got off to the wrong start, and I apologize. Could we, do you think we could begin again? I'm indebted to you after yesterday. I'd like to try. Phil and I discussed it at length this morning. I can be of help here—if you'll allow it?"

I hated to admit I was touched. "Well, okay, as long as we're all confessing our sins, some of your accusations weren't entirely wrong, William." Both lawyers sobered. "About feminism, no way were you right about one thing. But," I shifted in my seat, "I'm beginning to understand the shapeless anger that's motivated my life. My anti-war activism was grounded in absolute belief in nonviolence, but …"

"But?" both Phil and William prompted me, beginning to look alarmed.

"But there were times when an amorphous anger inside me needed venting." Neither one of them said a thing. In fact, they both appeared to hold their breath. "I mean, there were times when shouting back at the authorities, resisting arrest, even throwing whatever was handy, usually snowballs, at the cops as they closed in on our demonstrations, just felt good. Believe me—" Both lawyers looked so stricken I stopped. "What?"

"Your point, Kip?" Phil demanded.

"I'm saying that despite my philosophical position, sometimes fighting back, even violently when a cop or guard was swinging a nightstick at me or my comrades, felt good."

"You're talking about your case?" William whispered.

Oh, that explained the anticipation in their expressions. "No, no. I was simply trying to say that there were times, not many, when I felt so angry and full of dread at something unnamed that marching, protesting, hurling taunts at the cops who hurled worse at us, even a thrown fist or elbow, provided release. Despite the causes I believed in so passionately, sometimes my activism was just about me. I'm ashamed. I've never admitted it before, not even to myself."

Still my lawyers waited, perhaps for further explanation of my capacity for violence? "No, you misunderstand. Don't go reading into this. William accused me of enjoying anarchy and Phil—well, Phil wanted to know what was in it for me, all this joining of causes. I'm simply saying that on rare occasions I did get caught up in venting, that's all. I rarely struck back though I was beaten any number of times. Well, except that one cop who attacked Stan …"

What was I trying to say? "I was always a little on the angry side, that's what I'm saying. That's *all* I'm trying to say." Apparently trial prep for murder one was an ill-advised time to confess my propensity for violence, rare or otherwise. "Forget it, okay," I said, looking nonchalant. "So, shall we get on with my defense?"

Philomena at last made a thoughtful comment. "Sounds like some progress on the personal front, Kip." Did she mean: as opposed to the legal front?

CHAPTER FORTY

I knew with certainty who approached without glancing beyond my cell. Hesitant footsteps, bewildered by her surroundings, wanting to flee, making herself move forward. Only Samantha walked as if forward progress required intense circumspection. I'd noticed the faltering rhythm of my sister's gait before, but only now wondered what it said about her. Had Samantha come bearing more bad news?

"Kip," she cried as I rose to face her. "I'd have come sooner but …"

"But?"

"First someone here at the jail told us that you weren't allowed visitors—or was it phone calls?—but we found out that was wrong. Then, well, Raymond forbade me. He said I've been so distracted that I needed to stay away from you and the whole situation until I calmed down."

When the cell door shut with a clang that echoed off concrete, she nearly jumped into my arms. Samantha covered it by hugging me hard, even shedding a tear, which surprised us both. I returned the hug, wondering why we hadn't done more of this growing up? Of course, Sybel always frowned on any display of emotion.

I inhaled Samantha's lemony scent, something she used on her hair. "I'm glad you came, Samantha." I discovered in her hug that human touch felt reassuring.

Twirling about to examine the space, Samantha removed her coat, then pulled it back on and sat. Stuffing jittery hands in her pockets, she struggled to acclimate. "You're really all right here? It's so, so drab. And exposed. They don't even give you privacy to use the bathroom? Heavens, is that legal?"

"There's one female guard, but she only works weekends, so we've worked out signals."

Chagall's floating figure framed Samantha's head as she focused on the bars surrounding us. "You sound, I don't know, adjusted."

An instant burning at the back of my eyes formed my reaction to that description. "Would it help if I weren't? I try not to dwell on the things that for now cannot be changed."

Samantha shuddered, as if imagining herself living in this cage. "I brought some things from home," she changed the subject, "which the guards have and will bring back to you if they're allowed. Some books, toiletries—" Her eyes traveled my blue jailhouse uniform. "Extra clothing if they will permit …"

Realizing I hadn't been paying attention, I asked, "So what's new?" A jail cell really drove home the emptiness of normal conversation.

Samantha brightened. "I've been busy sketching out a new garden. Come first thaw, I'm going to do something really different. I've been thinking about it for, well, some time now, but finally got busy with actual plans and drawings."

"Hmm." I never shared Samantha's gardening bug, except for the final product. I loved flowers, as long as their scents weren't too cloying.

"You remember my garden, don't you, Kip? It was nice in its own way, I guess. I mean I used to love the way all the colors, species, and perennials were separated by borders. But—" Samantha smiled as if the project she described provided guilty pleasure. "—now I want something completely new. I'm going to rip up the walkways and replace them with steppingstones placed helter-skelter. I'm going to mix colors and varieties and, I don't know, toss seed willy-nilly and well, just see what happens. A book on English gardens inspired me."

Samantha pursed her lips with disapproval. "Raymond thinks it sounds crazy, ugly, I guess, and wild. But it's *my* garden, and he's never understood why I love 'working in the dirt,' as he calls it. He can't understand the feeling of creating something beautiful by muddying your hands a little. Well, that's just Raymond …" Samantha's enthusiasm faded. She checked her hands for mud. "Forgive me, Kip. How thoughtless of me, given this."

"It sounds beautiful, Sam." I sat across from her. "How's Dad?"

She shook her head sadly. "A mess. He's not handling anything well. He can't work, so he comes home. He can't be alone, so he wants Sybel and me there. He can't concentrate, so he moves around restlessly before going back to work, only to repeat the cycle. I guess no matter where he goes, he's reminded of his losses—at work, no Stan, his designated heir to the business; at home, no you, no Sarah …" Samantha gulped hard. "It's not easy for any of us, even Sybel."

"It should be hardest on Sybel, losing her husband, especially in such a publicly humiliating way."

"True, but as always, Sybel manages better than the rest of us. She's so strong." Samantha's assessment of Sybel brought Sarah's deathbed statements from the recesses of my mind: Sybel had to be medicated after mother died. *Talked of institutionalizing her.* " …listening to me, Kip?"

"Samantha, I want to ask you something. Do you remember what happened to Sarah's boyfriend, her fiancé, after Mother died?"

Samantha shifted on the hard cot and pulled her coat tight around her. "Why are you asking that now? Well, yes, I do remember Jerry. I was eleven or twelve after all, and he'd hung around the house for years."

"Why did Sarah choose the convent over him after Mother died?"

Samantha shrugged. "Within the year, Sarah was gone … and Jerry, too. I don't know what happened. No doubt she loved him, but she was always the most devout, too. Maybe the shock of Mother pushed her that way."

"Mere coincidence they both disappeared after mother's death?"

"What else?" Samantha played with her coat buttons. She was hiding something. I could always tell with Samantha. I waited, staring at her until she came clean. "You've obviously heard the rumors that have gone around for years. A town full of wagging tongues saying Daddy paid Jerry to leave. Surprise, surprise, imagine Daddy using his money—" A burst of cynical laughter from Samantha startled us both. Samantha colored. "You know better than to listen to town gossip, Kip, especially about our father."

I out-waited her again. "Daddy expected Sarah to fill Mother's shoes," Samantha admitted, "felt it her duty as the oldest. That's all I know for certain." Samantha unbuttoned her coat again. "They were both so young, Sarah just eighteen, Jerry not much older. He probably dropped her, or he left her behind when he went to college. You know Sarah, of all of us, would turn to the church after Mother's death and whatever happened between her and Jerry. It seemed perfectly natural she would take her vows."

"Wow. You believe it, don't you—that Dad paid the guy off?" Samantha's flitting eyes provided an irrefutable clue. "That must've broken Sarah's heart, especially after losing—"

"I'm quite sure—" Recovering her ingrained sense of family honor before all, Samantha sat forward to complete her thought. "—Daddy wouldn't intentionally hurt any of us, not even when we were all a little crazy with grief."

Crazy? "Do you remember Sybel being depressed back then?"

"No," Samantha answered without hesitation. "Sybel ran everyone and everything from the first as if she were born to it. That's what I recall anyways. Of course we still had our nannies then, but Sybel was always in charge. I think the nannies were also afraid of her, even at only thirteen or fourteen years old."

"'Also?'"

"Of course they were only eighteen or nineteen themselves and so far from home." Samantha ignored me selectively, suddenly leaping to her feet. "Daddy tells us you have a woman lawyer. Is she, you know, masculine? Can you imagine going to law school, with all guys in your classes? I bet no one told her not to be brighter than the boys."

"Whose advice was that, Sybel's?" I laughed, but sobered. Not our mother's? "You'll meet my lawyer soon enough, when she questions you. She'll surprise you."

Samantha froze. "She's not going to make me testify, is she? It'd be embarrassing to have to say what—"

"She'll want to, but don't worry. I haven't told her yet that none of my family is to be called as witnesses for the defense, even if it would save my hide."

Samantha plunked down on the cot. "I'm sorry, Kip. I don't know what I was thinking."

Family honor, of course. We'd been well schooled by ... "Speaking of Sybel," I switched gears, "she's evidently not all broken up by Stan's death. Why? What do you know about them?"

"Nothing!"

"Too emphatic, Samantha. Tell me."

Samantha began to pick at invisible lint on her coat until even she could see no more. She tugged her hair forward. "She loved him, at least at first. She was a completely different person while they dated. You should've seen her at their wedding—laughing, *crying*. But these last months, well, I don't know, she seemed less ecstatic, I guess. Probably just, you know, just an adjustment period married people go through." Samantha checked her watch. "I'm sorry, Kip, but I hadn't planned on staying long today. How do I get out of here?"

"Samantha, you just got here."

"I know, but Dad. And Raymond. I don't want him to know I was here, okay?"

Discovering I liked having a sister, someone other than prying lawyers to break the tedium, I turned away in disgust. *I'd think family would be a comfort,* Timothy had said.

"I'll stay a little longer, Kip." Samantha sighed, settling back against the bars. "There was something strange. You should've seen Sybel react when Dad told us he'd planned to leave his company to Stan. You'd think, since he was her husband, she would have been thrilled."

"Dad did what?" I was on my feet, close enough to catch Samantha's lemon scent.

She flinched at my closeness. "He planned to leave the company to Stan, in his control. Dad changed his will."

I staggered backwards. Had this been Stan's game all along, to distance himself from childhood fears of starvation, humiliation, and more recently, capricious employers by commanding a company worth millions of dollars? With the Sausage Company now coast-to-coast, its value might exceed a few million, in which case …

"Samantha, Sybel should've been thrilled, you're right."

"Well she wasn't—she came unglued. She called Dad 'an idiot' for trusting Stan more than his own children. That's exactly what she said. I was shocked and so was Dad. Still, he insisted it made sense. We'd never shown interest in the Sausage Company. Stan loved the business as much as Dad. Stan himself had suggested handling it this way to ensure its future as a family concern, as protection from those corporate competitors Dad always feared, who cut corners by using cheap ingredients and—"

"Fillers. Yeah yeah, I've heard it a few jillion times. Protection? What guarantees did Dad have that Stan wouldn't tire of the business, sell it, or run it into the ground? Even divorce Sybel?"

"Catholics don't divorce," Samantha snapped, a second reminder of my fallen Catholicism. She added, "Dad said that Stan had plans to take the company international, and he reassured us we had each been well provided for in his new will."

I hunkered down on the cot and propped my head on my fists. "I don't understand Sybel's reaction to her husband inheriting, unless—" I scrutinized Samantha. "—Sybel didn't trust him herself."

Samantha stood, buttoning her coat for, it looked like, the final time. "Kip, I really must go. I'll be late. Please get someone to let me out. I'll, I'll come back soon, I promise."

"I need clothes for the trial, Samantha, and I know exactly what I want. If you can't get them here, go wherever you must, Milwaukee, even Chicago. I want a dark pantsuit—blue, black, or brown—of good quality and material, no wide bellbottoms. Plus a couple conservative white blouses and low dark heels, pretty but comfortable." I clanged the bars for the jailer.

"Easy enough," she replied, wincing at the noise. When Timothy unlocked my pen, she hugged me quick and rushed out ahead of him. There was no hesitancy in her gait as Samantha made her escape from the Wausaukeesha County Jail. Only afterward did I wonder how Raymond took the news of Dad's will, not to mention Samantha herself.

Then again, it no longer mattered.

Part Four

To save the town,
it became necessary to destroy it.

– ANONYMOUS VIETNAM VETERAN –

CHAPTER FORTY-ONE

April 10, 1972

"You won't believe it, Kip, but there's a blizzard goin' on out there." When he returned for my untouched breakfast tray, Timothy's chitchat, intended to distract me, only emphasized what day it was: the opening day of the sure-to-be sensational Kip Czermanski murder trial. He eyed the tray with parental disapproval. "Hardly touched your food, Kip. That's no way to prepare yourself for today."

I was lost in thought, struggling to remember all the compelling reasons I had for rushing to trial, why I'd been so adamant about change of venue. Eight interminable weeks of living in a cage were suddenly over. I was about to be tried for murder by a jury of locals, if they could find twelve with no preconceived notions about me and my family.

"Oh, I'm not hungry, Timothy. The coffee I drank will stoke my energy no matter how long it goes today."

"Looking flighty and nervous from too much caffeine won't be helping your cause."

"Flighty and nervous?" We both turned to Philomena, who'd stolen into the cell behind Timothy. "He's right. You cannot appear either, especially today, first impressions you know. So eat your breakfast, Kip. Today's opening could drag on longer than you think."

She shook fast-melting snowflakes from the coat she slipped out of and tossed aside as she sat. Fluffing her weather-sodden hair with her fingertips, it fell compliantly into place. Maybe I'd try a pixie haircut like Phil's when I got out.

"It's really coming down out there, Kip. So late in the year, this can't be normal? Perhaps the weather will delay the trial?"

"No such luck," Timothy and I chorused, laughing at the thought.

"Not unless the wind's howling the snow into mountain-size drifts," Timothy observed.

I nodded agreement. "Storms have to really be wicked to halt anything around here."

Even in this cell, insulated from the elements, I could sense winter's unwillingness to let go.

Timothy picked up my breakfast, frowning at the tray. "Leave it for a while, would you?" Phil asked him, and to me, "I brought strong coffee you can wash it down with."

Timothy left the tray and disappeared until he realized he'd left my cell unlocked for the first time since my incarceration. He actually hurried back. As he fumbled with his thick knot of keys, I saw that my opportunity to make a break for it had just blown by like wind-driven snow.

Phil shook the dampness from the hem of her dark suit. Her boots gleamed like new. Suddenly sunny Santa Monica filled my mind, reminding me of all we'd both missed these last months—sunshine dancing on the quicksilver surface of the Pacific, its rays warming my skin, making me squint. I imagined dolphins cavorting in the surf. I sniffed in the must of the sea as my feet sank into the cool sand beneath its hot surface. I opened my eyes not to sand-coated feet but to the thick-heeled, sensible shoes I'd gotten for trial. I wanted to cry.

"This may sound strange, Kip," Phil was saying, waxing childlike, "but it's a beautiful day. The snowflakes are huge and fluffy. Maybe it's the California girl in me, or just the rarity, but they transform the world right before your eyes into a white, glistening, magical, winter wonderland. New York was rarely like this."

"I was about to apologize for dragging you into this—the case, the cold, the endless grays of a dying winter."

"Winter appears to be unaware it's dying. A storm like this in April is rare, isn't it?"

"It's April..." With little to mark the days or seasons, time had stood still for me. Time had stopped for me in February, fittingly my least favorite month.

"Don't apologize for dragging me here, Kip. I've enjoyed Wau-*sau*-kee-sha." She exaggerated the pronunciation.

I chuckled until it was evident she wasn't kidding. "You've enjoyed your *suite* at the Howard Johnson's, the tantalizing array of restaurant choices, the biting cold, the blinding sleet, the mind-numbing days without sunshine?"

"That's really how you see it?"

"I hate February," I cried. "The shortest month of the year was always the grayest and slowest to pass. With holidays long gone, springtime remained unfathomable due to the dirty snow, slushy streets, and monochrome fields and skies."

"But Kip, it's April."

"Right." I'd survived another Wisconsin February, barely aware.

Phil thought about it. "Who knows how I'd feel if I lived this year after year? But I've enjoyed the dramatic seasons in a place where I didn't need a car or a cab, where I knew most faces within a week, those faces smiling and saying hello, if only to cover their curiosity. Here I know the grocer, the laundryman, the drug store clerk, the bank tellers, not to mention the hotel and restaurant people, all by name. I don't know those same people at home where I've lived most of my life."

A contemptuous snort was my only response to that small town lack of privacy. "It cuts two ways, Phil, everyone knowing you and your business. There's something to be said for anonymity."

"But it's not without its charms, that's all I'm saying, Kip. The fact it has snowed so frequently only added to the experience. It's once in a lifetime, and I'm enjoying it."

"Oh sure, as long as you know it's 'once in a lifetime,' most anything is enjoyable, well, almost anything ..."

"... missed the rain and snow," Phil was saying when I tuned back in, "the changing seasons, it was pure humbug, concocted by people who begrudged LA its sunny climate. But you know …"

As determined to cheer and distract me as Timothy before her, Phil nattered on about the enchanting winter weather. No matter how harsh it was, I had to admit it would have been a vast improvement over the monotony of my cell.

Her delight reminded me I hadn't always hated winter. In fact as a kid I had loved Wisconsin's wintry silences when blanketing white absorbed all noise, as if in the magical fairyland each big snowstorm created, sound was unnecessary.

1954

It was just Wausaukeesha. I recognized our street and the houses—I was six after all. But covered in snowy whiteness, everything blurred into a beautiful shiny whole. I'd pretend I was visiting heaven, where everyone said my mother lived.

This heaven was very cold, bright, and silent, so before I could visit, my nanny dressed me in a ton of clothes—snowsuits with zippers, mittens clipped onto the sleeves so I couldn't lose them, wool hats with plaid scarves wrapped around them and tied under my chin, clunky rubber boots with metal fasteners tugged over layers of socks. By the time I got outside, I'd be sweating.

The kids in the neighborhood would come out to play after each snowstorm broke. We made snowmen and snowballs and pelted each other, though not many snowballs hit anyone. We built forts of snow, and castles. We lay in the snow, flapping our legs and arms to create snow-angels. Coated in white from head to toe, we never minded the freezing weather.

But secretly after the other kids went home, I liked being alone in the heaven-world made by each big snowfall. It was like being a ghost, or at least like being the only person left on earth—kind of like not being there at all. No one heard me, and I heard no one. The crunch of my boots packing down new snow reached my ears only, like my breathing heard inside my head. I exhaled clouds that disappeared on clear air as fast as I made them. I wandered my pretend kingdom of my neighborhood, being the first to mark smooth fields of white with my footprints. That felt like being a pioneer in a Western on TV, my lone tracks my claim to new territory, at least until someone stomped over them or the snow thawed.

Short winter days grayed quickly into twilight. Lights flickered on in neighbors' windows, creating a cozy glow from inside as the outside world darkened. I glimpsed tables being set, families gathering around a blazing fire, black-and-white flashes from TV sets, mothers in kitchens preparing dinner. These scenes inspired my favorite alone-time game, making up a story to go with what I saw. There'd be the mother and father drinking cocoa while their child told of the star she earned in school that day. Next door, the kids prepared for their grandparents' holiday stay, after which the youngest would go for a special visit to their house all by herself.

The twilight even more quickly gave way to nightfall. By then, my cheeks, my only exposed patches of skin, felt half-frozen and sluggish. The dropping temperatures froze the inside of my nostrils and sometimes hurt inside my head, like drinking something cold too fast. When the numbness reached the tips of my toes and fingers, it was time to leave my secret kingdom. Trudging home, knowing all my cold parts would soon be tingling and burning as they thawed, I continued to make up stories for the family inside each window:

Once upon a cold winter night, a family gathered together for a meal, and the mommy said to her youngest—

❧◦❧◦❧◦❧

"Don't cry, Kip. You'll be fine."

Phil pressed her hankie into my hand before I realized I needed it. I was crying over an innocent childhood game of … imagine a family.

"Be certain to acknowledge each of them—your sisters and father. And remember everything we discussed. Regardless of what is said in that courtroom, show no emotion." Phil wiped a tear from my cheek. "Control your reactions. Jot notes. That in itself should defuse them."

She rose slowly, hesitant to leave me undone. "I must go. I'm meeting William before court. Just remember we're behind you, Kip, both of us. Try not to worry."

"You're starting to scare me. Just go."

Phil assessed my mental state while bundling into her outerwear. "*We'll be fine.*" She bent down and surprised me with a kiss on the cheek. "As you've said all along, the sooner we get started, the sooner it's over and you're out of here." Phil trilled the iron bars for my jailer. "Chin up," were her last words before the jailhouse swallowed all traces of her—her quick footsteps, her spring-flower scent.

I hadn't moved when she reappeared. "Samantha brought everything we discussed? Sober pantsuit, comfy shoes?"

I extended the shoes I'd been breaking in beneath my powder-blue pants. Her failing to notice them was a good omen. "Modest white blouse, yes yes, don't worry. I'll look like a Youth-for-Nixon in court." And fool no one, I thought, not in this town. How stupid of me not to consider a change of venue. The hell with Sybel and her pregnancy and my right to a speedy trial if all it wins me is life imprisonment. Too late for second guesses now.

"… Kip. Ki-ip?" Phil, peering at me through the bars, called me back from my reveries. "None of your escapist daydreaming in the courtroom. I need you paying close attention while demonstrating your concern and seriousness. Remember to control your reactions. And Kip, eat your breakfast."

Chapter Forty-Two

Timothy's presence in the paddy wagon made my second journey to the courthouse more bearable. He insisted I be allowed to make the trip without handcuffs, agreeing to slap them on prior to my transfer from van to holding pen, aka the green room. Protocol actually required handcuffs from cell all the way to the defense table, but William picked up where Timothy left off, petitioning for and securing my hands-free entry into the courtroom.

This in Wausaukeesha, Wisconsin? I had squelched my amusement at these heated cuffing debates. *You mean to tell me, with no other prison inmates, no female prison uniforms, you guys are not making this up as you go along? There's been a murder trial in Wausaukeesha before?* Actually, that last I should have checked out.

Timothy kept up a running monologue of inanities to divert my sense of impending doom. We were ready, Philomena and William had reassured me, but *were* we? What did we have, really, outside freakish momentary amnesia on my part and humiliating circumstantial evidence? Still, as Phil so often stated, the evidence was *all* circumstantial, and she felt an accident interpretation was equally, if not more, believable.

"Reasonable doubt, Kip," she said repeatedly. "All the defense must establish is reasonable doubt. We need only one juror to doubt your guilt."

Timothy repeating my name made me aware the police van had stopped. He was telling me he'd have to cuff me since we'd arrived at the courthouse. So soon? I stood, obediently offering my hands behind me when he told me to put the hankie away first. Oh, I'd forgotten about Phil's hankie still clutched in my fist. As a pocket square in my breast pocket, it could be handy in court, not that my well-controlled reactions would give rise to its need. Shaking out the squished wad, I discovered monogrammed initials on plain white linen: PBH. Philomena Benedetti H. *H?*

I stuffed the hankie in my pocket and my jailer cuffed me, then helped me down the awkward step and steered me toward the entrance, obscured by huge snowflakes swirling in the air.

Winter was demonstrating its determination this year. Snow immediately accumulated on me. Phil might get her wish today. The transformative snow she so admired might well evolve into a trial-stopping storm. White out. A jarring surf tune screamed in my head as I was shepherded forward, seeking my footing. Not white out, "Wipe Out."

Chapter Forty-Three

The green room's tarnished mirror reflected the obvious: I needed a haircut. My frizzy locks, abetted by melting snow, had grown into absolute anarchy during my jail stint. Unused to inmates, particularly long-term ones of the female persuasion, my jailers offered the services of the local barber, who visited on Mondays when there were prisoners. Rather than risk my recalcitrant locks to the hands of a barber, I would face the court with an earth-mother look. Granny glasses would have been a nice addition.

Still, a good impression on judge and jury was critical, so several barrettes nearly dominated my dark whorls. To counter my jailhouse pallor, I'd applied the blush-on and lipstick Phil bought, compensating further with ultra-conservative dress. Buttoning my white blouse at the collar brought Katey Rudeshiem Beneke to mind. Sister Margaret would at last approve of me—well, my uniform anyway. My old overcoat from college, still emitting a mothball odor, wouldn't be seen beyond the green room, but I vowed I'd splurge on a winter coat as soon as I got out, even if I did live in Southern California. Should I now say, "lived?"

When the bailiff appeared to usher me from the green room to the courtroom, William accompanied him. William helped me to my feet with a reassuring smile. Timothy squeezed my shoulder as I was led away, saying, "Be right here, waitin' for you." Damned if that didn't make my throat seize shut.

William and I preceded the courthouse official down the long hallway leading inexorably to my fate. In his serious case-before-the-court gray suit from my arraignment, the same patriotic tie with diamond tie tack, William gave me one last encouraging nod before striding in ahead of me to the defense table.

We'd rehearsed this a thousand times. Following him in, I was to look "soberly" at the people in the audience I knew, nodding acknowledgement and making eye contact but without smiling. Phil had stressed this, my first act upon leaving the green room. In which year of law school, I wondered, did they teach the importance of being theatrical?

The buzzing from the crowded spectators fizzled as my presence was detected by the courtroom, escorted by the bailiff but cuff-free. I acknowledged those I knew but flinched when my eyes fell on Dad. I hoped my lawyers hadn't seen that. As Samantha had described, Dad looked as if he might not survive my trial. I began to believe Samantha, who said Dad had been too distraught to come to the jail after the few brief visits he'd made early on. She never offered an excuse for Sybel's absence.

In the two months I'd been jailed, Dad had shrunken into an old man. His tight curls glowed all salt under the lights, no pepper. His ruddy skin color had paled. Like his jacket and gaping shirt collar, his skin hung loose on his frame, Green Bay Packer mien diminished to frailty. I forced myself to sit, wondering if this experience had aged me as obviously. The green room mirror had suggested an answer: "probably."

But it was almost over. The thought occupied me, sitting beside William, Phil beside him on the aisle, both busily moving papers around.

I'd been warned the prosecution would fill the first days of trial, making its case against me, establishing the motive of jealousy while frequently alluding to my trouble-prone, violent history as evidenced by my police record. No matter how they smeared it, I was to listen with no visible reactions. This acting job could prove too much for me, a mere novice.

I was dying to check out my sisters, sitting directly behind me, as Dad had so absorbed my attention when I entered, but it was "inadvisable" to crane my neck to examine the spectators, so I perused the jurors before me instead. The one nearest me in particular scrutinized me in return. Perhaps the youngest of the bunch—fortyish, she was, as they say, pleasingly plump and motherly with dull hair and a worn housedress, but it was her eyes that held my attention. Light, intelligence, maybe some sympathy, shined there. Of the seven other women on the jury, she was the only one overtly curious about me.

The four men seated in the second row looked to be both town folk and farmers. The handsomest juror whose head towered above the rest with a tie on his plaid work shirt beneath a rumpled corduroy jacket appeared to be no stranger to fieldwork. His white-gray hair shining under the lights added a regal touch and nicely set off his tanned-leather skin.

William passed a note from Phil to me that read, "Don't stare down the jurors. It could be construed as challenging."

Geez! Look around, don't look around. Make eye contact, don't make eye contact. What's a girl to do? Imagine what I'll do when I get out of here. That sounded benign. I'd decided to take my time returning to California and my post at the center, if still available to me. Truthfully, I questioned whether advising unliberated women was right for me, advising anyone in fact. I would decide while driving cross-country through the Badlands, Death Valley, and other inspiring sights before settling down in Santa Monica with my black cat. Oh, Malcolm ... Will he even recognize me, let alone want to live with me again after all this time with Cece?

The smell of a Wisconsin winter seeped into my awareness as I wriggled in my seat with no safe place to rest my eyes. Stealing just a glance at the full house, I breathed in the scents of evaporating dampness, wet wool in forced-air heating, a hint of mothball mixed in. The familiar smells were a relief after the stagnant air of my cell.

All stirring ceased when the black-frocked judge was announced with "All Rise, Judge Ernest Fassbinder presiding. Be seated." Loose material swished around him as he took his seat behind the raised pulpit and from his high altar, banged my trial into session with his gavel.

"I don't get the arraignment judge," I whispered to William, "the young one with the long hair and sideburns?" Who might have better related to my activism.

"No no, he's far too young and inexperienced for murder," William whispered back.

Not much older than you, William, I thought. Only the big guns come out for murder.

I observed the judge, who along with the jury held my future in his hands as he consulted with courtroom officials. His bald pate gleamed under the overhead lighting. That halo effect should have been planned. He was a small man with quick moves. His gaze darted around the room and its occupants while in conference. But with his glasses reflecting light, his eyes could not be read. At last he folded his small, manicured hands and looked out from the one-way-mirrors of his lenses.

"Clerk, in the case of the State of Wisconsin versus Miss Kip Czermanski, you may swear in the jurors."

After their swearing in, the judge instructed the jury. "We will now hear opening statements. Jurors, bear in mind these statements are not evidence, merely what each side expects the evidence will prove. Prosecution, you may begin."

I drew in a deep breath as the Wausaukeesha County Prosecutor, Harvey Debick, assumed center stage of the courtroom. Beneath his peach-fuzzy skull, his pale blue eyes swept over my family behind me and paused on me. He straightened his dark suit and tie, seeming to gather himself before a storm.

"Thank you, Your Honor. Good morning, ladies and gentlemen of the jury. It's a good omen that the unseasonable snowstorm prevented no one from arriving this morning at the appointed hour. Now then—" A tone change signaled the end of pleasantries. "—the prosecution's case will prove to you beyond reasonable doubt that Miss Kip Czermanski, seated before you, murdered her brother-in-law in the early hours of Sunday morning, the thirteenth of February of this year. Not only that, we will prove the premeditation of the crime by this young woman." He paused for all eyes to bore into me.

"On the very night the Czermanski family gathered to bury and mourn the defendant's eldest sister, whose early demise occurred but a few days earlier, the defendant brazenly lured to her bed her brother-in-law, Dr. Stanislaw Szyzyck, who was married to her eldest surviving sister, Sybel. The crime of premeditated murder was committed in the defendant's bed in the family home with the defendant's entire family—including the victim's wife, the defendant's own sister—in residence.

"We will prove beyond doubt that the long smoldering rage toward her brother-in-law, who had tossed her aside to marry her sister, Sybel, resulted in Kip Czermanski bludgeoning Dr. Stanislaw Szyzyck to death, after seducing him."

His repeated emphasis on "brother" and "sister" stressed the heinous nature of the crime. I took another deep breath as William's glance warned me: *It's only the beginning.*

Standing before me for effect, the prosecutor continued, "Jurors will hear directly from the arresting police officer summoned to One Moraine Drive, the Czermanski household, early Sunday morning by a call to the police from the household, which had stated that Dr. Szyzyck, and I quote, 'may be dead.' The coroner will testify that Dr. Szyzyck died in the early hours of Sunday morning due to a massive hemorrhage caused by a blunt instrument strike to his head."

The prosecutor stared me down. "Where Dr. Szyzyck died is undisputed—in the defendant's, Miss Kip Czermanski's, bedroom, in her bed. This cold-blooded and audacious crime was all the more reprehensible coming on the heels of the family funeral that had reunited the family. That particular night provided the defendant her first opportunity for revenge, as it was the first time in years the entire family had slept under one roof. All due to the untimely passing of the eldest of the four Czermanski sisters, Sister Sarah Joseph, a nun."

I struggled to swallow a lump in my throat without being obvious.

"Miss Czermanski cannot deny a very public, sexual affair with her deceased brother-in-law throughout her years at UW Madison. Nor can she deny her equally public devastation when Dr. Szyzyck dropped her and left Madison." He swung around to me as if daring me to do so. "What would drive someone to commit so scandalous a crime at such a disrespectful time? Alas, Miss Czermanski, the beguiling young woman seated before you, has a history in Wausaukeesha, as the prosecution case will painstakingly demonstrate, for being a troublemaker and a constant challenge to her family and our community. Yet her troublesome youth proved a mere precursor to her lengthy criminal record earned during her college years.

"Jurors, I ask in advance for your forbearance as our case systematically develops the evolution of violence in the defendant's character that would eventually lead to the murder of Dr. Szyzyck. Upon completion of our case, I assure you there will be no doubt in your minds."

The prosecutor ambled back to his table in a sudden hush. He kept his voice low, saying, "When you've heard the testimony and examined the evidence, you will come to the unavoidable conclusion that Miss Kip Czermanski murdered Dr. Stanislaw Szyzyck with premeditation. And given that finding, men and women of the jury, the law of our state is clear. The crime of murder in the first degree must be punished by life imprisonment with no possibility of parole."

CHAPTER FORTY-FOUR

Judge Fassbinder banged his gavel, ending a stunned silence. "Defense," he directed, "proceed with your opening."

"Your Honor," said Phil, rising to stand before the jury box, "jurors, please forgive my scratchy voice today. I'm nursing a sore throat. The dramatic shifts in your weather have proven too much for me, a nonnative." The titters throughout the courtroom gave me a moment to admire Phil, not just for her chic, feminine, but professional appearance, but also for confronting head-on her being a suspicious outsider while acknowledging the heartier natives.

Phil's smile faded as she looked the jurors in the eye. "Stan Szyzyck died early that Sunday morning in February of a lethal blow to the head caused by a freak accident. According to the evidence gathered by the police at the scene, a very large and heavy vase toppled, striking the victim on the head and, most unfortunately, killing him. The shards that were scattered across the floor weighed in at over thirty pounds—without the water and flowers it had held. Consistent with the county coroner's findings, the vase striking the most vulnerable spot of the decedent's head induced the hemorrhage that took his life."

Phil seemed to speak directly to each juror as they examined her in return. She looked relaxed and at home in the courtroom, despite the spectacle a female lawyer created on both sides of the bar. You could hear a pin drop. A blouse in the color she favored above all others, a blue-green called celadon, alleviated the severity of her lawyerly black suit. The heels of her black boots made her more imposing while the pixie haircut and compassionate brown eyes softened her.

"This is a trial of maximum gravity," she said, her voice rasping, "I hardly need to remind you. A young woman's freedom—for the remainder of her young life—hangs in the balance of what you hear, see, and ultimately decide together unanimously." Phil cleared her throat. "The prosecutor has told you what he intends to prove in this courtroom, and prove it he must beyond any reasonable doubt in each and every one of your minds. In the civilized state of Wisconsin, the defendant is innocent until proven guilty—beyond reasonable doubt. Keep in mind the prosecution bears the burden of that level of proof."

She walked toward me, but turned back to the jury to speak. "Can the prosecutor *prove* why Stanislaw Szyzyck ended his relationship with Kip Czermanski three years ago? Remember, the prosecution admitted in its opening statement that their affair ended in college. Can the prosecutor *prove* why the deceased mysteriously turned up in Wausaukeesha," she pronounced it flawlessly, "mere months later during the summer of 1969, unbeknownst to the defendant? Can anyone tell us why the man my client thought was dead after his unexplained disappearance came to both work for her father and marry her sister, all unbeknownst to my client?

"Even under the best of circumstances when hearing directly from all the involved parties, could anyone prove such matters conclusively?" She veered toward the prosecutor to add, "I for one doubt it." Phil coughed and swallowed. I hadn't even realized she was sick until she'd mentioned it.

"The circumstantial evidence the prosecution will present could perhaps be interpreted as he's chosen. That same evidence, however, also implies the unfortunate but accidental death of Stan Szyzyck, as we are confident you'll find. That and nothing else is what you have to decide, based upon the case presented to you. Not whether you agree or disagree with my client's politics, her mode of living, or even whether you question the propriety of the situation that the prosecutor has pre-labeled for you as 'reprehensible.' I know you'll refrain from passing such judgments until you've heard all the witnesses and all the evidence. I'm confident your deliberations, reflecting that fairness and open-mindedness, will result in true justice."

Phil crossed back to the jury box and stopped before the housewife I'd noticed earlier. "Did Stan Szyzyck die at the hands of the young woman you see seated before you? Did she carefully premeditate, then carry out, his murder, choosing to do so with her entire family mere steps away? Or is it just as likely, if not more so, that he died in a gruesome accident?

"Defense will show the actual evidence irrefutably exonerates Kip Czermanski of murder, premeditated or otherwise. Our case will prove the defendant, an activist and *pacifist*, was, in fact, fighting off an unwanted attack by her brother-in-law. In so doing, the enormous vase of flowers placed bedside following her sister's funeral was upended. The vase that struck and killed Stan Szyzyck barely missed the defendant herself. Not only will you find the defendant innocent of crime, you'll find her a crime victim."

Phil came to a standstill before me and surveyed the jurors one by one. "Ladies and gentlemen of the jury, you must decide: Was this premeditated murder or the accidental death of a man who was in fact attempting rape?

The word 'rape' hung in the air as Phil took her seat beside William. Seemed like a good start to me.

CHAPTER FORTY-FIVE

During a five-minute recess the judge made copious notes, then restored order in the court by directing Prosecutor Debick to call his first witness. Debick charged to the fore, eager to debunk every word spoken on my behalf.

"Prosecution calls Wausaukeesha Police Officer Douglas Rankin." The ridiculously young policeman with the baby face who'd arrested me lurched forward. His nonstop blushing, in sharp contrast to his dark uniform as he ascended the witness box, made his oath, and seated himself, only emphasized his youthfulness. With cop-hat in hand, a cowlick was evident.

As if it hadn't already been established, Debick's first question to the gangly witness was: "Please tell the court your name and occupation," which he repeated. The prosecutor then walked him through his involvement the night Stan died, from the call he'd received in his squad car to his arrival at the house, being escorted to my room in the back on the ground floor where the family was gathered, to his examination of the injured man in the bed.

"Did you observe any evidence of sexual activity at the scene?" asked the prosecutor.

The officer's blush deepened still more. "Yes, sir. The, well, the victim was buck-na—uh, was naked, lying on his back, the lower half of his body under the sheets. But, well, beneath the covers one could see, that is detect, his, um, an erection."

With the witness coloring furiously, Debick allowed that to sink in before leading the witness through his phoning in his findings, ordering an ambulance, and questioning us one by one before taking me along in the squad car for further questioning at the station.

"What caused you to suspect Kip Czermanski, after questioning the entire family? In fact, you eventually arrested her on suspicion of murder, did you not?"

"Yes, sir. Well, all the other family members corroborated each other's alibis. Only Kip Czermanski was unaccounted for during the critical time period, and she couldn't remember too much."

"She couldn't explain her brother-in-law, dead in her bed?"

"No. She acted confused or stunned, maybe in shock."

"Or she wouldn't explain?"

"Objection," shouted Phil.

"Sustained."

"Your witness," Debick said, taking his seat as William rose from the defense table. The prosecutor and I did a double take when William, not Phil, approached the witness for questioning.

William had lost weight. He still tugged at his collar, but it no longer puckered the skin of his neck. We'd all been through a lot, and as he himself reminded me, it was only the beginning.

"Officer Rankin," he began, "you testified that the defendant acted confused. Did you mean 'acted' in the sense she might be obfuscating the truth?" William's voice sounded strained with nervousness.

Policeman Rankin looked perplexed. "Umm, what?"

William glanced at Phil, reddening slightly. He turned back to the witness in a way that included the jury. "Pardon me. I meant, did you think the defendant might be lying to you when she said she couldn't remember what happened?"

"I didn't think that, no. She was kind of out of it, confused, like I said."

"So she did not appear to be intentionally vague or perhaps hostile. In other words, the defendant was cooperating to the best of her abilities—"

"Objection, Your Honor," shouted Debick. "Counsel is leading the witness."

"Sustained," the judge pronounced. His glasses flared under the lights as his gaze traveled the room.

William walked to our table to look at his notes, seeming to need a moment. "Now, Officer Rankin," he continued, "you testified that the other occupants of the Czermanski household corroborated each other's alibis."

"Yes, sir. The defendant's two sisters and father all met up in the hallway upstairs after hearing a loud crash. They came downstairs to the defendant's room together, where they—"

"What caused that crash?"

"They all assumed, even the defendant herself, that the vase had toppled on the decedent in the bed, then rolled off and crashed to the floor, where it broke to pieces."

"All occupants of the household that night said the crashing vase awakened them?"

"Except for the defendant, yes, each told that story separately. That's what I meant by corroborate."

Was that tit-for-tat—corroborate for obfuscate? William seemed to be thinking the same thing. He narrowed his eyes at the witness before saying, "All the Czermanskis at the scene believed the vase fell on the victim, then onto the floor where it splintered. In other words, they *corroborated* the accidental death of Stan Szyzyck?"

"Objection. Counsel is asking the witness to speculate as to conclusions—"

"Sustained. Don't answer that, Officer."

"That will be all," William said, returning to his seat beside me. I saw Phil's almost imperceptible nod of approval for William's first performance of the trial, which was apparently helping her save her voice.

The prosecutor immediately called to the stand the Wausaukeesha County coroner. The girth of the man required him to squeeze his bulk into the witness chair, where he caught his breath after the exertion of his brief journey. After the swearing in, the prosecutor proceeded to plod through the duties tying him to the case—the receipt of the body after it had been pronounced dead at the emergency room and delivered to the county morgue, his subsequent autopsy findings. With a large handkerchief, the coroner mopped his face and the mounds of his neck, very ill at ease. Perhaps the tight fit of the chair? Only when he faced me directly did I realize the coroner was a young man, probably William's age.

"… yes, I found a head wound in the right temple area," he was saying. "No, by the time I examined the body, there was no evidence of the deceased's arousal, which of course could be explained by loss of blood over time. My full laboratory exam of the deceased determined the cause of death to be a brain hemorrhage induced by a blow to the temple with a blunt instrument."

Prosecutor Debick moved closer. "You've heard testimony describing a flower vase weighing thirty pounds that had shattered at the scene. In your expert opinion, after examining the head wound, could such a vase cause such a wound?"

"It's possible I suppose. A solid rap precisely placed with a heavy object could inflict a death blow."

"Precisely positioned, you say?" Debick repeated.

"Yes, the vulnerable area at the temple increased the chances the blow would bring death, beyond unconsciousness and/or concussion."

"But given the smallness of the vulnerable area, is it likely that a tumbling vase could land with such accuracy?"

"Objection," William shouted. "Leading and speculative."

Judge Fassbinder responded, "I'll allow it. The coroner is a witness with expertise on this subject. Please answer the question."

The coroner mopped his neck-rolls as his head shifted back and forth on top of them from judge to lawyer. "As I said before, it's possible but perhaps improbable that a freefalling vase would land just so on the vulnerable area."

"Improbable," Debick repeated, returning to his seat. "Yes, improbable. Your witness."

Again William assumed control. I couldn't catch Phil's eye to see why.

"Let me see if I understood your testimony," William began. "The wound you examined was dealt by a blunt instrument, which led to hemorrhaging in the brain, which you determined as the cause of death?"

"Yes."

"And the vase shattered on the floor of Miss Czermanski's bedroom—which in prior testimony was described as 'large and heavy'—this vase, which awakened the entire sleeping household when it crashed on the floor, it could, indeed, deliver such a blow?"

Mop, mop, pause. "Yes. Yes, it is possible."

"That's what I thought you said. Thank you. You're dismissed."

The bang of the judge's gavel startled everyone. "One hour lunch recess." Before he disappeared through a door behind him, the bailiff appeared to escort me to the green room.

I'd hardly finished arguing with Timothy about what I hadn't eaten of my lunch when the same man returned to take me back into court. He deposited me at the defense table, where I leaned in to ask my lawyers why William was doing everything. But the bailiff shouted for all to rise for the judge's return. I never got an answer.

"Prosecution calls Dr. Steven Millen."

Old Dr. Millen had been treating most of Wausaukeesha most of my life. I remembered the lollipops he administered after giving me a shot or taking my blood or sneaking some disgusting medication down my throat. Those lollipops really did make it better. His cherubic face hadn't changed much in two decades, though his hair, including the thick brows raining over the heavy frames of his spectacles, had gone white.

The prosecutor greeted Dr. Millen congenially. The doctor's smile made him look like St. Nick. When he answered the prosecution's question about his involvement in my case, he spoke so quietly, the whole courtroom strained forward.

"I examined Miss Czermanski late the evening of February 15th at your request, the county prosecutor's that is. I do this kind of work when called upon. 'Course, I've known Kip her whole life."

"Fine, Doctor. What did your medical examination disclose about Miss Czermanski?"

"I found no evidence of a foreign substance in her bloodstream."

"No alcohol, no drugs—nothing that would explain her amnesia of that time period? Okay. Was there any indication Miss Czermanski had been raped?"

"No. There were no contusions, broken skin, inflammation. No such signs."

"You're telling us that the defendant was not raped, inebriated, or drugged?"

"That's my medical assessment, Harvey."

"Thank you, Doctor."

Casting a smirk my way, Prosecutor Debick took his seat and William approached the witness box. "Dr. Millen, when was your examination of my client conducted?"

"Let's see, it was lined up for Tuesday morning, as I remember it, by Harvey. No, Wally called right after the arraignment hearing. I can tell you I was shocked to hear a Czermanski had been arrested and was being held for—"

"The Assistant DA called to arrange for the defendant to be medically examined the morning after her arraignment, and?"

"Oh, and I had an emergency that morning. I had to delay Kip's exam until Tuesday evening."

"How many hours after the fact was it? Let's see, two and a half days is sixty hours?"

"Yes, thereabouts."

"What did the Assistant DA tell you he was looking for?"

"He wanted inspection for sexual activity, and he asked for a blood analysis for alcohol or drugs."

"Is that even logical, Doctor," William posited, "given the time elapsed? You examined my client Tuesday evening. Her arrest occurred around three a.m. the previous Sunday morning."

"As far as detectability of most foreign substances in the bloodstream goes, it didn't make much sense sixty hours after the fact."

"Did the DA's office request you look for any specific drug?"

"No, William."

William pivoted toward the jury. "But the fact is, it wouldn't have mattered anyways, even if the prosecution had thought to specify. The fact is too much time had elapsed before the defendant's medical examination."

"For alcohol and many drugs, yes indeed," chimed in Dr. Millen.

William thanked him and told him he could step down.

"Prosecution requests redirect, Your Honor," Debick said, rushing forward. "Dr. Millen, let's be certain we all get our facts straight. Could a lapse of approximately sixty hours also affect the indicators you mentioned of rape? Let's see—" He glanced at his notes. "—'contusions, broken skin, inflammation.'"

Dr. Millen swiped a bushy eyebrow. "Even for a fast healer, there would still be detectable signs two or three days later."

"So, you stand by your previous assessment. The defendant was not raped?"

"Yes, I stand by that, Harv. Kip wasn't raped."

CHAPTER FORTY-SIX

"Prosecution calls Mr. Hubert Krousy."

Our next-door neighbor, Mr. Krousy, eased into the witness chair in the clothes he'd worn his whole life: graying sweater buttoned over a faded Pendleton shirt. I could almost smell the cherry-scented tobacco from his ubiquitous pipe, now a bulge in his back pocket. His answers to the prosecution's initial questions which established his connection to my case mirrored the deliberateness of his movements.

"Yes, I've known Kip since before she was born." He chuckled at that statement, bobbing the thinly covered scalp that also hadn't changed in my lifetime. "I've known all the Czermanski girls. They lived next door since Sarah, the oldest, was just a tot. Still see the comings and goings at the Czermanskis just about every day, living just across our joined driveways."

The prosecutor encouraged this witness to expound. "Kip was friends with my youngest, Lanny. They were close in age, a few years between them's all. They dated once or twice, nothing serious to it ... Yes, I seem to remember some brouhaha over a high school dance they went to, way back when."

I bolted forward in my seat, seeking Phil's attention but failing to get it. The prosecutor wasn't really going to dredge up that humiliating dance—

"Were you aware, Mr. Krousy—" Debick moved in, careful not to block the jurors' view of the witness. "—that your son's date for St. Hedwig's senior dance, defendant Kip Czermanski, was observed on the dance floor at the bottom of a pile of dancers?"

"I 'member hearing something about—"

"Did you also hear that when she emerged from the floor, it was in nothing but her underwear?"

"I heard there was some kind—"

"Yes or no, Mr. Krousy?"

William objected, "Your Honor, relevance?"

Debick responded, "As stated in our opening, prosecution intends to demonstrate the evolution of the defendant's character, Your Honor. Given the natural inclination to be lenient with a young woman, it is essential that the steady progression of her violent, trouble-prone nature be seen for what it's come to—a true threat to society."

Now Phil was on her feet. "Sidebar, Your Honor?"

My two lawyers and Prosecutor Debick along with Wally Werner, Assistant DA, collected on one side of the judge's bench. I'd wondered whatever happened to Wally. Imagine, "weird Wally" a lawyer. When they returned to their respective tables, I thought my side looked most unhappy. Judge Fassbinder directed the prosecution to continue.

"Mr. Krousy, as a lifelong neighbor of the Czermanskis, would you say such incidents characterized Kip Czermanski throughout the years you observed her from right next door?"

"Objection!" both Phil and William protested. "Leading, speculative, and irrelevant."

"Withdraw," said the prosecutor. "Mr. Krousy, were you aware that the defendant was ejected from the Immaculate Conception Catholic Elementary School for violence on the playground, resulting in another student's injury?"

"Of course I knew all about it, Harvey. It's a small town, I don't need to tell you."

Debick reared back at his familiarity. "*Mr.* Krousy, would it then be fair to surmise that such incidents were not uncommon for the defendant from a very early age?"

"Troubles in school?"

"Objection, Your Honor."

"I suppose trouble seemed to find her more'n most."

"Yes indeed, 'more than most.'" Debick repeated.

"Your Honor, objection."

"But she was a nice kid at heart. A little troubled maybe."

William tried to object a third time, to which Debick responded to the judge, "I withdraw the question, Your Honor," and sat down, relinquishing the witness to the defense.

William weighed something as he slowly moved toward the witness. "Mr. Krousy, as the Czermanskis' next-door neighbor, you testified to seeing the 'comings and goings' of the Czermanski household. Given your proximity, the fact that your driveways are contiguous, did you see or hear anything unusual the night of Sarah's funeral?"

"Nope, nothin' unusual. Couple cars in the drive all night, but we know why they were there."

"The cars you noticed in the Czermanski driveway all night, did you know whose cars they were?"

"Well, let's see, Samantha drives the green Olds and Sybel drives some black foreign car, a Mercedes I think it's called. Stan drove a red Corvette—yep, it was there too. And … yes, Raymond's Cadillac, the white one, was there, too. JJ parks in the garage so his new Cadillac wasn't out. That's it."

"Just one more question, Mr. Krousy," William said, demonstrating more self-assurance with each moment before the court. "You labeled my client 'a nice kid,' just 'a little troubled.' Why?"

Mr. Krousy kept his eyes on me as he said, "'Cause Kip … she never knew her mother. That was hard on her, hard on 'em all." Making to elaborate, Mr. Krousy opened his mouth several times, then changed his mind. William encouraged him to continue, but Mr. Krousy clammed up. He was thanked and dismissed.

"Prosecution calls Mr. Horton Charmers."

"Who?" I leaned over William's list. My lawyers pointed to the name on the witness roster, the principal of Wausaukeesha High School, though not when I attended. Now this man's predecessor—I'd known him rather well.

Principal Charmers, in a rust-brown suit of a stretchy material that bubbled at the knees and elbows, scurried to the witness box. A tiny man with delicate features and startled eyes peered about from a whippet-thin face. The principal pledged to tell the truth and alit on the edge of the witness chair. His whole body appeared to tremble as he patted down his slicked-to-the-skull hair, first with one palm, then the other. After stating his name and occupation, the prosecutor handed a file to Principal Charmers for his identification. I imagined the hair grease he'd leave on it.

"This file contains the high school records for one Kip Czermanski," the principal squeaked as if his voice hadn't yet changed, "a student at Wausau-keesha High School from ninth through twelfth grades, ending upon her graduation in June 1966. Yes yes, I'll read from the record. Expelled once for smoking in the men's room with …"

Leaning toward William, I clarified, "I wasn't smoking—"

William ignored me. "Your Honor, we object to these continuing, outrageous irrelevancies."

"Is there a point, Mr. Debick?"

"Establishing the defendant's long-standing discipline problems from the points of view of the community, as well as an educational expert, provides essential insight into her character development," Debick argued.

Judge Fassbinder made a curt nod, an exasperated I'll-allow-it-but-get-on-with-it, which for an instant doused the gleaming reflections shielding his eyes. Somber gray eyes stared out. "Summarize for the court, Mr. Charmers, Miss Czermanski's disciplinary offenses, their nature, and the punishments administered."

Mr. Charmers set the file aside. "Kip Czermanski," he began, glancing at me, "was notated on the DWL, the Disciplinary Watch List, from her first year, the ninth grade, on. In the vernacular, she was a troublemaker. In total, she was expelled from Wausaukeesha High eight times, mostly in her last two years, for everything from this incident, smoking in the men's room with a number of young boys, to cheating on her Latin final."

"Cheating? I gave my answers to the guy next to me who was flunking out of school." Phil's circumspect glare, fraught with meaning, silenced me.

The principal added, "She was truant any number of times and caught forging excuse notes from her father."

Before defense could again object, the judge stemmed the chuckles this testimony produced by directing the prosecution to make a point or release the witness. For the first time, Judge Fassbinder showed a favorable reaction: irritation with the prosecutor.

"As a professional in the field of education, Principal Charmers," Debick laid it on, "what do these records suggest to you about the defendant?"

"She consistently ranked among the highest disciplinary problems for the school." The witness sighed. "With each passing year, she grew more defiant."

"A troublemaker… Each passing year, more defiant," Debick repeated. "Thank you, Principal Charmers." He turned to Phil. "Your witness, Miss Benedetti."

Was it naïve on my part to wonder how such witnesses could be worth taxpayers' dollars? I relaxed with the prosecutor's overreach. If all Harvey Debick could stir up against me was a broken zipper and truancy, I'd be heading for California within the week.

Instead of Phil, William exaggerated the production of getting around to cross-examining a witness we hardly took seriously by lining up pencils and papers, stacking files, sighing, and pushing back his chair. William reluctantly rose and after a pause for effect that had the witness trembling harder, William asked Mr. Charmers how long he'd been the principal of Wausaukeesha High School.

"Oh, so you came to the school *after* Ms. Czermanski had graduated and gone on to university. You don't know her personally then, only from papers in a forgotten file?" William stopped in front of the jury box. "So what else have you learned about my client from that file you're holding?" When the witness didn't bite, William asked, "Does it also reveal classes taken and academic scores, Mr. Charmers? It does, good. Then could you tell us Ms. Czermanski's grade average and standing."

"Objection, Your Honor," said the prosecutor. "Academic scores are not relevant—"

Phil stood and William pivoted, but the judge ruled before they could counter. "Overruled. You introduced the high school record, prosecutor." Debick slid onto his seat.

"Grades," said Mr. Charmers, but for this, the principal had to fish through the file. "Yes, here. She finished high school with a low A average."

"An A average for four years of high school?"

"A *low* A average."

"Thank you, Mr. Charmers. In what percentile of the student body would that put my client? Upper ten percent, upper five?"

"Upper five is close. Of course, she would have been in the top one or two percentiles if she hadn't flunked gym repeatedly for unexcused absences."

"Gym?"

"Physical education," the principal corrected himself.

William turned to glare at me with a sternness that elicited giggles from the gallery, even the jury. "Are most of your discipline problems, your 'troublemakers,' such excellent students, Mr. Charmers?"

"No," the diminutive man admitted sadly, "not commonly."

Eyeing me with mock disgust, William returned to the table, took his seat, and only then thought to excuse the principal who scurried passed us, eyes straight ahead. My lawyers and I stifled our smiles. The witnesses so far gave us all a boost of confidence. Even in my hometown, summarizing my attendance records in high school was an impossible leap to premeditated murder. Right?

CHAPTER FORTY-SEVEN

Samantha had told me my closest friend through the years, Amy Gruden, had been subpoenaed from Minneapolis to my trial, and was the next witness the prosecution called. Even my sisters and father were on the prosecution's witness roster, a fact Phil discounted as an obvious bluff. She didn't totally get Wausaukeesha or my family if she believed my dad and siblings were a gamble for the prosecution. They might not overtly testify against me, but in true Czermanski style, they'd let me look bad. When I'd insisted none of them be called for the defense, Phil's exasperation had exploded, but I knew them and hung tough. Still, Debick would probably give them the opportunity to skewer me by putting them on the stand.

Amy sauntered from the back of the courtroom in a tight white mohair sweater that revealed her lack of curves. Her polyester bellbottoms approximated the color of a ripe banana. She sat on the stand, twining clumps of her straight black hair around her finger, a lifelong habit similar to Samantha's except Amy didn't yank them out. How little she'd changed since our Immaculate Conception days, except for the mod clothing. Amy's ready smile and brown-eyed innocence had always fooled the adults. Behind the innocence that so reassured them, Amy always knew what was going on long before the rest of us Catholic school kids got it—like the intricacies of sex she'd observed in her poodles.

Debick established that Amy and I had been friends since morning kindergarten at four years of age. "And you two have remained friends, Miss Gruden?"

"Of course. Even after Kip started at Kosciusko, the public grade school, we stayed best friends. I don't see much of her since she moved to California, but we talk on the phone a lot. I'm going out to visit her this summer." That statement gave Amy pause. "Anyways, she was my roomie at Madison our senior year, so we've known each other for, like, forever."

"Was Miss Czermanski a good student at the university?"

"Are you kidding? Kip was a great student. She aced anything that interested her. She tutored me in psychology, which I totally, like, never got at all. We weren't alike really, not much, especially in that way. I was into partying and boys and beer, even if it was only that watered down three-two we could get until we hit twenty-one."

She giggled at that slip before hurrying on. "And you know, like Kip was into issues and causes and serious stuff like that. She studied and marched for one thing and another. She was passionate about the war and blacks' and women's rights and … you know, that kind of thing."

Harvey Debick straightened his tie as he leaned against the jury box, facing Amy. "Would you call Miss Czermanski a good roommate your senior year?"

"Oh, the best. She paid half the rent and was hardly ever there, certainly not much at …"

"Night?" obliged the prosecutor.

Amy colored. William stood and said, "Move to strike, Your Honor."

Debick was on his feet. "We've been over the rationale for this testimony, Judge. Either defense will allow prosecution to develop its case—"

The judge didn't seem happy about it, but he ruled, "I'll allow this line of questioning, Counselor, but make your point."

Debick turned back to Amy, who twirled her hair around her finger. "Now then, where was the defendant at night while you two shared an apartment senior year?"

Amy froze. "Um, I really don't know."

"Come now, Miss Gruden. You and Miss Czermanski have been friends since grade school. She wouldn't tell you? You didn't worry when she was out all night?"

"Kip had lots of friends she could stay with."

"Boyfriends?"

"Well … Oh, this is so unfair. You can't imagine how screwed up she got after Stan left. I mean, it was really heavy. She was utterly bummed, and she, like, kind of went crazy. She freaked. She slept around some that year for the first time in her life. But she always let me know where she was."

"She 'freaked?'" Debick paused. "Meaning she overreacted to the devastating loss of Dr. Szyzyck. She went 'crazy?'"

"That's just a saying, you know, I—"

"Did your roommate, Miss Gruden, regularly experiment with drugs during this period?"

"Objection." William leaped to his feet. "Hearsay."

"Let me rephrase, Your Honor. Did you, along with your roommate, experiment with drugs?"

"Answer the question, Miss Gruden," the judge directed.

"Not really, not like most kids, no. For all her far-out dress and hippie friends, Kip was way straight, know what I mean? She like wasn't into ludes or coke or anything heavy, though they were sure available if you wanted 'em." Giggle, blush, bright smile, hurry on. "She could hardly smoke dope. Kip's always been hypersensitive to smells, and well, she was more intellectually rebellious, I suppose you could say."

While Amy looked proud of that last depiction, shocked silence followed in the courtroom. Was everyone wondering, like me, whether she testified for or against me?

William's perfunctory cross did little to counteract what had so far been established: I was a radical activist with a long and violent police record in trouble since childhood who was no virgin by my desperately liberated senior year of college. Was he succeeding, the prosecutor, in showing the evil seed of my character as it grew and branched out over the years? Was truancy to delinquency to free sex to first degree murder becoming less far-fetched with every witness for the prosecution?

I wished I could study the faces in the gallery. Those of the jury revealed too little for me to know the answer with any confidence.

CHAPTER FORTY-EIGHT

I wondered again why William handled every witness while Phil had simply sat by since the opening statements. I'd get to the bottom of that as soon as possible. Several jurors fidgeted—I wasn't the only one bored to tears with this irrelevant but embarrassing minutiae. Perhaps we'd break soon. I hated to admit, I was getting hungry just like Timothy had warned me.

But again the stern prosecutor stepped forward as Amy was dismissed and called "Ralph Jeffrey." Phil and William double-checked the witness roster as an unrecognizable man lumbered toward the witness box from the far side of the gallery. He stopped and whispered something to Wally, who whispered to Harvey Debick until the judge called a halt to their private conversation.

"Excuse me, Judge. I meant to call Jeffrey Ralph to the stand."

Amid snickers, the bulky man restated his name and, thick fingers on the Bible, swore to tell only and all of the truth, so help him God. He settled back in the witness chair, his patched-at-the-elbows jacket spreading wide to reveal shirt buttons tested by his belly. The man incessantly wiped his hands on his jacket sleeves and pant legs. The prosecutor established the man's connection to the case: He'd been Stan's landlord in Madison. Only then did I recognize him. An adorable, chubby dog had trailed him throughout Stan's building. Pugs. His name was Pugs. Or was it Pugsy?

Jeffrey Ralph testified to "observing me night and day" at Stan's apartment, where I "frequently spent the night, despite curfews for females in the dorms." His description of my frantic search for Stan through the fall semester of my senior year felt more damaging.

"She was desperate," he testified, "harassing me repeatedly for information about Dr. Szyzyck for months. She couldn't cope with Dr. Szyzyck's leaving. She seemed crazed in her determination to find him. I told her repeatedly I had NO information about him, no forwarding address, nothing. I think I understand why."

For the first time, Philomena led the objection. I noticed Debick craning to watch her. Phil questioned how a mere landlord, not even the defendant's, could possess insight into motive. The jowly man produced a bundle, tied in string, from his jacket pocket and held it aloft. I feared I knew what he held— my postcards to Stan from Europe—as Phil moved to suppress evidence not previously disclosed to the defense.

The judge demanded an explanation from the prosecution for this "discovery violation," to which Debick requested a "sidebar," courtroom-ese for lawyers conferring in private with the judge at his altar-bench. My impression of the courtroom veered from churchly pulpit to theatre stage and back until the two became indistinguishable in my mind.

When their muffled, gesticulating exchange ended, the judge allowed into evidence my stolen postcards, written to my lover in Madison from all over Europe the summer he disappeared. Long-distance lust was about to be added to my portrait the prosecution was painting. And Stan never got my postcards.

Debick invited the witness, whom he referred to interchangeably as Mr. Jeffrey and Mr. Ralph, to explain what he could about my "frantic" behavior. The man thumbed through my postcards before selecting one to read. Clutching my private picture postcards in the sweaty hands he swiped on his pant leg gave me a severe case of the creeps. I itched all over, drinking a whole glass of ice water to gulp down looming humiliation.

"'I feel so free here,'" he read, a leer lighting his features as he did so, or was it just my dread at hearing my intimate words replayed in public? "'I don't know, sort of undefined and unrestricted, even more so than in Madison. This far from home, the possibilities look endless. But every inch of me aches for you. When I get back, don't plan on leaving your apartment, no, your bedroom, no, your bed, for at least a week. And I promise you this: we'll never be separated again. There will never be a reason good enough to part us again.'"

The landlord held up another postcard, this one of the Eiffel Tower, and, in his raspy voice that heightened the desperation of my words, continued to read. "'The fact you can't call or write me, the time and distance between us, makes me lose all sense of myself. Though I've seen so many amazing things, I need you, almost more than food and air, to feel alive and connected to earth. I'm desperate for your touch. The romance of Paris is a total waste without you. Be well rested when I get back. You'll need your strength—both threat and promise. I'll never let time or space—anything—separate us again. Ever. Ever.'"

Hearing my words, pure horny drivel, years after they were written, brought tears to my eyes. I suddenly remembered loving Stan that way, urgently, with every cell of my being. All of which had brought us to this. Stunned by crushing sadness, I didn't care who saw me react.

Following a quick exchange with Phil, William went forth to cross-examine Stan's landlord, glaring at him as he hunkered down in the witness chair, gathering my postcards together for the prosecutor as evidence. Evidence of what? I wondered. Loneliness? Love? Lust?

The man began to sweat more profusely as William circled for some moments before opening his cross-examination with, "Mr. Ralph, how do you happen to be in possession of private United States mail which obviously does not belong to you?"

"The building they were addressed to is mine. I mean, my mother owns it and I run it. As caretaker, I collect all unclaimed mail." He leaned back in the chair, his shirt buttons straining to the extreme. "The addressee left with no forwarding address. I could've tossed them back then, but well, the truth is,

I've never seen those places pictured. The postcards are pretty." He held one up for all to see the "pretty" walled city of Krakow, Poland.

"And you just happened to read them, then keep them—for years?"

"I read them back then when they came, checking for the addressee. My eyes might've wandered …" The witness lost his place when he locked onto my eyes. He swiped both hands on his pants. "I … I started lining the mirror in our entryway with them, stuck them up there as they continued to arrive from all those foreign countries. We loved seeing those exotic photographs every time we entered our apartment, Mother and me, places I figured I'd never see firsthand."

"How did you know who wrote them?"

The landlord scoffed, "Most of them were signed 'K,' circled by a heart." That childishness brought heat to my face. "I knew who they were from." He pointed at me. "She always had that lovesick look when she was with Stan, which was a lot. I knew her, the defendant, by name."

"How?"

"She was very nice to me in the beginning. She introduced herself and always stopped to say hi. But she changed. Once Dr. Szyzyck moved out, she turned pushy and demanding—downright rude. She really wasn't nice at all." The landlord bit his lip, creating a pink protrusion in the midst of his sweaty face.

William wrinkled his brow for effect. "Tell me," he said, settling against the far edge of the jury box so all the jurors had a clear view of the witness, "how did you feel about Ms. Czermanski?"

"Feel?"

"Yes, feel. Did you like her? Have feelings—a crush on her perhaps? Did you read those lovelorn and suggestive postcards and perhaps fantasize about—"

"Objection," shouted the prosecutor.

"No," shouted Jeffrey Ralph. But William just waited, staring him down as the judge allowed the question. "A little crush, maybe, once, when she went out of her way to be so nice to me, more than nice. But … no … I just …" The red-hued landlord blundered to a halt.

"Witness is dismissed," William snorted contemptuously. Mr. Ralph skulked back into the gallery, eyes downcast as he passed.

The judge banged his gavel and announced, "Court is adjourned until eight-thirty tomorrow morning."

Wow. I sat dazed, vaguely aware the bailiff waited for me. *It was your dog, Mr. Ralph, your cute little dog that attracted me.*

CHAPTER FORTY-NINE

"Why did William handle the witnesses in court today, Phil?" I smiled at him. "Not that you weren't good. Actually, William, you were great."

We sprawled on our accustomed cots in my cell after the opening day of trial, perhaps prematurely relaxed. We'd agreed the day's proceedings had done little more than establish my love affair with Stan, something I'd never denied. All in all, day one hadn't amounted to much more than embarrassing as hell.

"William did well indeed," Phil agreed. "We told the judge before court that my sore throat required rest. We'd decided to let William handle the early trial to avoid tipping my hand before necessary. If curiosity about the 'lady lawyer' from California in any way distracts our opponent, let's sustain it as long as we can."

"But you really do have a sore throat?" I asked.

"Of course," Phil answered.

Debick zeroing-in on Phil at her first objection came to mind. "You're intentionally distracting the prosecutor?"

"And he us. I'm still reeling from that procedural anomaly with the post-cards he so innocently explained away. He's sneaky, but he tipped that hand early."

I sat up straight. "Whatever happened at the bench that allowed my stolen postcards to be entered as evidence, and by the way, evidence of what?"

"Harvey Debick convinced the judge he knew nothing about the postcards, even after interviewing and calling the witness," Phil answered.

"Further, he argued the postcards could offer glimpses into your state of mind, your 'growing psychological imbalance.' He reminded the judge that the unanticipated evidence could go against the prosecution as easily as for it. Like any good lawyer would let that happen. Still, today was a propitious start, wouldn't you agree, William?"

William resumed his ramrod posture on the cot and issued a warning. "Don't count Harvey Debick out yet. Never count Harvey Debick out. He was heavy-handed today to the extreme, borderline ridiculous, which only makes me wonder what he's cooking up."

Phil and I exchanged worried glances. "His was a weak start though," Phil insisted as if to convince herself.

"It would seem so," William admitted, "unless it's critical to his case to establish that many little wrongs inevitably led to one big one."

"Quite a leap," I offered.

"Truancy to murder," Phil scoffed. "I'd say so."

William considered. "It's Harvey's overly meticulous style, leave nothing out that might strike a chord with even a single juror. You know he's studied the jury. He'll try to appeal to each one of them in some way." His pessimism deflated us as William came to his feet. "Time to get home. I want to review interview notes from your family members tonight. They're on prosecution's docket for tomorrow."

With that statement, I slid into thorough depression. "You're not to cross-examine them, remember. I don't trust them. The less said the better from each of them."

"We are well aware of your irrational demands on this subject," Phil snapped, anger flooding her cheeks, "but as your lawyers, we must maintain the right to question statements that don't agree with prior interviews or don't jibe between them. Allow us to do our job, Kip, to take advantage of whatever possibilities present themselves in court. It's why you have lawyers."

"Fine," I said, sounding anything but fine. "But don't try to wheedle testimony from my sisters and father that you think might assist me. It won't. Even if they wanted to help me—trust me, they only wish to preserve the family's reputation and no more—they will only make things worse, I guarantee it."

This particular disagreement had grown more bitter every day. Seething, Phil bit back a retort while William signaled the jailer. "You're going to have to trust someone, Kip," he said, pausing at the cell door. "Perhaps you could start with us."

Feeling slapped by his words, I stared straight ahead long after the sound of William's footsteps had faded. But it was my lawyers who refused to trust *me* on the subject of *my* family. Phil rose, muttering about the work she had before court reconvened.

"It's not that I distrust you, Phil, nor am I trying to tie your hands. But ..."

She stopped packing her case and looked at me. "But?" she repeated.

"But you don't know them. I do, and I think, in fact I know, it's for the best."

She slammed her briefcase shut. "You're the psychology major turned counselor, Kip. Think about it. From any perspective, it's a mistake, starting with: It just looks bad. Then overlay the legal ramifications. It's insane when you consider the bare facts of your case: you in the house with the deceased, your two sisters, and your father, period. And we can't talk to the only other people who could possibly have firsthand knowledge of the incident? Why? Because they might try to harm you? They don't have to try. You're already in jail, accused of murder in the first. You stand to go to prison for life. What further harm can anyone do to you, Kip?"

"But I'm not guilty. I won't go to jail."

Phil plunked her heavy case on the cot and shook her head. She took a deep breath before extending a hand to me. When I shifted out of reach, she yanked on her coat. "Use your head, Kip. This hands-off-your-family requirement of yours not only looks fishy, it stinks. Are you protecting someone? Is that what this is about?"

"Only myself."

Phil banged the bars for the jailer. "See you in court." But as she waited for him, she began to chuckle. "Who knows, you might be right. I've never heard of the prosecution calling the defendant's immediate family to testify. If he actually does put them in the witness box tomorrow, you might be right. It makes no sense otherwise."

As she exited, panic rose in my throat. Phil was leaving angry. "Phil, Phil wait." She hesitated as the jailer locked up and continued on ahead of her. "The H on your hankie? Your initials are PBH?"

"Harrison."

"You use your middle name, not your last?"

"I use my maiden name professionally, not my married."

"You're *married?*" I stumbled backwards with that shockwave.

"Why, yes—"

"You … you don't wear a ring, you've never talked about a, a husband. It's just never come up? You weren't hiding it from me, were you?"

"Hiding it? No. I rarely travel with my wedding ring since I cannot wear it at night. I'm always scratching myself on the diamond. I won't risk leaving it in a hotel room again. It's never come up because …" Phil looked genuinely perplexed. "… it's never come up. We've had plenty to talk about, haven't we, and not much time to do so."

She emphasized one more of my burdensome demands. "There's no grand plan to deceive you, Kip. We're not all conspiring against you. You really do need to trust someone."

"I thought, just assumed, you were a feminist—not a feminist like I'm a feminist, but a kind of precursor. You're a lawyer, the center's lawyer, a woman tough enough to go it alone in a very sexist field in our sexist world. You …"

She waited, tapping the floor with the toe of her boot.

"I mean, okay, why would a woman of such accomplishment and independence need a husband to tell her what to do and not do? Or need the government to make your union all legal? Or did the church sanctify your marriage?"

Phil's jaw dropped. "I wanted to formalize my commitment to my husband. There was no church, which, given my Catholic upbringing, proved difficult for my parents." She stomped away, but circled back. "You make a lot of assumptions, don't you, Kip? You assume my husband tells me what I can and can't do. He doesn't, he wouldn't dream of it."

She glanced at her watch. "And I didn't need what you've insinuated. My husband loves and encourages me to be me, to do what I want, no, what I must. He loves me for the very qualities that scared most men off, like the ones you mentioned—accomplishment and independence. I'm here, aren't I? Haven't been home in two months, and no telling when I will be. It's more than enough for him that I'm deeply involved in your case."

"But marriage. It's so …" I choked back the word bourgeois. "Next you'll tell me you have kids, perhaps a daughter, just my age." My lawyer blanched, her reaction abrupt and severe. "You have kids too?"

"No." Phil shouted, dropping her briefcase with a thud to grasp the bars between us, straining for control. "No, I do not have kids." Her gaze was so defiant, I backed away. "Nor will I apologize for my marriage, Kip. I will tell you we're both lawyers and our marriage, a simple legal ceremony, confirmed our life partnership, our devotion to each other, a quite singular …"

A glimmer of something singular stole across Phil's features. "He's hardly a yoke I'm forced to bear. And if you must know, had I been able, we would have also committed the grievous crime of having a family as well. So what does that prove? Where do you get these ideas?"

Phil snatched up her case but circled again, wanting but not quite able to go.

"Can't a feminist who believes in a woman's right to pursue her dreams be what she wants, answer to herself and her own inner stirrings? Can't a feminist like men, especially liberated men, feminists themselves? Is liberation meant to preclude a choice so basic as to how and with whom one lives? Does your brand of feminism bring its own set of proscriptions and restrictions?" She shook her head in disbelief. "You call that liberation, Kip?"

My gaze faltered, remembering Peter Replogel's hand in mine, stealing along Bascom Hill as feminist chants grew more violent: *Male Chauvinist Pigs. Kill the Pigs.* How he and I had laughed about such misplaced hatred, right before we made love. Had that stridency somehow infected me?

"But marriage—it's so, so, so *bourgeois*." There. I said it.

Phil's contempt and disappointment frightened me. She checked her watch and chose her final words with care.

"Think of it as one option for a relationship that you and your partner define in your own terms. I must go, Kip. We can talk about this some other time if you wish. But for now, as you said, we best stay focused on your trial."

CHAPTER FIFTY

April 11, 1972

I spent the night between the first and second day of trial restless with worry, not over my fate strangely enough, but over Phil's anger—worse, her irredeemable disappointment in me. I wasn't sure why it seemed to matter so much.

Only the anticipation of my family testifying pushed that concern from my mind as trial reconvened. "Prosecution calls Samantha Turner." With that, Phil's theory about the prosecution bluffing by including my family on its witness list was laid to rest.

Everyone craned to watch Samantha emerge from the first row behind the defense table. I took the opportunity to check out Sybel, who appeared self-possessed and cool, seated beside Dad. My dad wasn't nearly as collected. I quickly scanned the rest of the courtroom. Samantha's husband was nowhere to be seen. Impeccably-bred-but-penniless Raymond Turner III made clear his resentment through his absence. Why hadn't I confessed and spared them all this degradation as he'd suggested? Because I'm innocent? I faced front to watch Samantha's halting ascent to the witness box.

Samantha still looked like a Life magazine Breck-blonde, only after a hard patch. Glowing tresses smooth to their gently curled under ends brushed her shoulders as she moved, the barrette clipped to one side the same color as her eyes, true blue. The white blouse cinched at the waist by a loosely hanging dark skirt looked frumpy, as if she strove to underplay her looks, perhaps as an offset to her husband's accustomed flamboyance. Still, against her wishes, her quiet beauty shined forth for all to see. Only her thinness and furtive glances hinted at the pressure she struggled under.

Instead of Harvey Debick, the assistant district attorney stepped forward to question Samantha. Perhaps Phil's sore throat was catching? When Samantha smiled at Wally Werner, it seemed to confuse and embarrass him. Hadn't she dated Weird Wally in high school? The judge urged things onward: "Your witness, Mr. Werner." Yes, they had dated.

"Mrs. Turner, where were you the night of February 12th?"

"Home. Well, Dad's home. My childhood home, you know, Wally, on Moraine Drive."

Wally's neck and face darkened to the carrot color of his hair, which looked like his freckles were melting together. "Yes, Mrs. Turner."

Watching Assistant DA Werner handle Samantha's interrogation called up young, carrot-topped Wally, riding his bike past our home a hundred times a day, hoping for a glimpse of shy Samantha. When he got one—when I wasn't the only one in our yard spending as much time outside the house as possible—Wally sped by, legs pumping wildly, his shirttails flapping behind. But he never rode by fast enough for us to miss the deepening red of his face, and not from exertion. Once old enough to figure it out, I'd shout at the top of my lungs, "Hey Wally. You again, Wally? You lost, Wally? You lose something, Wally?" So funny, wasn't I?

Grown into a red-haired, freckled Don Knotts look-alike, bobbing Adam's apple and all, Wally handled Samantha self-consciously, as if he hadn't outgrown his childhood crush. "Tell the court why were you there, Mrs. Turner, and for how long?"

Samantha swallowed hard. "My sister, Sarah, was buried that day. Everyone was at the house afterwards, you know, a gathering of friends and neighbors after the services. I planned to spend the night in my old room. We were all there, mostly to comfort Dad and, and each other, of course."

"'We?' Please remind the court who was there with you."

"Well, Dad of course, Sybel and, and… Stan, her husband, her …" She swallowed hard again. "And Kip. That's it, just the family."

"Your husband, Mrs. Turner, where was he that evening?"

"Like most everyone in town, Raymond was at the house earlier, but he went home for the night … to feed the cat. I, I wanted to stay on at Dad's. I was … felt needed."

"Fine, Mrs. Turner." Wally circled back to the prosecutor, who made a sort of subtle signal before Wally continued. "Now would you, in your own words, Mrs. Turner, describe what happened that night after Sarah's funeral and burial, after the guests had left your home and the family had gone to bed."

Samantha uncrossed and recrossed her legs, then pulled her hair forward over her face before responding, "I was asleep. It'd been a long day, a long month with Sarah sick and … Anyways, sometime during the night I awoke to a loud crash. I listened for a moment for something that would indicate where it came from, what had happened. When I heard nothing more, I slipped out of bed and peered out into the hallway. Sybel was hurrying toward Dad at the top of the front stairwell. I, I ran after them, and we all went downstairs to Kip's room together. Dad whispered he thought the noise had come from there."

Wally prompted Samantha, "The three of you descended the stairs to Kip's room, and then what happened?"

"We listened at Kip's door but heard nothing. When Dad eased the door open, we heard a strange noise, like a dripping faucet. Dad pushed the door wide open." Wally prodded Samantha to go on. "I, I made out Kip standing on the far side of her bed. Then Sybel flipped the light on, and we all, I don't know, gasped, I think."

"Your father, sister, and you gasped? At what?"

"At someone in Kip's bed. Kip didn't seem to know what was going on. She stood in a soaking wet nightie, staring down at the, the person in her bed." Samantha retreated behind her hair, twisting a few strands around her finger. "Sybel figured it out first, I guess. She pushed Kip aside and started yelling at, at the person in bed. 'Stan, get up this minute. I mean it, Stan. Get up now.' That kind of thing."

"Your sister, Sybel Szyzyck, recognized the person in Kip's bed?"

"We all did. It was Stan, that is, Sybel's husband."

The courtroom buzzed until the judge enforced silence. "Please continue Mrs. Turner," Wally urged.

"Sybel … Sorry, but could I have a glass of water?" After a few gulps, Samantha placed the glass on the witness box and continued. "Sybel tried to wake Stan up, sort of pushing and pulling at him, but he didn't respond. So she rolled him over on his back." Samantha blushed purple, finished the water and replaced the empty glass on the witness stand. "We all kind of gasped again because, well, well Stan was still … well, beneath the sheet you could see that he was, um, aroused. Sybel really yelled for him to get up and cover his … himself. I think she yelled at Kip, too."

Sybel had hissed, 'What have you done now?' That memory was clear. I relived those moments as Samantha described them, haltingly but in detail, for the courtroom—from Sybel's inability to hear Stan's heartbeat, initially due to the curlers she pulled from her hair, to extending her bloodied fingers before us, to turning his head for us all to see it bleeding.

"Uh, more water, please?"

Wally refilled the glass, asking Samantha if she felt well enough to go on. Wide-eyed and pale, she said she could continue if necessary. "I'm afraid it is, Mrs. Turner."

"Well, there was some debate, discussion, you know, about how this was going to look, town gossip and all. But we called the police … to report the accident and, and to ask for help for Stan, even though Sybel said he was passed needing it. Sybel said Stan was, that he was … dead. I checked Stan's pulse myself and feared … was afraid she might be right." Samantha asked as her tears seemed imminent, "Am I excused now?"

"Thank you, Mrs. Turner, I know how hard this is for you, but please tell the court what happened that night after the call to the police."

"Um, the police came, that young officer from yesterday, who called the ambulance that took Stan away. That same officer took my sister away—for further questioning, he said."

"Which sister, Mrs. Turner?"

"It's not obvious?" Samantha snapped. "Kip."

Wally did a double take. "Thank you, Sam—Mrs. Turner. Defense witness."

The witness rose as if to flee but thumped back into the witness chair as Phil approached her. Why not William all of a sudden? I wondered, suspicious about the verity of Phil's sore throat. A surreptitious glance revealed an entire room galvanized by Phil's every move. In my mind I heard Samantha asking me, *What's this lady lawyer you hired like? Masculine? Bet no one told her not to be smarter than the boys.* Samantha struggled to return Phil's smile.

"Mrs. Turner, you testified to hearing a dripping sound when you opened the door to Kip's room. Also that your sister, Kip, was somewhat dazed, standing in a wet nightgown. What do you think caused that?"

"I'd put funeral flowers in all the rooms. The house was overflowing with flowers from Sarah's services. Everyone was so kind … I, I'd found a huge old crystal vase I'd never seen before Sybel's wedding and filled it with flowers called amaryllis, really different, just the kind of thing Kip would most appreciate."

A brief chuckle from the gallery startled Samantha, but Phil nodded encouragement.

"We noticed, well after the initial shock, that is, we noticed shattered glass on the floor of Kip's room on one side of her bed, and strewn flowers and spilled water soaking the bed and dripping on the floor. Plus, the vase no longer stood on the nightstand where I'd put it earlier that night. I think we all assumed it toppled on the bed, hit Stan, then rolled off to splinter on the floor. That's what woke the whole house."

"Yes, the coroner testified that a blunt instrument was the cause of death. Please describe this vase for the court."

"It was cut crystal and so heavy I could barely carry it myself. No way could I have carried it upstairs. I had to add water and flowers after placing it beside Kip's bed. It was probably, well, thirty inches high, a yard even, and very old. It was a lone survivor of a pair my parents had been given as a wedding gift."

"Thank you, Mrs. Turner. The shards from that vase weighed approximately thirty pounds, without the water or flowers it held. You also mentioned a debate that ensued about how this aroused body in bed 'would look,' something about 'town gossip,' before the police were called."

Samantha nodded again, but the judge directed her to speak her answers for the record. "Yes."

"Were you concerned about how this incident would reflect on you and your family, Mrs. Turner?"

"Um, yes, no, well I suppose, but Sybel, of course it was her husband, she was … most concerned."

"And what did your sister, Sybel, suggest in that regard?"

"She wanted to wait, you know, until it went down. His …"

"Penis?'

Samantha reddened. She had said how this testimony would embarrass her. Wasn't doing much for me either. "Yes," she muttered.

"An odd reaction for a wife whose husband lay bleeding to death—to wait until—"

"Objection, Your Honor. Witness is being led to speculate—"

"Withdraw, Your Honor. So once you all realized that Stan was seriously injured, his wife, Sybel, called the police?"

"N-no. I, I made that call. She, well, Sybel likes to think things through first, you know, thoroughly."

"No, I don't know. In fact to me, hers was a very strange reaction for the wife of a dying man." Upon reaching the defense table, Phil pivoted back to the witness. "Just one last thing, Mrs. Turner. You testified your husband went home to feed the cat. But your neighbor, Mr. Krousy, testified to seeing your husband's car in the driveway throughout the night."

Samantha thought back. "He did say that. But Raymond walked home.

His car was hemmed in by all of ours, and he couldn't get everyone to move their cars during the reception when he wanted to go. So he just walked home and picked up his car the next day."

"Thank you, Mrs. Turner. We're through with this witness at this time, Your Honor. However, defense retains the right to recall Mrs. Turner at a later time." Samantha looked alarmed, but the judge told her to step down and called the morning break.

I passed the quarter-hour recess in the green room, encouraging Timothy to eat the donuts he'd gotten me, trying not to think about Sybel, next on the prosecution's witness list.

CHAPTER FIFTY-ONE

"Prosecution calls Mrs. Sybel Czermanski Szyzyck." Prosecutor Debick had inexplicably replaced assistant DA Wally. The prosecution appeared to be effectively utilizing the defense lawyers' distraction tactics.

Sybel rose in the row behind me, adjusted the clingy skirt that just covered her thighs, and buttoned her form-fitting black jacket, called a peacoat. A black turtleneck, black tights, and shiny black boots completed her ensemble. She moved to the aisle and up to the witness box, all eyes on her. When she pivoted, her hoop earrings glimmered and her shag haircut's choppy yellow bangs fell around her brilliant blue eyes, framing them perfectly. Always on top of the latest fashion trends, Sybel brought a mod new meaning to mourning clothes.

"Mrs. Szyzyck," Prosecutor Debick began, "you heard your sister, Mrs. Turner, describe the events of February 12th and 13th following funeral services for your eldest sister, Sarah. Did her account accurately describe your recollections of that time period?"

Sybel nodded at the prosecutor, staring straight at him. "Let the record show the witness nodded in the affirmative. After all you've endured, Mrs. Szyzyck, there will be no need to put you through a recounting of those events."

Prosecutor Debick picked up something from the table and held it out to the witness as he approached her. "There's only one additional area for which I need your testimony. Do you recognize what I'm carrying?"

Sybel studied what the prosecutor held for a moment and nodded, but the judge directed her to answer for the record. "Yes, I recognize it."

"And what is it that I'm holding here?"

"It is an ice hockey stick, for playing ice hockey."

"Yes, Mrs. Szyzyck, and whose ice hockey stick is it?"

Debick held the stick overhead for the defense table's first clear view. I, too, recognized it—light wood, shellacked to a gleam except where scraped-up at the foot, red and gold stripes denoting the Wausaukeesha Weasels. I'd had a stick just like it in high school when I played fourth string on the girls' ice hockey team. It was something to do after school besides going home to Sybel.

"Mrs. Szyzyck, whose ice hockey stick is it?" Debick repeated. My lawyers busily scanned files, searched lists, and exchanged glances.

"My sister's." Sybel responded.

The slightest irritation colored Prosecutor Debick's overt awe of the beautiful and amazingly composed widow when he asked, "Which sister, Mrs. Szyzyck?"

"Kip."

Yeah, who else would freeze her ass off on the sidelines for four years of high school? I was a terrible skater with my weak ankles.

Debick thought for a moment before asking, "Would you, in your own words, Mrs. Szyzyck, tell the court how I happen to be in possession of your sister Kip's ice hockey stick."

Sybel released a martyr's sigh. "I was home last Sunday afternoon when you and Wally came by. Actually, I'd moved home—back to the big house on Moraine Drive—after, after my husband's, uh, untimely death. I didn't want to be alone in the house Stan and I … and Daddy needed me."

"You refer to myself and the Assistant District Attorney, Walter Werner, calling at the Czermanski home last Sunday, two days ago?"

"You're asking me? Of course. Anyways, you asked to view the crime scene, or some such words, one last time. There was no use saying no. You'd just get a warrant to see whatever you wanted. So I let you in and led you back to the nanny's quarters off the kitchen which Kip used as her rooms for years."

"Yes," encouraged Debick, "and then?"

"You and Wally poked around Kip's bedroom for some time, then the bathroom and storage closet in the hallway to the kitchen. I wondered, working in the kitchen, why you two were rummaging in the broom closet. I hadn't checked it since my move home and worried what chaos you'd uncover."

"Yes yes, Mrs. Szyzyck, please go on."

"Did you not say 'in my own words?'" she chastised the prosecutor sharply. Not knowing Sybel well, Debick looked surprised. "You pulled Kip's ice hockey stick from the back of the broom closet," she went on, "where it had probably been forgotten for ages."

"And then?" Debick oozed solicitously. Sybel had this effect on men.

But Sybel grew bored with this game. "As if you don't remember. You asked me if you could take the stick along for further examination. You promised to return it when you were done. Are you done?"

"Not just yet, Mrs. Szyzyck, but I am with you. Thank you very much."

Debick spun on his heel and said, "Your Honor, prosecution wishes to enter into evidence the defendant's ice hockey stick."

I tried to get William's attention to ask what my old hockey stick had to do with anything, but he bolted to his feet, shouting, "Objection," barely beating Phil to the punch. "Your Honor, this is the second incident in as many days of prosecution not properly pre-disclosing evidence to the defense."

"Explain, Mr. Debick," ordered the judge, "and it better be good."

"The stick was taken on a hunch, Your Honor, as you heard from the witness, only the day before yesterday. It was sent immediately to the crime lab for analysis. Only as court began today did the lab relay its findings. For that reason my assistant conducted the first examination this morning, as I was still reading through the lab report I had just received. There simply wasn't time to disclose. My apologies, Judge."

"And the report—"

"Your Honor," Phil's voice shrilled with outrage, "defense has had no opportunity to examine this evidence, nor study the lab report that it would appear you are allowing."

"We'll enter the lab report as well," Debick slipped in, "if we may. However, allow me to summarize for the court?"

"Get straight to the point, Mr. Debick," demanded the judge, and to Phil, he added, "I'm aware of your situation, Miss Benedetti."

The prosecutor stood midway between judge and jury to read from the lab report: "The ice hockey stick bears traces of hair, skin, and blood of the type matching Dr. Stanislaw Szyzyck. Evidence of attempted removal of those traces are also present. Fingerprints of all members of the Czermanski household found as well, along with apparent attempts to remove them."

A buzz became a roar as my lawyers objected and the entire courtroom shifted and commented. What had just happened? At the heart of the ruckus, Harvey Debick held aloft my ice hockey stick as if blood, skin, and hair were visible. The judge, threatening to clear the courtroom, at last quelled the outburst and summoned the lawyers to his bench.

I watched their heated discussion from behind the four attorneys lined up before the judge's pulpit, making myself breathe while clutching the table, trying to make sense of what was happening. The gavel boomed over the silent gathering. Speaking over the lawyers' heads, the judge announced, "I will allow this new evidence, but warn the prosecutor that any further procedural missteps will be dealt with severely."

"Motion for mistrial, Judge," Phil countered, sounding angry as hell.

"Noted, Miss Benedetti, and denied. Clerk will accept prosecution's evidence, both the lab report and alleged murder weapon. Court stands adjourned until next Monday at nine a.m. to allow defense time to analyze this evidence."

What? Monday morning, five and a half days away. Barely time to— Wait— "Murder weapon?" Did the judge refer to my ice hockey stick as the murder weapon, the *alleged* murder weapon? They think I killed Stan with my old ice hockey stick? That I stashed it in the broom closet outside my bedroom after not quite wiping clean the evidence?

Chapter Fifty-Two

"I haven't touched that hockey stick since, I don't know, since high school." My lawyers were trying to believe me, I had to give them that.

"This changes everything," William muttered to the spot on the floor of my cell he'd been staring at, unable or unwilling to look at either of us.

"A manslaughter fallback is no longer viable." Phil sighed, her exhaustion evident. "The blunt instrument of the coroner's report would no longer appear to be the vase that accidentally toppled during a struggle. Assuming it all checks out, and there's little reason to suspect it won't, it appears someone murdered Stan quite intentionally."

"The vase was a cover-up after the mur—Stan's death." William barely breathed.

"You still can't remember, Kip?" Phil leaned across the gulf separating lawyers from the accused. "This new information doesn't jog from memory any more details of that night?"

I shook my head, wanting to bury it under the poor-excuse-for-a-pillow on my cot. "That stick stood in the corner of my room since my high school hockey-playing days, my sitting-on-the-sideline days, I should say. It was still there when I came home from college, I'm pretty sure. Yes, in fact, I used to hang my coat on it when it was too damp to put away. That's right. I never moved it from the corner, never touched it. And since I painted the nanny's quarters orange, Sybel refused to come back there altogether, allowing me, as she called it, 'to wallow in my bad taste.' So it's not likely anyone moved it." My lawyers' concern disconcerted me. "I just can't say for sure it was still in the corner when I came home to say good-bye to Sarah."

"Right," said Phil unhappily. "Kip, I have to ask. Did you agree to meet Stan that night after the household went to bed, or perhaps imply your bedroom door would be open for him?"

"No."

"Did you allow him in when he did show up?"

"No way."

"You didn't change your mind once he got there?"

"No."

"You didn't have a change of heart with him and try to make him to stop, maybe pick up the stick in the corner and—"

"No, no, and no. Damn it, I've told you all of this."

"You weren't jealous of his marriage to your sister?"

"I don't know. It sickened me but—"

"Enough to want to hurt him and the sister who stole him? Did you accidentally—"

"No." I leapt to my feet, flailing my fists, so fucking angry and frightened and sick of these questions and people not believing me and this cell and no sunlight and crappy food and a cot for a bed and a whole town just waiting to watch me fall. "No, I did not kill anyone with a vase or a hockey stick or with anything. God knows why I still can't remember that whole night."

Perhaps with rage like this coursing through me, I could kill someone. Disgusted by my defenders' suspicions, I lunged at the cell bars, grabbing hard to control my urge to punch, kick, and claw. But punishing the bars did nothing to avert an avalanche of tears.

"I'm sorry, Kip," Phil soothed, "but the prosecutor will do much worse. If we put you on the stand, he'll goad you into demonstrating a killer temper just like that. You have to be prepared if we have to call you. And we needed to be sure. Come sit down. We'll think of something."

My uncontrollable sobbing seemed to inspire William's abrupt need to get away. "I should go pick up the lab report on the hockey stick," he said. "Copies should be ready by now. I'll leave one at the Howard Johnson's for you, Phil."

He scurried out as soon as he could. Phil stood, saying something to William through the bars about making copies of something else, I think I heard my "medical exam."

My tears began to slow, but my mind raced. "I'm going to jail—for life. Scapegoat to the bitter end. My whole life I've always been to blame, no matter what. You're looking at *the* fall guy. I'll be found guilty," my voice cracked. "It's my role."

"You believe you're guilty?" she asked, seating herself. "Is that what you're saying? Or that you might be?"

"What the fuck difference does it make? Fucked up family needed a fucking victim—me." I kicked the metal bars, hurting my toes. "Ow. Raised by a witch who's hated me since I was born. Dad, Mr. Consummate Breadwinner, didn't give a shit what happened in his household. Don't bother Dad, he's got bacon to put on the table, wieners in his case." I kicked again, then hopped to my cot and threw myself on it. "You have no idea what it's been like. Whatever you do won't make a lick of difference, Phil, not in this town."

"Yet you wouldn't consider change of venue."

"Don't remind me. I wanted to get it over with and out of here. Can you blame me?" Phil didn't respond. "Okay, I probably wasn't thinking right. I can feel it, their eyes on me during court, anticipating my last and most spectacular fall." Phil's nonreaction struck me as an accusation. "Oh, you'll never understand. No one has. No one will."

Phil took her time in replying. "I see why you say that. It had to be difficult without your mother or father steering your household."

"Don't use Psych 101 on me again, unless you really mean it."

"I do mean it. I am sorry, Kip, sorry it's been so hard for you." Instead of calming me, Phil's empathy brought out more tears.

Phil moved to the cot beside me. "You know, Kip, I've learned the hard way that the worst times of my life steered me in a direction previously unimagined."

"Jail for life is too imaginable," I sobbed.

"In retrospect, I've thanked my lucky stars for the things I thought I wouldn't survive while they were happening. My life would have played out so differently."

"Oh, right. Something good is just around the corner. Thank you very much, Mrs. Harrison, but Pollyanna prognostications are a bit out of line here in my jail cell."

Phil fell silent, more saddened than offended. Phil wasn't the enemy, I reminded myself, watching her disappointment. Here she sat, even after our disagreements, talking me through it, metaphorically holding my hand. Why was I trying to bite it?

"We've had a serious setback today," she said, rising. "I'll leave you—"

"No, Phil, don't go. I'm just … I'm being miserable. I am miserable." Tears spurted with my admission. "Don't go … It's just that maybe …"

"What?"

I hugged myself, trying to get smaller and disappear. My cell felt freezing. "It's what, Kip?"

"I don't know what I'm trying to say. Just that, well, what if everyone knows something, has always known something, about me?" Phil was not following. "What if everyone is right?" I whispered. She leaned close to catch my words and I almost slumped against her. "All my life I've been punished for being bad, just for being … What if something inside me, I mean, what if they're right about me? What if I deserve it?"

Phil handed me her hankie. My head ached, and surely I could cry no more. "Listen to me, Kip," she said, tilting my chin up until we were eye-to-eye, "they're not right. They're not. You accepted your role as scapegoat because they were bigger than you, they supposedly knew more than you, and it was the only role offered. You were just a child who needed a mother and a father, and you did your best with neither." Phil let that sink in. "Perhaps your sisters and father did their best, too. But you most of all needed their wisdom and protection and got none of it. You are least responsible, you must know that."

Seeing my attention riveted on her, Phil continued. "It's time you reject the role you've played, the role you accepted. It's time you found yourself a new role. Of all your family, you are most able to do that. I see that in you, Kip. I believe you can do it. Muster all the courage you have and resist being the scapegoat you've been molded into."

Sniffling, I hung on her words.

"What you do now, Kip, during the worst of times will color and shape the rest of your days."

With the bars closing in around me, I could barely breathe. "But what can I do?"

Phil stood, patted my shoulder, and signaled the jailer before she responded. "You can get lots of rest. You can eat. We need you healthy. Jot notes on anything and everything that occurs to you." She touched my cheek, and I leaned into her hand. "You can be courageous in the face of fear and defeat. You can do all that, Kip. Be your own cause for a change. Use that passion and commitment of yours for yourself. Fight this defeatism."

Phil followed the jailer out but paused to add, "William and I will be in and out for the rest of the week. We have a lot of work to do and very little time. Kip, I know it's difficult to be philosophical right now, but it's the most critical time of your life to be just that. Do not give in. Do not give up."

CHAPTER FIFTY-THREE

Sunday, April 16, 1972

During the remainder of the week the defense had been given to "examine" the new evidence, I hadn't seen my lawyers once. Messages passed to me by various jailers explained their "unavoidable absences. In Madison reinterviewing potential witnesses, questioning medical experts, seeking more information about your arrest." Et cetera.

I tried not to dwell on the fact that someone had murdered Stan with *my* hockey stick in *my* bed with *me* in it. Bleak was too optimistic a word for how things looked. But left alone to stew in my worries and guesses only increased the challenge of adhering to Phil's advice to remain philosophical. As each day in my cell dragged on, my mind stuck on a phrase she'd tossed out: "the role you accepted." It made no sense—like I had a bunch of choices?

She's a lawyer; she should stick to law. But why did it bother me so? Because I'm alone in this cell with no night or day, powerless to do anything real about my future. I should be … Hell, I had no idea what I should be doing. "Be courageous in the face of fear and defeat," she had said. A hell of a lot easier said than done. I'm going crazy, aren't I, stir-crazy? I can't take much more alone time. I can't—

Footsteps—not a jailer—hurrying to my cell. Not Phil's. William's? Yes, William's gait for sure.

Once locked in with me, William barely contained his excitement, despite the dark circles under his eyes, magnified by his glasses.

"Nice of you to drop by. Where have you been, both of you?"

"You didn't get our messages, Kip? We left word. I've got great news. Phil was right. You just have to keep digging. Sometimes a chunk of gold turns up. Where is she, by the way? Her last message to me said she'd be here all Sunday afternoon."

"How the hell should I know? I'm just the client." When William didn't notice me sulking, I went on the offensive. "I haven't seen her since Tuesday—neither of you. Since Tuesday—that's five days sitting on my thumbs in this cage all alone. Even Timothy has been on vacation."

"She planned to visit the coroner again, the doctor who examined you after your arrest, the library, God knows. Anyways, do you remember Kimberly Kempinski?" Pulling the name out of the stale air, William conjured a vision that stunned me into nonresponse mode. "Maybe I should wait for Phil. She's going to want to hear this."

"William, you can't pop in here and stop in the middle of *good* news. What in the world does Kimberly Kempinski have to do with anything?"

"You do know her?"

"Could anyone forget? Brilliant red hair down to her ass—ah, bottom, freckles, huge green eyes."

"Quite striking, you're right. She's agreed to testify on your behalf, albeit reluctantly."

"Testify for me? About what? She never gave me the time of day. Kimberly was far too cool to notice the likes of me."

"About Stan, about him drugging her, and others." My mouth would not form a question. I sank onto my cot before I keeled over. "She says she was just one of the girls Stan drugged for sex. Her story checks out. I was able to subpoena the student medical center's records after she came forward. It appears he drugged and raped her, and others, according to her. She contends that's why the university fired him. I'll verify that first thing in the morning. I finally got a subpoena for his personnel records. The university has been adamant about confidentiality, but they'll have no choice now."

Kimberly Kempinski. Others. Drugged? Raped?

"I tell you, Kip, Phil will be so relieved. She's been over and over your blood tests taken after your arrest with multiple experts. She had a hunch, but 'no foreign substances' could be found. She repeated to me, 'Here's Kip, so bright and overly observant, a survival skill learned early on with her family, yet she's blank about the whole incident of attempted rape and death. Shock? I don't think so. She's too tough.' When all that could be found was a trace of alcohol, not enough to classify you as 'under the influence,' she was deflated, but only for a moment."

Time to face facts. Phil was far more of a shrink than I. Survival of the overly observant. She was right on, again.

"… pieces come together with this. I must find Phil. We were, I can admit to you now, running out of angles."

Wound up like a top, William sprang from my cell the moment the jailer unlocked it. Alone again, I curled up into the fetal position as Kimberly Kempinski, in all her redheaded glory, materialized before my mind's eye.

1968

We hadn't slept in days. On a cold spring afternoon near the end of junior year, what started as a Black Power rally on Bascom Hill mushroomed into a fiasco. Black militants and sympathizers, protesting the lack of black studies, black teachers, and black scholarships, called for a strike. Blacks fought disproportionately in the trenches in Vietnam, a fact that made the anti-war movement overlap frequently with their cause. A couple thousand people had gathered to listen to Panther speakers defend their strike, which kept students from classrooms.

The campus cops, reinforced by the Madison Police, meted out crowd control with a heavy hand. With shields and clubs, they pushed and herded students who'd broken no law. Acrid clouds of tear gas wafted over the anti-war and black leaders who addressed the milling masses. Almost inevitably, a scuffle broke out between the peacekeepers and some roughed-up protestors, prompting University President Fred Harrington to call for Governor Knowles to send in the National Guard.

The overreaction of armed Guardsmen surrounding the Hill drew thousands more protestors, enraged at the police-state mentality. With students cramming the Hill from all sides, tensions grew palpable. Round-the-clock vigils, stoked by outrage, tear gas, and frayed nerves, ensued. Stormy rhetoric filled the air until the air itself felt flammable. Normal campus life ground to a halt, which freed more students to gather and mill.

Still, after a few days and nights, even the most ardent activists slipped off for some sleep and real food. I was among the last to leave, shaken by these provocations by our university president, the governor, the National Guard, Madison Police, and the campus cops. We had legally assembled to peacefully vent our beliefs. Who brought guns, bullets, tear gas, and billy clubs to this party? Why such a show of force?

Walking through our thinning ranks, I realized I hadn't seen Stan since his address on the Hill the day before. His speech, an incendiary mixture of indignation at institutionalized bigotry and solidarity with the black cause, had enraptured the crowd, even the passersby and first-time demonstrators. Students never seen at rallies or marches assailed him with questions when he stepped down from the makeshift podium before the statue of President Lincoln, the emancipator of slaves. We were separated in the throngs long before I stepped up to the loudspeaker to deliver my thoughts.

A strange thing happened when I faced thousands of expectant students spilling down the Hill. In the background, the illuminated dome of the state capitol mystically hovered over the storm cloud of breath rising above the gathering. The fear and anger I saw in students' eyes inexplicably caused mine to dissipate like the vapor they created. I was left with unexpected sadness. When I spoke, it was quietly, about renewed commitment to nonviolent change.

"How tragic," I began, "that threats and violence speak louder and more influentially than nonviolent words and actions. Is this humanity's shared truth, our shared burden? Will we never learn to talk, to exchange viewpoints peacefully, before it's too late? Could we, the leaders of tomorrow, begin a new chapter by writing a peaceful page in history today?"

I'd lost them, the whole crowd. I sensed it in the sudden quiet. Their outrage required an object and I wasn't up to supplying one. The subdued crowd clapped politely for me when I relinquished the mic and stepped down. Here and there I caught an expression that might indicate someone thinking instead of thirsting for action. But I'd disappointed them, no question. A fiery young comrade of mine, followed by several black speakers, soon reenergized the rally, but failed to reenergize me.

I asked around the Hill for Stan, but no one had seen him. Trudging across campus in the cold that seeped in with the dark, I made for his apartment. My bulky plaid overcoat pulled up around my ears did little to keep out the ferocious winds gusting off the lakes. My footsteps slowed near the crest of the hill where Stan's apartment building perched. Its entry doors flew open and Stan stepped onto the sidewalk with the sorority girl I sat behind in Poli. Sci. 202. Even from a distance, I recognized the straight red hair that fell well below her hips. Her thick tresses mesmerized me in class, like most of the guys, but for more practical reasons. I wondered how she held it to dress, to get into a car, to sit on the can.

Surprised more than suspicious, I stopped to watch. Her crimson hair flared out when she pirouetted to accept a stack of papers from Stan. Spinning again on her heels, flying hair wisped across Stan's face. She sauntered toward me, and as always, walked by without acknowledging me. I turned to watch her red locks swing languidly back and forth across her butt at the place where her tights met her miniskirt. How long would it take to learn that undulating hip-and-shoulder maneuver and grow out my curls? Forget it. Not in this lifetime.

Stan wrenched his eyes from the disappearing redhead as I approached. "Kip, I heard you were wonderful, your speech."

"You didn't hear it?" I asked, pulling at the kinks of my Afro.

In a khaki shirt, hugging himself against the cold, Stan pulled me close and kissed me passionately. Tired to the bone, I leaned into him and let him. "Come in," he whispered. "Causes can wait."

"Why didn't you hear my speech?" I demanded, climbing the stairs to his apartment. "Where have you been? And what was what's-her-face doing here?"

Stan slid a supporting hand down my backside, indicating what he had in mind when we reached his place. "Hm?" he said. "Oh, we ran out of leaflets on solidarity with the black strike. Can you believe the crowds we drew? It's exciting to think of all the new minds we reached."

"You came here with her for leaflets?"

"Actually, I've been back and forth several times during the last few days." Once inside, Stan drew me to his arms and murmured, "My poor, tired, pacifist baby. Let's get you a glass of something hot and put you to bed."

I let my coat slip to the floor in a plaid puddle, sniffing an aroma like hot chocolate that made my stomach cramp with hunger. I was too tired to think, but still something niggled. *Help me distribute flyers ...*

Exhaustion and Stan's coddling encouragement to drink the proffered mug was winning out when I remembered swinging red hair. "Wait a minute. What about what's-her-name? How long was she here?" Stan wasn't wearing his headband; why did that detail seem important?

He held me at arm's length and laughed. "Do I detect jealousy?" He hugged me and spoke into my hair. "'What's-her-name' heard my speech and wanted to help. She came back with me the last time our leaflets ran out. Now drink up before it spills."

Stan steered me onto his bed and concentrated on loosening my layers of clothing. But I required reassuring answers before a prone position in a warm bed with hot milk in an empty stomach finished me off for at least the night.

"A convert?" I yawned, searching Stan's face.

"Absolutely." His loose brown locks covered his features as he struggled to unwind the strings of my combat boots. "Totally inspired by what she heard on the Hill. Kimberly mentioned your speech to me, in fact—"

"Kimberly?"

"Yes, that's what's-her-name's name, Kimberly Kempinski. She called you the most compassionate of speakers."

"Made a real impression all right. Kimberly didn't recognize me when she brushed by me a moment ago."

Stan ripped the covers back, retrieved the mug, and lifted my legs onto the bed. He lay down next to me, fully clothed. My mind grew dull and heavy. "Stan, isn't that how we got together?" He kissed me as I mumbled my way into peaceful oblivion.

One day later, normal campus life resumed.

In Professor Szyzyck's class, a comment by a fellow student on the politics of the last world war incited an alarming tangent in our professor. Kimberly Kempinski's seat was empty before me, so I had a clear view of Dr. Szyzyck, scoffing, "History? You're assuming history is an accurate record of prior events?" I hated it when Stan got all professorial and talked down to us, asking questions that allowed no answers. "Who writes history? The defeated and downtrodden? The dead? You Americans and your naiveté." At such times, Stan reverted to the world-weary Polish war-survivor, forgetting he, too, was now an American.

"Good God, can none of you think for yourselves? Yet?" Grasping the sides of the podium, Stan steadied himself, his feral eyes beneath the head-band boring into our mass stupidity. When he calmed himself, his contempt expressed itself in a scornful tone. "The downtrodden are too busy eking out their existence to write history. The dead are forever silenced. History is written, and rewritten, by the survivors, by the winners, by the last ones standing." His manic laugh sent a chill down my spine.

"If history proves anything, it's that the end justifies the means. The last ones standing," he repeated, "bestow their interpretations, biases, and rationalizations on the apparently unsuspecting generations to follow. And those gullible enough call that history." Stan seemed to be singling me out, or was he searching for the recent convert to the cause, Kimberly? "Is there a better reason," he appeared to ask directly of me, "to be certain you're one of the winners?"

CHAPTER FIFTY-FOUR

April 17, 1972

My dad was billed as the final witness for the prosecution. Mr. Debick had been building to this day since my arrest. No, he'd been building to this day for decades. My lawyers had badly misjudged the prosecution's "bluff" in calling my family to testify. What else had my lawyers misjudged?

I went through the ritualized transfer from jail to the courtroom feeling especially pessimistic. Historically, the townsfolk thought me to be a fuck-up of the first order. But never for one second did I believe they'd think I could kill someone. Now it looked as if everyone believed it with no hesitation.

Until I was escorted to the defense table, I hadn't seen Phil since the court had recessed for five days. I avoided eye contact with her now. During those days of separation, I'd vacillated between anger at Phil's glib advice and worry over my attack on her marriage. I hated to admit I missed talking with her, and it unsettled me that Phil had taken priority over all my pressing worries. I didn't know whether to shout at her for ignoring me, or beg her forgiveness for my being, well, for my being narrow-minded and judgmental.

I stole a glance at her when she rose as the judge called court into session with his gavel. I noticed the way her silvery blouse beneath a dark jacket highlighted her pixie haircut's silver strands in a most flattering way.

"Your Honor," she said, her low alto commanding the court's full attention, "defense moves to strike the hockey stick previously entered into evidence due to illegal search and seizure."

While Debick bolted to his feet to defend his actions, the judge replied, "Mrs. Szyzyck allowed the DA and his assistant the search."

"Yes, Your Honor," Phil admitted, "but even with consent, the stick by the DA's own admission was not in plain view. Mrs. Szyzyck hadn't specifically consented to closets being searched—"

"I'm afraid not, Miss Benedetti," the judge broke in, rifling through papers before him. "Consent as I recall was … yes, was for the former nanny's quarters. Evidence stands. Motion denied. Prosecutor may begin."

Phil exhibited little concern over the ruling, as if the motion had been no more than lawyerly posturing for reasons I didn't understand.

"Prosecution calls Mr. JJ Czermanski."

As he journeyed from the first row behind the defense table to the witness box, Dad masked the aged frailty besetting him since the deaths of both Sarah and Stan, not to mention my humiliating arrest and trial. Expanding into his customary role of dominant fish in the small pond, even his "I do" at being sworn to tell the truth sounded blustery. It was good to see the dad I'd always known, to catch his Old Spice scent when he passed by. He leaned forward in the witness box, battle-ready, letting the world and Harvey Debick know he was no one to be toyed with.

After the preliminaries, Dad's age-old nemesis started in with, "Mr. Czermanski, would you say your household has been in, shall we call it, disarray since the tragic death of your wife some twenty years ago?"

"Disarray?" Dad looked both indignant and perplexed. Philomena and William, in their furtive glances, shared his perplexity. "No, I would not say that."

"Really? Surely four young girls had a difficult transition after losing their mother. Surely you all did."

"Your Honor," said Phil, rising, "relevance?"

Debick countered, "The atmosphere and relationships that developed within the Czermanski household are of paramount importance. They help establish motive as well as the defendant's capability to commit the crime of which she stands accused—murdering her brother-in-law." The judge allowed Debick to continue.

He squared off before Dad. "Mr. Czermanski, tell the court what transpired in the running of your household after the passing of Nor—of your wife?"

"We pulled together like a family. That's what families do."

"Could you be specific?"

"Well—" Dad looked irritated as he thought back. "—first of all, Sarah being the oldest, out of school and all, was expected—She took over primary responsibility for running the house. But Sarah had this calling—to Jesus, to God, to the convent. Many Catholic girls feel the call, sooner or later, but most of the time it passes." Dad was startled by chuckles from the gallery. "Sarah's calling was real. It didn't pass. She left for the convent within a year after Norma's passing, but Sybel, the next oldest, stepped right up to fill her shoes. A good job she did and not more than thirteen or fourteen years old herself."

Dad and Sybel exchanged warm smiles and Sybel sat up straighter. "Course, the girls were too young to be unsupervised while I spent long days building our business, so I hired a nanny, the first one a second cousin from Poland, to come live-in and take care of them. After that, the old nanny lined up the new one from the girls in the village. They'd change places, so to speak, at the end of every school year, the new one staying a year and so on." Dad sat back and eyed Debick with suspicion. "What you're implying about disarray is, as usual Harv, way off the mark."

Debick pivoted away from the spectators to mask his reaction to Dad's retort. "But wasn't Sarah, your eldest, engaged to be married when Mrs. Czermanski died?"

Unbelievable. Was I the only one in Wausaukeesha who hadn't known that before Sarah's funeral?

Dad shifted on the hot seat. "They were kids. It wasn't … didn't work out. Sarah was always super-religious. I suppose she just saw the writing on the wall."

Debick took his time getting to his next question. "So … Sybel stepped in, aided by a revolving door of nannies from Poland. Still you must have had qualms, burdening a fourteen-year-old with supervision of your large home and younger children?"

"Burdening? You still don't know about families and hard times, do you Harv? When my dad couldn't work—our last year of high school, you remember, which allowed you to just step right in as captain of the football team—I gave all that up 'cause that's what it took. You do what you have to."

Dad's slow burn migrated up his neck. "No one asked me if I wanted to quit high school. We lost the farm and moved to town to one of those ramshackle cottages down by the old rail station. We used to call it Trampdale."

Dad chuckled bitterly. "Bums hangin' around … To this day, I can't hear a train whistle without bracing for the roof to come down on our heads, the trains came so close …" Dad remembered himself. "*I* sacrificed, and from peddling my *matka's* sausages door to door in this town, grew a national business. Done pretty damn—darn well, by my girls and my folks." He leaned toward the prosecutor. "So I guess that makes me the last of the dumb Polacks, eh, Harvey?"

The judge's gavel boomed. He warned the two combatants that in his court of law, they could leave their childhood rivalries behind, "or the prosecutor will dismiss himself immediately."

"Sorry, Judge," said Dad, "but Sybel did a good job handling the household. There was no 'disarray,' that's all I'm saying."

"Move on, Mr. Debick," the judge ordered.

"Of course, Your Honor, my apologies. I merely meant that fourteen years of age sounds young for such responsibilities. I never questioned Mrs. Szyzyck's abilities." Debick cleared his throat. "Let's move on to the night of Sarah's funeral and the reception afterward at your home. We've heard that all your daughters stayed overnight at the house, Sybel with her husband. Did you observe anything unusual at the reception, interactions between your daughters, for example, or between them and their husbands? Anything involving the defendant, Kip, and Stan?"

"Nah. My girls' interactions were par for the course, far as I could tell. I saw nothing unusual with anyone in the family, except for sadness."

"So you all went to bed. Tell me where everyone slept."

"In our rooms. Sybel with Stan in her room, first left after the bathroom at the top of the stairs. Samantha in her old room next door, where the hall turns toward my bedroom. Raymond went home, I can't think why just now. And me at the end of the hall, next to the empty room that was Kip's. Kip slept downstairs in the room behind the kitchen."

"Kip once occupied the empty room beside yours?"

"Not since high school. She wanted to move down to where the nannies used to stay when she was younger. Girls hit a certain age and they need all sorts of privacy."

"Mm-hmm." Debick consulted his notes, letting Dad dangle. "Please tell us what you heard and saw that night after the family had gone to bed."

Dad shifted in the chair. "I got up and went to the bathroom during the night. Too much brandy, I guess," he confessed. "When I came out of the bathroom, I heard something. I stood, listening, and heard it again. Voices? I couldn't be sure, but decided it was voices, or angry whispers from below. I felt my way along in the dark when all of a sudden there was a loud crash. I froze at the top step, thinking: burglars. Should I go search out my old hunting rifle? Nah, it hadn't been fired in a decade or more. Call the police? I was still debating when Sybel caught up with me. 'What was that, Daddy?' she whispered. Samantha followed right behind her, looking downright scared to death, even in the dark. Well, it's a man's job to protect his family," Dad said, puffing out his chest. "I thought I better just get on down there and see what's what. The girls followed me, though I kept waving them back. And, well, it was," Dad gulped, "just like Samantha described."

"You mean, of course, the three of you found Stan's body in Kip's bed with Kip standing over him. Mr. Czermanski, did you notice the ice hockey stick in the room or vicinity? Perhaps notice it no longer stood in its accustomed corner of the defendant's bedroom?"

Dad shook his head until, at the judge's insistence, he answered, "No, didn't notice." The witness box was beginning to drain the fight out of Dad, I could tell.

"Please tell the court when and how you met Stanislaw Szyzyck."

Dad rallied for this subject. "Let's see, it was back in the summer of '69. As a long-standing regent of Wausaukeesha College, I am frequently involved in recruitment, and not just for the Czermanski College of Animal Husbandry either. We were looking to expand the social sciences department and needed a political science teacher, er, professor. Don't know exactly how we came up with Stan's résumé, but I headed the subcommittee interviewing candidates. That's how."

"Correct me if I'm wrong, Mr. Czermanski, but Dr. Szyzyck never worked for the local college."

"That's right. We liked Stan right away—bright as they come, top university credentials. We voted to go to the second interview, which is usually lunch or dinner with one of the committee members, its head in this case, me. Over a Czermanski Sausage lunch at Kleinschmidt's, it just kind of came to me, how much I needed a guy like Stan at the Sausage Company. I mean, my sixtieth birthday was just two years off …" Dad lost his train of thought. Oh, right—Dad's sixtieth was also Stan and Sybel's wedding. "Turned out Stan was raised on homemade sausages like me, way back in Poland before the war. We even spoke in Polish …" Dad's smile was wistful. "He was a gem, a natural, for my business."

"So you hired this 'gem'?"

"Had to discuss it with the regents first. There were other applicants, so no real problem, no conflict of interest. Yes, I hired him, brought him in, showed him around, and he took off running. He *was* a natural. Had big plans to take the company—"

"Mr. Czermanski," said Debick, jerking Dad's chain, "did Dr. Szyzyck disclose why he'd left the University of Wisconsin in Madison during your hiring process?"

"Sure. He admitted that his politics had run afoul of the administration. He explained his, I guess you'd have to call them, radical politics to the subcommittee at our first meeting. He was only four when the Nazis overran Poland. Lost his dad early in the war. Lost his mom in the camps. Barely survived himself. It left quite a scar, but it sure explained his strong feelings about war. We could accept that," Dad added magnanimously.

I shook my head. Not just eighteen-year-old girls were seduced by Stan's war story.

"He'd 'run afoul' of UW's Administration," Debick reiterated. "He'd been fired for his politics?"

"Stan was forthright about all of this. Said he'd been fired for leading campus demonstrations against the war in Vietnam."

"I see. Were you grooming him for management of your company?"

"At first, I wanted to see how he fit in and handled things. But in the back of my mind, I had a pretty good intuition he'd be the successor I'd been looking for. Yep, I was grooming him."

"How did he come to marry your daughter, Sybel?"

I followed Dad's glance to the daughter in question. Managing to look both bereft and in control at the same time, Sybel wore a short black jumper, a fuzzy black mohair sweater beneath, with black tights and boots again. She'd done a major wardrobe overhaul for trendy mourning clothes.

I turned back to Dad when he said, "I introduced them not long after he'd come aboard. Brought him home for dinner once, then many times, then regularly. They just kind of took off as a couple, you know, from there—though it still took two years till they married. But it was time, past time when you think of it, for both of them to settle down. They weren't getting any younger, and well, it sure made my succession plan easier. My son-in-law, my successor—keeping it all in the family." Dad's beaming faded quickly. "That was the plan anyhow."

"Your succession plan at the Czermanski Sausage Company," Debick finished for him. "Had you formalized your plan for Dr. Szyzyck to succeed you?"

"I own the company, Harvey," Dad smiled. "I can do what I want."

Debick sucked in a deep breath. "Of course, Mr. Czermanski, but upon your death, did you ensure an orderly transfer of power within your national concern to your son-in-law? You do have another son-in-law, do you not—" Glances proved Raymond was still AWOL. "—plus three surviving daughters?"

Dad furrowed his brow, trying to decide if he'd been insulted in some way. "I put it in my will, my last will and testament. I changed my will, oh, 'bout a month or two before … before all of this."

"You changed your last will and testament to leave the Czermanski Sausage Company—as you yourself called it, a national concern—solely to your son-in-law, Stanislaw Szyzyck? A month or two before his death?"

Phil distracted me with a just audible gasp. William went studiously blank at the same time.

"I just said that, didn't I? If you must know, I left Stan fifty-one percent and each of the girls an equal share of the rest."

Debick walked toward me, pausing to stare me down. "How did your daughters and your surviving son-in-law react to being cut off from control of the multi-million dollar asset your company represents?"

"I'd only got 'round to telling Sybel at the house after Sarah's funeral. She was looking so down, I thought it'd cheer her up some."

Debick pivoted to face Dad. "And did it 'cheer Sybel up some?'"

"Objection," both Phil and William shouted. "Witness is being asked to speculate," Phil finished.

"Sustained," ruled the judge. "You needn't answer the last question, Mr. Czermanski."

"When did you tell all of your daughters and surviving son-in-law about this momentous revision to your last will and testament?"

"We discussed it shortly after the funeral. I assured them they were all well cared for, despite the change. Which is, uh, moot now anyways, isn't it?" No one but me paid attention to Dad's mispronunciation, moot sounding like mute.

"Mr. Czermanski, characterize your daughters' reactions. Were they pleased at their inheritance being pulled out from under them in favor of your son-in-law of a mere six months?"

"Object, counsel is leading and antagonizing the witness."

I wondered why it had taken so long for my lawyers to object to this interesting but irrelevant line of questioning, when its relevance slammed into my gut like a fist, knocking the wind out of me.

"I'll withdraw," Debick injected.

"I assured them all that I took care of them," Dad determined to explain, "but I had to do what's best for the company, didn't I? I wanted to leave the company I'd built from nothing intact. My girls and certainly Raymond— none of them were interested in the business."

"But it would be natural for them to be concerned at the great diminishment they'd suffered in your will?"

"Objection."

"I suppose, but they weren't—"

"They might even be angry? Furious?"

"Maybe, but—" The judge's gavel rapped louder and louder.

"Might even be driven to protect their interests, get rid of the interloper who'd married in and stolen their inheritance?"

"I, I—"

"Your Honor," Phil shouted over Debick and Dad. "This is outrageous!"

At last, Debick relented. "My apologies, Your Honor." The judge directed the jury to disregard the interchange, and Debick pulled himself together by studying his notes. "What you are saying Mr. Czermanski, if I understand your testimony on your succession plan, is that between Dr. and Mrs. Szyzyck, they would have jointly controlled more than sixty-seven percent of your company, leaving your other children virtually powerless."

Dad looked stunned. "I guess so, but—"

"I'm done with this line of questioning," Debick cut in. "Let's move on." Debick's tone lightened. "Were you aware, Mr. Czermanski, that your youngest daughter, the defendant sitting here, and your son-in-law, Sybel's husband, Dr. Szyzyck, were lovers?"

"I heard the testimony from that guy from Madison who kept pawing those postcards."

"Did you know they were lovers before this trial?"

"Only since Kip's arraignment."

"Your daughter, Kip, didn't tell you? Nor your son-in-law, Stan, whom you worked with everyday? Nor did Sybel tell you about it?"

"Don't know that Sybel knew, but no, none of them told me."

"Now why, I wonder, wouldn't Kip mention it the first time she heard Dr. Szyzyck's name, or at the very least admit she'd known him, especially if she were in fact surprised to learn of his whereabouts and his new situation in Wausaukeesha. Plus, Stan, whom you've characterized as 'forthright,' failed to mention it also. It's almost as if they both intentionally hid something."

"Objection."

"Sustained! Mr. Debick, you will refrain from leading the witness to speculative conclusions. I will not warn you again, Prosecutor."

Debick paused before the jury box. His weary expression said that dredging up this muck was so distasteful, but alas, it was his job. Returning to the prosecution table and sliding onto his chair, he offered the witness up to the defense.

CHAPTER FIFTY-FIVE

Philomena, not William, rose before my father, each sizing the other up. "Mr. Czermanski, you testified that you discussed with all your daughters the change you'd made to your will some time after the funeral. Please be more specific."

Dad thought. "It was a few days after the funeral and the … incident with Stan. That's as specific as I can be."

"But wasn't your youngest daughter, Kip, being held at that time in the Wausaukeesha County Jail—held in fact since the 'incident with Stan,' first for arraignment, then for trial?"

"Oh yeah, Kip wasn't there, that's right, just Sybel and Samantha."

"You're stating that Kip was not a party to the discussion of the change made to your will," she repeated for the benefit of the jury. "Did Kip even know about this change before your testimony today?"

"I guess not. Oh yes, she did. Samantha told Kip when she visited her in the jail."

I noticed Phil blink a few times. "Fine, Mr. Czermanski. But Kip did *not* know you changed your will, leaving controlling interest in your company to Stan until she was *already* in custody following his death. That is your testimony?"

"Yes, I agree with that."

"So any insinuation of the change to her inheritance being motive for the defendant is after the fact *at best*. When Stan Szyzyck died, my client had no knowledge of your new will." Phil let that sink in by rustling papers in a file. "You testified that Dr. Szyzyck was 'forthright' in telling you about his work history when you first met him in mid-1969. Surely the local college, if not the Sausage Company, checked prior employment and verified his statements?"

"Wausaukeesha College never got that far with this candidate, but yes, my secretary phoned the university in Madison to verify employment dates and so forth."

"Your secretary verified that Stan Szyzyck was fired, as he led you to believe, for his radical politics?"

"Not exactly. All the university gives out is dates of employment, nothing more. I don't have to tell you how litigious this world is becoming, do I?" Laughter erupted throughout the courtroom, and surprising everyone, Phil joined in. "There was no reason not to believe him," Dad added, visibly warming to Phil. "You should've seen him back then—hair down past his shoulders, a headscarf wrapped around his head like some Indian chief. Even though he was trying to tame it down for us, he was still a hippie, plain and simple. Why wouldn't I believe what was written all over him?"

Phil nodded. "Can you think of a reason this son-in-law whom you so obviously admired wouldn't mention his previous history with your youngest daughter, or why she herself hadn't mentioned it?"

Dad cocked his head. "Well, Kip had moved far away. I suppose that to Stan it was ancient history, you know, water under the bridge. It probably ended as these things often do, with everyone just moving on."

"Thank you, Mr. Czermanski." Phil walked back to our table, looking at me hard, debating something with herself. She turned back to address the judge, "Your Honor, again I'll dismiss this witness while reserving my right to recall him later in the trial."

Dad assured Judge Fassbinder that he wasn't "going anywhere," and stepped down. Only those as close as I could hear his literal deflation as he plunked into his seat between my sisters.

The judge directed the prosecutor to call his next witness. Debick stood and paused for so long that the entire defense table tensed for yet another of the prosecution's innocent bombshells. But through clenched teeth, Debick at last yielded. "Prosecution rests."

Before adjourning for the day, the judge directed the defense to be ready to commence its case first thing the next morning. Now it was all up to us.

CHAPTER FIFTY-SIX

Speeding back toward jail, my police transport hurtling through the potholes shook loose a realization. I had witnessed Dad at the funeral reception trying to "cheer Sybel up" with the revision to his will. Their argument in the corner of our living room following the funeral had silenced the rest of us, and eventually them.

"They were talking about Stan taking over the Sausage Company," I proclaimed aloud. "And Sybel was anything but cheered by it—but why?"

"Say what, Kip?" Timothy leaned across the aisle of the bouncing van. "Musta missed something."

"Nothing, Timothy, nothing." We've all missed something, I thought, but what?

"You forgot?" Phil and William watched me closely, waiting for an answer.

My back to them, I stared into the dull foil mirror hung over the sink, pulling barrettes from my hair. Freed, it sprang into its own unique version of an Afro. Secretly, I was watching them watch me.

"I did. I forgot. Samantha mentioned Dad changing his will just as she was leaving my cell and I guess …" I sighed as I sat down to face them. "I got all hung up on her knowing the guy Sarah had been engaged to and the rumor about the two of them."

"Rumor?" Phil arched her brow.

I hadn't intentionally kept my lawyers in the dark, had I? Was Phil's insinuation that I accepted, even enjoyed, my role as scapegoat, subconsciously at least helping them convict me? The mere words weighed me down with fear and revulsion.

"What rumor, Kip?" William asked.

"That Dad paid Sarah's boyfriend or fiancé, Jerry Andersen, to leave town so Sarah would replace Mother and run the household for him."

Phil questioned William, "Do you know who they're talking about, Jerry Andersen?" When he shook his head, she said, "Look into it, will you? There might be something there." To me she asked, "Did your father pay him to leave?"

I shrugged. "Probably, though Samantha wouldn't admit it."

"Anything else you've forgotten to tell us, Kip?"

"I'm sorry. I never dreamed Debick could construe the change to Dad's will as motive." I kicked off my ugly sensible court shoes. Everything ached, from my feet to my head.

"Construe it convincingly," Phil pointed out. From her curtness I sensed her head must ache too. She handed me several notepads and pencils. "Kip, I've asked you to note things that occur to you, and now you see why. It's essential we know everything before it comes out in court. By now that should be obvious."

"I guess I get hung up on unimportant details like why wasn't Sybel happy that her husband would inherit Dad's company? I mean, with her third of our forty-nine percent, they could do anything they wanted, overruling Samantha and me completely."

Phil and William glanced at each other. "Did Samantha have an idea about that?" Phil asked.

"She thought they were going through some newlywed adjustment period."

"We must put her on the stand." Phil said, anticipating my refusal.

"Sybel? No way," I snapped. "You don't know her. She'll only make things worse, I guarantee it."

"Samantha then," William tried.

"None of them. You can't trust any of them. You can do this without them. You're going to have to do this without them."

"We are on the same side, aren't we?" Phil asked testily as she rose, signaling the jailor with vehemence. "We're late for our meeting with our witnesses. See you in court."

"Yeah," I grumbled, wanting to hold her back, explain, apologize, ask her forgiveness. But "See you in court," was all I could manage before she stomped away.

CHAPTER FIFTY-SEVEN

April 18, 1972

Defense opened its case by calling Kimberly Kempinski. The hush that fell over the courtroom emphasized the clicking heels of each undulating step taken to the stand. Swinging red tresses hypnotized an entire room. As she passed the defense table, I picked up her scent, White Shoulders. She sat— she did have to lift her hair to do so—and faced the room wearing a bright red suit, her green eyes as striking as the rest of the visual.

William would begin the defense case. Phil claimed another sore throat from the radically changing spring weather—from blizzard to heat wave and back. There had to be some deeper strategy behind it to which a mere client wasn't privy. Standing before Kimberly, William seemed to forget why he was there. I, too, was suddenly struck dumb by a question that popped into my brain. Why did Stan seek out Polish women?

With difficulty and dignity, Kimberly told her story, her throaty voice breaking repeatedly. "Professor Szyzyck came on to me in his office in North Hall. I walked out, disgusted. He detained me after our next class meeting— actually Poli. Sci. 202, the class I was in with Kip, the, the defendant. He apologized profusely to me, and I believed him ... then. When I offered to help out at a demonstration, that's when it happened, the rape." A furious blush crawled over her skin. "We went to his, Professor Szyzyck's, apartment to get more flyers to pass out on Bascom Hill. There he offered me a beer. We'd all been up for days by then—that's what I thought when a few sips made me woozy. What happened before I left his apartment with the flyers is still a blank."

William asked, "You don't know what happened, Ms. Kempinski?"

"Not exactly, but I knew something was wrong. I felt sore and … not right. I went to the Student Health Center late that night because I was … uncomfortable and bleeding. The examining doctor asked when I'd last had, uh, sexual relations." Her coloring jumped up a notch. "I bluntly told him: never. The doctor … he said that was impossible, based on my exam and … my troubles. Then I knew.

"I reported it to university authorities. Their lack of surprise provided the first clue that I wasn't alone. Professor Szyzyck was fired a few weeks later. He left campus just as the spring '69 semester ended."

Where was I during all of this? Oh yeah, asleep in Stan's bed, which Kimberly had just vacated.

William thanked the witness for the difficult testimony that brought tears to my eyes, then asked, "How do you explain your inability to remember what happened to you? Surely one beer could not render you so incapacitated."

"One of my sorority sisters, she's in pre-med, the one I confided in and who encouraged me to go to the university authorities, knew about a drug used for something she called 'date rape.' I'd never heard of such a thing, nor the drug. When I reported the incident to them, their questions—who was I with, what had I been drinking or eating, could I be certain nothing had been sneaked into my beer—made her theory more likely."

"Do you know what this date-rape drug is called?"

"GHB."

"The date-rape drug, GHB, left you with no memory of Stan Szyzyck's assault, even after you realized your situation and received confirmation at the campus health center?"

"That's correct."

"That's all, Ms. Kempinski. We thank you again for your brave testimony today."

"I can go?" she asked, rising from the chair, red hair tumbling forward.

"Cross, Your Honor." Harvey Debick was already before the witness. Kimberly sat down slowly. "Miss Kempinski, you testified you knew Miss Czermanski at the University?"

"Sort of. She sat behind me in Professor Szyzyck's class."

"Were you aware that Miss Czermanski and Professor Szyzyck were lovers?"

"Of course, everyone knew, well, assumed. Kip was smart and outspoken, but whenever he came near her in that lecture hall, or when she thought no one paid attention, she went positively gaga over him. It kind of entertained the class—"

"Objection."

"Sustained."

"Miss Kempinski," Debick oozed, "characterize what you observed from the defendant toward your professor during class?"

"Just that she was, uh, head over heels for him. Crazy in love."

Debick stalked back to me and paused, looking from the witness to me and back. "'Crazy in love,' you say."

"I meant—"

"We get your meaning. Did you observe Dr. Szyzyck's feelings for the defendant as well?"

"Yes, no, I don't know. He was always after the girls, flirting I mean, you know, testing the waters, seeing who would bite. He was fond of Kip, and they were amazing as *the* couple in the anti-war movement. I'm sure … Well that's all I observed."

"He was not so crazy in love perhaps?"

"Objection, Your Honor."

"Sustained."

"Sorry, Your Honor," Debick said before turning back to rephrase. "Dr. Szyzyck had many relationships then, other than the defendant?"

"I don't know that. He was flirtatious, as I said. But he and Kip spent a lot of time together, that much everyone could see."

"Now back to the question of rape by Dr. Szyzyck. Your medical exam proved you'd had sexual relations, but there was no hard evidence of your being drugged?"

"Well, yes."

"Didn't you say you'd been involved in a campus protest and up for days when you ingested the beer that Dr. Szyzyck offered you?"

"Yes."

"So Miss Kempinski, is it not possible that exhaustion and alcohol, perhaps some feelings of attraction toward your professor, might have led to a more consensual situation?"

"Absolutely not." Kimberly's fury flooded her face. "I wouldn't be here if—"

"Thank you, Miss Kempinski. You may step down."

"And Dr. Szyzyck was fired for drugging and raping coeds," she stormed. "The university let me know how they'd handled my complaint after he left."

"Dismissed," the prosecutor shouted over the witness. Kimberly rose and set her jaw before descending from the stand. She paused at the defense table as if she wanted to clear something up between us, but moved on. I smiled my appreciation at her for the gutsiness she'd shown on my behalf.

"Judge Fassbinder, defense calls Albrecht Fenster," said William. I didn't recognize the name until I saw the dean of UW's Political Science department, Stan's former boss. Instantly, his tight-assed and -lipped secretary who'd gloated over my misery when Stan disappeared flew to mind. The dean took the seat after his swearing-in and smiled at me with sympathy. The gesture recalled my first impression of him, his resemblance to the photos of sickly Grandpa Czermanski, balding and pale, and I relaxed a bit.

Having established the dean's connection to the case, William asked him if he recognized the file he held. He identified it as Stan's university personnel records as the file was placed in his hands. "Would you please read to the court the document within the file that covers Stan Szyzyck's dismissal from the University of Wisconsin."

Dean Fenster made a wry smile upon opening the file. "I think I'd best summarize. It's lengthy, but I wrote it myself. Dr. Szyzyck's employment was terminated on May 19, 1969." He closed the file and continued, "for repeated complaints against him by coeds who claimed to have been drugged and raped. The story was almost always the same: an unsuspecting student was given something to drink by Dr. Szyzyck under innocuous circumstances. The student blanked out for a period of time following, and usually wound up at the campus health center or a doctor's office. Subsequent examination proved sexual contact." He removed his glasses, polished the lenses, then nibbled on the frame.

"How many such incidents were reported, Dean Fenster?"

"More than a dozen, but only eight—did I say only?—could be verified." His smile was anything but amused as he replaced his spectacles. "By that I mean witnesses saw the victim with the professor, could corroborate the timing of the incident with the medical information, and for that same time period, Professor Szyzyck could not provide a sound alibi."

"What was the final act that caused Stan Szyzyck's dismissal?"

"I was asked by the chancellor's office to observe Professor Szyzyck closely. As some of the complaints alleged that the rape had occurred in the professor's office, I was asked to drop in unexpectedly, use my key to unlock his office if required. The university would tolerate none of this, especially on its own property, but had to have sufficient and airtight grounds to fire a tenured professor."

"I see. So you dropped in, used your key, and what did you find?"

The dean looked down before he responded. "I caught the professor with a coed. She was out—drugged, unconscious, and partially clothed. I called the health center, and they came for her, examined her, and were able to trace a date-rape drug in her blood, a small quantity of which I recovered from a desk drawer in that office."

"What was the drug you recovered?"

"GHB. Dr. Szyzyck was let go, fired. I called him to my office and told him if he signed his termination agreement, the university would not pursue further action against him, though I couldn't guarantee one or more of his victims wouldn't. He signed and left the area almost immediately. Until you subpoenaed me and his records, I never knew what had become of him."

"And now you know. Your Honor, defense will submit the personnel file of the decedent into evidence. Thank you, Dean Fenster. Prosecutor, your witness."

Debick began his question en route to the witness stand. "Did Dr. Szyzyck explain the GHB you said you found in his desk drawer?"

"He said use and/or possession of GHB was not illegal, first and foremost. He claimed he used it for bodybuilding purposes, and that it helped him sleep."

"Did Dr. Szyzyck offer any alibi or explanation concerning these alleged rapes?"

"He claimed that having consensual sex was, likewise, not a crime. But that didn't ex—"

"Why did none of his alleged victims—eight I believe you said that were verified—press charges against Dr. Szyzyck, Dean? Not a one."

"I suppose the adverse publicity—"

"The same reason the university itself chose not to take legal action against an alleged sexual predator on its payroll?"

"Without the witnesses coming forth, the university's case would have been difficult to prove, although I—"

"Difficult indeed. No further questions. You're dismissed," Debick informed him before he said anything else.

CHAPTER FIFTY-EIGHT

William wasted no time. With my head splitting from the revelations of the last two witnesses, he called, "Dr. Oswald Olsen." Who? It was all I could do to keep up.

His dapper, citified appearance suggested that Dr. Olsen did not hail from Wausaukeesha. Chicago, I'd bet. Neatly trimmed and combed dark hair with sideburns of a respectable length, the doctor was clean-shaven and wore wire-rimmed glasses perched on his nose. His clothing—navy suit, blue shirt, gleaming shoes—all reeked of expensive tastes. A deep tan added to his startling handsomeness. If a Chicagoan, he was a snowbird.

The doctor appeared poised and relaxed on the witness stand. Raising his right hand exposed a thick watchband that captured the light. After stating his name, he added, "I'm afraid most people call me 'Ollie.' Can't seem to shake that childhood nickname." I found that hominess, in contrast to his overt sophistication, comforting.

William ignored his comment. "Dr. Olsen, please tell the court your training and employment background."

"I'm an MD and a Ph.D. in chemistry, both degrees from the University of Chicago, where I'm employed. Along with teaching responsibilities, I'm currently researching the bio-chemical responses to a range of neurotransmitter drugs, including gamma-hydroxybutyrate, GHB, a central nervous system depressant. Some of my research is for private pharmaceuticals and governmental agencies, as well as for the university and my personal interests."

"Would you characterize yourself as an expert on the drug GHB?"

"Gamma-Hydroxy-Butyrate, yes. Unfortunately, I've appeared as an expert witness in too many rape cases. In fact, GHB is quickly becoming known as the 'date-rape' drug. My research and training certify my expertise in this area." For some reason, he chose this time to check out the defendant, and I squirmed in my seat. At that moment, I could have killed Stan.

"Tell us about this drug."

"First synthesized about a decade ago in the early Sixties as an anesthetic, the drug triggers a range of effects in the human body by temporarily increasing GABA—gamma-aminobutyric acid—and dopamine in the brain. That can alter the user's mental state from normal to something similar to inebriation, all the way to coma. It's claimed, and we're still verifying, that GHB aids weight loss, increases strength, improves sleep, and can work as an antidepressant. Moderate doses of GHB induce relaxation, euphoria, and uninhibitedness similar to alcohol, while at the same time increasing the libido. Higher doses induce sleep, even coma, with euphoria giving way to sedation. We're analyzing other effects and usages such as diet supplementation and bodybuilding, but it would appear from all the research that GHB is both nontoxic to the liver and kidneys and nonaddictive."

"I'm sure Dr. Szyzyck's victims appreciate that."

Debick leapt up. "Object, Your Honor."

"Sustained," the judge ruled, advising the jury to ignore defense counsel's last statement.

William moved on. "Is it fair to say, Doctor, dosage is critical to its safe usage?"

"Absolutely. Too much could be dangerous. Most foreign substances introduced in the body carry a chance of adverse reaction."

"It's fair, then, to say it's extremely dangerous to slip this drug into someone's food or drink without knowing how they might react, let alone what they may have previously ingested. What does happen when the drug GHB is used in combination with alcohol?"

"That scenario is fraught with risks," Dr. Olson attested. "Serious consequences could result, even death, although to my knowledge, no such occurrence has been reported to date."

William sought out Kimberly sitting far in the back of the courtroom before commenting, "You heard the testimony of the previous witness, Dr. Olsen, who said Stan Szyzyck gave her a beer before she blacked out and was raped. He could've killed her with that combination—"

"Objection. Now it's the defense who is leading and speculative," cried Prosecutor Debick.

"Sorry," William acknowledged before the judge ruled. "Would someone familiar with this drug through regular usage likely understand the risks associated with its use in combination with alcohol?"

"Anyone who obtained it OTC, over the counter, would see such a warning on the label. Unless he was home-brewing it in his basement, alcohol would be specifically warned against. And were he brewing his own, he'd probably be sophisticated enough to be aware of the chemical-reactivity risks."

"I see. But someone who repeatedly used this 'date-rape' drug by sneaking it into his victims' drinks, alcoholic or otherwise, would, in your opinion, be flagrantly courting danger for his unknowing victims."

"I'd certainly agree with that."

"Why GHB, Doctor? Aren't there other substances available that could reduce inhibitions and increase libido?"

"Yes, of course. Alcohol itself can have these effects, but it's hard to slip a quantity of alcohol into someone unnoticed. GHB comes in liquid or powder form, it's odorless, colorless, and basically tasteless. Further, unless someone knows what to test for in a timely manner, GHB is undetectable in the blood of a victim, it being excreted within a few hours of ingestion."

"You're saying GHB is an ideal date-rape drug because unsuspecting victims cannot detect it by taste or smell, it works quickly to reduce normal inhibitions and increase libido, and cannot be traced in the victim afterward."

"Exactly," the doctor confirmed.

"So if he doesn't kill his victims, the rapist generally gets his way with them *and* gets away with the crime," William stated with revulsion. "Dr. Olsen, could you be more specific about the drug's effect on memory?"

"Again, depending upon dosage, memory in the victim would be spotty to nonexistent. You might compare it to alcohol's effect on memory. Alcohol sometimes erases moments here and there, and at other times, can erase a whole evening."

Like a memory black hole, I thought, with swirling events not quite in focus.

William paused before the jury. "In your expert opinion, Doctor, is it likely that someone drugged with GHB could turn violent? Say, pick up a weapon and beat someone to death with it?"

The scientific method was almost visible as the witness considered first one side, then the next, pondering and dismissing. "Not likely," came his pronouncement. "The drug's effect on inhibition leans toward the libidinous. I've never seen any evidence of GHB going the other way—toward violence. No, I would go so far as to testify that GHB has never provoked a violent reaction, regardless of dosage."

William returned to our table before he offered up the witness to the prosecution.

"Now Ollie," Debick began, all smiles at our expert witness. "You did say people call you that? Do you mind if I do?"

"Not at all. I'm afraid I'm quite used to it." Instantly, Master-of-the-Undermine Debick took control. Dr. Olsen, MD, Ph.D., and Professor at the University of Chicago, became just Ollie, as in the TV puppet show *Kookla, Fran, and Ollie...* "Now tell me, you say Dr. Szyzyck could purchase this dangerous drug you've been describing 'OTC' over any drugstore's counter? No prescription required?"

"It's been sold over the counter as a dietary supplement since its discovery ten-odd years ago."

"Right. That's what I thought you said. As the defense itself previously established, possession of GHB is not illegal. Dr. Szyzyck could have kept the small quantity found in his office for anything from bodybuilding and dieting to sleep inducement, as the defense witness said he claimed, could he not?"

"Yes."

"Now why, if this drug is as dangerous as you describe, would it be so easy for anyone to get a hold of?"

"Only now—"

"Don't we have the Federal Drug Administration to protect us and our children from such dangers?"

"Yes—"

"Can aspirin kill you if you take too much, Ollie?"

"Yes of course, but—"

"So to characterize the deceased, Dr. Stanislaw Szyzyck, as wantonly distributing a lethal drug, is tantamount to calling any mom who gives her kids St. Joseph's Aspirin for Children a potential killer. Is that what we're to believe, Ollie?"

"No, of course not."

"All of which is especially troublesome when Dr. Szyzyck's intentions and use of GHB can never be proven. You're dismissed, Ollie."

William bolted out of his seat. "Redirect, Your Honor. Dr. Olsen, before letting you get back to your medical research and professorial responsibilities at the University of Chicago, a few last questions. In your expert opinion, is it likely that Dr. Szyzyck was slipping his victims GHB to aid his preys' weight loss regimens?" The laughter from the gallery brought down the judge's gavel.

"I would seriously doubt it," Dr. Olsen smiled as laughter waned, "as evidenced by multiple victims' medical examinations pointing both to sudden, unexplained memory loss, as well as to rape."

"Thank you, Dr. Olsen. You may step down."

Dr. Ollie Olsen rose, straightened his suit that needed no straightening, and descended the witness stand, smiling at me as he passed. Despite his suave appearance, the smile seemed grandfatherly and protective. It made me wish I could crawl into a hole to hide my humiliation.

CHAPTER FIFTY-NINE

As the witness came forward, her gym-floor squeaks and jocky gait called attention to her thick-soled shoes and anything-but-sheer nylons. In contrast to the previous witness, this witness's ill-cut beige suit emphasized her large frame in all the wrong places. Bobby pins poked out from her gray permanent curls.

After stating her name, "Barbara Jean Howenhauser," the witness made her preference clear: "But I go by 'Babs.' It's how everyone knows me." When asked her occupation, Babs ad libbed. "I'm a journalist and a lifelong friend of the defendant's family. I grew up with Kip's mother and father. Attended their wedding way back when, as well as Samantha's to Raymond and Sybel's to Stan."

William tried to focus her. "Aren't you employed by the—"

"Yes yes, everyone knows me as the social chronicler of Wausaukeesha."

"You write for the Wausaukeesha newspaper," he directed Babs through her signature verbosity, "known as—"

"*The Dairyland Diary*, yep. Society editor. Everyone knows that."

"Fine, Ms. Howenhauser, but just for the record, you understand."

"Call me Babs."

"All right, Babs. You wrote a detailed article for your paper on the wedding of Stan and Sybel Szyzyck, did you not?"

"Just doing my job, but it was a good piece, wasn't it?" As she described the dual birthday party/surprise wedding, Babs misted up, dissolving into tears when she recalled how Sybel looked like my mother's twin, wearing

Mother's wedding dress and walking down the aisle on Dad's arm. "It was like seeing a ghost." Babs rummaged for the Kleenex she found tucked in her pocket and honked into it like a goose. "Truly, if I do say so myself, one of my best examples of *reportage.*"

I almost choked on her Frenchism-cum-Wisconsin-nasal-twang, but William pressed on. "In it you said that Mrs. Szyzyck, Sybel, was most like her mother."

"In looks."

"Not in other ways?"

Babs straightened and glowered. "I should say not."

"Their personalities were different?"

"In the extreme." Babs leaned over the witness box conspiratorially. "You're too young to know, so let me just tell you, Norma was a saint. Beautiful, sweet, caring, a generous friend and quite a catch for JJ, I tell you. Most popular girl at Wausaukeesha High when we were there. Everybody loved her, the girls and the boys." Babs surveyed the room. "Half the men in this room would've given their eyeteeth to be at Norma's side." Did I imagine that Babs defiantly lingered over Harvey Debick? "But personality-wise, lovely Sarah, Sister Sarah Joseph, the eldest sister and nun, was closest to her mother, a saint herself. Genuinely good would about sum it up."

"So Sybel is not like that—*genuinely good, sweet, caring, generous, a saint*?" Debick was on his feet, objecting, but William defended himself. "This witness has known the family intimately since the defendant's parents were themselves children. The prosecutor has insisted all along that relationships and interactions are critical to establishing motive and the defendant's ability to commit the crime. Judge, we've had to listen to testimony from witnesses much further removed from the Czermanski family. The prosecution cannot have it both ways."

"Overruled," the judge determined. "Defense may proceed."

Babs seemed to remember herself. "Not that I'm bad-mouthing Sybel. She's a tough woman, that's all. Some find her highfalutin, but she's competent and strong-willed and always has been. Maybe she had to be—taking on so much so young. She can be downright steely, but with her workaholic Dad, like I say, she probably had to be …"

William produced the letter Babs had sent me in jail. "Do you recognize this letter?" Babs went uncharacteristically silent, bobbing her head. "For the record," William stated, "the witness nodded in the affirmative. In this letter, you offered to be Kip's voice to the community, did you not?"

"Well, yes. I figured she could use me to state her side if, if she wished."

"Why did you think she'd need you to 'state her side'?"

Babs looked confused. "Well … Kip was sort of the forgotten child, much younger than the rest of her siblings and on the wrong side of most issues with her family. I just thought she might need … someone to make her side known."

"You, who have known the family intimately your whole life, are saying Kip never had a champion, even within her own family?" William unfolded the letter. "May I quote you? 'I never trusted that Stan. But since he became not only Sybel's husband but also your father's right-hand man, I'm certain you'll need a friend in the community to stand up against them both.' What did you mean by all that?"

"Hmm." Babs looked at her lap for a while. "Sybel and Stan stood on the highest rung of Wausaukeesha society. JJ practically owns this town, I needn't tell you, William. Half the folks here work for him directly, the other half indirectly, supplying him and such. I meant nothing disrespectful—" She glanced at Sybel. "—just that the Czermanskis are at the top of the heap. Kip might've needed a friend, that's all."

"Kip is a Czermanski. Why wouldn't she be at 'the top of the heap' as well?"

Babs shook her head. "That's just not the way it worked. The pecking order was JJ and Sybel, and Stan once he entered the picture, then Samantha, then Kip." Did anyone else besides me notice she'd forgotten Raymond altogether?

"So what you're saying is Kip has always been the outcast." William stopped in front of me to read: "'I never trusted that Stan.' Tell us why you wrote that?"

Babs pursed her lips thoughtfully. "Something about him. I've got a really good sense for these things, for people. It's my job. Over my years in journalism, I've had to meet and mingle with everyone from the Czermanskis to the cherry pickers who come through seasonally. You have no idea what a journalist must go through.

"Anyways, this Stan shows up one day like some hippie, flashing his degrees and college affiliations all over the place, acting the intellectual. Then in no time, he's turned himself into JJ's double—cuts his hair, shaves his face, buys some wingtips, and goes all corporate. He woos Sybel, and that actually takes. Maybe it's the reporter in me, but I just wondered what we weren't seeing. And through this trial, I do believe my instincts have been proven right. He did have secrets, didn't he? I bet Sybel could just …" Babs went pale and silent.

"Could just what?"

"I'm, I'm just sure this has been hard on her. That's all I meant to say."

"It must be hard on the whole family. You single out Sybel as his wife?"

"Sybel is, has always been, extremely … Yes, because she's the wife."

William crossed back to the defense table to buy some time, but all he added was, "Thank you, Ms. Howenhauser. Babs. Your witness."

Debick was up before William took his seat. "Babs, let's be honest. You don't like Sybel Czermanski Szyzyck, and you never have."

"I wouldn't say it like—"

"Remind me. You have a son around the age of Mrs. Szyzyck?" Babs glanced down. Of course—hitting my fist on the table startled my lawyers—it's impossible to hide anything in a small town. "Do you or do you not have a son around the age of Sybel Szyzyck? Babs, this is not a difficult question."

"Thomas. Tom. He's thirty-three."

"In other words, the answer is yes." The prosecutor circled and came in for the kill. "Isn't it true that your son, Tom, was in love with Sybel Czermanski

Szyzyck most of his life? They dated in high school, maybe college, didn't they? But she never returned his feelings. Isn't that why you don't like Sybel, truth be known? Nor the man who won her heart?"

"Now Harvey, that is really oversimplify—"

"That will be all, Mrs. Howenhauser. I'm done with this witness, Judge."

Babs struggled to her feet in her creased suit, dazed. I knew she'd been nosing around for gossip with that letter of hers. "My voice to the community," my ass. She was hoping for some dirt for her column, the more embarrassing for Sybel, and possibly Dad, the better.

Our society editor, it would seem, didn't much care for the "top rung" of Wausaukeesha society.

CHAPTER SIXTY

No sooner was I sprawled in the green room for the lunch recess, my blouse unbuttoned at the neck, my shoeless feet raised on a chair, when my lawyers appeared.

"We're going to have to call you, Kip," Phil announced. "We've got little else to go on without your family members. Remember what we've discussed. Be careful when you're crossed. Think before you react or say a word. And Kip, William will have to handle your examination today. I'm afraid," Phil added, "I'm saddled with this recurring sore throat through today."

I rose upon hearing my name called, determined to be the most convincing witness ever to grace a courtroom. I had to be. My defense had come down to me and me alone.

I sat in the witness box in my prim dark suit, my kinks and whorls besieged by barrettes, feeling the riveted eyes of my judges and accusers. I blocked them out by focusing on William, answering his questions about my convictions concerning war and civil disobedience, sexism and racism, the causes of my life and times—the very things this young lawyer and I had violently disagreed on not many weeks before. Surreptitious glimpses of bored, unimpressed faces suggested that establishing my philosophical underpinnings was far less interesting to jurors and spectators than Harvey Debick's sensationalized slants on my life had been.

"Ms. Czermanski, the court has heard about your involvement in the anti-war movement. Does that explain your police record in its entirety?"

"Yes. Acts of civil disobedience, especially nonviolent acts of civil disobedience, are not only a right under the Constitution of the United States and the Bill of Rights, but a duty."

"Your involvement with one of the anti-war movement's leaders, a much older, more experienced man, your professor in fact—who only much later became your brother-in-law—began as a meeting of like minds and developed into a love relationship?"

My fantasies of Stan as I sat in his lectures came to mind, but we first hooked up through the war movement, that was true. "Yes."

"Now, your behavior, especially your senior year in Madison, has been painted in this courtroom in the most salacious terms. How would you characterize your actions your last year of college after Stan's disappearance?" William asked.

"Acting out."

"And 'acting out' means?"

"It's a lay psychological term, meaning my deep hurt, my deeper fears of abandonment, played out in all sorts of, well, immature and desperate activities, sex partners, for example. But it is also relevant to keep in mind the sexual revolution fomenting all around me—love the one you're with, that kind of thing—as well as other counterculture influences. Plus, it was a year of my life when, yes, I was a lost and heartbroken kid."

A twinkle in William's eye told me he approved of my choice of words so I rushed to add more. "Stan was my first, my only, love. At the time, I believed we were meant—"

"Thank you, Ms. Czermanski," William cut me off with a glare. Right, answer in as few words as possible. You'd think I'd remember that after listening to Babs Howenhauser, social chronicler.

William gave us both time to regroup by walking to the defense table, where Phil sat alone, nursing her dubious sore throat. "You were saying you were in love with Stan during the time of your involvement with him. Did you have other sex partners during that period?"

"No." I knew it sounded corny and old-fashioned, but admitted, "Stan was my first and only lover until his disappearance."

"Were you aware Stan had other sex partners during the period from early in your second semester of your freshman year through your junior year, roughly from the winter of 1967 through spring of 1969?"

"I am now." Laughter, gavel banging, uneasy quieting. "I wasn't at the time. I thought I was his only …" Talk about sounding old-think.

"You had no inkling of the testimony we heard earlier about Stan drugging women for sex during your two and a half years together, actions which ultimately cost him his post at the university?"

"No idea."

"Now that you know, how does it make you feel?"

"Stupid. Used, big time. And naïve. And sad …"

William paused to allow my sadness to make the impression he hoped for. "Ms. Czermanski, you've heard your sisters and father tell their story of what happened that night at the family home. What's your version of those events?"

"I locked the doors to the house after finishing up in the kitchen, turned off the lights, and went to bed. Next thing I recall was dreaming about Stan when we were together, then struggling with him for real. I remember struggling … Next, I was standing beside my bed, soaking wet, wondering who's in my bed and why, when my family materialized at the door." I shuddered, remembering the chill of standing half-naked in a wet nightgown. "Next thing I recall is Sybel helping me dress in the college castoff clothes that still hung in my bedroom closet. Then I was going to the jailhouse for questioning, and then, well, eventually, I wound up here."

"So your memory is both spotty as well as completely erased for a period of the night of your sister's funeral. What happened right before you locked up that night?"

"Sybel and I were doing dishes when Stan came into the kitchen, carrying brandy for us both."

"Did you drink that brandy, Ms. Czermanski?"

"Yes. I was so tired and sad, but agitated, like I'd never sleep, thinking about the sister I'd just lost. Maybe it would help me unwind, I thought, and drank it down."

"Did your sister, Sybel, drink the brandy her husband brought in for her?"

"I don't think so. She made a comment about hating brandy after Stan left."

"How would you explain your faulty memory of that night?"

"I couldn't explain it until I heard the witness, Kimberly's, horrifying tale. And then of course, Dr. Olsen's testimony about GHB, the date-rape drug they found in Stan's office."

"Yet repeatedly we've heard that GHB wasn't found in your blood during your medical exam."

"Right, but Dr. Olsen testified the drug is excreted within hours. I wasn't examined for two and a half days."

"Yes, our expert witness, Dr. Olson, did testify to GHB's untraceability." William crossed to the jury and leaned toward them, "We know Stan had, at least eight times according to his UW personnel file, drugged and raped women, a fact which led to his dismissal from UW right before he showed up here in Wausaukeesha. Do you believe Stan, with his demonstrable record of doing that very thing, drugged you that night?"

"Objection."

"I'll allow it," responded the judge.

"Now I do. He hung around the kitchen, encouraging Sybel and me to drink up." *Na zdrowie*, he had said, *or as they say in these parts, bottoms up.*

"But yet, he didn't rape you, isn't that what the medical report showed?"

"He didn't succeed."

"How do you explain resisting him if you were drugged with GHB?"

"I believe Dr. Olsen said much of the effect of the drug depends upon dosage. I must not have had enough, or it must've begun to wear off before Stan could ... do his worst."

"Do you believe, as you now look back, that he had drugged you before?"

"I doubt it. He had no need to." My audience guffawed. "But now when I think back on it, I see Stan's irrational temper when he didn't get his way. Stan wouldn't take 'no' for an answer."

I paused, remembering such a time. I was leaving Madison to go home for the last weeks of summer.

1968

The summer session had ended, and Stan and I had said our good-byes well into the previous night. Amy was due to pick me up any minute to give me a lift home, but I was running way late, still packing up to check out of the dorm forever. Next year she and I would live in an apartment. Hurrah. I figured the ringing phone was Amy to say she was downstairs in a no parking zone and to get down there fast, but instead, it was Stan.

"How long until you leave?" he asked. "I'm just back from my last class. Come over for another good-bye. I'll make it worth your while, baby, I promise."

"Stan, I really can't. I'm way behind and Amy—"

"Just a quickie, then. Come on. I promise not to waste a minute. There, I'm already getting naked. Get over here. You won't be sorry."

"Stan, stop it. You know I can't. Besides, last night should carry us both through the rest of summer." I actually blushed, reliving the night. Thankfully Stan couldn't see.

"Kip, I mean it. One last send-off, a quickie. I need it even if you don't. I'm giving you five to get over here, five to get ready—"

"Stan, I can't. Amy was due fifteen minutes ago. I've got to pack and catch my ride home. I can't, I'm sorry. I love you. I'll be back before you know it." When he didn't respond, I said, "Okay, Stan? I love you. It'll be even better after a forced separation. Stan?"

He exhaled a long, angry sigh. "You're really not coming? Then don't bother looking me up when you do come back to town." He slammed the phone down in my ear. He never picked up when I dialed back repeatedly, which made me even later.

Once home, I called from Wausaukeesha for days, getting the coldest of shoulders when he did at last answer the phone. After a dozen additional attempts to explain and apologize, I just stopped calling. It was only a few weeks until I returned to campus for the fall session, but weeks of endless worry.

I went straight to his office when I returned, and eventually, his threats were forgotten. We went on as before—in fact, better than before—just as I'd predicted.

"In retrospect, an underlying fury, maybe an instability, was always there," I testified to the quiet courtroom.

William was satisfied with that answer. "Please tell the court why, with what we've heard about your memory that evening, you remain certain you couldn't have murdered Stan, accidentally or in the heat of passion."

"To start with, it's *so* not my nature. If I'd killed someone every time I felt mistreated—" Oops. William glared a warning at me. No ad libbing. "I believed in and practiced peaceful protest and resistance, talking versus fighting through issues. Plus, not only was I dazed, I was in a soaking nightgown when my family entered my bedroom that night. The logical explanation for my being drenched was I was trapped beneath Stan when the vase toppled on him and spilled its contents."

"Your entire nightgown would not have been soaked had you been standing beside the bed wielding an ice hockey stick." William moved to the far end of the jury box. "Ms. Czermanski, you're not a large woman. Was Dr. Szyzck half a foot taller?"

"A bit more."

"It seems unlikely a small woman like you could overwhelm a larger man. Was the ice hockey stick positioned, say, ten feet from the bed, or even further in the hallway broom closet beyond your closed bedroom door?"

"If it was there, it's less than ten feet to the corner of my room."

"Expert testimony stated that in the uninhibited state of arousal induced by GHB, turning suddenly murderous would be unprecedented." William appeared to anticipate something—an objection? When none came, he drew himself up to ask, "Were you, or are you still, in love with Stan Szyzyck, Ms. Czermanski?"

"No. My work at the center helped me see things more clearly. I'd begun to understand my feelings for Stan were rooted in a deep longing for connection. The early loss of my mother, not having a mother to be more accurate, and my distant relationships with my father and sisters were fundamental to that sense of disconnectedness I desperately tried through Stan to put behind me." I peeked over William's shoulder to observe my family's reactions to those words, but both William and Phil at the table behind him blocked my view. "His actions toward me after his marriage to Sybel hurt and disgusted me."

"What actions specifically?"

"At the hospital after Sarah died, Stan accosted me, pretending to comfort me in my grief, then coming on to me. He held me, tried to kiss me, and suggested we carry on as we had during the years of our love affair."

"What was your response?"

"I told him in no uncertain terms to stay away from me, that I wanted nothing to do with him, ever. By the time I'd returned to Wisconsin to see Sarah for the last time, I no longer loved Stan. Perhaps I never did. I'd grown up some."

"So you rejected him. How did he react?"

"If looks could kill …"

"You mean he was furious?"

"Extremely. Insanely."

William appeared deep in thought, walking from me to the jury box. "You rejected Stan after the pass he made at you and left him 'furious.'" William looked all too weary when he commented to the jury, "And we all know how Stan Szyzyck overcame resistant women, don't we?"

"Objection, Your Honor."

"Withdraw the question," said William.

My attorney retreated to the defense table before reluctantly offering me up to the prosecution. I couldn't decide if planting reasonable doubt had been accomplished with the jurors. The jury foreman wouldn't look at me. Debick may hold only circumstantial evidence against me, but was it more persuasive? I couldn't be sure.

With Harvey Debick looming before me, I recalled Phil exhorting me to "resist" with everything I've got to the bitter end, or by default, I would be accepting the victim role. *Resist Kip, resist.* I sat up and zeroed in, but Debick just stared for so long, I finally took the bait. "You wished to ask me something?"

He smiled a smug, infuriating smile. Over his shoulder, meaningful glances from both my lawyers said: Don't lose it now, Kip. Phil rose to protect me. "Your Honor, this is not the first time the prosecutor has intimidated and discomforted witnesses with his theatrics. None of these people spend their days in the courtroom as he does. They're uncomfortable to start with in this spotlight. They shouldn't be made to squirm—"

"Sustained. Question the witness, Mr. Debick, or I'll dismiss her myself," the judge said sternly.

"Miss Czermanski, you just testified that Dr. Szyzyck was 'your only love.' Isn't that what you said, Miss Czermanski? Your sister's husband was the only man you have ever loved?"

I sighed. Even I couldn't help digging myself in deeper. "It's what I said. I haven't been in love since Stan, but that's not to imply—"

"Just answer the question, Miss Czermanski. Now you've admitted to your rebellious, troublesome youth and your radical politics. You've led protests and demonstrations, some of which—despite your 'philosophies'—did turn violent. You do in fact hold a lengthy criminal record which includes assault and battery of a police officer in Madison, do you not?"

"He ambushed Stan, and with his cop buddies surrounding him, was beating Stan mercilessly with his billy club."

"So where Stan Szyzyck was concerned, you did, at least once, have a violent reaction?"

"He was outnumbered and—"

"Yes or no, Miss Czermanski?"

"Yes."

"You're not denying that your longtime sexual affair was consensual either, are you?"

"No, of course not. I already said—"

"Nor do you deny your strained relations with your entire family. So let's see, you've admitted to having loved your dead brother-in-law, to your sexual involvement with him, to never loving another man. You've further corroborated that you yourself locked the doors to the house before you went to bed and only the family remained in the house the night your brother-in-law died in your bed. Am I stating this correctly?"

"Yes," I said, sounding irritated despite my best effort not to react.

Debick leaned on the witness stand, all chummy. "So what do you think happened? We know you conveniently can't remember salient parts of the night in question. We know there's no proof that you were drugged, but there *is* proof that you were *not* raped. So what do you think happened that caused Stan to die in your room in your bed with you there at the time?"

Resist Kip, resist. "I still can't remember several hours of the evening and several more are spotty, much as Dr. Olsen described. I thought the vase crashed on Stan, hit his head, and killed him. I can't explain the hockey stick. I can't really explain anything else, except I know I didn't hit him with it. I didn't kill him. I wouldn't, ever."

"Even if he was, as you've implied, attempting to rape you?"

"No. Well maybe if he were attempting rape, but then I would hardly be bedside wielding a weapon."

"Of this you are certain," Debick scoffed for the jurors' benefit. "Okay,

I'll play along. Then who did it, Miss Czermanski? If not you, the rebellious, anti-war agitator with the criminal record who loved this man who dumped you for your sister whom you've never gotten along with, then who did fatally strike Dr. Szyzyck?"

I determined to meet the prosecutor's accusatory stare. "I don't know."

With another staged snort of contempt, he turned his back on me and walked back to the prosecution table. "We've heard that the vase beside your bed that you assumed killed Dr. Szyzyck was heavy and filled with water and funeral flowers. So heavy, in fact, that had you tried to pick it up, you'd have difficulty. Is that correct?"

"Yes"

"For the moment, let's say you had tried to pick it up. Being unsuccessful might cause the contents to spill all over you. Might your nightgown have gotten wet that way?"

"But I didn't try—"

"You don't remember hitting Dr. Szyzyck with an ice hockey stick? You don't remember picking up the heavy vase, sloshing water making it slip through your hands perhaps? You don't remember trying to make Dr. Szyzyck's death look like an accident?"

"No, I—"

"Your Honor, we vehemently object—"

"Sustained."

"Dismissed."

I was so wiped out, I hadn't heard my dismissal until the judge adjourned for the day. As I stepped down, I saw only Prosecutor Debick's self-satisfied expression. It was more than self-satisfaction. It was excitement, as if the scent of blood aroused him.

Part Five

Freedom's just another word for
Nothin' left to lose.

– JANIS JOPLIN –

CHAPTER SIXTY-ONE

"Kip." Timothy, almost hurrying to my cell, sounded dire. "Your sisters're here to see you."

"Both of them?" I tried to hide my horror.

"Yep, both."

I took a deep breath before nodding for him to show them back. I peered into the mirror, fluffing my hair out to full-force Afro, certain to offend Sybel. I'd already changed from my courtroom suit into my boxy prison blues, guaranteed to further affront Sybel's fashion fastidiousness. I found I simply didn't care anymore what anyone thought. I had nothing left to hide.

I listened to their footsteps, easily identifying each sister by the rhythm of their strides: Sybel's—quick, determined, unhesitating—like a freight train building steam; Samantha's steps echoed more softly, tentative and ambivalent. Recalling my impression that Sister Sarah's feet never touched the ground, I imagined her being exposed to the humiliating courtroom testimony, the details of my sex life, from Stan to the embarrassing number of boys I practiced sexual liberation with my senior year, trying to forget him. I felt a searing blush and thanked heaven Sarah had been spared. She would've changed her mind about me being "the healthy one."

"Are you okay?" Samantha cautiously entered the cell behind Sybel. "You look flushed." The rest of my look being beyond polite commentary. Sybel's eyes widened at my appearance. Like twins, my sisters wore dark slacks and nearly identical blue sweaters, way more appealing than the jailhouse powder-blue I wore. Sybel had dispensed with her mourning black, worn faithfully everyday in the courtroom. "You don't have a fever, do you?" Samantha asked me.

"No, no. I'm fine. Just … Uh, nice of you two to drop by." *Lame, Kip.* "Well, sit down." Samantha seated herself beside me with Sybel opposite. An awkward interlude ensued where some of the more vivid details of my life broadcast in court replayed in my head.

Sybel cleared her throat and forced a smile. "Your lawyers have indicated that Daddy's presence at court during your trial is essential, as is mine and Samantha's, to demonstrate support for your story—" Her voice ratcheted up conspicuously on the word. "—such as it is. But after these sordid days of … testimony—" Her lips pursed in disdain. "—I'm not sure I can agree any longer."

I studied my hands in my lap for the time it took to think of a response. "More than anyone needed to know, especially Dad." I fought back further waves of embarrassment as Samantha took my hand.

"Indeed," Sybel agreed. "So I'm for telling Miss Benedetti and Billy Beneke that Daddy's too ill to attend the proceedings. If you both agree, I can convince Daddy that his learning the repugnant details of his youngest daughter's higher education is too embarrassing for Kip, that she wants him to stay away. You'd both have to back me up on this though." Sybel frowned. "Daddy's getting a bit difficult to control."

"But, but the show of family support?" Samantha spoke up. "What about it? Won't this hurt Kip?"

"You're worried about Kip, Samantha?" Sybel scoffed. "What about your own father? You've seen him, how he's aged in mere weeks. We could lose him, too, Samantha, the way it's going." Sybel rose but found nowhere to go. "I should think you might worry about that, at least as much as you do about Kip." She spit out my name, all harsh consonants. Sybel slammed back onto the cot, spewing, "We all know our little Kip lands on her feet. Her lawyers will get her off, I'm betting, self-defense." Sybel's shrilling laughter spiked the hair on my neck. "Our young Kip's a survivor, on that we can all count."

An uncomfortable hush descended until Samantha blurted, "But I just think we should talk to Kip's lawyers first. She might end up in serious—"

"Jesus Christ, Samantha." Sybel launched herself to standing again, swaying unsteadily over us, "Shut up." We both gasped, Samantha pinching my hand. "Why anyone worries about Kip, I'll never understand. Everything's about Kip. Poor baby Kip, motherless since age three. Poor Kip, kicked out of Catholic school, raised by a 'revolving round' of nannies, the little afterthought baby—who always wound up center stage. Just like now, Kip. Your disgusting affair with my husband. *My husband*, Kip, not yours."

"Sybel—" Samantha began.

But I cut in, "It had to be hard, Sybel, listening to all that's been said about Stan in court. But it's not easy for me either. And my history with Stan predates by years his being your husband."

"So that's that, right Kip?" Sybel hovered over us like an avenging angel, eyes flashing, fists clenched, off balance. "You're sorry? So let's just forget all about it, shall we? Kip's sorry, Samantha, you heard her. She's sorry she fucked up our lives. She'll be terribly sorry from the safe distance of California while forever and ever we'll live with every word spoken in that courtroom. For the rest of our lives, do you hear me, Kip? Every bloody word." As Sybel's murderous rage intensified, Samantha tried to squeeze the life out of my hand.

I was struck dumb until the building pressure of Samantha's hand closing around mine forced a reaction. "Ouch," I cried, confusing Sybel. Samantha, realizing what she'd been doing, glanced at me and giggled. That incongruous giggle, undoubtedly nerves, proved the final blow. Sybel exploded.

She lunged at us, fists raised. Anticipating a barrage of punches and slaps, I hunkered down to defend myself but the blows never came.

"Samantha apparently doesn't get it," Sybel seethed. "Samantha, Kip hasn't caused the death of your husband—yet—has she?" Samantha dropped her head, but Sybel with one finger forced Samantha's chin up until their eyes locked, Samantha's glittering with tears. "But you seem to forget that Kip's killed before—our mother. Now she's killed again and Daddy's at death's door. I advise you to be wary, dear trusting Samantha. Be wary of baby sister. She'll—"

I recovered from my shock to shout, "Sybel, are you crazy?" Her face, contorted by hatred, was no longer beautiful. Her demonic expression brought Sarah's words to my mind. *So distraught she had to be medicated … talk of institutionalizing her … Sybel's running … You'll see it if you really look.*

"I hate you," Sybel hissed, releasing Samantha to focus all her loathing on me. Still holding onto me, Samantha recoiled against the bars, pulling me backward with her as my mouth fell open. "I hate you, Kip," Sybel stormed. "Everything you touch, you ruin. Everything, from the day you were born. Stan and I were happy until he told me he knew you. Then things began to change. I thought he was the one thing, the one thing, that would be mine alone," she sobbed. "But no, no, he'd been tainted by baby sister. I should have known where that would take us. We've been there before …"

Sybel staggered backwards until she tripped onto the cot, staring into space through trickling tears. Samantha squeezed my hand again while we watched Sybel's unfocused eyes overflow. She mumbled to herself, snippets here and there audible: "… too late … I never told … I didn't know … I didn't mean it." Sybel doubled over, wailing, "I didn't mean it."

"Sybel—" Like my voice, I shook, convinced Sybel had suffered a breakdown right before our eyes. "—I'm not, we're not, following you."

"I didn't mean it," she moaned, her face buried in her arms on her lap.

Samantha leaned forward. "You didn't mean what, Sybel?"

"That I hated her."

Samantha smiled meaningfully at me. "Of course. Kip knows you didn't mean it."

"No!" Sybel screamed, her red eyes bulging when she sat up. "I never got to tell her. She died. She died because she wasn't supposed to have more children. The doctors told her, everyone knew. But the church in its infallibility … Mother had Kip, and it killed her. You killed her, Kip, just by being born. And I," Sybel sobbed, "I never told her I was sorry, that I didn't mean it."

"You mean Mother?" I filled in. "You told Mother you hated her?"

Sybel's voice softened, became almost childish, as though she relived a haunting scene from long ago. "Mother called me to her room, asked me to sit on the bed beside her. She held my hand." Sybel gazed at my fingers entwined with Samantha's. "She said she was proud of what a fine lady I was becoming, that she knew I'd grow into a wonderful woman soon." A moment of pride dissolved with Sybel's quivering chin. "Mother told me she felt more and more tired, and that very soon, she would need to sleep for a long time. But she wasn't worried. That's what she said, she wasn't worried because she knew I'd help Daddy and Sarah run the house and raise the younger girls to be as nice …

"She scared me," Sybel whispered. "I didn't want Mother to sleep. And I wouldn't help so she could sleep. I snatched my hand from hers and jumped off the bed. I told Mother I was sick of her always being in bed. 'Ever since the new baby came home, you've been in bed,' I told her. 'It's time you got up and acted like my mother, too. I need a mother, too. I don't want to help Daddy and Sarah. I won't.'

Sybel's breathing was ragged when she continued, "'You can't do this,' I screamed. 'Get up. Get up.' I tried to pull Mother out of bed, make her stand, make her be my mommy like before. But she couldn't stand, and she started to cry. I screamed at her, 'I hate you. You shouldn't sleep. Get up. Don't sleep …'"

Before Sybel slipped into a world she couldn't come back from, I put a tentative hand on her knee. She focused on it, as if she had no idea why it was there or who I was. "I ran from Mother's room," she said, her voice trembling, "and slammed my bedroom door. I kept the lights on all night, determined not to sleep. If I could do it, maybe Mother could, too—not sleep.

"When Sarah knocked at my door the next morning, she told me something bad had happened to Mother. I knew she'd fallen asleep. I had, too. I told Sarah, 'Mother said she was very tired and needed to sleep. Go wake her.' But Sarah was afraid, so I raced to Mother's room and shook her. 'Get up, Mother. I'm sorry. I will help. I'll take care of everyone, I promise. I didn't mean what I said. Please get up, Mommy, please.'" Sybel squeezed her eyes against the vision in her head, sending water down her cheeks from her wet lashes.

My first reaction was as a group leader at one of my assertiveness sessions at the center where participants' life stories often moved me to tears. I'd always felt blamed for Mother's death, that and every other bad thing that happened, but this was my first glimpse at the guilt that had driven Sybel's life. Sarah had been right, Sybel was running, still.

"And it's all your fault," Sybel's thirteen-year-old fears gave way to the cold steel infiltrating her voice. "Your being born made Mother sick, bedridden, and finally killed her. It's your fault I said those terrible things I could never take back. You killed her, and you've killed again. I wish you'd never been born."

My second reaction was far less professional. Here was the sister who'd spent a lifetime blotting out her own shame by making my life a misery. Sybel's guilt trip over her parting words with Mother excused her cruelty, the terror foisted on me, my whole life?

"Like I asked to be born, Sybel? Like I chose to grow up motherless, under your control? I've paid every day of my life for your shame." An erupting volcano of anger catapulted me to my feet to tower over her. "How pathetic, Sybel. Well, I'm done paying for your guilt."

"Now, Sybel," Samantha said, trying to defuse the volatile situation, "you know what Father Dubchek said. It was God's will that Mother was called—"

"Zip it, Samantha." Sybel snapped. "What the fuck does a priest know about it? About as much as most men or the nuns." Samantha was as stymied by this Catholic heresy as I. "What kind of God takes a beautiful woman like Mother, leaving the four of us who needed her so? And Daddy—" Something akin to disgust clouded her face. "—so lost he was as good as dead until he poured his guilt into building our company."

"Sybel," Samantha cried, raking her hair forward over her face, "that's blasphemy. You don't mean it."

"I mean every word. I'm sick to death of all the pathetic preachings that have never done one thing to make our lives more livable. What do these 'men of God' know? The priest, who in his wisdom commended our mother's fate to God's hands, cared nothing about the danger to her. Even Daddy, who knew the risk, chose the church's dictates over his own wife's safety, which he had jeopardized in the first place. Go ahead and give them lip service, it doesn't hurt. But you have to figure it out on your own, like I did—" She narrowed her eyes. "—and saved all your asses doing so."

"Poor Sybel," I sneered, "the self-martyred Czermanski sister. I should feel sorry for you? Forgive your every unjust act, your rages and tantrums pawned off on me because your last words with Mother were like all your words with me?" I reared back and slapped her with all my might. "I've wanted to do that my entire life. I hate you, too, Sybel."

Sybel's hand covered the cheek I'd struck. I'd never hit back before.

It felt so good.

It felt terrible.

"I won't feel sorry for you," my voice broke. "At least, you, Sybel, you knew Mother. You have memories of her." I backed into the corner of my cell, as far from my sisters as possible. "It was your guilt all along, words you couldn't take back, that earned me my title of scapegoat. Not one of you—nor Sarah, nor Dad—ever stood up for me, your defenseless baby sister, though you certainly saw how she treated me. I've never felt a part of this family, and you're all to blame for that. Better you'd raged at God all this time, Sybel, than take your guilt out on me since birth."

Samantha sobbed into a Kleenex. Still pressing a hand to her cheek, Sybel gazed blankly at me as decades worth of revenge spilled forth. "Poor Sybel, too busy running our lives 'with a vengeance' to have one of her own. Go to hell, Sybel, all of you, go to hell!"

I clunked my head against the cell bars, wishing more than any time since my arrest that I could escape to California or beyond, and never look back. Who needed them? But not only couldn't I escape, I was about to be locked up for the rest of my life for the murder of a man who seduced me, used me, dumped me, married my sister, then crept uninvited into my bed and, somehow, died there.

Wait a minute. Sybel must have known Stan wasn't in bed with her. Sybel was the lightest sleeper on earth.

"You did it, didn't you, Sybel?" I accused her. "You knew Stan wasn't where he was supposed to be and came looking for him. When you discovered him in my bed, in a rage you grabbed the ice hockey stick in the corner, hit him over the head, then toppled the vase for good measure. Maybe you hoped the vase would kill us both."

Sybel's eyes followed my every move as I badgered her.

"Admit it, Sybel, it's you who killed your husband and pinned it on me. You and Dad—and you, too, Samantha?—you're all willing to see me go to jail for it. Your scapegoat to the bloody end."

With nowhere to run or hide, I turned my back on my sisters. But words so often spoken in my sessions at the center taunted me: *Think about the ways we contribute to the negative patterns that shape our lives, accepting, even condoning them …* One of Phil's philosophical conundrums followed quickly on its heels: *Resist or be complicit in accepting your role.*

Rattling the bars with both fists, I argued with myself. *Forget it. I was a kid. I was in no position to assert myself. And I'll be damned if I'll thank Sybel for her "sacrifices" in running my life.*

Avoiding my sisters, I stared through the bars only to have Sarah materialize outside my cell. She grasped my hands on the bars in her bony fingers and implored me to *look, look.* I smelled the stench of her disintegration as hospital monitors bleated mournfully in the background.

I collapsed on the end of my cot and buried my head in my hands. Could I have asserted myself? Did I like being the scapegoat? Were these even logical questions? Damn you, Phil, don't I have enough to contend with?

But the answer would not be pushed away. Of course I preferred being the nettle in Sybel's life to being ignored altogether. I preferred the problems I caused and the ones Sybel created for me to being completely forgotten. And it sure kept her running. Sybel never had a life.

Damn. That last thought proved a painful insight. Sybel derived as much from her martyrdom as I did being her crown of thorns. Living at home until six months ago when she married Stan, Sybel truly never had a life. Always the quasi-wife, the old-maid daughter, the substitute mother, the witch of a sister—revealing titles all. No wonder family- and self-image obsessed Sybel even more than Dad. Family relationships defined her.

Not ready to forego the revenge I dreamed of my whole life, I resisted this train of thought, closing my eyes, covering my ears with my hands. Still, unwelcome insights could not be held back. Did I, on some level, believe I deserved Sybel's wrath? Had I unconsciously accepted that I killed Mother "just by being born?" Had I tried to absolve that guilt by accepting their blame and punishment?

Sybel grabbed my arm and startled me, rousing me from my soul-searching. Her storm-gray eyes bore into mine. "Are you saying you didn't do it, Kip? You didn't intentionally lure Stan to your bed? Kill him—by accident or otherwise?"

I shook off her hand. "I wanted nothing to do with your husband, Sybel."

"Those postcards …" Her gaze softened. "Did you really feel that way about him?"

Telltale heat coursed through my body to burn my cheeks. "Stan was the first man, no, the first person, I ever loved completely, no reservations. Yet after nearly three years together, he just walked away, never bothered with good-byes or explanations." I waited for control over my voice. "I've been afraid to ask, but what … what happened to him? I mean, where is Stan, his body?"

Sybel and Samantha glanced at each other. Sybel answered, "I lost that argument. Daddy insisted we bury him in the mausoleum, opposite Sarah, on the other side of Mother …"

"No."

"It was a small service," Samantha added. "The young priest said a simple rite for the family and few friends at the mausoleum."

"Don't forget Doris Schnagle," Sybel interjected.

I was dumbfounded. "Doris Schnagle? She attended Stan's service?" Poor Doris, whose derogatory nickname since puberty had been Whoris Doris. "Oh no, not Doris too. Stan's in the mausoleum with Sarah and Mother. How could Dad defile their tombs?"

It was good to remember how Stan came to disgust me. "When Stan just as abruptly resurfaced two years after his disappearance, I don't know what I felt. The news was overwhelming. But after I came home and he suggested we continue 'as we'd been' in Madison—right at the hospital, right after Sarah passed, mere months into your marriage, Sybel—I was beyond stunned. I was pissed. I warned Stan to steer clear of me."

I slid off the cot and circled the suffocating cell over-occupied by three sisters.

"I awoke that night from a deep sleep, struggling. Stan was there, determined to seduce or rape me. There's no way I could've hit him over the head with a hockey stick. If I'm guilty of anything, it's wobbling the bedside table with the vase on it in our struggle."

Sybel, who had been following my every word, abruptly turned away from us. Samantha sniffled into her Kleenex, looking scared, perhaps anticipating God's thunderbolt after Sybel's blasphemy. A momentary calm ensued after the storm. I glanced over my shoulder as Timothy's footsteps neared.

"Everything okay back here?" he asked. "Heard some racket before it got real quiet."

Sybel raced to the cell door. "We're done. Let me out. Right now."

Once unlocked, Sybel dashed out without another word. Samantha sprang to her feet, looking from me to where Sybel had vanished and back to me, finally rushing out after her.

A flurry of footsteps abruptly ceased, all of which jangled my overloaded brain. I brushed at the place on the cot vacated by Samantha, blonde hair sprinkled around it like she'd begun to shed her winter coat, wondering: Now what have I missed?

Chapter Sixty-Two

"I'm fucked. Totally."

Philomena started to placate me, but I cut her off. There was no more time for philosophizing. Fish or cut bait. Fight or die.

"We'll have to put her on the stand. I was adamant before," I admitted, "and know she'll try to hurt me, but Sybel must go on the stand. I want you to call her. I demand that you do. And Samantha and Dad and Raymond, too. Let 'em all do their worst."

Another meaningful glance traveled between my lawyers that rubbed me the wrong way.

"We've debated this subject daily, Kip," Phil said. "It's risky. Sybel's rather unbalanced. I'm not sure we can control her. She's a wild card."

"What else can we play?" I asked. "So far everyone has corroborated the prosecution's contentions that I'm a bad seed who blossomed into sex, drugs, and anarchy, *crazy* in love with a man no one in their right mind would trust, who, having driven me beyond sanity by marrying my evil sister, just happened to die with a hard-on in my bed."

"Yet now you wish to give voice to this 'evil sister?'" Phil plied one of her typical gambits. Though she'd waited impatiently for me to arrive at this inevitable conclusion, she still insisted I consider all consequences methodically.

"Wish to give voice to her? No. But unless you've got the joker up your sleeve, Sybel's the last card, my only hope. She'll smear me with a lifetime of rebellious antics, but under pressure, she just might make a mistake and inadvertently help me somehow. Sybel, the consummate light sleeper, is the only one who must have known Stan was not in her bed where he belonged. She's holding something back, I sense it. But I'm open to a better plan if you've got one."

"We came to the same conclusion long ago," William admitted. "But Phil wanted you to realize not only the necessity, but the danger, on your own." Always being last to figure things out around here truly bugged the shit out of me.

"We'll put her on first thing tomorrow," Phil added, "but here's the risk. If we're too hard on her, Sybel might choose to make her pregnancy known when it's most damaging to us. We'll look bad and the jurors might blame you for causing her future child's fatherlessness. Yet if we don't pressure her, she'll smear you, to use your term. We could lose all around."

I studied William, the one this strategy would haunt long after Phil and I left Wausaukeesha, one way or the other. "Are you ready for this?" I asked him. "As a local, is it worth the gamble? To you?"

"Phil asked me the same question. It's difficult." He sat back to think. "The partners won't approve of any rough handling of their client's favorite daughter. They've been sending mixed messages since the day they convinced you to take me on—actually, since the day I heard about this case and rushed home for the arraignment."

Now Phil and I exchanged surprised glances. William explained, "I've thought it through again and again. Maybe I'm way off base, but it's as though the partners wished to both distance themselves from the case and keep close tabs on their key client and his business—their only business—through me."

William jumped up to pace the small circles inscribed by the cell. "Did you hear what I just said? The partners are using me to spy on you while keeping their key client safe from predatory law firms. Should the trial's outcome be less than JJ Czermanski requires, Polanski & Stelzl will not be responsible. I will. *I* will."

William stopped in mid-circle. He clunked his head with his palm. "Of course ..." William assumed the voice and manner of his boss, Bob Stelzl, nailing the man to a T. "Had to let him go, JJ. A real disappointment, that one, after his schooling and our extensive hands-on training."

"A sacrificial lamb," I commented.

"How long have you known?" Phil asked.

"I didn't," William said, "or maybe I did from the beginning. It was odd, Kip, what you asked me the first day. 'Wouldn't my father want one of the partners to handle my case?' Something wasn't right. They pried into everything we were working on from the start. I stopped answering, actually began obfuscating the truth about what we were doing."

He rapped his head even harder. "What an idiot I've been, believing their story about me being the only criminally trained lawyer in the firm. I am too young and too green for something like this." He looked meaningfully at me. "We all knew that. I was proud of their faith in me."

William chuckled bitterly. "But in truth, they didn't want a big Milwaukee or Chicago firm coming in to steal their nationwide client, Polanski & Stelzl's *only* client. There is no Polanski & Stelzl without Czermanski Sausage Company. JJ should've taken them in-house years ago."

With a shake of his head, all the pieces fell into place. "You can't imagine how happy they were when Kip hired you, Phil. 'Some girl lawyer from California,' they said upon hearing. 'Lone practitioner,' they added, which struck me as odd, even then. 'JJ will wet his pants,' they laughed. And still I didn't catch on."

Phil broke in. "But once all parties signed the confidentiality agreement I insisted on, they at least stopped using you to spy, didn't they?"

"They ignored that agreement from the first." Before Phil could respond, he added, "But I didn't. I couldn't ignore a legal document I'd signed. I practice the law." William paced, antsy and riled. "You asked me a question, Kip: 'Is it worth the gamble' putting Sybel and your family on the stand? My answer is, it's essential."

Phil had been right—about William, too. How had she known? Have I grown up half as much as he in the same time period? "What do you intend to do tomorrow with hostile witness Sybel Czermanski Szyzyck?" I asked him.

"She'd respond best to me," William said. "Don't you agree, Kip? Sybel seems to dismiss and underestimate men."

It was my first good laugh in weeks. "Sybel's attitude toward men is a real love-hate, I'd have to agree." Her cynical words about priests and Dad himself echoed in my head. "I'm so glad someone else sees it."

"I'll handle her questioning then," William offered, "despite the partners' disapproval. If I can disarm her, she might slip—"

"Or crack," I added, Sybel's meltdown in my cell before the lawyers arrived still vivid.

"No," Phil said, "you've handled yourself brilliantly, William, but it's time I stepped back in. We don't want a man harassing the pregnant widow any-way. Sybel was the only other occupant of the house that evening with an obvious reason to want Stan dead."

"Other?" I protested.

"From the jury's point of view." Phil nodded at William as if they'd pre-agreed to lay something heavy on me. Her eyes traveled back to mine. "If this fishing expedition doesn't result in Sybel's admission of guilt, Kip, if no reasonable doubt is driven into Counselor Debick's wall of circumstantial evidence—"

"One step at a time," I stopped her.

"I want you to think about a mental competency defense. If we convince the jury you were most likely drugged, then by definition you cannot form criminal intent."

"But that means admitting I killed Stan?"

"Well, yes, but—"

"No. I didn't and I won't. I'm done being the scapegoat."

My lawyers rose to leave, William signaling the jailer. Just as the cell door was opened for them, I held Phil back. William seemed to understand. "We'll talk later, Phil. Night, Kip."

I waited until we were alone. "Phil, I've been meaning to, that is, I, uh, I want to apologize for that day in my cell, for labeling marriage bourgeois, for, you know, being kind of narrow-minded." I tripped over the last words.

She sat down. "You surprised me. You, this crusader for liberation, so harshly judging, so limiting and limited."

I could feel my face flushing, so I made a production of getting comfortable on my cot. "I know. I'm sorry. Really. It was inexcusable. Guess I'm as programmed as the next. I've thought about it a million times. I'm ashamed."

"Thank you, Kip. I appreciate your telling me." We sat in silence for a moment.

"Phil, can I ask you what you meant that day, about not being able to have children?"

The dramatic shift in her expression was an answer in itself—this was forbidden ground. "I wasn't … couldn't, that is, I was physically unable to have children."

"Wow. Why?"

"It's a long story, Kip. And these things happen for a reason. We have to believe that."

"What things?"

"You're the inquisitive one, aren't you?" Phil said, standing to pull her coat on to leave. Then she stopped to face me. "I'm not proud of this—at all. If I tell you, don't you dare spout clever feminist rhetoric. This goes much deeper than slogans and pop attitudes."

She sat down before me, searching my face. "You promise to just listen and not react." I nodded.

"I had just been accepted at Stanford Law when, when I realized I might be pregnant." She studied her hands for a moment. "Imagine losing your virginity and getting pregnant at the same time. It was thirty years ago, Kip, 1942, a time not at all like these. An unmarried law student carrying a baby would have created a scandal the likes of which the school would never tolerate. The mere hint of it would have barred me. I'd have to give up law school or … So I did what women did in my day, a back alley abortion … For one night with a man I didn't really love.

"Anyway," Phil forced herself to go on, "the abortion worked so well, I was scarred for life, left unable to have kids." She forced a smile. "At the risk of sounding sappy, I've imagined a daughter, scrappy and smart like you. So now you know. She, he, wouldn't be much older than you." Phil stood and I rose with her. She placed her hand on my cheek.

I pressed her hand with mine, and with everything I had, fought back all further reaction, as promised.

CHAPTER SIXTY-THREE

April 19, 1972

Philomena studied the beautiful Widow Szyzyck as she took the witness stand and was reminded of her oath. Poised before the hushed courtroom, Sybel's shaggy blonde haircut, lit from above, formed a glowing crown. In her first departure from strict mourning black in the courtroom, Sybel wore a flattering, fitted midnight-blue pantsuit. Her appearance was as cold as red-headed Kimberly's had been hot.

Phil smiled as she approached Sybel. In return, Sybel blatantly studied my attorney—from her polished brown boots to her dark brown suit and shimmery blouse beneath. An interesting battle of wits was taking shape.

"Mrs. Szyzyck, you've heard your sister's testimony earlier that your late husband offered the two of you brandy as you were cleaning up in the kitchen following Sarah's services." Sybel remained still as a statue, the Goddess of Revenge perhaps. "Did you drink the brandy, Mrs. Szyzyck?"

Cold stone came to life. "No. I hate brandy."

"Your husband didn't know that?"

Sybel morphed from the haughty witness into the courageous widow. "Evidently not, but you must remember, Miss Benedetti, we were married just six months before this … tragedy."

"True," said Phil. "But you'd known Stan since soon after his arrival in Wausaukeesha, since the summer of 1969 or two years before you married. Then again," Phil conceded, "we never can know everything about one another, can we?" Sybel sat back with eyebrows arched, openly reevaluating Phil. "What did you do with the glass of brandy your late husband offered you?"

"Took one swallow—I don't know why, except we did all need ... something that day—then tossed it down the drain and washed the glass."

"Whereas my client said she drained her glass."

"I was busy washing up—"

"You didn't hear her earlier testimony?" Phil interrupted.

"Of course. According to Kip, she drank it down and handed me her empty glass."

"But you can't corroborate that?"

"It hardly seemed significant. As you might imagine following the funeral of my sister, I had other things on my mind."

Phil gave Sybel a hard look, then walked toward the jury box. "Given, Mrs. Szyzyck, the testimony you heard from Miss Kempinski, that she was just one of the women your husband drugged—"

"You think Kip was drugged? And me too, I suppose?"

"You don't?" Phil countered.

"*I've* suffered no memory loss." Sybel's eyes scanned the courtroom. When they locked on Dad's, she softened her stance. "But anything is possible, I suppose."

"You doubt Ms. Kempinski's story, as well as your own sister's? Miss Kempinski's has been verified. Your husband lost his job over it—was fired by the university for just such activities. He didn't contest the allegations once they were presented. He left the campus quietly and willingly, relieved I'd imagine, that none of his victims pressed charges and the university was satisfied to muzzle bad publicity."

"I know!"

"You knew all that?" Phil asked.

"I mean, I heard the testimony."

The defense, smelling an almost-slip, allowed Sybel to dangle until, risking direction from the judge, Phil moved on. "Mrs. Szyzyck, did you quarrel with your husband in your bedroom later that night?"

Sybel startled. "I really don't remember a quarrel—"

"Something about you being the Ice—"

"Well, yes," Sybel blurted, sitting forward to glare at Samantha. I twisted in my seat to check her reaction, but Samantha's head was ducked low. "Now that you remind me, I do recall an argument." Sybel drew in a steadying breath and cast her most winning smile at my lawyer. "Stan always … I mean, after Sarah's funeral, I was too emotionally drained to, to perform wifely duties."

"You argued with your husband about having sexual relations that night?"

Sybel squirmed at the rephrasing. "Yes, we argued about it. But after the funeral, the days at the hospital, all the planning and people at the house, everything I had to do, imagine him acting shocked at my refu—my exhaustion. As if, after all that, he expected me to be waiting with open arms." Sybel's indignation began to show.

"You sound surprised at what he expected, Mrs. Szyzyck, when he was your husband."

Sybel clenched her jaw. "Which does not give him the right to demand sex when only he wants it. This is the Seventies, Miss Benedetti."

"'Demand sex,' which you refused him. And this on the very night he was found in your sister's bed?"

"Oh for heaven's sakes." Sybel glared at Phil, anger blotching red on her skin. "It's hardly unusual for married couples to disagree about … on timing, that is. Stan held some outdated, old-country values, insisting a good Catholic wife couldn't deny her husband."

"And on the night in question, with your husband insisting upon sex, you responded?"

"What I always responded, forget it. This is America, land of the free, not to mention that a good Catholic wife might expect her husband to act like a good—I mean, under the circumstances, Stan had to understand I just couldn't."

"Your late husband didn't act like a good Catholic husband? What do you mean?"

Sybel exerted steely control in replying, "Stan held radically different views on matrimony than, shall we call it, the mainstream."

"Your late husband had extramarital affairs during your brief months of marriage?"

"Affairs? Dalliances. One-night stands. His way of life changed not one iota with marriage, which is why I'd turned him out of my bed months before. He … it disgusted me."

"So," Phil circled the stand, "you argued about sex, and he called you the Ice Queen of Wisconsin, a reference to the fact you'd turned him out of your bed some months before due to his ongoing sexual 'dalliances.' Do I have that correct?"

"Yes."

"Then what happened, Mrs. Szyzyck, after your argument?"

"He got in the other twin bed in my old bedroom, and we went to sleep. A crashing noise somewhere in the house awakened me, and you know the rest. My father, sister, and I met up on the stairs and went down together to investigate."

"Did you hear Stan leave your bedroom before this?"

"No."

"Really?" Phil pondered for a moment. "Would you describe yourself as a sound sleeper, Mrs. Szyzyck?"

"Light. I am an extremely light sleeper, as a matter of fact."

"So how did Stan manage to get out of bed, open and close the bedroom door, and leave you, a self-confessed 'extremely light sleeper,' alone without your knowledge?"

"I may be a light sleeper, but everyone was exhausted and emotionally drained after the weeks we'd been through and that long, sad day." Sybel strained for control.

"Could a swallow of GHB mixed with brandy explain your uncharacteristic deep sleep?"

Sybel sat back and thought about it. "I have no idea if that's possible, or with a sip, even probable."

"You heard Dr. Olsen testify to the effects of GHB?"

"Okay, okay, it's possible, all right?"

Phil didn't flinch at Sybel's contempt. "Mrs. Szyzyck, is it fair to say that your husband had an active sex drive which continued well after you refused him sex? And that his long-established pattern of satisfying that sex drive wherever he wished—with or without the consent of his partners—also continued?"

Sybel cocked her head to affect boredom. "Your words, not mine."

Phil returned to the defense table. Beneath her feigned boredom, Sybel's anger smoldered at this unpleasantness publicly forced upon her. How dare we, all of us, put the grieving widow through such a grilling.

The low murmur of Phil and William's tête-à-tête, their heads touching as they whispered, drew the attention of the judge, who directed Phil to proceed or release the witness. Philomena ignored Sybel's glower as she stalked back to the witness.

"Characterize your relationship with your husband for the court, please."

Sybel leaned in to take Phil head on. "Normal."

"After testifying you'd turned him out of your bed months into your marriage? When was it exactly that you stopped sleeping with your husband?"

"Hmm, October-ish."

"You were married in August, married only two months before you stopped sleeping with your husband?"

"Yes."

"'Normal' sounds odd in this context, Mrs. Szyzyck. Plus, your husband didn't tell you about his relationship with your younger sister. That's normal?"

"He told me, just not in detail, because ..."

"Because?"

"... because—"

"Did your husband still have feelings for your sister?"

"No. Well—" Sybel glanced at me. "—I have no idea. You'd have to ask him." Sybel's callousness caused a gasp in the gallery.

"Fine, Mrs. Szyzyck," Phil said and moved on. "Your late husband was romantically involved with your sister, Kip, at the University of Wisconsin for almost three years. That's been well established. Unusual name, Czermanski. How many Czermanskis live around here?"

"Just us—in Wausaukeesha, that is."

"In the state? The country?"

"Just us that I'm aware of. Daddy was an only child. Both his parents emigrated from Poland without their families, so we never had relatives around. Why?"

Phil showed mild amusement at Sybel asking questions from the witness stand. "You wonder why I ask? Your husband knew your uncommon last name, knew it quite well before meeting you or your father. Given the national reach of the Czermanski Sausage Company, he probably knew it before meeting Kip. Yet from the first he never mentioned to either your father, with whom he worked, nor to you that he knew Kip. I'm just wondering why?"

Sybel toyed with the top button of her jacket, unbuttoning, buttoning, unbuttoning. "I have no idea."

Phil's brow broadcast perplexity to the courtroom. "It's not unusual, maybe even suspicious, to you?"

Sybel buttoned up. "You're implying what? That Stan used us, Daddy *and* me? He was after our money, the company, all along?"

I pounced on this opportunity to seek my dad's reaction to these implications and found him transfixed—deer-in-the-headlights stunned—by Sybel's words.

"It's just curious," Phil said. "I don't know what to make of it, and thought perhaps his wife would." Allowing Sybel's irritation to build, Phil took her time in adding, "But Mrs. Szyzyck, your husband couldn't have ulterior motives with you." I swiveled back to watch Sybel wait for the other shoe to drop. "If he were after the Sausage Company fortune, he could simply have stayed with Kip."

If Sybel hadn't been sitting, she'd have keeled over. She grabbed the witness box with both hands. "Yes," she said in a small voice, frown lines marring her forehead.

"After all," Phil continued, "your father treats all his daughters equally, doesn't he?"

Sybel blinked several times. "Equally in what sense?"

"In the monetary sense?"

She cleared her throat. "Of course, although ..."

"Yes?"

"Although Kip didn't accept his support after college."

Phil directed her next rhetorical question to the jury. "Kip forswore her father's money?" She swung back to Sybel. "When Kip moved to California, she walked away from the family fortune?" Phil walked toward me. "What you're saying, Mrs. Szyzyck, is that Kip was not a viable conduit to the Czermanski Sausage Company, isn't that right?"

"Objection," the prosecutor shouted. "Assumes facts not in evidence."

"Withdraw, Your Honor. Mrs. Szyzyck, as you testified, your youngest sister had long before these events rejected her father's support and claims to the family's assets. Does it seem reasonable to you, as has been implied here, that she'd murder for it?"

"I wouldn't know." Sybel tossed her head as if sweeping the long locks that were no longer there over her shoulder.

"Please think again, Mrs. Szyzyck. Would someone, anyone, who'd refused her father's money, commit murder for it?"

Sybel stared back at Phil, insolence written all over her, before she admitted, "It sounds illogical in my opinion."

Phil moved on. "You played an important role in your household after the death of your mother. How old were you when she died?"

"Thirteen."

"So young, and such a difficult age for a woman. So many changes in your body. So confusing and even frightening. You must have missed her terribly."

"Of course I did. As for the rest of what you said, far too many practical matters occupied my mind."

Phil returned Sybel's contemptuous gaze with pure astonishment until Sybel glanced away. "Practical matters indeed, like a three-year-old to raise, an eight-year-old sister, a big house, not to mention your schooling, your father, new nannies every year. It's a wonder at thirteen you held it all together."

Sybel sized Phil up, seeking her deeper meaning, or at least, her ultimate direction. "Thank you," she said dismissively.

Phil laughed, which startled more than just Sybel. "You're a strong woman, Mrs. Szyzyck." She wandered back toward the defense table, pivoting as she changed tacks. "You were married for six months, Mrs. Szyzyck?"

"Yesss," Sybel droned.

"How old were you when you married?"

"Thirty-three."

"And you had no serious beaus before Stan?"

"I had many beaus, as you call them. None had moved me to marriage."

"You gave up a lot to raise your younger sisters, didn't you?"

Almost imperceptibly, Sybel succumbed. "Yes I did. I had to. No one else was going to do it. And my father needed me. They all needed me."

"And you him, I'd imagine."

Sybel had to think about that one. "I suppose."

"You're very devoted to your father, aren't you?"

"Of course, he's the only parent I've had for twenty years."

"You still miss your mother very much."

Sybel's rigid features perceptibly softened. "She made everything understandable. Why someone like that had to die …"

Phil asked, "Why did she die? I've never heard the reason."

Sybel looked straight at me, but Phil outwaited her. "An undiagnosed post-delivery problem after having Kip, part of the afterbirth never fully detached. Slow bleeding over time led to other complications. Mother's decline lasted three long years following Kip's birth."

"And you resented Kip for it, perhaps even blamed her for your mother's death?"

"Of course not." The return of her stone mask held in all emotion.

"Yet you two weren't close. Worse, you could barely tolerate each other from the beginning."

Sybel looked surprised that I might have described us so. "She always needed something. Another meeting with her teachers, trouble with the nuns, the priests, expulsion from school. Good Lord, I never had a moment."

Phil nodded agreement at Sybel. "Why didn't you seek help from your father, expect him to help parent his own children?"

Sybel looked baffled by the stupidity of that question. "Daddy was building our business. And, and I promised." The mask slipped, but Sybel recovered. "I could handle it, and Daddy needed me to handle it."

"'Our business.' Is that how you think of your father's company, as yours and his?"

"It is ours. All of ours," Sybel rushed to add. "I did as much as any wife. I enabled his success as much as any … one."

"How did your father's change to his will, leaving sole control of the company to your husband, make you feel?"

"Pis—Shocked." Rage lit up Sybel's expression. "Daddy didn't consult me. No, he told me after Sarah's funeral, as if that would cheer me up. 'He's your husband. I thought you'd be pleased.'" She mimicked my father perfectly.

"You didn't like your husband very much, did you?"

Sybel's eyes grew wide. "'Like?' I guess not, after a while. People like Stan and Kip, they bring all this trouble on themselves. No show of respect for appearances and proprieties, the church, the powers that be in general. My God, his disgusting needs. Never atoning for his sins. No, after we married and Stan's true colors became apparent, I suppose I did stop liking him. Maybe I still loved something about him. He could be irresistibly charming, so smart, handsome, and worldly. There was no one like him in this town."

"Your father encouraged your relationship with Stan, I take it."

Sybel nodded. "Daddy was euphoric when we began to date. He wanted so much for us to marry. He considered Stan a *wunderkind*. It influenced me."

"So when your father told you his plan for leaving the company to Stan, you weren't, to put it mildly, pleased?"

"Of course not, but Daddy wouldn't understand. Stan almost got our company—why? Because he's a man, a Polish-speaking, sometimes Catholic man, just like—" Sybel blushed. "And, and I, being a woman, could never succeed my father, though I could run that company with my eyes closed, just like I've always run everything else."

"Your father wouldn't understand, not even your marital problems?"

Sybel guffawed. "Such details are at odds with the male worldview, not to mention Daddy's plans. Men expect the wife to make things work—turn a blind eye, give it time, whatever it takes." She erupted into cackles at some private joke. "Give 'em money and send 'em back to Poland."

That additional slip caught more than just my lawyer's attention, but what did it mean? Was it something about Sarah's fiancé?

Phil bore in. "That is how your father reacted when you told him about Stan's brazen infidelities?"

Sybel sobered quickly. "No, of course not. I never told Daddy."

"How sad," Phil said, catching Sybel so off guard, she verged on tears. "So you had to take matters into your own hands, once again, to make things right, didn't you, Mrs. Szyzyck? You knew Stan wasn't in bed beside you that night. You followed him to Kip's bedroom and there, finding your husband with your sister, you picked up the ice hockey stick standing in the corner and—"

Before the prosecution could intervene, Sybel reacted emphatically. "No WAY. I hear what you're implying, Miss Benedetti, but you're dead wrong. I had no need to kill Stan to set things right. I planned to tell Daddy all about Stan and make sure he changed his will again, or I would have forced Daddy's hand by divorcing Stan. My father would have reviled that—Catholics don't divorce." Sybel caught her breath. "After burying Sarah, all I could do that night was go to bed. As for the inheritance issues you mention, I had plenty of time to correct them all."

Phil retreated to the defense table slowly. Tough questions made Sybel fray at the edges, had forced reactions she couldn't completely control. Still nothing of value for my defense had come of it. Of the five people in the house that night, one was dead, one on trial for it, and the other three perfectly corroborated each other's alibis, even under pressure. Phil studied me intently before abruptly doubling back to the witness.

"Are you pregnant, Mrs. Szyzyck?"

My jaw dropped in shock along with Sybel's. She steadied herself, grasping the witness box. This was definitely NOT the strategy. What was Phil doing?

Sybel looked down at her lap to double-check whether she showed. She blinked at Phil in bewilderment. Her mouth moved before sound came out. "I … I'm … yes."

The whole room reacted: murmurs, whispers.

"How far along are you in this pregnancy?"

"Close to three months."

"Three months," repeated Phil for the jury's benefit. "But you told us, Mrs. Szyzyck, that you'd turned your husband out of your bed in October of last year, almost six months ago now. How could you be just three months pregnant?"

"Yes, well Stan … he managed—"

"Did he rape you, Mrs. Szyzyck? Maybe drug you beforehand?"

Sybel couldn't look at Phil for a moment. "It's not rape," she asked when she glanced up, "is it? Not when you're married."

I didn't realize I'd been holding my breath after Sybel's heartbreaking question until Phil began again in a soothing tone. "Why have you kept your pregnancy secret, Mrs. Szyzyck?"

"I hadn't decided …" Sybel mumbled.

"Decided what?"

"I …" Sybel bit her lip, glancing around, then down at her lap. "Too much going on, I guess."

"Yes indeed, Mrs. Szyzyck. Yes indeed." Phil remained at the witness's side, giving them both a moment before surrendering her to Harvey Debick.

CHAPTER SIXTY-FOUR

"**Are you able** to continue, Mrs. Szyzyck?" the judge asked as the prosecutor stood.

A ragged intake of breath. "If I must," Sybel responded. "Let's get this over with."

As Phil took her seat at the defense table, I caught not only my father contemplating Phil with surprise, but both Stelzl and Polanski exchanging alarmed glances. *Being underestimated almost always works in your favor,* she had said when we met. Yet, though her gutsy examination revealed what a sick jerk Stan was, none of it justified his murder, nor pointed to another perpetrator.

Prosecutor Debick either felt protective toward this Czermanski or he plotted to win her over with his compassion. He leaned into the witness box as though ready for a neighborly chat across the fence, opening his cross-exam with an offered shoulder.

"This has been a most trying time for you, hasn't it, Mrs. Szyzyck?"

Sybel bobbed her head, forming a brave but unstable smile. "Very," her voice trembled. "First my sister's death, then my husband's, now all this."

"I understand. I won't keep you long. You testified to your husband's affairs, 'dalliances' as you termed them, after your marriage. What did you know about your husband's history with your youngest sister before you were married, Mrs. Szyzyck?"

"I was unaware Stan and Kip had known each other until he and I talked about Daddy's sixtieth birthday. When Kip's no-show was discussed, Stan mentioned 'remembering her at the university.'"

"When did you learn of their affair?"

"Stan told me—Well, Daddy's birthday party preceded our wedding ceremony. I planned both celebrations, back to back, catching everyone by surprise," Sybel bragged. "Anyways, on our honeymoon, Stan told me he'd been 'deeply involved' in an anti-war group at the university with Kip. He didn't want to upset me with the gory details we've been exposed to here." She glanced meaningfully in my direction, then tossed her nonexistent locks again.

"You mean, their sexual involvement?" Sybel glanced down while Debick, empathy in his pale eyes, patiently waited.

"I should say so. But when Kip came home to see Sarah, I noticed her reaction to Stan and something in Stan, too, though I couldn't put a finger on it. I figured there was more—assumed it, knowing Kip. And now, of course, we all know everything."

"'Knowing Kip?'" Debick repeated.

"Well, yes. With Kip, there was always more to the story, some detail conveniently forgotten, until things blew up in our faces."

"So you suspected there was more, that neither Dr. Szyzyck nor your own sister had told you the whole truth about their past?"

Sybel zeroed in on me as she answered, "Yes, and why? I have no idea." Scanning the crowd, her gaze tripped over my father again so she quickly added, "Actually, Kip lived in California since finishing college. We hadn't talked much until she came home to see Sarah. Then with the funeral and all …"

"Really?" Debick mused, "If it weren't for distance and the events you mention, Kip would most likely have told you about her involvement with your husband?"

Sybel looked amused. "I wouldn't say that about our relationship."

"No? How would you characterize your relationship with your sister?"

"Which sister?"

"The defendant, Kip," Debick replied with some impatience.

"Saying we're sisters doesn't say it all?"

Debick pretend-chuckled. "I'm afraid not, Mrs. Szyzyck. You two weren't close?"

"No. Kip is ten years younger, and frankly, we were more like mother and child than sisters, due to our circumstances."

"You mean the death of your mother?"

"Yes and—Yes."

Debick swiveled from observing the witness to observing me. "One might assume such circumstances would make you closer than mere sisters."

"Hmm," was the best Sybel could do as I determinedly returned the prosecutor's glare.

A gentle tone oozed from the prosecutor's voice when he turned back to Sybel. "Weren't you close to your mother?"

"Objection, Your Honor," William interrupted. "Relevance?"

"Again, Your Honor," Debick said with frustration, "the familial relationships within the Czermanski household establish contributory factors in this case."

"Overruled," the judge pronounced. "Please answer the question, Mrs. Szyzyck."

"Very close. Extremely. My mother was …" Sybel stumbled over the emotion her voice betrayed, "… the most beautiful and kind woman I've ever known. I loved her more than anyone. Except Daddy, of course." Her eyes sought out my dad, whose ego she had recently and publicly bruised.

"It's clear her death was quite hard on you."

Sybel uncrossed and recrossed her legs, resuming an erect posture that in effect resurrected her protective walls from such intimate invasions. "Of course," she answered coldly.

The prosecutor retreated a few steps as if feeling a sudden chill. "But you and your youngest sister didn't share a similar feeling for each other? Why?"

Sybel opened her mouth to speak when William cut in. "Objection, Your Honor. Prosecution is now asking the witness to testify for the defendant."

"Sustained. Disregard the question, Mrs. Szyzyck."

Debick smiled at Sybel. "Tell us why you didn't feel that same sort of closeness for the sister you raised as if you were her mother."

"Well," Sybel chuckled bitterly, but thought again. "Kip was different from the rest of us—difficult, hard to control, prone to trouble."

"Ah yes, 'prone to trouble.'" For the first time Debick's unmeasured smile flashed at me.

"Mischievous—"

"We understand, Mrs. Szyzyck. Would you say Kip, feeling her difference from the rest of you, was jealous of you—"

"Your Honor!" William jumped up and rounded the table as if he intended to make Debick stop. "This is preposterous."

The judge commanded the lawyers to approach the bench. I could see only the judge's facial contortions and his mirrored eyes as four lawyers gestured, their movements jerky like a silent movie. They looked like reprimanded but unrepentant school kids when they stomped back to their respective tables. William flopped down beside me, still clenching his fists.

The prosecution abruptly dismissed the witness. "Thank you, Mrs. Szyzyck. You may step down."

Chapter Sixty-Five

"Appeals process."

My cell at the Wausaukeesha County Jail took on a whole new appearance once my lawyers uttered those words. Among other things, it meant transfer to the state penitentiary. No more Chagall to give my imagination a window out on the world, no more vegetarian diet, no more strong coffee smuggled in openly. No more Timothy and our lame, wonderful canasta games that helped wile away the measureless time. Most of all, it meant the likelihood of my imminent conviction of premeditated murder.

"So that's it?" I sighed, taking in my accommodations at the single-prisoner jailhouse with new appreciation. "Waupun, is that where they'll send me?"

William didn't react while Phil made a desultory attempt to bolster my spirits. "Kip, we've still got tomorrow. We'll stick to our plan, call your sister, Samantha, then your father, although—"

"Although we hoped it wouldn't be necessary." I said, stating the obvious.

Neither lawyer responded. That had been our hope, but Sybel had not confessed. Maybe in the black hole of my memory loss lay guilt. Maybe, somehow, I had done it.

"'Anything is possible,'" I mimicked Sybel.

Phil's smile was so sad, I fought to hold off the much needed release of tears or hysterical laughter or both. Later, I told myself, I'll have plenty of time for that later.

"That's right, Kip, anything is possible," Phil said, trying to rally us all.

"We're not done for yet. We've got tomorrow and the next day or two. One step at a time. Oh, we've added Raymond Turner III to the witness roster. Someone may yet incriminate Sybel."

"Weren't you the one a moment ago advising me to be realistic?"

"We have to be prepared for the appeals process, Kip, we do. But let's put the rest of your family on the stand and see what comes of it. Let's stay open to all eventualities."

I agreed. "Might as well stay open and let this drag out. There's certainly no reason to hurry the end now."

On the drive from the courthouse in the police van not an hour ago, Timothy too had tried to cheer me. He told me he'd made sure I was getting Sara Lee banana cake for dessert tonight. The time was nearing for my last piece of something I loved for a long, long time, a lifetime.

"Fine, call Samantha and Dad, then Raymond. So how long does the appeals process take?"

Phil and William exchanged glances, a signal I'd learned meant more bad news. William ventured, "It could take a year. Or two."

Stunned, I remembered that was only the appeals process. Failing again meant the rest of my life in prison, and my upcoming twenty-fifth birthday celebrated in a penitentiary.

The scent of overcooked broccoli preceded the night guard delivering dinner. My lawyers pounced on the opportunity to get back to work as he entered. A sudden insight flashed before me as the door slammed shut.

I blurted, "'Send 'em back to Poland.' Sybel's slip in court today—it wasn't about Jerry, Sarah's fiancé—but Leeza."

Phil stopped short outside the cell. "The comment Sybel made on the stand today? 'Give 'em money—'"

"—and send 'em back to Poland.' Sybel was talking about Leeza, our last nanny."

Phil checked her watch. "Is this pertinent to the case, Kip?" When I shook my head no, she pressed, "You're certain this time? Just in case, write it down, this Leeza-thing."

"That's it." I congratulated myself, collapsing onto my cot. I reached for the plastic utensils on my dinner tray while my mind churned backwards fifteen years.

1957

By nine years old, I could open my bedroom door without making a sound. Dad, in the room next to mine, wasn't the light sleeper in the household, but Sybel from her room down the hallway heard everything. She was a really light sleeper. Maybe Sybel didn't sleep at all.

I became expert at avoiding all the creaky floorboards as I tiptoed down the dark hall between my room and the bathroom beyond Sybel's and Samantha's bedrooms. But that didn't work for long. Sybel told Dad my "nocturnal flushing disturbed" her rest and convinced him that my nighttime trips to the bathroom were no more than "childish attention-getting behavior." At nine years of age, she said, I should no longer be so indulged.

From then on, leaving my bedroom once I was sent to bed was forbidden. Sybel thought I'd learn to stay in bed and hold it till morning like a normal little girl. But I couldn't. Well okay, maybe I didn't want to.

Though I was scared of the stairwell at night, where all kinds of boogeymen crouched in the shadows, I made up my mind to use the downstairs bathroom, the nanny's bath, between her bedroom and the kitchen. Necessity as well as stubbornness beat out my fears of the dark. In truth, I'd come to like the freedom of the sleeping household when no one watched my every move or bossed me around.

With the banister clutched in one hand and my nightgown bunched up in the other, I crept down the spooky stairwell and took my time in Leeza's bathroom. I dawdled among her bottles and jars, in no hurry to return to the creepy stairs. In fact, I decided I needed a glass of water from the kitchen before heading back to bed.

I let the flushing toilet go silent before easing open the bathroom door. A sound just outside startled me. Giggling? Couldn't be Sybel. I froze in the doorway as a splinter of light from Leeza's room widened across the wall opposite as her door opened. What was Leeza doing up so late, I wondered, when Dad's squat shadow moved onto the wall.

I held my breath. Dad would be so mad, finding me here. The light shrunk and disappeared as my nanny's bedroom door closed, which is why Dad didn't see me until nearly tripping over me.

"What the f—What are you doing up, young lady?" he sputtered.

"Dad, I had to go to the bathroom. And I'm thirsty. I know I'm not supposed to leave my room at night, but I had to, Dad, really."

He stared at me, and I could just make out the watery gleam where his eyes would be. When he didn't react, I asked, "What are you doing up, Daddy?"

"Go on and get your water," he said, sounding mad as he turned me toward the kitchen and fell in behind. "You should be in bed. Hurry on back up there before—"

Lights flashed on as we entered the kitchen. My eyes adjusted to Sybel swooping in, her nightgown billowing behind her, pink foam rollers covering her head.

"I've told you to stay in your room at night, Kip," she snapped at me. "What are you doing up?"

"I'm thirsty and I had to go. I can't be keeping you awake. I didn't even squeak the floorboard in front of your room or the one at the back stairs either."

Sybel eyed Dad before ordering me to bed. "I'll deal with you tomorrow, Kip," she promised.

"Just a minute, Sybel," Dad responded, holding me by the shoulder. "The child needed a drink, didn't you, Kip?"

I wondered about Dad's red face as he filled a glass at the faucet and handed it to me, spilling water on both our hands. Dad concentrated on something near my feet as I drank so I couldn't catch his eye. Did he want me to stick around since Sybel seemed more upset than usual? But Dad said no more when Sybel warned me to get moving.

I crossed the kitchen to the back stairs, balancing the glass in both hands and stopping on the first step to take a sip before my climb. I overheard Sybel whisper, "This has got to stop, Daddy. Leeza's only eighteen—younger than I am. If anything happens, we'd be personally humiliated in this community, not to mention the effect a scandal could have on our business."

I didn't hear my father's response, though I lingered on the stairs. When it hit me what they must be talking about, I spilled more water, hurrying up to bed. I was still awake, trying to imagine my Dad doing with Leeza what Amy Gruden said our parents did to make babies, which was what the Grudens' two poodles did a lot. I burned scarlet when, hearing Dad's bedroom door close, the picture formed in my head. Yuck.

Long before I could look at my dad or Leeza again without blushing, I got another shock. Entering the kitchen after school some weeks later where the sausages Sybel warmed spiced the air, Sybel told me to go say good-bye to Leeza. Good-bye? Leeza wasn't supposed to leave till the end of the school year when the old nanny leaves and a new nanny arrives from Poland.

"Leeza's going home early," Sybel said, "for personal reasons. And Kip, just so you know, there will be no more nannies in our house. At nineteen, I am perfectly capable of managing the household and all its occupants myself."

Her self-satisfied grin scared me. This was the worst news I'd ever heard—Sybel in charge with no one to referee when she spun out of control?

I rushed down the back hallway past her bathroom to knock on Leeza's bedroom door. She yanked it open, threw her arms around me, and pulled me inside. She kissed and hugged me, crying. I felt for the bulging at her waist that Amy Gruden said was the sure sign that parents had made a new baby. Amy Gruden was right. Yuck and double yuck. How embarrassing. How could Dad and Leeza look at each other after doing *that*? I tried not to stare at her stomach while Leeza whispered for me to watch out for Sybel—like I hadn't been all my life?

"Don't go," I begged her, forcing my eyes to her face. Her watery blue eyes, streaked red, her shock of white-blonde hair all matted and messy, made her hard to look at. My eyes settled on the dead Jesus on the gold cross she always wore around her neck. "Please, don't go."

"I must, Little Kip, but you'll be okay," she lied, neither of us believing it. Sniffling, she promised to send me a postcard from Krakow once she got home.

I trailed her to the kitchen in her her grape jelly-scented wake, fixing my eyes on my last nanny's stocking-seams. Sybel and Leeza stared at each other. How alike yet how different they were. Sybel's yellow hair was pulled back in a ponytail that hung down her back. She wore bobby socks with gray suede loafers and a gray pleated skirt. Leeza, about the same size and height, equally pretty and a year younger than Sybel, looked old and tired in her loose-fitting suit of scratchy fabric, her thick stockings and worn shoes.

"I'll be taking you to the airport," Sybel told her. "Put your bags in the car in the driveway. I'll be right out."

When Leeza asked if Mr. Czermanski would be home to say good-bye, Sybel said, "He's far too busy, but he sends his good-byes as well a generous something extra to help you get started back home."

Sybel slipped an envelope into Leeza's handbag. Leeza's skin went as pale as her white hair. She bit her lip and walked out. I followed with her other bag, but Leeza said no more to me, sliding into Sybel's car and slamming the door behind her.

As Sybel drove off with Leeza sunk down in the seat beside her, I watched from our driveway, imagining a little sister or brother to play with, to befriend and stand up for. I think I would have liked a new mother as nice as Leeza.

Soon, the cold March wind forced me back inside.

Thinking back on it, I wished I'd told Leeza how I felt, but there had been no time for regrets. Sybel's initial thrill at taking complete control of our household soon gave way to the arduous reality. Her resentment increased with time. With no more nannies, war broke out among the Czermanskis, Sybel and I in opposing camps, Dad and Samantha occupying the extensively mined middle ground, while Sister Sarah had made her retreat years earlier.

It stunned me to realize that the war begun long ago only now was reaching its decisive battle.

CHAPTER SIXTY-SIX

April 20, 1972

With freedom no longer taunting me from beyond the close of my trial, I no longer cared how swiftly it passed. But it would end, and soon. With that inevitability, I began to see the ritualized courtroom proceedings as if for the first time.

"All rise," thundered the disembodied voice of the bailiff.

We rose for the robe-swirling entrance of the judge-priest, whose monkish pate gleamed under the overhead lights as if aglow with divine knowledge. He took his seat at his altar high above, the better to hear God's Own Truth, and from where he would mete out Its brilliance for us unworthy mortals for whom it was his mission to intercede. Hallelujah for infallibility.

"Be seated." We sat.

Maybe I should go to confession. I could still go, couldn't I—once a Catholic, always one? That is, confession could come to me, surely. Father Dubchek—no no, the new priest from Sybel's wedding write-up—he was at the funeral—Father ... Father Biaggio. An Italian priest, perfect. But what would I confess? If I have something to confess, now would be the time and the place to do so.

"Defense calls Samantha Czermanski Turner."

Forgive me Father for I have sinned. I was born to a dying mother and I wasn't tall or blonde and I was too helpless to raise myself but too stubborn to quietly submit to everyone else's way of doing so. I killed my mother, that's what they all believe. I was born a murderer, yet it's taken nearly twenty-five years to rig the trial they longed to put me on. I stand before my judges to be sentenced, once and for all, for my particularly heinous original sin. I plead guilty to "just being born."

William grasped my arm and shushed me. I'd spoken aloud. "None of that now, Kip," he whispered, squeezing my arm hard enough to get my full attention.

Allrightallready.

"Samantha Czermanski."

Surprised, Phil stopped before the seated witness. "Your full name again, please."

"Sorry." Samantha tugged some bothersome wisps of hair from her head. "Samantha Czermanski Turner." Samantha, rubbing her fingers to release her pluckings, was having trouble with her name.

"Remember that you are still under oath to tell the truth, the whole truth, and nothing but."

"I, I remember."

In a thoughtless wrinkled white blouse tucked unevenly into a dark skirt that overwhelmed her thin frame, disheveled Samantha had climbed to the witness stand in boots bearing salt residue rings. She'd clipped her hair gone stringy with two bobby pins. Why had Sybel allowed her to appear in public like this? "Poor Samantha." I barely breathed the words out loud.

William's severe look told me he wasn't kidding. Then his expression changed. He stared at me as if I'd just answered the $64,000 question, then forgot me altogether. William focused on Phil, interrogating sister Samantha in the hope she'd incriminate Sybel, since Sybel hadn't so obliged. Dad was up next, then Raymond, and then who or what would we try?

"Mrs. Turner, do you recall earlier testimony concerning an argument between Sybel and her late husband, Stan, which occurred on the night of Sarah's funeral?" Samantha smiled blankly, making no response. "Mrs. Turner, did you understand my question?" Phil asked.

"Oh yes, an argument." Phil did a double take at that spaced-out answer.

Poor Samantha, I dared not whisper again.

"You overheard the argument from your bedroom next door?"

"Uh-huh," Samantha answered with a vacuous smile.

"You overheard it because you weren't sleeping, or because Sybel and Stan were loud?"

Samantha puzzled over that one. "I wasn't asleep yet, I guess."

"So they weren't that loud, loud enough to wake you or anyone else in the house?"

"I don't know. I, I guess not."

"What did you hear after the argument ended?"

"Nothing. I suppose I fell asleep."

"You didn't hear the door to the bedroom right next to yours open and close, slam maybe? You didn't hear Stan leaving, perhaps stomp out angrily, move down the hallway, go down the stairs?"

"No, no I didn't hear any of that." Samantha's smile turned tremulous and vanished, her lack of knowledge apparently making her miserable.

"But Mrs. Turner, if you were awake enough to hear a low-volume argument going on through your bedroom wall, an argument you heard clearly enough to make out your brother-in-law labeling your sister the Ice Queen of Wisconsin, how could you not have heard the immediate aftermath? You fell asleep instantaneously upon their argument ending?"

"That's all I heard," Samantha snapped. "I, I don't know," she added. "I can't explain it, except we were all so tired …"

"Yes," Phil allowed.

These lawyerly fishing expeditions had grown meaner in spirit with each witness. Would this nightmare ever end? Would any of us be left standing? Who would write the Czermanski family history? I wondered, thinking back on that strange lecture of Stan's on that very topic. Or should I say, who would survive to rewrite it?

Phil and William hated this witch-hunt as much as anyone, but did their duty to me regardless. And William would have to live in this company town after the trial. *Forgive me, Father, for I sinned, again. I've damned William's future.*

"… until a crash downstairs brought us all out into the hallway," Samantha was saying.

"Your father described getting up to use the bathroom. That means he would have to pass by your bedroom, as well as Sybel's. You didn't hear him pass your door?"

"No," Samantha insisted, irritation growing.

"So after hearing a crash, you found your father already standing at the head of the staircase opposite the bathroom when you entered the hallway, correct?" Samantha nodded, then remembered to say yes. "And where was Sybel?"

"She was hurrying toward Dad."

"In other words, you were the last to arrive, you who were awake enough to hear a private argument in detail, then so sound asleep, you missed all these comings and goings taking place right beyond your bedroom door. One would presume a door is a far less effective sound barrier than a wall."

Samantha seemed to be replaying Phil's statement at slow speed for comprehension. Blinking, she said, "I'm sorry, but I'm a little lost. What are you saying?"

"I'm saying, Mrs. Turner, that your hearing was highly selective that night."

"Well, maybe no more selective than being awake or being asleep after a terrible, exhausting day."

"All right, Mrs. Turner." Phil pivoted to watch Mr. Turner during her next question. "Your husband left his car at the house and walked home that night, we've heard."

The courtroom's attention shifted to Raymond the Third, seated behind me with the family, natty as ever and still tinkering with his monogrammed cuffs. After his notable absences, his presence in court meant no more than he'd been subpoenaed and would testify himself soon.

"Um, yes, he went home. Raymond likes to sleep in his own bed. And the cat, someone had to feed him. I, I wanted to stay around for Dad, you understand?"

"Yes, Mrs. Turner, I do," Phil acknowledged. "Does your husband have a key to the family home on Moraine Drive?"

"I don't think so." Confused, Samantha studied Phil, then Raymond.

"Who has keys to the family home on Moraine Drive?"

"I do, and Sybel, of course, and Dad. Maybe Kip, I'm not sure. No one else I can think of. Maybe Dad's cleaning lady—no, Sybel always meets her to let her in. That's all, I think."

Though most wouldn't detect it, Phil returned to our table dejected. This pushing and probing was getting us nowhere, but until all avenues had been exhausted, Phil wouldn't relent. "Your cross, prosecutor." Available avenues were dwindling rapidly.

"Mrs. Turner," Debick began, straightening his black tie and starched collar, "we've heard a lot about your family and the goings-on of your household during this trial." Even at that nonquestion, Samantha blushed and pulled her hair forward around her face. "Funny thing, though, we haven't heard you mentioned much throughout all of that. I've wondered why?"

Her hue deepened. Phil, not realizing she'd gasped, shared an acknowledging nod with William. I shook my head at my lawyers. They'd begun to divine each other's thoughts.

"Isn't it true that you were the one sister who got along with everyone, who made the peace and smoothed things over between the contentious factions in your household?"

"I don't, I mean, well … maybe."

"Describe for us your relationship with your sisters and father."

She looked at me. "I'm as close to Kip as anyone, the closest in the family, I guess." A long strand of hair twirled around her finger was freed with a yank. "And Sybel and I have always gotten along. I understood her responsibilities and intentions, regardless of how, on occasion, they came off. And Dad, well, Dad had to work a lot. I tried to make his home when he was there as pleasant as possible. I just wanted us to be a normal family."

"What about your sisters' relationship?"

"Sybel and Kip? Well—" She made a dry chuckle. "—they never understood each other. They were always at odds, you might say."

"Did they like each other underneath it all?"

Samantha looked horrified at the question. "N-n—Probably not. Kip seemed to push Sybel's buttons from the first. Kip was always in trouble and being punished."

"Sounds as if they hated each other." Before Samantha could respond or my lawyers object, Debick added, "There's a peacemaker in every war." He thanked and released the witness.

Samantha wasted no time vacating the spotlight, but Phil rose before she could get away. "I'm sorry, Mrs. Turner, Your Honor. Defense requests a redirect."

When the judge instructed Samantha to return to the witness chair, she hesitated so long, the judge had to direct her once again. She sat down hard, her displeasure obvious. She studiously ignored Phil's presence, fiddling with her hair with both hands.

My lawyer watched her carefully as she asked, "To review previous testimony, during their argument that night from the bedroom next door, you overheard your brother-in-law call Sybel—"

"Yes yes yes, Stan called Sybel a nickname he sometimes used for her, the Ice Queen of Wisconsin." Even sweet Samantha had reached total exasperation. "Yes, that's what I heard—as I've told you."

"Right." Phil thought a moment. "Did you just say 'a nickname he sometimes used for her?' You'd heard it before?"

"N—Y—Hmm, maybe."

"Yes or no, Mrs. Turner? Which is it?"

"Umm, yes, I guess."

"You'd heard it before. Since Sybel turned her husband out of her bed?"

"Uh, I, well I'm not sure." Samantha glanced around, her eyes glancing over me, my family, her husband, and back to Phil.

"But you'd heard it before the night of Sarah's funeral and their argument. Now where would you have heard something so intimate and unflattering about your sister before that night?"

I swiveled around to check Sybel's reaction. Sybel would die before she'd repeat something like that about herself. Appearances came before everything, especially among sisters. Sybel sat forward, fixing Samantha with a frown.

"In fact, Mrs. Turner," Phil was saying, "you apparently knew it was your brother-in-law's 'nickname' for your sister."

Samantha pressed as far back in the witness seat from Sybel as possible. "I meant that Sybel, she must've told me."

Phil singled Sybel out as she moved toward her, leading all eyes in the courtroom to do the same. Sybel's rigid reaction contradicted Samantha's knowledge, gained though a sisterly confidence.

"Oh, I doubt that very much, Mrs. Turner," Phil said, eyes on Sybel. "But of course we could call Mrs. Szyzyck back up here to testify whether she'd shared that secret with you."

Samantha braved another glance at Sybel before exclaiming, "Stan must've told me. He might've, I don't know. How important is this anyways?" Meek Samantha's mood swings astonished me.

"Why would your brother-in-law tell you something like that, Mrs. Turner?"

"How should I know?" came Samantha's retort. Phil let her words hang in the air until Samantha met her stare. "Gee, I don't know, do you suppose …" Samantha froze. "He, he must've needed someone to talk to about it."

Phil moved in closer. "Your brother-in-law needed someone to talk to? He confided to you his marital problems with your sister?"

"Umm, maybe, once."

"Once?" Phil repeated.

"I mean, he needed someone, I mean—"

"You mean Stan Szyzyck needed you?"

"No! Yes! No, not exactly. I, I really don't know what you're getting at."

"Stan needed you to confide in. Is that correct, Mrs. Turner?"

"I guess, he just, yes, he needed someone to talk to."

"And he chose you?"

"Oh, isn't it obvious?" Samantha shouted, leaning forward to take Phil head on. "Stan needed someone in this closed-minded, company town to talk to once in a while."

Phil fired immediately, "Mrs. Turner, were you involved with Stan Szyzyck?"

Samantha stared at Phil. I couldn't breathe as time seemed to stop and the whole courtroom froze. I swear I wanted Samantha to scream with righteous indignation: *No fucking way. You're whistling up the wrong tree, Missy.* Save yourself, Samantha, quick, before it's too late.

"'Involved?'" Samantha mimicked Phil's enunciation. "You make that word sound just plain dirty." Samantha grinned. "'Involved,'" she repeated with a chilling laugh. "No, mine was a bigger mistake than being 'involved.' I fell in love. Can you believe it? That's more than his wife or his college conquest can say. I loved him." Samantha glared at Phil, defying us all.

My senses shut down, or the courtroom fell into foreboding silence. Murmurs penetrated my cocoon when the entire courtroom stirred as Raymond beat a hasty retreat for the exit.

Laughing, blotting her eyes and nose with her Kleenex, Samantha called after him, "Bye-bye, Raymond. Bye-bye. Daddy, say good-bye to Raymond. Raymond, don't leave without a proper good-bye for my father. Let's see now, who will miss whom the most—Raymond will miss your payroll, Daddy. But then again, Daddy will miss Raymond Chauncy Turner the Third's pedigree." Samantha laughed so bitterly, I couldn't watch. "Whoops, have I said too much?" she asked and giggled. She glared at my father. "Guess it'll be a draw."

Phil stepped to the witness box. "Mrs. Turner, do you need a moment?"

Please take a moment, Sam, please.

"What the hell," Samantha exclaimed through a twisted smile. "I loved him. Stan saw me, the real me. To him, I wasn't just background scenery for the never-ending Czermanski dramas. He loved me, Sybel, and I loved him." Samantha burst into tears.

"No," Sybel muttered from behind me. "No."

Phil handed the witness her hankie and offered her a glass of water. "Mrs. Turner—"

"PLEASE. Don't call me that. Just Samantha, okay?"

"Samantha, drink the water. Take a deep breath." Phil retrieved the emptied glass from the witness as if she couldn't be trusted with it. "Samantha, how long were you romantically involved with Stan Szyzyck?"

"Not long, not long at all …" She sniffed loudly, then blew her nose in Phil's handkerchief. "Just before Sarah came home, Stan confided in me that Sybel had stopped sleeping with him. He was hurt and confused about it, going a little crazy. It was natural to console him, to try to explain Sybel to him. Then somehow—" Samantha stared at Phil in bewilderment. "—somehow a sisterly hug turned into something different." Samantha's expression hardened into defiance. "We fell in love and needed to be together, both of us."

I stole a glance at Sybel, who was looking at me in amazement. When she turned back to Samantha, her expression changed from shock to loathing. Were there tears in Sybel's eyes?

"That was in January?"

"Yes, January. At the end of that month, Sarah came home. At first, with everyone focused on Sarah, I hardly noticed that I was becoming invisible again. But when I needed comforting, I found Stan had forgotten all about me." She faced Phil in complete confusion and sobbed, "I became invisible again, and I still don't know why. And now I never will, will I?"

"More water, Mrs.—Samantha?"

That this pained Phil was obvious—this, the very thing we hoped against hope would happen. Only it wasn't Sybel who incriminated herself, but Samantha, the middle child, the peacemaker, the pleaser of the family. The sweet one.

Alas, a gut-wrenching hallelujah for universal fallibility.

Phil moved on cautiously. "Tell us what really happened that night after you buried Sarah, and everyone had gone to bed."

Samantha's story tumbled out like Phil was the friend she'd longed to confide in. "I sent Raymond home. He wasn't much for funerals or family messiness, and frankly, I was glad to be rid of him. Raymond demanded constant reminders that the universe revolved around him. I guess I'd grown tired of it … I, I managed to tell Stan, as the last guests were leaving, that I'd leave my bedroom door unlocked for him. I thought maybe now things could return to normal, I mean, between us, to the way they'd been before Sarah. Listening to the argument between Stan and Sybel through my bedroom wall, I expected anytime he'd stomp out or sneak away to be with me. It'd been so long …

"Their argument ended, but nothing. Nothing happened. I thought I heard Stan leave the room, but wasn't sure. I waited and waited but still no Stan. Maybe he'd misunderstood. I should find out if he's waiting for me somewhere in the house." Samantha looked at Phil. "I could always say I needed water or something if I ran into anyone. When I could wait no longer, I crept from my room and down the back stairway."

"The back stairway." Phil repeated. "Please describe its location for the court."

"There's a door across the hall from my room to the back staircase which leads straight down to the kitchen and the nanny's quarters beyond, Kip's room. The house is old, old-fashioned I guess you'd say, with back-to-back staircases separated by a solid wall. The front stairs lead down to the entry hall, the living room to one side, the dining room through to the kitchen on the other. Such a lovely old home, one a family should've loved and enjoyed …"

Samantha required prompting from Phil before continuing, "Stan wasn't waiting for me, not even close. No, Stan was forcing himself on Kip—Kip, who didn't even want him." She turned to me as her tears bubbled over. "Imagine. I'd done everything but kidnap the man, I wanted him so badly.

And you—you resisted with everything you had.

"Stan didn't notice me, even when I tried to pull him off, when I hit him as hard as I could. I couldn't stand it. And he was hurting Kip." She glanced at me, then back to Phil. "And I'd become old, invisible Samantha again, only angrier than I've ever felt. How dare he. I wanted to hurt him—like I hurt. And make him stop with Kip ..."

Samantha wiped her eyes with the hankie. "I must've remembered Kip's old ice hockey stick in the corner of the room. Before I knew what I was doing, I slammed it down on Stan, hard, on the head, just as he turned to see who was pestering him. He saw me all right, one last time.

"Dear God, what had I done?" Samantha cried. "I stumbled backward in shock, watching Kip's struggle continue under Stan's weight. The flailing arm she'd freed struck the nightstand with the vase on it. I watched the table and vase wobble, as if in slow motion, until the vase fell over on Stan. Water splashed, flowers flew. Then the vase rolled off the bed and crashed on the floor. The noise—" Samantha shuddered. "The crash of glass splintering in a million pieces on the floor, it, I don't know, kind of woke me up."

Samantha's eyes grew wide with fright. "Now everyone would see me. I was scared to death. I dashed up the back stairs to my bedroom. I didn't know I still clutched Kip's hockey stick until I entered the upstairs hallway just as Sybel flew by, running for Dad. I crossed to my room, stashed the stick between the mattress and box springs, and ran after them. They were whispering at the top of the front staircase about what they'd heard. I just slipped in behind them." Samantha's tears trickled. "Of course, they never really noticed."

Stan, that an unspeakable opportunist, had found Samantha easy prey, like me. Yet we were lucky in one sense. Un-easy prey he drugged and raped. No one refused Stan Szyzyck. Poor Samantha. Her need to smooth all ruffled feathers, to please and placate, had mired her in this. Still I couldn't ignore the fact that Samantha was willing to let me take the blame to save herself. I proved the exception to her deep need to appease.

Phil asked her, "So you wiped the stick clean and secreted it into the broom closet later?"

Samantha's laugh was unbearably sad. "I planned to sneak back home, remove the stick from its hiding place, and burn it in the fireplace. I didn't know what else to do. It seemed riskier to try to take it to my house. Besides, Raymond never let me light a fire. Too messy, he felt.

"I'd finally found the house empty, which was difficult after Sybel moved home with Dad after, well, after. I pulled the stick from under my mattress. I never thought to wipe it clean. Maybe pushing and pulling it between the bedding appeared like I had. Stealing down the backstairs, I heard Sybel fumbling keys at the rear door. I slipped out of sight into the hallway to Kip's room as Sybel entered the kitchen with grocery bags, shouting my name.

"I panicked." Samantha gasped for breath. "My car was in the driveway. Sybel had clearly seen it. I shoved the hockey stick in the broom closet and went to help Sybel with the groceries. I never got another chance to spirit it away. No matter when I showed up at the house, even those times Sybel said she would be doing one thing or another, someone was always there, usually her. Weeks later, she told me Wally and Mr. Debick had come by and found Kip's ice hockey stick in the broom closet 'of all places,' she said, and that they'd taken it with them for some reason."

Samantha cowered in the witness stand. "Every day since, I expected to be arrested. And every day that I wasn't, I started to think maybe this would all go away." Samantha's eyes moved slowly from Phil to me. "Kip gets blamed for everything, but she always bounces back. I figured this might be like that—Kip getting blamed, but bouncing back somehow."

She spoke directly to me. "I never understood how you did it, with everything against you. You were amazing …" As if she just heard her own words, Samantha cried, "Please forgive me, Kip. I'm sorry for what I put you through. I knew you'd get off on self-defense, or figure some other way. You always did. Oh Kip, I'm sorry." I could only stare back.

Samantha's gaze swept the room, coming back to Sybel. "Oh Sybel, I am so sorry. I … you …" I twisted to catch Sybel's reaction. She stared back, much as I had, at the surprising source of this heartache, until Sybel's stunned mind started to churn. Her expression settled into cold, hard hatred.

"I trusted you more than anyone on earth," Sybel said, spitting the words at Samantha. "I cared for you, protected you. And this is the thanks I get? I should have seen through that goody two-shoes act of yours ages ago. You, you—"

My father reached for Sybel's hand to stay or comfort her, but Sybel snatched it free, shouting, "The next time I see you, Samantha, I hope it's standing at your grave."

The gasps throughout the courtroom caused Sybel to remember herself. She closed her eyes and squeezed her hands into fists, falling silent.

Harvey Debick rose to request of the judge, "Allow prosecution and defense to approach, Your Honor?"

Swatting back tears, Samantha watched the lawyers go forward to huddle. Then she, too, shut her eyes and appeared to hum to herself, swaying to the music.

I glanced back at Sybel and Dad. Unabashed tears coursed down Dad's cheeks while Sybel remained shut off from all reminders of betrayal. We all jumped when the judge's gavel banged abruptly. Samantha glanced around the room in fear.

Judge Fassbinder announced, "Miss Benedetti, your client has been cleared of all charges. Miss Czermanski, the charges against you are dropped. You are free to go."

Phil addressed the judge while I struggled to comprehend his words. "Your Honor, if you will, it's Ms. Czermanski and Ms. Benedetti."

This feminist declaration from my lawyer baffled the judge. He brought the gavel down several more times to mask his unenlightenment, then stumbled on. "Mrs., yes, it is Mrs. Turner, you will be held for arraignment in the death of Stanislaw Szyzyck."

Blinking at him, Samantha's fear fluttered into incomprehension. The judge, sounding the gavel one last time, pronounced, "Court adjourned."

"All rise."

The bailiff's command sounded after the judge had already vanished. Still, we rose. The guard approached Samantha, helped her to her feet, and led her toward the back of the courthouse. As if a gentleman had come to assist her over an icy patch, Samantha smiled up and took his arm.

I suppose I was waiting for the bailiff to lead me out of court. Only when he didn't come for me did I realized it had happened, the miracle we'd been hoping for, but not really expecting. I'd been exonerated. I was free, at least free to leave the court, the jail, my family, and this town. With that momentary elation came the crashing weight of what I would carry with me for the rest of my days—the final disintegration of a family, played out in a courtroom.

My family.

CHAPTER SIXTY-SEVEN

Phil folded me in her arms. "You were right all along, Kip. You knew you hadn't killed Stan."

I melted against her and sobbed in her ear, "You were right, too, Phil." She pulled back. "I did play my role—willingly—in the family, taunting them, causing trouble. I got their attention, and attention, good or bad, had to substitute for love."

When the full impact of Samantha's confession rolled over me like a wave of nausea, Phil supported my weight. "I thought of myself as the forgotten child, but did Samantha, too? Did we all feel alone?"

Sensing their eyes upon us, Phil and I turned to Sybel and Dad standing in the first row. Dad, trailing tears, shifted his weight and his gaze as if there were no comfortable place left for him. I noticed his clothing and skin, loose and hanging. He'd become old. Sybel stared at the door Samantha had passed through, and then, glancing at me, leaned toward Dad to whisper, "Let's go. Let's go!"

With the remnants of my ruined family before me, I mumbled to myself, "Who would ever believe *I* was the lucky one."

Phil wrapped her overcoat around my shoulders. "You'll change the world, Kip. I know you will. I'll see you back home."

She kissed my cheek and nudged me, like a chick from the nest, out into the great big world, as prepared as she could make me. I needed a push to leave behind the woman to whom I owed my life. Glancing back at her, I stumbled into William.

He shook my hand, then grabbed me up in a great hug. "Congratulations, Kip. Kip, I want to thank you. I'll never forget what you did for me." He swallowed his surging emotion.

I hugged him hard, trying to control my own feelings. "William, you saved me. Thank you."

What would happen to him now? Could he work for the sleazy bosses who, speaking of scapegoats, certainly had him lined up for the slaughter, but only if absolutely necessary? I studied his unworried face and knew he'd be fine.

"Good luck, William," I whispered and kissed his cheek. Two steps away, I turned back. "William, would you get my poster from Timothy and send it to me?" He could only nod. Before I stepped into the center aisle, I added, "And tell Timothy to catch one for me."

For the first time, I pushed through the gate that separated spectators from court officials and criminals, coming face to face with the immobilized on-lookers. My father reached out for me as I passed him. I stared at his hand on my arm until he released me. My voice, when it materialized, carried through the silent courtroom.

"Why, Dad, why did you blame me? Why would you, of all people, blame me for Mother's death, and allow my sisters to do the same? You must know that if I could have I, I would have chosen not to be born."

Tears slid down my cheeks as it hit me: *This is what I didn't want to feel. This is what I never wanted to face.*

Dad marshaled his reserves for a final bluster. "Now see here, Kip, I didn't blame you. Father Dubcheck said it was God's will that took your mother."

"Easier than blaming yourself or your religion. Blame it on God when you knew Mother couldn't sustain another pregnancy and did nothing to save her. Safer yet, blame me, the end result." I lurched past him.

But Dad grabbed my hand and spun me around. "Don't Kip, please. I've, I've made some mistakes with you, with all of you."

Dad's eyes darted from me to Sybel, who pounced on the opportunity to say, "Daddy, everyone is listening. We can talk at home, Kip. Now let's get out of here."

When neither of us moved, Sybel whispered, "Oh God," in her martyred tone, and flopped onto her seat. But she continued to watch for any opportunity to whisk Dad away. He'd come to his senses sooner or later, she knew, and only she could prevent further family embarrassment. It was her job.

Reading her thoughts, observing her wariness, I suddenly pitied Sybel. She stiffened at my nearness when I leaned down to whisper, "Mother knew you were terrified of her dying, Sybel. She understood what you said and why." Sybel cast a sidelong glance at me, never letting Father out of sight.

I pushed past them for the double doors at the rear of the courtroom, and freedom. A window cracked open in the back let in the first fresh air I'd breathed in weeks, perhaps ever. I filled my lungs with the loamy scent of a Wisconsin spring—snow-saturated mud.

A pretty blonde with tears standing in her eyes lofted a kiss to me from two fingers pressed to her lips. Immediately I recognized Katey Rudeshiem Beneke, who had witnessed her husband's courtroom triumph. No one else stirred as I slowed, nodded at her, then walked on, unwilling to look back. I already felt like stone.

"Kip," Dad shouted, chasing me down the aisle. "Don't. Wait, Kip, please. I'll make it up to you—all of you—if you just give me a chance. Kip, can't you at least give me one more chance?"

I circled, coming face to face with my father, as distraught as I'd ever seen him.

"I can't lose you, too, Kip. I've done—we've done—too much of that." He peered around at the door that had swallowed Samantha. Words choked him. "I'm being punished for letting my wife die. I'm losing my daughters, one by one."

What a botch we'd made of our chance to be a family. Could we figure a way to move on from here? I was too tired to imagine it.

"I never forgave myself for going along with the priests," Dad confessed, "for doing nothing for Norma. After your birth, when she started to fail, then was gone, well I guess you did remind me of it. I didn't mean to hurt you, Kip."

I watched Babs Howenhauser sidling in to catch the conversation as Sybel made her move. She rushed down the aisle and grabbed Dad's arm. "You're making a scene, Daddy," she whispered. "Hush. Kip, Daddy, let's go."

Sybel pulled on her coat and tried to steer Dad to safety. As he hesitated, somehow my sadness took form in words.

"We were all lost when Mother died," I said. "You running from your guilt set the pattern we all followed in our different ways. But we were just kids, Dad." I struggled to go on. "We needed love, guidance, and just a little light to grow. I need …" I tried again. "I need what you can't give me, Dad. I need a mother and a father. Real sisters. I need my childhood back."

A thought overtook my mind: Did we owe it to Mother to make something of the wrecked lives that had cost hers? What would that mean now? But I was unable to deal with it.

Sybel inserted herself between us and in a harsh whisper said, "That's just about enough, Kip. Haven't we been humiliated enough in this courtroom? Daddy, get a hold of yourself."

"Sybel, you still can't see? Samantha's crime, it was our fault—we're all to blame."

"Speak for yourself," she shot back. "I'm going, Daddy, and if you know what's good for all of us, you'll leave with me. Oh, just let her go, Daddy. Kip has been nothing but trouble to us. They've all been nothing but trouble. Let Kip leave, and good riddance."

Dad vacillated between us, dropping his eyes and staring at the floor. Without another word, Sybel took my father's arm and led him up the center aisle, heading for a side exit. My father made no further protest. Before the door closed behind them, Sybel looked back at me, glued in place in the aisle. A triumphant smile spread across her lips just before the door closed behind them with a click.

I pivoted and pushed through the swinging doors at the rear of the courtroom. Stepping through them caused an onslaught of confusing emotions. I caught the doors to gaze back at the courtroom, at the door Samantha had disappeared behind, the one Sybel and Dad escaped through, at the somber faces of neighbors, friends, and foes. Like me, all were struck dumb.

Pushing the doors with all my might, I strode out into the dim hallway, distancing myself from judges and jailers with every step. But the swinging doors, cutting smaller arcs with each swing, made a swoosh-swoosh sound that accompanied my footsteps: Open. Close. Open. Close. Open …

Sunlight, though momentarily blinding, felt like a benediction on my skin after the darkness of the courthouse, the corridor, the jail, the trial. Life. Only the deepest shadows on the courthouse steps harbored the last, stubborn clumps of snow, gray like ash. They wouldn't last the day.

Winter's annual battle had finally turned in favor of spring.

www.agsjohnsonauthor.com

ACKNOWLEDGMENTS

In the years that have passed in the creation of this work of fiction, from taking the voice that disturbed my sleep one night many years ago all the way to a completed novel, hundreds of people have inspired, criticized, encouraged, questioned, reacted, laughed, and cried with me along the way. It would be impossible to acknowledge each one by name even if my memory were perfect. Literally every person I brushed up against added some small or large piece to my understanding. I thank you all, specifically Ann Fitzpatrick, Amy Liston, Nancy Simmons, Ann Kiley, Jerry Gross, Doris Coleman, Donna Smallwood, Carol Millen, and my deceased aunt, Sophie Surmacz.

I thank my friends for at least pretending to believe I would find the end after a dozen years. And of course, Johnson, your literal support made it all possible. Your line editing wasn't bad either.

My writing buddies since our first class together in grad school in 1999, Nancy Ellen Dodd and James J. Owens, accompanied me on this fantastic and difficult journey every step of the way. Dr. James Ragan gave me a chance I worked hard to deserve.

Ellen Reid and her team of specialists—Dotti Albertine, Laren Bright, Don Herion, Pamela Guerrieri and Kevin Cook—you are gods among those who help to create books and realize dreams.

My sisters Jo Ellen, Nancy, Carol, and Sharon; and my stepkids Leanne, Lisa, Laura; my sons-in-law Brian, Ryan, and Darren—gone but not forgotten; I thank you all for fueling the fires of complex, karmic relationships that form the foundation of everything important.

And to my grandkids, such an unexpected joy in my life, Lindsay, John, Brooke, Aidan, Kylie, and Will who, like my cats and dogs, allow me to glimpse unconditional love.

Song Permissions

A portion of the proceeds
from the sale of this novel will be donated to
The World is Just a Book Away,
a charity that builds libraries for children in developing countries,
changing their lives forever through access to books.

Should you wish more information please go to:
www.justabookaway.org